G000272994

HABITAT MAN

D. A. BADEN

Habitat Press

Paperback ISBN: 978-1-7399803-0-6

eBook ISBN: 978-1-7399803-1-3

Published by Habitat Press (www.habitatpress.com)

DISCLAIMER

A delightful number of incidents presented in this book are true (ish), and characters are definitely based on people I know or have known, but attributes have been shuffled and reallocated across the characters, so anyone who guesses who exactly is who in the right combination can send their answers to me and get a star! The issues covered though are definitely real. Thank you to all the wonderful people, projects and organisations that have inspired this work of mostly fiction. I hope you enjoy reading it as much as I enjoyed writing it.

Dedicated to the real Habitat Man (he knows who he is) who works tirelessly and at no charge to offer assistance to the undervalued nematodes, beetles, worms, springtails and microorganisms that are the building blocks of life.

CONTENTS

PROLOGUE

A tiny wren, tail cocked, trilled its liquid song from the new willow fence. Nearby, a chiff-chaff chanted the repetitive call of its name. A queen bumblebee burred, her legs loaded with balls of pollen for her hungry offspring. A brimstone butterfly fluttered by, investigating the flowers on the willow bower, its bright yellow wings a flash of sunshine.

We gazed into the hole I'd dug. Next to the bones was a new body, the shallow pond-shaped hole like nature's opening arms pulling him back to the earth.

FIFTY

I walked resolutely, deep in thought. It starts today, I vowed, because if not now, then when? Monday actually would make more sense. But either way, by this time next Saturday it will all be different. Probably I'll still be going to the local with Jo, but... but what?

I sighed, and stopped to watch a bluebottle feeding on a smear of excrement on the pavement.

'That fly has a more productive life than I have, Jobo,' I declared. 'Cleaning up our shit, pollinating plants.'

'Such an accountant,' she mocked. 'Mid-life crisis at fifty years precisely.'

I glanced up. With her grinning face, rotund form and baggy orange jumper, she reminded me momentarily of a space hopper. I returned to watching the action on the pavement, where another fly had alighted on the excrement.

'Has a better sex life too,' I informed her, 'although the earthworm copulates for three hours at a time.'

'No one can compete with that. Anyway, you don't want to be bothering with all that slimy nonsense.'

'I do.'

The soft cooing of collared doves floated on the autumn air. They mated for life, and a pair nested in the front garden of the young couple who always walked to the pub holding hands.

We walked on past a hedge of sparrows who were unashamedly polygamous. The swaying poplar tree by the pub was alive with the din of starlings roosting together for comfort and warmth after a summer in pair bonds.

'I must be the only species shacked up with a lesbian, who doesn't even pay rent.' I proclaimed.

'Don't worry, mate. My software will make me rich and sort out your mid-life crisis.' She pushed through the door and headed for our table.

I got the drinks in automatically. I did worry. Too much was riding on it. The Costing for Nature software had been held up for the last three years as the shining beacon that would redeem my job, reverse my complicity in the climate crisis, and justify Jo's rent-free status. Jo had done the coding, and I'd spent evenings and weekends inputting the environmental data. It was ready at last and on Monday I'd be pitching it to my firm of accountants.

'I've been thinking…' I said, after the first long gulp of beer.

'Oh no…'

'I'm fifty, Jo, I've spent half of my life in a job I hate. I've been getting by on the hope that the new software will solve everything, but they probably won't go for it.'

'You'll be fine. Show me your pitch. Pretend I'm the head honcho,' she slurped her beer expectantly.

'Okay.' I psyched myself up into sales mode and loosened up, moving my shoulders and easing my neck out. I took a gulp of beer then gazed at Jo, imagining her to be the head of accounting, Martin Brigham. 'The Costing—'

'Too much going on with the eyebrows, Timbo.'

'Huh?'

'The tilt is too pronounced, makes you look anxious.'

'Okay.' I pushed my eyebrows back into horizontal mode. 'We need to include nature—'

'Take the pleading look out of your eye. You need to be confident, assured. This Costing for Nature accounting software is the best thing since sliced bread.'

'Right. The CFN measures environmental—'

'We already do loads for the environment. We do our best,' said Jo as Martin.

I lowered my eyebrows until they glowered forcefully. 'It's not enough to do our best,' I boomed, 'we must do what is necessary!'

'Too Churchillian.'

'Is that bad?'

'Depends if you can pull it off.' Doubt entered her eyes. 'Forget it for tonight, it's your birthday.'

'Forget it? If I don't make a stand at fifty, when will I? I was complicit in the financial crisis, but I refuse to be complicit in the climate crisis.' I banged down my glass.

'You do all right financially though don't you?' She drained her pint and nodded towards the bar.

I gazed at her, eyes narrowed, suddenly suspicious. Had she been dragging out the software on purpose? Was it just an excuse not to find a new job? She was chronically lazy after all and it was no surprise when she was made redundant three years ago. It had followed the incident when she'd hastened into the lift at ten am. 'Late?' the man in the lift had enquired. 'Always,' Jo had cheerfully responded, unaware she was talking to the CEO.

'What?' enquired Jo, noticing my look.

'I'm just thinking you haven't changed since I first met you.'

'Really?' She looked surprised, which was fair enough. Thirty years ago, she'd been petite, long-haired and hyperactive. Now she was just short. Short hair in a blokey cut, plump from beer and crisps and doing nothing, and plain until her face lit up with mischief. One thing hadn't changed though, I still couldn't tell if she had my back or was just exploiting me.

'Do you even care about the software?' I asked.

'I know what you're thinking,' said Jo.

'Really?'

'You're worried about cocking up the pitch. I gave up three years to work on it; but, mate, I did it for you as much as for me, and it was fun working with you on it. Best case, this software will sort out your mid-life crisis, make my fortune, and save the world. But if it doesn't, I won't blame you.' Her eyes shone with sincerity. She rattled her glass.

By pint three, Jo had jollied me out of my trepidation, and was taking the mick out of the Rugby. On the pub television, New Zealand was playing England in the World Cup and the All Blacks were performing the haka.

'It's supposed to be fearsome, a Maori battle cry,' I told her.

'Pah! That's nothing.'

'What do we have then?'

'Morris dancing.'

'Morris dancing?' I spluttered.

'Bring it on then!' She stood up and did a hop and a skip and looked at me expectantly.

I glanced around. People were looking over. 'I'm not doing the haka.'

'Fight, you lily-livered cringeling.' She grabbed some napkins smeared with ketchup from the neighbouring table and fluttered them in my face.

I shouted with laughter and fell back in my chair, clutching at the table to avoid tipping. I wiped my cheek and my hand came away red with ketchup.

Jo jigged on the spot, bright-eyed with victory.

'Okay, morris dancers win.'

We'd attracted the attention of the old man at the bar, a seemingly permanent fixture. He raised his pint in acknowledgment. Jo sat down finally and raised hers back.

'What's the difference between him and you?' she nodded over to the guy at the bar.

'What?'

'Ten years and me.'

'Huh?'

'Well, if I wasn't around, that would be you wouldn't it? Sat at the bar, all alone, muttering into your pint.' She sat back, happy to have proved her indispensability to my life.

My laughter died on my lips. She was right. All that stood between me and lone-man-at-the-bar was her and my work, and I hated my work. Now the pitch was imminent, I saw clearly I'd been hanging too much on it. Even if they bought the software and put me in charge, I'd still be single, still working a sixty-hour week, sat at a desk, day in, day out.

'Cheers for that, Jo, lovely observation, thanks.' I wiped away the ketchup with a clean napkin.

She downed her pint and looked at me expectantly.

'Forget it, if you want another you get it. It's my birthday and you didn't even get me a present.'

'Yes, I did. I forgot. Hang on.' She produced a crumpled voucher from the back pocket of her baggy jeans with a flourish.

'Happy fiftieth.'

I looked at it. It was a voucher for a life coaching session. I sat up.

'Oh my days! That's what I need, a new life.' I beamed at her, heartened suddenly. 'This is unusually thoughtful. I've felt so trapped, it would be nice to talk to somebody. They help you reframe things don't they? Deal with your past. It would be hard to talk about, but maybe it's time. Then go forward into a new future—'

'One thing though, Timbo, it's Charlotte.'

'What? Your niece?'

'She's started a life coaching course.'

I slumped back in my chair. 'What does she know about life?'

'But you'll do it right? She said she needs a good mark for the practical.'

'So basically my fiftieth birthday present is Charlotte's homework. Cheers.' I drained my pint and banged it down next to hers.

'Go on then, I'll sort you another, if you want to take it to pint four?'

'I feel obliged to.'

'Cos you've turned fifty, to prove you can take it? Cos we both know, Timbo, on pint four there's a tendency to get over emotional.'

'No, because you're buying.'

We called it a day after the fourth pint, which Jo had wangled on the house on account of my birthday, and staggered home.

Outside in the fresh air, I brooded on her words.

'Look at them.' I gazed with envious eyes at the couple ahead of us, turning into the house with the lovely garden. 'I don't even have a garden.'

'Oh no. I touched a nerve. Come on, Timbo, it's just cos you've turned fifty.'

'But you're right,' I burst out. 'Other people have stuff in their life they're passionate about – their partner, their garden, their work. I'm half dead most of the time, and most of the time I don't even realise it but…' I tailed off, not wanting to admit that those moments of random hilarity with Jo were the only times I felt alive. An image of a little boy crying flooded my consciousness suddenly. An image printed indelibly on my memory – the boy I'd hurt, bawling. Crying so, so much. He'd be an adult now, probably with his own kids. We'd left the next generation such a mess. If I could just make it better… It hit me with the force of a great revelation how much I needed the environmental software to work. I grabbed Jo and gazed earnestly into her eyes. 'I'll give the pitch my best shot.'

'I know you will, mate.'

'It has to work. Otherwise I can't do it anymore, Jo, I can't take the guilt.'

'Emotional.'

I looked up into the sky, the grey clouds parted for a moment revealing the stars beyond. A nip in the autumn breeze roused a sudden confidence. I could do it. They were accountants after all, and it didn't matter which bottom line you looked at, environmental bottom line, social bottom line, financial bottom line, this came up trumps each time. 'I can do it a hundred per cent.'

Jo checked my eyebrows and nodded, satisfied.

I rehearsed my pitch on the train all the way to Waterloo, drawing strange looks from the couple sitting opposite, who were no doubt wondering why my mouth was moving silently and my eyebrows were wavering between imploring, glowering and deadly serious.

At Waterloo, I approached the usual mix of homeless, beggars and *Big Issue* sellers, rummaging in my pocket for some change. The smart-suited man ahead of me made the mistake of giving a fiver to the bolshy guy at the end. Or maybe it was on purpose. I'd noticed the more money he was given, the longer his tirade would be.

'Fiver wouldn't even pay your dry-cleaning bill, you rich tosser,' Bolshy Guy hurled at him, deftly pocketing the note.

Smart-suited man shook his head, shuffling from polished black shoe to polished black shoe as the tirade continued.

'The world would be better off if you didn't exist. If you didn't bother with your dry-cleaned suit and stayed at home and did sweet fuck all. Smart-guy-city-tosspot,' he accused, peering up through overgrown eyebrows and shaggy hair.

He had a point. I'd calculated the environmental impacts of laundry using Jo's software and could have informed them about the high carbon footprint of washing clothes and the contribution of dry cleaners to air pollution. I decided not to interject and walked on past 'smart-guy-city-tosspot', who stood patiently accepting the abuse. The tirade might go on for a while and I couldn't afford to be late. Anyway, I didn't need my daily dose of psychic self-flagellation, because today I would be part of the solution, not part of the problem. Instead, I gave a fiver to the friendly chap by Waterloo Bridge for a *Big Issue*. His cheery smile of thanks was mirrored by the wagging tail of his dog that I couldn't resist patting. I smiled at him reassuringly. 'It's all going to be okay,' I told him, 'lovely dog.'

I walked the familiar route over Waterloo Bridge and gulped in a lungful of the bracing wind, taking in the open vista of the Thames and the Houses of Parliament etched against the cold grey sky. A cormorant perched on an old barge, drying its wings. Gulls circled raucously above. I could just make out crabs picking among the debris on the muddy banks where the tide had receded. Nature in the heart of the city.

Last week the bridge had been occupied by Extinction Rebellion protestors. Part of me had been thrilled to see them. Hordes of young bearded, pierced and tattooed protestors beating drums, chanting and waving banners: 'Save the Earth', 'Rebel for Life', 'Wise up, Rise up'. There had been families too, mothers with pushchairs, dads with toddlers on their shoulders. But no amount of smiles and thumbs up on my part could disguise my city suit and complicity. They'd chanted, 'This is the sixth mass extinction,' and in my paranoia and guilt I'd been sure it was aimed at me.

I got to work with twenty minutes to spare. I made a cup of tea and sat on the plush sofa. I ignored the pile of *Financial Times* and car magazines scattered over the low table and got out the *Big Issue*. With a shock, I took in the headline: 'Parakeet Mystery still not solved'. Oh my days! It must be a sign. I read quickly. Parakeets may have beautiful plumage, but they were destroying habitats of garden birds. They'd taken over in Surrey and London and were now spreading across the UK. For years, Jimi Hendrix had been blamed for freeing a pair of parakeets in Carnaby Street in the sixties, but now it seemed that it wasn't his fault after all. The article concluded that there were several incidents across the years, but the tipping point seems to be a pair of parakeets set free in Surrey in the mid-eighties. My stomach lurched and I ran for the toilet.

I hated our office toilets, the scent of the air freshener worse than what it disguised. And they were pretentious, with toilets that automatically flushed the moment you got off them, or, unnervingly, when you moved on the seat. I washed my hands quickly. It must be nearly time for my pitch. I hoped Simon, the financial director, wasn't going to be there, with his intimidating beard. Jo would often reassure me that there was nothing wrong with being a 'baby face', but then she'd smirk. I regarded my pale freckled face in the mirror and longed to be more hirsute. I didn't even want a beard necessarily, just the feeling that beneath my skin were follicles of thick, dark, bristly hair bursting to come forth. Then I'd feel equal to the task.

I headed to the conference room and sat amidst the pot plants in the waiting area. 'By valuing the ecosystem and everything that depends upon it, we will protect it,' I whispered earnestly to the Areca Fern and Rubber Plant. 'Unless we cost for nature…'

I stopped quickly as several suited men and a woman trailed out, leaving Martin and Simon at the table. Through the glass walls, I saw Simon open up his laptop and show something to Martin. They talked animatedly, probably working out how inputting the environmental and social impacts of each project would affect the overall costs. I stood and paced to relieve my nervous tension, muttering under my breath, trying to control my eyebrows. Just as I'd pushed them from an anxious forty-five degree tilt up, down into a menacing glower, Martin beckoned me in. I forced my brows horizontal and entered with the gait of a confident man who was bringing them the best thing since sliced bread.

'Hi there. Right, er…'

'That's us on the beach,' Simon was saying.

'Looks lovely,' murmured Martin.

'Four-star resort but we wouldn't go back.'

I sat at the table opposite them and placed my laptop on the top pointedly. Martin eventually looked over.

'What are we meeting about again, Tim? Remind me.'

Remind him!

'This is to talk about the Costing for Nature software that will transform the way we do business. For the better,' I added quickly.

'Okay, go ahead.'

'We need to cost for nature.' Simon was still swiping through his photos. I paused, but he showed no sign of looking up. 'For example, when we cost a project for time and money, we factor in the carbon cost too, and allow money to offset.'

Martin looked doubtful.

'I know it's not a perfect solution, but at least the environmental costs would form part of the cost-benefit analysis.'

No reaction.

'My degree was in biology, I don't know if you knew that? So I've been able to feed the latest environmental data and predicted carbon costs into the algorithms.'

'Sounds expensive,' Simon finally looked up.

'No, erm, my… er a qualified software consultant I know, developed some software that calculates it all for us.' I searched in vain for a sign they'd checked it out. 'There was a link in my email?'

I waited while they murmured among themselves. It was a short conversation.

'Thanks for your idea, but it's not something we'll be taking forward right now,' said Martin.

'Right.'

That seemed to be it.

I went to my desk, sat in my ergonomically designed chair among a sea of similar chairs and desks in the open-plan office and gazed at my screen. The screensaver showed endless forests against a startling blue sky. I tapped a key and up came accounts for a global IT company we were helping to make richer. Standard financial modelling indicated that designing products to fail with parts that couldn't be replaced was the most profitable business model. I gazed blankly at the numbers as it sank in. They hadn't even looked at my CFN analysis that costed in the e-waste, unnecessary carbon emissions, and health costs from sweatshop conditions and toxic ingredients that seeped into the water. A new screensaver sprung up. A tropical island with clear turquoise sea filled with colourful fish. I was suddenly furious. They hadn't looked at any of the sample scenarios. I grabbed my laptop and marched back in.

They were still there exchanging holiday horror stories.

'Bali was crap too. You couldn't swim in the sea,' Martin informed Simon.

'It's not more expensive,' I declared loudly, striding in and banging the door behind me. Well I tried to, but it was a glass door on a hinge designed to shut gently. I opened my laptop and pointed to the example scenario.

'See that,' I pointed at a graph showing two lines comparing current costs with costs using the CFN.

'What's CFN?' Simon deigned to glance over.

'It's Costing for Nature accounting software,' I told him through gritted teeth.

'Well it costs more, doesn't it?'

'Now look.' I typed three years into the time box. The two lines for standard cost and CFN costs came together. 'Now look.'

I typed five years into the box and the CFN line shifted below the standard cost line. 'CFN saves them money. This scenario is for the construction companies we deal with that we walk past every day coming into work. Simply switching to green cement, for example, substantially lowers CFN construction costs due to its lower carbon footprint.'

'I drive,' Simon said.

'What? Why would you drive?'

'I've got a Ferrari.'

I looked at him in his perfectly cut suit, luxuriant beard, clipped to precision, shoes too polished and shiny for public transport and hated him.

'Way overpriced for what you get. Now if it were a Porsche —' began Martin.

'But the point is,' I shouted over him, 'for every company we deal with, in the short term, yes it costs money to properly cost in environmental impacts, but in the medium to long term it costs way more not to.'

'I'll tell you what costs too much money,' Martin said.

'What?' Simon asked.

'A Ferrari,' said Martin.

'No, two-week holidays swimming in plastic,' Simon retorted.

'Ouch.'

I took a deep breath, determined to stay calm, to do justice to our CFN software that would save us from ourselves, restore the planet to perfection and enable me to saunter past XR protestors head held high. The daily commute, the hours sat at my desk gazing at the screen, the inane conversation in the coffee room about cars – all would be redeemed if I was working for something worthwhile. Simon clicked on his laptop and slowly an image of him with his perfect beard and smiling wife and young son came into view. I lost it.

'I don't care about your car or your two weeks' holiday on your tropical island.'

'The holiday was shit anyway,' consoled Simon. 'We had to return early, my son got asthma and the hospitals were full.'

'Don't you see we're the engines of all this?' I cried. 'Plastic didn't get in the sea by magic. The asthma didn't just happen. It was the pollution from clearing rainforests. The whole of bloody Indonesia has breathing difficulties. We crunch the numbers and depending on what goes in, out comes the decisions. If we added waste and air quality and climate change to our numbers you wouldn't get plastic in the sea and asthma. You must see that? It's us, it's all us! It's all our fault.'

They looked at me aghast as my voice hit soprano pitch. 'I know it hurts to admit it. I understand that. I tell you what... Okay... I've not told anyone this, I've never admitted it to a soul, but I'll tell you now.' My heart was pounding. Dare I say it? I must. I must set an example and own up. I tried to look them in the eyes as I made my confession, but looked away at the last minute. 'I set the parakeets free. It was me. There. I've owned up and you know it feels good. My bad. I did it. It wasn't Jimi Hendrix, it was me and now they're taking over. They're an invasive species. I'm not jealous of your Ferrari or your holiday, or your beard.' Simon looked up sharply and stroked his beard possessively.

'Well maybe the beard,' I admitted recklessly, still riding the confession wave.

Simon shot Martin a look. Was it guilt? I pressed the point home. 'Surely you must see it's our fault? But that's okay, because the Costing for Nature software can put it all right. We crunch the numbers, what goes in is what comes out.' I knew I was repeating myself but was unable to stop. 'We're not just complicit, we're guilty, but we can make it right!'

'Mmmhmm,' soothed Martin. I petered out, finally deciphering the look in their eyes. It wasn't guilt. It was pity.

I fell silent and packed up my laptop and left the room.

I returned to my desk and fell into my chair. Twenty-five years. I'd been in this job for twenty-five years. My fingers hovered over the keyboard, but nothing happened. I couldn't type a word. I tried to close down the file I'd been working on but fell at the first hurdle. 'Save', 'Don't Save'. I gazed at the simple question. Eventually I realised it wasn't that I couldn't decide, it was that I didn't care. I clicked on another tab and another screen of numbers popped up. I tried to close it and was faced with the same query 'Save', 'Don't Save'. Over twenty windows were open. I pushed the power button hard until it gave up the red light and went home.

I walked back across Waterloo Bridge to Waterloo station where I handed the bolshy guy a twenty-pound note and gazed at my black polished shoes as he told me at great length how the world would be better off without me.

Travelling home off-peak, I had my choice of window seats. I sat in the nearest and gazed blankly at the passing scenery. The London Eye gave way to tower blocks, then Battersea Power Station, then rows upon rows of back gardens. After Woking, the Hampshire countryside came into view and my eyes rested upon fields, woods and blue sky with breaks every twenty minutes of office buildings and shops as we passed through Basingstoke, Winchester and finally Southampton. When I got home, I headed straight for Jo's room to break the news. I didn't care what she said. I'd done my best. If she needed money, she could get work easily enough.

There she was, sat at her computer, absorbed in the screen in the same position she'd been in for years.

'Sod off out of here,' she said, not turning round.

'Bit harsh.'

Jo jumped and looked round. 'Sorry, I was talking to the Persians, they've just attacked my capital.'

I looked at the screen and my heart sank. It was Civilisation 6. Jo had lost several years to Civilisation 2. In the end, we'd had to wipe it off her computer and smash the disc. But she'd been back when the next version allowed her to play online with real people. Each new version meant I'd pretty much lose her for a full year until she had exhausted all permutations and achieved victory over all.

'How'd it go?' she asked, still tapping into the computer.

'They said no.'

'Did you tell them about your expertise? That you worked at the Environment Centre for years, and keep up to date with all that?'

'They didn't give me a chance. Anyway, I put all that in the original email.'

'Did they test the software?'

'I sent them the links to try out in the email.'

'Oh, for God's sake.'

'What is it? The Persians?'

'No, you. No one reads past the first sentence.'

'I sent you the email to check before I sent it off, but you were too busy playing Civ, I presume.'

'You probably put the important bit in the second sentence.'

'I did my best,' I told the back of her head.

'Yes!' she cried, tapping at the keyboard. 'Got the bastards.' She turned her head towards me, but kept her eyes on the screen. 'You can always try again another day.'

'I'm not going back.'

I meant it. In the blankness of my mind since I left the conference room, wheels had been turning deep inside. I couldn't do one more day, not even to empty my drawer. I waited for Jo to turn around, to express some surprise, some emotion, some sign of caring about costing for nature, about what a difference it might have made, about me.

'Bloody hell!' she exploded. I could see over her shoulder a battle occurring on screen.

I thought back to her comment in the pub. Was Jo now all that stood between me and the lonely guy at the bar muttering into his pint?

'Buggery bollocks!' she shouted at the screen.

I noticed the life coaching voucher on the desk and picked it up.

'Transform your life'.

THE LIFE COACH

From: *MakeLifeCount@outlook.com*
To: *Tim Redfern*
Subject: *Your life coaching session*

Dear Tim
I'm delighted to confirm your life coaching session for next Thursday.
Before you come, please consider the following questions:

1. *What are you good at?*
2. *What does the world need?*
3. *What brings you joy?*
4. *What can you be paid for?*

I must admit that looks professional so far.

From: *MakeLifeCount@outlook.com*
To: *Tim Redfern*
Subject: *Your life coaching session*
PS It's me Charlotte!
PPS Cheers for this

PPPS My flat's a bit messy, can I come to yours?

Oh well.

Charlotte arrived in tiny black shorts over black tights, high-heeled ankle boots and a frilly white blouse. She took her iPad out of a glittery pink handbag and placed it on the kitchen table.

'You're going to be a life coach then?'

'Yeah, well, everyone says I'm good with other people's problems,' she said, undaunted by my doubtful tone.

Charlotte and Jo looked very different, one tall, fashion-conscious and skinny, the other short, plump and permanently in baggy jeans, but they shared the same brash confidence, and air of knowing it all.

'Anyway, it's this or McDonald's.'

'Tea?' I hovered over the kettle.

'Coke, please.'

'No Coke, I'm afraid. Water?'

Charlotte shook her head. She glanced down at her notes then sat up straight with an air of business and launched into her spiel. 'Life coaching changes lives through inspirational conversations, and a voyage of self-discovery.'

'Okay.' I munched a biscuit.

'And helping you to transform your life. Together we will create meaning and purpose in your life.' She looked up from the screen to hit me with a wise and sincere stare. I brushed the crumbs from my mouth and returned her solemn look. She looked back down.

'Oh, and through structured exercises.'

'Is that it?'

'Erm…' She scrolled down, tongue sticking out, muttering to herself. 'We'll skip that bit… that bit's boring… right. Tim.'

I jumped to attention and put down biscuit number three.

'Yes?'

'You left your job recently I heard?'

'Not formally yet, but yes.'

'Right, we'll do the structured exercise to explore new possibilities.'

She swung the screen to face me and I saw a Venn diagram.

'All you have to do is think of something you'd like to do that fits in the middle.'

I gazed at the diagram. My mind was utterly blank.

She read them out loud slowly. 'One. What are you good at? Two. What does the world need? Three. What brings you joy? Four. What can you be paid for?' Between each one she fixed me with an enquiring look.

I gazed in vain over the four adjoining circles.

'Anything?'

'Sorry, I can't think.'

She peeped at her notes. I waited patiently, pretending I hadn't noticed.

'Let's try dropping one,' she said eventually.

I scanned them again and came to rest on the last one. *What can you be paid for?* I thought about everything I wanted and didn't have.

'Skip the last one.'

'Really?'

'Yes, really.'

Charlotte shot me a disbelieving look, thinking no doubt of the many handbags and groovy boots money can buy. 'Let's skip number four then. So what are you good at? What does the world need? Erm...' She refreshed the screen to bring up the Venn diagram again and peered at it. 'What brings you joy?'

I gazed out of the window. The leaves on the trees over the road on the common would soon be turning to autumnal russets and browns. After decades forcing myself to sit at a desk, now I couldn't bear to be inside at all if I could help it. I turned to Charlotte. 'Would your boots handle a walk?'

She agreed that they would, and once outside, walking through the common, it was easier to think. We strolled, taking in the dogs chasing squirrels up trees and the rustle of birds in the bushes. I heard a familiar screech and saw a bright green flash as a pair of parakeets swept across the sharp blue sky.

'Wow! Are they parrots?'

'Ring-necked parakeets,' I said tersely.

'Aren't they pretty.'

'No they're not. They're an invasive species, taking over habitats.'

'Like grey squirrels?'

'Yes. It's bad news for the local bird population that they've reached this far.' I was reminded of the Extinction Rebellion protestors and their chant that we were causing the sixth mass extinction. They weren't wrong. Songbirds were a rarity now. It was years since I'd seen a hedgehog in the wild, and butterflies seemed much less common than when I was a kid.

'What does the world need?' she prompted.

Maybe I should become a protestor? A tubby fifty-year-old among the twenty-somethings. I couldn't see it.

'What are you good at?' she pressed, desperate to make some progress.

I thought hard. I didn't want to say accountancy because it certainly didn't give me joy.

'My grade depends on this.'

'Scrabble? In fact, games with Jo can get quite vicious.'

She sighed. 'Can we go back in now? These boots aren't great for walking.'

When we arrived back, Jo was up, unperturbed at being seen in pyjamas and dressing gown at eleven-thirty in the morning.

'Aunty Jo, what's Tim good at?'

'It's obvious,' Jo said, pouring muesli into a bowl.

'Is it?'

'Think what your *Mastermind* specialist subject would be.' She added the last of the milk.

'Invertebrates,' I said immediately.

'That's creepy-crawlies to you, Char.'

'Really?'

'Yup. Got an appointment with some Persians.' She took her cereal and left.

Charlotte glanced at her notes again and turned to me with a determined expression. 'So, when was the last time you felt joy?'

It was depressingly hard to think of a time.

'The last time I felt joy was…' I had to go back almost thirty years. 'My practical project for my ecology module, getting my hands dirty, creating habitats for wildlife, working with nature, helping it.'

As I remembered, my body lost all its tension and I found myself smiling. Investigating the university's wildlife gardens, the heady feeling of my book learning coming to life. By then I knew the names of the plants and their preferences with regard to soil and light, which were native, which weren't, which ones the minibeasts liked, which they didn't. I remembered the feeling of taking it all in, the interlocking ecosystem, revelling in my knowledge, eager to learn more, feeling part of something good.

That's when it all fell into place.

Dear Martin
I am handing in my notice as of today and will not be returning. I know the usual notice period is two weeks, but I have more than two weeks' holiday owing so you should be quids in. I remember when Gary was fired and was escorted out by security in case he got disgruntled and caused trouble, although he only became disgruntled because he wasn't allowed to clear out his own drawer. Anyway, I'm disgruntled, so it's best I don't come in. You can have the chocolate biscuits in my drawer.

I paused over the keyboard. There was a lot to say. That I was off to atone, that I felt happy for the first time in decades, that I had lots of trepidation but no doubt at all. That I could grow a beard now as I'd no longer have to endure the painful banter when it went through its early stages, although to be fair, Jo was worse than Simon or Martin. No, I wouldn't waste a moment more than I needed to.

I can't believe I gave you 25 years – half of my life, but that's on me.
Yours sincerely
Tim Redfern

Send.

I set two pints down on our usual table. Traditionally the first pint was spent moaning, but things were different now. Possibly the norm of me buying the drinks also needed to be addressed, but I was still on a high from the new life stretching before me.

'What do you think of the term Green Garden Consultant?' I asked Jo.

'Not enough punch. How about Worm Man?'

'Shut up. Anyway, it's more than worms, it's the whole ecosystem. How to restore biodiversity and increase the wildlife value of back gardens. Obviously worms are crucial—'

She cut me off before I could rhapsodize about earthworms as is my wont.

'Habitat Man!' she boomed.

'It's stupid, it sounds like some kind of Marvel hero.'

She shook her head and I could see it had been decided.

'Habitat Man,' she repeated firmly.

Over the second pint we debated the terms of my work.

'You should definitely charge.'

'If I charge then people won't do it, especially those who can't afford it.'

'They'll think of you as a free gardener, mate, they'll take the piss.'

'Compromise, I'll advise only, but I won't do any gardening.'

'You don't want to undervalue yourself. You're a skilled ecologist are you not?'

I shrugged modestly.

'You're too easily taken advantage of.' Jo spoke from long and rewarding personal experience.

'How far is your desire for me to get paid,' I took a leisurely swig of the pint she'd just bought, 'related to your fear of buying your share of the drinks?'

Over the much-disputed third pint we resumed discussion of logistics.

'You don't want to be doing a ton of paperwork.'

'Which I'd be doing if I got paid, because of tax and all that.'

'But they won't value your work if it's for free, they'll mess you around.'

She had a point. I mused for a while. In the gents, as is often the case, the answer came to me. I needed an intermediary. I'd charge a token fee to address Jo's point and donate it to an environmental charity and they could promote the service and liaise between me and the people who wanted my services. The question was who.

'Transition Group?' Jo suggested when I put it to her.

'Not a bad idea.' We had a thriving Transition Group in Southampton that ran all kinds of projects: a repair café, a clean-air group that campaigned against the cruise ships that disgorged pollutants into the air, tree planting project and a campaign to prevent expansion of the local airport. 'In fact, Jobo, it's perfect!'

From: Transition Southampton
To: Member list
Subject: Green Gardening Consultancy
Gardens are important for nature. A local ecologist, Tim Redfern, is kindly offering a wildlife gardening consultancy for one visit. He will give his time for free, but requests an advance donation of £10 to Transition Southampton for each site. All advice will be in response to the wishes of the participants and reflect the potential of the specific garden concerned. The coming autumn provides a good opportunity to consider how to enhance the wildlife value of your garden. If you'd like to participate, see our website.

From: Transition Southampton
To: Tim Redfern
Subject: Green Gardening Consultancy
Attachment: Lori, Bitterne Park

Dear Tim
Your first customer (details attached). Good luck!
Karen

3

LORI

Bitterne Park, a suburb of Southampton, retains a village feel. A clock tower situated in the triangle between Riverside Park, Cobden Bridge and the local shops gives an extravagant air to the mini community. You never knew who you might encounter under it. Sometimes a group of Buddhists from the nearby meditation centre, sometimes a group of Christians praying for peace. Occasionally a band sprang up attracting a crowd, delighted at the unexpected entertainment. Today it was hopeful Jehovah's Witnesses. I locked my bike to the park railings, and crossed the road quickly before they could press a leaflet into my hand.

I slowed my pace as I approached Lori's house. The final words of my so-called 'life coach' rang in my ears, *this is the first day of the rest of your life*. I'd cringed at the cliché; it hadn't felt true at the time. But today it did – if all went well that is. Time for my first... ah! I hadn't even got the terminology sorted yet. First... customer? Not being paid. Victim? Have some belief in yourself, man!

The sky was bright blue, but ominous clouds approached from the west. I suddenly had cold feet. It was a long time since

I'd dealt with actual people in my work. Jo was one of the few people I felt comfortable with, and when she was deep in a new game, we barely spoke for days. The thought of her mockery if I bottled out propelled me forward. I took a deep breath and steadied myself by assessing the property.

Standard three bedroom, semi-detached. Weeds growing out of the path – promising, indicating someone who doesn't believe nature needs to be hammered into submission. I straightened my back and adopted a posture that said 'I'm a trustworthy expert in my field and not a rapist or estate agent' and strode up the path to the door. I paused at a menacing vampire bat knocker.

I sprang back in shock when the door was flung open in my face and an angry black-clad spectre ran out, shouting.

'Stop trying to control me, you fucking cow!'

A teenage boy stormed past me, throwing me a dark look. Frantic barking signalled the arrival soon after by a pink-collared Yorkshire terrier that thought it was a Rottweiler. Bared teeth hurled themselves at my ankles, but drew back each time a millimetre from making contact. She caught my eye and brief looks were exchanged. The flash from her brown eyes informed me that she felt she had to go the extra mile because she'd been slow on the uptake, being momentarily confused by the shouting boy. Mine said, I'm admiring your precision and I'm not concerned. She tailed off her barking and growling in fits and starts until I was thoroughly checked out and deemed acceptable. A pink tongue licked my hand and she looked up at me.

Liquid brown, kohl-rimmed, emotion-filled eyes begged my forgiveness for the overzealous greeting. They beseeched me to understand it's just what she had to do. Their brown moistness reassured me I was now welcome to stroke her if I should so wish. She tipped her body sideways a fraction in the tiniest of hints to admire her silky ears, her honey-coloured fur, all shades of white, grey, gold, silver and brown. Wavy, but short and velvety, recently cut. Her tail thumped softly in the sure knowledge that I'd have to bend down and have a stroke.

I squatted down, stroking her back and ears. 'Aren't you the most beautiful—'

An ear angled itself towards the hall landing as running sounds were heard.

'You murderer!'

What? I stood up quickly to leave, but I was too late.

'Oh. Er, hello.' The voice was like warm caramel.

I looked up and there she was. A human equivalent. The same deep brown eyes, contrasting strikingly with the lighter hair. One could say it was the hair of someone who wasn't worried about letting her grey grow through. But having just seen the dog, it seemed like a statement of extreme style and panache. The colours, mingled grey, silver, honey and gold were like an impressionist work of art. The mesmerising eyes moved quickly through a range of expressions – anger, outrage, embarrassment, apology, then wry humour.

'Sorry about that. Teenagers!' She shrugged. 'It's all the testosterone, I'm told.' She put out her hand. 'I'm Lori.'

I straightened up and took her hand. 'I'm Tim, erm... Habitat Man.'

'This is Florence.' I nodded down at the dog. She was gorgeous, and Lori too. But the boy had thrown me completely. Such suspicion and anger in those deep-set black eyes. He'd looked at me like he hated me. And what had she meant by 'murderer'?

In a blur, I followed Lori into a kitchen. Large Velux windows from an extension let in light over a kitchen table. Clear autumn sun streamed through glass patio doors. Lori opened them and ushered me onto the decking, exuding a benign, encouraging air, along with the remnants of an apologetic smile.

Outside in the crisp autumn air, I took a deep breath and regained my composure.

'Are you okay?' she asked.

'Yes, yes of course.'

The sun caught her hair, creating a halo effect. I dragged my gaze away and leant against the decking rails to survey the long, narrow back garden; a shaggy rectangular lawn, concrete slab path, messy flower beds, a new-looking shed at the back, all surrounded by lap-board fencing. Like a million other suburban gardens.

'Erm, what do you want to achieve in the garden, Lori?'

'To be frank, I don't have much time for gardening, so to make me feel better, I thought at least I could make it good for wildlife.'

'The good news is that generally, the less you do, the better for nature, so you're off to a great start already.'

'Brilliant.' She flashed me a heart-stopping smile.

'Let's have a look then.'

She nodded and I followed her down the steps and into the garden. On the right-hand side was a tall thicket of bamboo, grown so high it cast shade over most of the garden. An invasive species. Non-native.

'Are you plotting against my bamboo?'

I checked her expression – a hint of a smile. I risked it.

'A bit. It's your garden so I'm guided by you, but I'd get rid of it and replace it with a deciduous native species – maybe a small flowering tree, a rowan or wayfarer tree?'

'Really?'

'Native species host much more insect life than imported species. The flowers will attract insects, and the berries will feed the birds.'

She didn't look convinced so I dropped it.

'No worries, it's your garden and there's still habitat potential.' I walked towards a pile of garden debris and rotting logs at the bottom of the garden. 'This is fantastic. You can create two habitats right here.' I pointed to two big green bags stuffed to bursting with vegetation. 'There's no need to take these down the dump, just pile up all garden debris in a pile next to the logs.'

She nodded enthusiastically. 'It's not a mess, it's a habitat. I'm happy with that.'

An earthy patch overtaken by weeds separated the lawn from the dumping ground.

'The old shed was where the logs are now,' she explained. 'That was the old flower bed in front of it, but I've let it go a bit.'

'You can screen the messy bits by creating a false back to your garden with a hedge, so the debris will be hidden behind it,' I told her. 'Hawthorn would work well, cheap, easy to grow, native species, and it will provide food and a nesting site for birds.'

'Easy to grow sounds good to me. As you can see I'm not a natural gardener.'

'That's not always bad. Bees will like your dandelions and clover, and your nettles and thistles will attract butterflies.'

I pulled a small trowel out of my pocket, squatted down and dug into the soil to get a sense of the depth and texture. The trowel was going in easy enough, no problem with depth. I rubbed the grey soil between my fingers... I dug another spadeful, still looking. A lone woodlouse, what had happened to the rest? Where were the worms, the springtails, the beetles, the millipedes? These were the building blocks of the food chain. I felt a jolt of anxiety in my gut. I'd not dug in soil for twenty years. Statistics were one thing, but the soil was barren. Where has all the life gone?

Florence trotted into the garden and squatted down, gazing serenely into the distance.

'Do you use a wormer on Florence?'

'Yes?'

'That will kill all worms it comes in contact with.' I held some unmoving soil in my hand. 'How about flea treatment?'

'Is that bad?'

'Pets rarely get fleas in winter so maybe give it a rest till summer.'

'The vet recommended it each month just in case.'

'It's a good income stream for them, but one typical flea treatment has enough pesticide to kill millions of insects, not just fleas, but bees too, and it gets into the water supply, affecting aquatic organisms and amphibians.'

'OMG, I feel like a murderer now.'

'Look for less toxic alternatives. If they don't work you can always do a stronger treatment if problems occur.'

I straightened up and spotted a large tree stump. There was little point treating stumps with stump killer as they won't grow once cut down to that level, but commercial gardeners often did anyway. If the poison made it to the roots as it was designed to, it would also have affected the surrounding soil. I rubbed the soil from my hands and peered round the garden. A few decking boards and panels from the old shed lay among the logs.

'The treated wood from the old decking and shed should be removed as it will be toxic to wildlife.'

'So a trip to the dump after all. And the logs? I meant to burn them but then this area became a clean air zone so they've just been left.'

'Perfect. Insects love rotting wood, and that will attract the birds.'

I turned a log over with my foot to illustrate. On cue a robin appeared on the fence, head on one side, checking to see what might be revealed. We were both delighted to see a large earthworm wriggling around.

The robin shot us a quick glance, then looked at the worm.

'I'm not sure who to root for,' Lori said. 'Probably the robin. What about you?'

'I confess to being a member of the Earthworm Society.'

She laughed and we watched, united in needing to know the fate of the worm.

There was a peaceful silence, that wasn't really a silence at all. The momentary chatter of magpies in next door's oak tree. The sonic boom of a flock of swans flying overhead to reach the river nearby. The quiet murmur of traffic elsewhere sounding distant and irrelevant to the minidrama before us. The robin jumped down to the worm, who continued to wriggle, ignorant of its peril. A rustle in the bamboo caused the robin to look sharply around and fly off.

The sky went dark as clouds obscured the sun. It started to rain, hard.

The bamboo waved its fronds at me as we rushed back. It had got away with it this time.

Florence settled into her faux fur dog basket. I sat at the kitchen table, looking round. The kitchen was cosy and unpretentious. It spoke of a woman with more interesting things to do than housework, yet sufficiently clean that I felt happy to accept the offer of tea and toast. I nodded thanks as she set down a mug of tea in front of me.

She sat opposite me. 'How long have you been a gardener?'

'I'm more of an ecologist than a gardener, but I've done a bit of guerrilla gardening.'

'Ooh, have you?'

'Oh yes,' I said, mild pride in my voice.

'What's guerrilla gardening?' The way she said it made it sound far more dangerous than it was.

'You plant fruit trees and edible plants in public spaces without permission, and even,' I decided to play up the romance of it, 'in people's gardens.'

'I knew a guerrilla knitter once.'

'What? Someone who gets rid of nits.'

'No, a knitter, someone who knits.'

'Ah, yes of course.' Stupid idiot.

'She knitted this patchwork shroud and put it over the statue of Lord Palmerstone in Palmerston Park.'

I laughed out loud at the image it conjured up in my head.

'I think it was a feminist protest against all the statues being of male imperialists.'

'There should be a statue of her.'

'Knitted,' said Lori. We burst into laughter. 'No one ever saw her after that.'

'What? You mean…'

'There's a bit of conspiracy theory around her actually, because she was never seen again.'

'Very mysterious.'

The rain picked up, drumming down on the Velux windows.

I noticed the guttering outside her patio doors, which led onto the decking. 'I didn't see a water butt – do you have one?'

'No. Oh dear maybe I should.'

Did she sound defensive? Tim, you idiot – cardinal rule, don't make people feel guilty. Here was I, sat at her table drinking her tea, berating her for not having a water butt.

'Sorry, no, I didn't mean, look I can get you one. We could put it on the decking to catch the rainwater.'

'Yes, that would be handy for watering the plants in summer. But I'll get it, I don't want to take advantage.'

'Right, yes, okay.'

She nodded, amused.

'I'll put all my suggestions in a report listing all the advice and materials needed.'

'That would be great, I'd just been thinking I should have taken notes.'

'No need.'

While Lori buttered toast, I surveyed the garden out of the patio doors, mentally compiling my report. The hawthorns would be tall enough by next summer to screen off the habitat area behind it. The garden material piled at the back would decompose providing a habitat for invertebrates, which, in turn, would provide food for birds.

'This is a great project you're doing. I'm so glad you came,' Lori echoed my thoughts.

'You were the first...' I paused, still wondering what term to use.

'Beneficiary of your skills?'

'Beneficiary of my skills – I like it.' I smiled at her as she handed me a plate of buttered toast. Florence appeared at my feet, and gazed up at me with loving eyes.

'Was it good for you?' Lori laughed.

'Thank you, it was... yes.' I felt my face getting red. 'Erm, you'll need bare-root hawthorn saplings. It'll create a hedge with a high wildlife value. I'll email you a link. Plant them the moment you get them.'

The clock tower chimed. Twelve already. I paused. Jo had been insistent. 'One visit only, no actual manual labour.' We'd shaken on it.

'I could help plant them if you like?'

4

THE D

The pub was unusually lively – a group of twenty-somethings were clustered round the bar, laughing and talking at the top of their voices, upsetting the man at the bar with their jollity. Jo waited to order, caught between a group of girls on one side and the old man on her other ranting at them.

She eventually returned and set the beers down in front of me.

'What did lone-man-at-the-bar have to say tonight?'

'He was shouting something about forgiving Jesus.'

'He doesn't like it when the young girls come in.'

'I do.' She smiled over at the girls who smiled back. Despite being a loner at heart, Jo had the ability to make superficial friendships instantly. A friendly quip, a jocular aside and they immediately thought of her as their best friend. She rarely remembered who she'd made friends with, so called everyone 'mate' just in case. It rankled sometimes when she called me the same, but I knew better than to say anything, preferring to deny her the pleasure of mocking me for being overly sensitive.

'Habitat Man!' she boomed, raising her pint.

'There's no need to bellow Habitat Man like that.'

'How'd it go?'

I filled her in on my first appointment. Jo was very interested in Lori. Before she could express disapproval of my offer of a return visit, I enquired about Charlotte's life coaching course.

'I bet Charlotte got top marks for her case study – i.e. me.' I sat back and enjoyed a long gulp of my beer, waiting for the glowing feedback. I must have been a life coach's dream. What a turnaround to report on.

'She got a D.'

'What?' I choked on my pint.

'She's well pissed off, but it's not your fault, mate.'

'How could it be?'

'She said you shouldn't take it personally, she knows what a sensitive soul you are.'

'I do take it personally. It's supposed to be a transformative experience. How much more transformative could it get than me giving up a six figure salary to work essentially for nothing?'

'That's the problem. They're worried that Charlotte egged you on in an irresponsible manner without checking your financial situation.'

'I've paid off my mortgage, I can last till my pension, I can live simply, especially now you're buying the drinks.'

This elicited a sharp intake of breath from Jo.

'Yeah, well you don't have to justify yourself to me. Anyway, it wasn't just that.'

'What then?' In my righteous indignation I'd edged into soprano which would normally result in Jo taking the piss. It seemed like this time I'd got away with it, which should have warned me.

'What then?' I repeated in a deeper voice.

'She said she was marked down for not providing enough psychological context.'

'What?' Back in soprano.

'Like why you stayed so long in a job that you hated?'

There was a short silence, she continued tentatively.

'She asked if you'd be prepared to fill in some background.'

'Like?'

'How come you never married, had kids, changed job?'

'You didn't tell her did you?'

'Course not.'

The thought of strangers assessing Charlotte's homework, i.e. my life, was more than I could bear. It wasn't a story that looked good on paper. Only Jo understood the truth, and I was happy to keep it that way.

'Well, I'm not going to tell a bunch of strangers my personal financial details am I?' I said in the end.

'Certainly not,' Jo agreed. 'Your round.'

From: Tim Redfern
To: Walker. L
Subject: Green Garden Consultancy – Final Report – Lori Walker

Hello Lori
Please find attached your report; please let me know if you have any questions. Thanks again and lovely working with you.
Tim
PS Would you like a hand planting the saplings? No charge.

I was too effusive. I should have said 'nice working with you'. Was I too forward with the saplings?

It was strange to have time on my hands. I'd spent much longer than I needed to on Lori's report, and once I'd sent it off, I was at a loss.

I wandered into Jo's room but she was immersed in one of her online games.

'Jo?'

'Go on then, tell your mum!' she jeered at the screen.

I hovered.

'Jo?'

'What?'

'I thought now I've got time I might start cooking properly. I've signed us up for a seasonal organic vegetable box.'

'Mmm?'

'No more ready meals or takeaways. Fancy a vegetable stew later?'

'In a minute.'

I gave up and started cooking. Root vegetables were in season so I spent a while peeling and chopping swede, turnip, parsnips, carrots, celeriac and potatoes and cooking them all up with a tin of tomatoes and baked beans for protein. I'd hoped that Jo would join me for lunch but she just grabbed a bowl and ate in front of her computer.

I found myself brooding over the D I'd got for the life coaching course. It was totally unfair – my life had changed beyond recognition. What about the secondary impacts in terms of Lori's garden? As a result of the changes made, there'll now be more habitats for wildlife. I should take before and after pictures, as a record. And what about the water butt, conserving water for the dry spells? Although she might never install one, it was just advice I gave after all. I checked my email hoping Lori had responded, but nothing yet.

Bored, I returned to my notes and wrote them up in earnest.

I had to bully Jo to eat dinner with me. Normally I wasn't home from work till eight and she was used to eating in front of her computer, but I was desperate for some stimulation.

'You need to learn how to relax,' she commented, then picked up the bowl. 'I'll finish this in my room.'

'No you don't. You can talk to me. Honestly, you're spending too much time gaming.'

'You should have a go.'

What? The Multi Guild of Runecraft.'

'That's the one,' said Jo grinning.

'Not my thing.'

'You'd be crap at it anyway.'

I wasn't having that.

The next day I constructed my avatar. Chuckling at my own cunning, I made myself a beautiful female. Women always did better in negotiations.

For a while I wandered round, admiring the way my auburn tresses swung becomingly. I soon realised that before I could do anything interesting I'd have to gather resources so I chopped some wood. That got tedious after a while so I mined for gold.

'It's boring,' I declared to Jo later over lunch.

'It is when you start but I skip that bit.'

'How?'

'I lure newbies into the wilderness and nick their stuff.'

'What?'

'It's only virtual, Timbo, don't look at me like I'm a criminal.'

'The actual players are real behind their avatars.'

'Or I do a bit of whoring,' Jo enjoyed my look of shock. 'I made myself utterly stunning and I've several boyfriends who I suck up to so they give me stuff.'

I thought of how gorgeous I was and hid a coy smile.

'But,' I said sanctimoniously, 'it's true to life in that you have to work and do a bit of the boring stuff before you move onto the excitement.' I caught a glint in her eye and stopped quickly in case she thought I was having a pop at her for not working – she didn't take criticism well as a rule, overt or implied. This time it looked like I'd got away with it.

After lunch, I checked my emails, still nothing. Disappointed, I had little else to do but have another go. After spending hours laboriously chopping wood and mining for gold,

I hastened forth on a quest, light of heart and looking groovy in my spangled tight-fitting lime green bodice and flared pink tutu. At last, I had a treasure trove full of resources and the Runecraft world was my oyster. I wisely avoided an invitation to accompany a man into the dark woods and instead followed a cobbled path towards a shining lake. I was approached by an avatar even more beautiful than me – tall and slender with the long, yellow hair of a princess.

'Please, do you have a golden sword?' she implored me.

'No,' I typed into my speech bubble. 'What's that?'

'It's magic,' she replied. 'I would give anything, all my gold, all my wood, all my treasure for a golden sword.'

I took a look, and she had a lot of treasure to give. 'I've wandered for years in search of the golden sword,' she said walking off.

I carried on and saw a sign for a market and headed in that direction. Soon I came upon an old woman.

'Golden sword for sale,' she croaked.

I couldn't believe my luck, but surely it would be more than I could afford as a beginner.

'How much?' I typed.

'Just a hundred pieces of wood, and fifty gold,' came the response.

That happened to be almost exactly what I had and I eagerly made the trade. Jo always said I was unworldly but wait until she found out that I'd got hold of a golden sword so early in the game. My stomach told me it was dinner time, but I contented myself with a bag of crisps and rushed back to find the beautiful princess to sell it on. She was gone. I hunted around desperately but it looked like she'd signed herself out of the game. I was suddenly nervous that I'd sold everything I had for this one object. I spent hours wandering from place to place, looking for a buyer. In the end I sold it for a couple of bales of hay and gave up.

When I finally stomped downstairs at two in the morning, Jo was there making tea and toast to fortify her for the next few hours gaming into the night. She grinned when she saw me.

'Golden sword?' she croaked.

From: *Transition Southampton*
To: *Tim Redfern*
Subject: *Green Gardening Consultancy*
Attachment: *Dawn, Highfield*

Dear Tim
I'm sorry things have been slow. I'm sure it's just the stormy weather, but this should cheer you up. We got a £10 donation and a request for a visit from Dawn (details attached). We're putting it towards setting up our new Share Shop, so if you need to borrow anything like gardening or DIY tools, let us know. I know you said you wouldn't be doing actual work, but the offer is there if you need it.
Karen

PS I also got an enquiry from Geoff from Woolston, asking about habitats for bats and frogs, I'll send details once he's paid.

I responded immediately to set up a visit. I was glad for more to do but it wasn't the email I was waiting for.

5

THE POLYAMORIST

I heaved my way up the hill on my bike, turned into Dawn's road and leant the bike against her fence. With the sound of my bike silenced, there was a slight hush in the air, the birds seemed to sing extra loud, calling their mates back to the nest. I allowed myself a moment to savour the peace and quiet, marvelling at how a few trees and the sound of birdsong and wind rustling through branches can transform an urban suburb into an oasis of calm.

The doorbell was answered by a comfortably plump, black-haired woman, wearing multicoloured silk pyjama bottoms and a loose shirt that exposed a generous cleavage.

'Dawn?'

'Habitat Man?' She looked me up and down, her eyes glinting for a second, then she beckoned me in.

I smiled nervously and followed her into the house. I'd always associated Highfield with academic types, and the very proper ladies from the Highfield Women's Institute. They certainly wouldn't answer the door wearing pyjamas.

'What would you like me to do?' I asked, once the kettle was on.

'I'm looking for a compassionate way to get rid of rodents.'

'Ah. I try to preserve wildlife and habitats, I'm more about how to get animals into your garden.'

'Even rats?'

'No. Rats are social and intelligent creatures, but they can easily take over.'

'I thought I had mice so I tried to trap them with this.' She showed me a small plastic bottle with a tiny toy plastic ladder stuck to the side and a lump of cheese in the bottom. 'But it turned out to be rats.'

I jumped when she pulled a huge dead rat out of a bag by its tail.

'I called the rat man but he just took the mick and wanted to poison them.'

I stifled a smile, the rat was many times larger than the bottle.

She dropped the rat back in the bag and handed me a mug of hot tea. I took it gratefully, glad of a chance to gather my thoughts after the misunderstanding.

'Erm… what *would* you like to see in your garden?'

'Hedgehogs perhaps? I haven't seen them for ages.'

'Wonderful, we can try.' I stood up, tea in hand. 'Shall we have a look?'

Dawn swapped her fluffy slippers for wellingtons and led me outside.

'First thing is to avoid slug pellets and pesticides, they're a key cause of decline of many species, hedgehogs included.' I followed Dawn into her back garden.

'Also they need to gain access.' I looked around. The fence on one side had come down, presumably blown over by the recent storm. A seed of a plan was growing in my mind. It all depended on the answer to my next question.

'Would you consider a hedge here? It won't provide an instant barrier, but it has four advantages.'

'Do tell.'

'Firstly, new fences are often coated with a wood preserver which hedgehogs often lick and will poison them. You can get environmentally safe water-based products, but even if you do, hedgehogs need to roam, so if your garden is fully enclosed like this one, there's no space for them to get in, or out. Three, hedges are good for providing habitats and food for birds and bees.'

'Birds and bees, yes…' Dawn's eyes gleamed as she held my gaze. 'And four?'

'There's a minimum order of twenty-five a bundle for bare-root saplings which would cost about thirty pounds. You'd only need ten to cover this gap, and they'd take a year or two to grow into an effective barrier but I know someone who may have ten hawthorn left over. I'd be happy to collect them.'

'Sounds good, I can bung her a tenner towards it.'

'Fantastic.' Another visit to Lori to hand over the money.

Dawn looked a little taken aback by my enthusiastic response.

'Last thing is create a nesting site, a compost heap would do the trick, and would also provide a habitat for the kinds of creatures hedgehogs like to eat.'

Dawn shook her head. 'Apparently it's the compost bin that's attracting the rats. I'd better stop putting in food waste.'

'Don't do that. Everything biological should be composted.' I saw her compost bin hidden in the corner of the garden. 'Let me take a look, I can probably rat-proof it. I'm good with my hands.'

'I like a man that's good with his hands!' The glint in her eye was suddenly pronounced.

I was saved having to respond by the doorbell.

She rushed inside. 'Back in a mo, hun, you do your thing.'

I checked out the compost bin. The ground underneath was uneven, allowing rats access.

When she returned, I told her my plan. 'Move the bin onto the paved area in front of your shed, then the rats can't get in. It also makes it easier to shovel out the compost from the bottom.'

'It could go there, no problem.'

'Then use the area where it was to pile up your old leaves and garden debris to create a safe spot for hedgehogs to nest.'

I lifted the lid of the compost bin to take a look. It was almost full. 'It would only take half an hour to empty out the compost, re-site the bin, and re-add the compost.'

She glanced up at the bedroom window. I wondered who'd been at the door.

'That would be wonderful, thanks, hun.'

Oh. I hadn't meant to imply I was going to do it myself. I looked at Dawn's silk pyjamas, and sighed. 'Okay. I'll give you a shout when I'm done?'

'If you're sure?'

'Do you have a spade?'

'Here you go.'

I was conscious of her eyes on me as I bent over the bin, dug out the compost and put it in a pile. I hoped I didn't have builder's bum. I straightened up and raised my arms above my head to stretch out. Dawn's eye strayed to a patch of hairy stomach that had appeared as my shirt lifted up in the stretch. I felt myself beginning to blush and bent over the bin again. I prayed fervently she didn't plan to stand there watching me work.

'Okay, cheers, hun. I'll be upstairs. Shout when you're done.'

Thankfully, she headed back inside. Lugging the top level of food scraps and grass cuttings over to the paving slabs took a while. I took the opportunity to shovel out the rich fertile compost from the bottom of the bin, and pile it up round the back of her hedges, plants and trees. Once it was empty, I dragged it over to the paved area, and shovelled the top bits back in. Taking out the compost and putting it back in would do it good, creating pockets of oxygen that would help the process along. I noticed some lovely reddish-brown, wriggly worms left on the ground and popped them back in. Job done!

I peered in the compost bin satisfied, and amazed, as always, by the chemistry that translates grass cuttings and food waste into rich, earthy soil that nourishes the garden. And it was all down to the humble earthworm. If I were ever to write a poem, it would be to the worm that aerates and enriches the earth. Its tunnels of air, castings and water, weaving a life-giving magic. Its slimy undulations turning the waste of the world and plain mud into rich, textured soil, food from which the roses can grow. The humble worm! I replaced the lid and raised my arms above my head to stretch, then brought them slowly down, breathing in the invigorating autumn air. I dreamt of a world where we award this humble worm all the respect it deserves. I had a brief mental image of the worm with a medal round its neck, nodding modestly to the applause.

Pleased with this vision and my work, I trudged up the garden feeling the pain in my back from the bending and shovelling. It was lovely working outdoors, but I wouldn't want to be a gardener. I rotated my hips clockwise and then anticlockwise to ease out the kinks. I gazed up to stretch my neck and noticed a net curtain twitch in the bedroom. Was I imagining that eyes were upon me?

I walked up to the back door. 'Hello!' I ventured. No answer. I took off my boots and stepped into the kitchen. I was desperate to wash my hands, but the sink was full of washing up.

I heard a television on upstairs. Who else lived here? Did Dawn have a husband or family? Jo had berated me for thinking of people as hazards, but after so many years dealing with numbers, I was finding it strange being in other people's homes.

I walked up to the bottom of the stairs. 'Hello! Er, Dawn!'

An upstairs door opened and the television was heard more clearly. Dawn's face appeared.

'Hi, Dawn, I'm done, can I wash my hands?'

'Of course, hun, up here, the bathroom's on the left.'

I hastened up the stairs and into the bathroom to wash my hands. I emerged, and jumped in shock as a piercing scream came from the bedroom. Dawn was standing in the doorway unperturbed.

'Kerry and I like to snuggle up in bed and watch an Agatha Christie.'

I nodded, heart still racing from the unexpected scream. I could hear Miss Marple in the background. 'You are in dire peril, my dear.' Dawn was still standing there, gazing at me steadily with that glint in her eye.

'Has the Wizard been in touch?'

'Who?'

'From Woolston.'

'I've had a Geoff from Woolston.'

'That's him. Tell him I said "blessed be".'

Oh my days! He wanted bats and frogs. What was he planning on doing with them? I remembered that one of the collective nouns for bats was a cauldron of bats. My wild imaginings were brought to a sudden halt by her next question.

'Fancy coming in to play?'

Play? Monopoly? Scrabble?

'Me and Kerry have been watching you and we think you're sexy.'

So I hadn't imagined the glint. The question crossed my mind whether Kerry was a male or female. Best not to ask in case she took it as interest.

'I looked at my watch. Why did I do that? Now she's going to think it depends on how much time I have. I was paralysed. This was definitely one to tell Jo. What better example of potential hazards was there? Although, I already could hear the response 'what's so hazardous about someone wanting you to join in a threesome!' Frantic sounds from the television ended my paralysis. 'You had better get away from here as fast as you can!' urged Miss Marple. I took her advice and ran.

6

PANSYGATE

From: Walker. L
To: Tim Redfern
Subject: Re Green Garden Consultancy – Final Report

Hi Tim,
Thanks again for your help. The report is wonderfully detailed. I
ordered the hawthorn saplings – they'll arrive Friday so will plant
them on Saturday morning if you're free? No worries if not.
Cheers
Lori

Yes! I forgot to mention adding some RootGrow Mycorrhizal Fungi to nourish the saplings. I'll order that right now.

When I approached Lori's house, I was delighted to note that Florence marked my arrival with a wagging tail rather than a volley of barks. Lori answered the door and I was almost bowled over by Florence's exuberant welcome.

'Come on, Flo, leave the poor man alone,' Lori pulled Florence away. 'Are you here to help me plant some hawthorn?'

'I am.'

'That's very kind. Come on through. Tea?'

'Always.' I followed her into the kitchen.

'Milk no sugar?'

'Yes please.' I smiled, delighted she'd remembered.

'Is it okay if I take some before and after shots of your garden?'

'Go ahead.'

I stepped out on the decking to take a few pictures. On impulse, I took one of Florence who'd come out to join me, then snuck a quick photo of Lori while she wasn't looking to show Jo. I returned to surveying the garden, keen to become acquainted with the wildlife that lived there already. Magpies occupied the tree dividing her garden from next door, and pigeons cooed in the distance. A bird sang, probably the robin we'd seen last time. In autumn, it would already be defending its territory. The sounds of Lori making tea mingled with the wind in the trees and the robin's song. I felt completely at peace. I'd made the right decision, I knew that now. Soon, because of this project, there would be extra food and shelter for the birds and the bees. It may have been a freebie gift, cheeky even, but thank goodness for that life coaching session, although the D still rankled.

Lori brought out cups of tea which we drank while making our way down to the bottom of the garden. We laid out the hawthorn saplings, teasing out their roots to separate them.

'I'll dig the holes,' I suggested, 'you sprinkle in some RootGrow, then I'll plant the saplings and you fill in the earth.'

'Sounds very efficient,' she smiled.

I squatted down and dug down to about six inches, then looked up. 'Look,' I nodded towards the robin who had appeared on the fence, alert for any goodies we may unearth.

'No worms yet,' Lori told him and squatted down next to me. 'Done any guerrilla gardening lately?'

'Not for years,' I said, grabbing the first sapling.

'Why not? It sounds fun.' She sprinkled in RootGrow.

I gently placed the sapling into the hole. 'We got taken over by the Bassett ladies. They'd see a space that had a lovely bit of scrub, dandelions, great plants for wildlife that thrive in such conditions. And they'd pull it up to plant something pretty.'

'They sound pure evil, Tim. What did you do?' She watered the hole and we both shuffled twelve inches to the left to get the next hole ready.

'Me and some others left and formed a splinter group. But I quit when they started breaking the law.'

'What like?'

'They'd plant fruit trees and vegetables in land listed for development. Then came AppleGate.'

'AppleGate?'

'They mapped all the fruit trees in the area, then they'd gather up any fruit that wasn't being harvested and leave it out in boxes for people to take for free. Trouble was that they didn't care if the trees were on private property.'

'You disapproved?' Lori sounded surprised. Clearly she'd find my visceral fear of getting in trouble with the law rather wet.

I shrugged noncommittally, and grabbed another sapling.

'You can plant fruit trees in my garden if you like.'

'But it would have to be secretly, under the cover of darkness to be true guerrilla gardening,' I joked.

'Ooh yes please.' Her eyes twinkled for a moment, then she looked worried. 'Better not, my son's got an air rifle.'

'What?' I stopped in the act of digging the hole.

'The other day he shot a magpie.' She patted down the earth furiously.

The murderer accusation suddenly made sense.

'Hang on, I haven't put the hawthorn in yet!'

She looked down and laughed. 'Sorry.'

'Couldn't his dad have a word?' I congratulated myself on my subtle approach of finding out her status.

'He's the one who got him the air rifle for God's sake.'

'Oh my days!' Still, by her tone, it sounded like they'd split up.

'Yes, and—' she stopped abruptly, and adopted a teasing smile, 'and, er, are the evil pansy-planters of Bassett still going?'

'I don't like your mocking tone,' I reproved her. 'They lost interest when the pansies died because no one watered them. There's nothing more useless and ugly than dead bedding plants.'

'PansyGate,' declared Lori, making me laugh.

I'd dug another hole before I realised we'd planted all the saplings. 'Looks like we're done.'

We got to our feet and stepped back to admire our work. Two rows of hawthorns stood thin, young and trembling, creating a natural barrier between the lawn and the area at the back where Lori had raked the rotting wood and vegetation.

'Prune them next autumn when they get to waist height and they'll bush out and create a natural screen so you don't see the wild area behind.'

'Thanks, Tim.'

'My pleasure.'

My back was already protesting, and I stretched out extravagantly, confident now in any bits of my torso revealed.

Lori counted the saplings. 'We've got ten left over.'

'I know someone who'd be happy to take the spare hawthorns off your hands for a tenner.'

'She can have them for nothing.'

'She's happy to pay.'

'No I insist, just take them.'

'All right.' I packed them away and we carried them back up the garden. I looked around for another reason to return.

'Have you considered a pond?'

'There's not enough room really.'

I bit back a comment about even tiny ponds also being useful for wildlife. I mustn't be pushy.

Florence thumped her tail in greeting from her basket when we got back to the kitchen.

'Thanks for helping out, and for bringing the RootGrow. What do I owe you?'

'Nothing. I had some anyway.' I sat down at the table. 'Does your son...'

'Ethan.'

'Has Ethan any interest in wildlife?'

'Only to kill it. Otherwise he seems to live online, except for when he storms out to places I don't know, doing things I've no idea about.' Her brow furrowed. 'So no, except... he likes vampires?' We laughed.

Lori put the cups in the sink. I noticed she hadn't put the kettle back on. I felt a jolt of disappointment and realised this was the most fun I'd had for a long time. I'd actually felt completely relaxed and at ease all morning in the presence of a seemingly single, non-lesbian woman. I got up again. 'Right well, Lori, thanks for the tea.'

'You off?'

Damn! She wasn't kicking me out. 'Well...' I sat back down.

Lori went to refill the kettle then hesitated at the sound of stomping on the stairs.

'Ethan's up.'

The stomping sound got closer. Seeing the tension in her face, I spared her having to say it.

'I'll be off then.'

Lori and Florence saw me to the door. I bent down to give Flo one last pat. Lori opened the door for me. I saw the vampire bat knocker and had an idea.

'I could make you a bat box?'

7

A GREAT IDEA

I smiled broadly, enjoying the sight of Jo at the bar. Saturday night down the local – probably the only thing about my life that hadn't drastically changed. I was glad because Jo and I had barely spoken in the week. I hadn't realised how much time she spent gaming. I'd naively supposed while I was at work, she was doing useful things too. I'd also assumed that once I was at home we'd interact more, but she was set in her ways and most of my conversational greetings were waved away with an 'in a minute,' or ignored.

Jo set down two pints of beer hurriedly.

'What's up?'

'Human dog at one o'clock.' She grabbed her phone, and took a photo.

I looked out of the window. A man with long brown hair and a long grey beard was being pulled along by an Afghan hound that looked just like him.

'Check out that beard. And the dog!'

'I've got a good one.' I showed her the photo I'd taken of Florence. 'Isn't she the most beautiful dog you've ever seen?'

She put on her glasses and had a peer.

'Oh yes! Part teddy bear, part sex-siren.'

I swiped left. 'And that's Lori.'

'Oh my God.' Jo grabbed my phone and swiped to and fro, comparing the photos. 'This is perfect for my dogs-who-look-like-their-owners collection.'

'You're not posting them.'

'Go on, mate, I've got to keep my followers happy.'

'Too bad, but aren't they both lovely?'

'I know what you're thinking, Timbo, we're not getting a dog.'

It wasn't what I was thinking but now she mentioned it...

'Well I'm at home a lot now, I'd have time to walk it.'

'We don't have a garden. Anyway, what happened to the one visit rule? How many times have you been at Lori's?'

'I haven't got much else to do.'

'As long as she's not using you.'

'What? Because that's your job?'

Jo ignored my comment and appraised me for a moment. 'You're different.'

'I feel different.'

'You're more annoying.'

'What? I'm doing the cooking.'

'You haven't progressed since student days, it's always lentils and rice or vegetable stew. And you expect me to be grateful for it.'

'It's healthier. You know, Jobo, your lifestyle could be better.'

'That's another thing. Now you've gone and transformed your life, you're starting on me.'

'Well you're gaming almost all your waking hours now we're not working on that software. It's not healthy, to be fair.'

'No, you're right, I quite miss working on that.' She finished her beer and slumped back in her chair.

'Me too.' I remembered the evenings and weekends we'd dedicated to developing it. Jo had written the software and I'd supplied all the content: carbon footprint, water footprint, biodiversity metrics, resource costs. It had been exhausting – for me anyway as, unlike Jo, I was working the other five days. But it had also been fun. For the first time I allowed myself to acknowledge the deep disappointment I'd felt when they'd turned it down. It looked like Jo felt the same. I loved my new life but I needed more to do. We both did.

Jo sat upright and tapped the table. 'We could... no... get the pints in, mate, while I think.'

I didn't have to wait long at the bar. Our local was quiet again this week. It looked like the youngsters had decided not to make it their regular, put off perhaps by the old man at the bar ranting at them. Today he was muttering quietly into his pint. Ever since Jo had said that could be me one day, I'd taken more of an interest.

'Sorry what did you say?'

'Sewilemunimmeyed,' he informed me, gazing at me though bloodshot eyes. I nodded politely. The landlord set two pints on the bar top and I made my escape.

'There's no way it's ten years between me and the guy at the bar,' I declared, setting the pints down. 'Twenty at least.'

'You'd be surprised. Drink adds decades to the face.' She took a large swig. 'I'm thirty!' I looked at her double chin and crinkly eyes and laughed.

'Don't laugh too hard, mate, you're no spring chicken yourself.'

I stopped laughing before she could elaborate.

'I was thinking while you were chatting up the man at the bar, we should be more creative with our cooking.'

'I could try new stuff. Maybe experiment with some quinoa instead of rice. Mange tout instead of peas?' I suggested.

'This is lapsang souchong all over again.' Jo's words held an implicit threat.

I remembered the torture she'd put me through when I'd

once brought back a packet of loose leaf lapsang souchong tea. As punishment for being pretentious, she'd insisted that I had to get through it all before I was allowed to have a normal cup of tea.

'Well you asked for a change,' I cried, before she got the idea of making me eat bucketsful of quinoa. 'I got so fed up of lapsang bloody souchong.'

'Tasted shit, mate.'

'It seemed to last forever.'

'That's because I was secretly refilling it,' she laughed, a gleeful look in her eye.

'Oh my days!'

Her laughter was infectious. I tried to be cross but every time I thought about it, it set me off in giggles.

'I can't believe I didn't realise.'

'Four bloody packets I splashed out on.'

'You total—'

'Not cheap either,' her laughter paused, as she followed the shapely outline of a woman heading for the bar. Jo ogled women in a way that I would never dare, but like me, rarely made a move.

'Still you told me off for being stuck in a rut, but when I tried something new, that's what I get.'

'I know it's so unfair, but it makes me think.' She leant back, taking a thoughtful swig. 'I've got it! A way to be more creative in the kitchen and make use of the Costing for Nature software.'

'Go on then.' She had the animated air that boded the arrival of a Great Idea.

'We create columns of ingredients ordered by food type, then the program randomly selects ingredients from each column.'

'Like a random recipe generator?'

'Exactly. That's what we'll call it. Program it to choose up to three ingredients from each food type, and weight the probability that they'd come up based on their carbon footprint.'

'Weight those that are in season, so you'd get nuts in autumn, root veg in winter, berries and spring greens in summer.'

'And you create a dish based only on those ingredients that come up randomly.'

'No way. We've got to eat it, at the end of the day,' I protested.

'The rules are that you're allowed to drop one item and add one item,' she allowed graciously.

'But water, salt and oil are free.'

'The Random Recipe Generator is go!' Jo declared.

From: *Transition Southampton*
To: *Tim Redfern*
Subject: *Green Gardening Consultancy*
Attachment: *Daisy, St Denys*

Dear Tim
Here's another request for your skills. This came from Daisy in St Denys.
Cheers, Karen
PS There's a free pond basin going if you can find a use for it.

8

DAISY FROM ST DENYS

'Daisy in St Denys' sounded fun. Not just for the alliteration, but, next to Bitterne Park, St Denys was my favourite area, in my favourite city, which might surprise those who know Southampton. It was all about the people. Southampton as a city is diverse, with a mix of academics, students, sailors, dock workers, numerous ethnic groups, mostly Indians but also Africans, Chinese and Europeans. Many cities have great diversity, London obviously, but in Southampton, it seemed to me that the various groups were relatively at ease with each other.

St Denys was home to the eccentrics and alternatives – greenies, hippies, old timers, plus a mini-community of house-boaters who lived on the river. Occasionally I'd felt the lure of the countryside, but it was this side of the city that kept me in Southampton.

Perhaps having been bombed to pieces in the war, Southampton was very open, with none of that tall-building, closed-in feeling you can get from other cities, including the ever-trendy Brighton. Southampton wasn't trendy, but it was authentic and it was green. You could cycle from North to South or East to West across the city and never leave a park. I thought of the statue of Lord Palmerstone in Palmerstone Park that was knitted over and laughed again. I'd love to see a photo, but that was back before everyone had cameras on their phones.

I was glad I'd decided to cycle. The road was edged with parked cars on both sides, without a break. One house stood out among the row of Victorian terraced houses, the tiny front garden adorned with woven objects, artfully arranged piles of pebbles and pine cones and sumptuous wreaths made from dried flowers. This was it, but I saw nowhere to put the bike. This was the slightly grimy side of St Denys. I wondered if I could get away with hiding it behind the discarded sofa in the front garden a few doors down.

'Bung it here if you like.' A man next door wearing a saffron robe pointed to where I could lock it to his gate. Grimy yes, but friendly. I smiled my thanks and wheeled it over.

'Cheers.'

'No worries.'

I returned next door and looked round for the bell. Numerous wind chimes, a dangly thing – I struggled for the word – 'dream catcher', no bell and no doorknocker. I patted the wind chimes, setting off a range of harmonies that transported me for a moment to the Alps, where goats and cattle roamed. The door was opened by a girl, a student perhaps? Orange hair, purple trousers, colourful top. It should have clashed, but somehow it didn't.

'Hi, are you Daisy?'

'Yes – Tim?' I nodded. 'Come on in.'

The smell hit me the moment I entered, a heady, yet warming mixture of incense and spices. I followed Daisy though the house into the kitchen, where an old man in baggy trousers and a loose top stirred a curry. Colourful, knitted, patchwork blankets covered a two-seater sofa in the corner, on which were woven baskets full of potatoes and carrots. The windowsill was crowded with jam jars full of herbs, a mini Buddha, joss stick holders, wooden carved animals and polished stones.

'That smells lovely.'

The old man peered round at me. 'All home-grown vegetables,' he said proudly.

'Wonderful.' I was heartened. This looked like a good start. I was keen to see what the garden looked like.

'What brings you to our neck of the woods?'

'This is Tim, Grandad, he's come to check out our garden.'

'What for?'

I sensed a withdrawal of his goodwill, and wondered if he'd been told about the green garden project.

'I'm here to help create habitats for wildlife.'

'Hmm.'

'You don't mind do you, Grandad?'

He stirred and it was hard to read his expression. 'Okay, but go easy.'

I felt a bit deflated, I'd liked seeing myself as a kind of habitat hero – 'Habitat Man come to help nature!' Jo had boomed down the pub, taking the piss. Even so, I'd liked the image. Now I felt on uncertain ground. Daisy though was keen to get going and led me into the garden.

It was a magical place. Like the house, it was quirky and full of hidden areas. A couple of squirrels chased each other up a hazel tree, under which sat a stone Buddha, hands in lap, eyes blissful and half-closed, meditating. There was little lawn, most of which was overgrown. The low autumn sun brought an extra richness to the light, like the world seen through golden spectacles. The red and yellow leaves from the hazel tree glowed against the deep blue of the sky. A graceful willow tree at the bottom of the garden, its leaves a mix of yellow and green. A witch hazel next door shared its strong, sweet fragrance and flame-coloured ribbon-like flowers with the garden. An elderflower tree on the other side was already bare, leaving a carpet of leaves, a mosaic of colours on the ground. A vegetable patch by a mixed hedge. Ancient terracotta plant pots hosting chili plants, aloe vera, kale, and a variety of herbs. Daisy pointed to two woven chairs and a bench that surrounded a homemade table, which seemed to almost be growing out of the garden.

'Hand-made by my grandad with our own willow,' her voice was full of pride.

I stopped to admire the chairs. One was high-backed with curved armrests like a throne, and the other had curved rockers on the bottom. A start had been made on another willow creation, about six feet long.

'What's this one?'

'Something Grandad is working on. He won't say what it is.'

'Did you have anything specific in mind when you asked me round?'

Daisy sat on the throne. 'I want to create a Feng Shui garden.'

I hadn't a clue what she meant, other than it sounded oriental. 'Do you mean like a Japanese garden?'

'No. I don't mean exactly Feng Shui, but drawing on the principles of using space to create a sense of harmony and spiritual well-being.'

'That sounds interesting, I think you've made a great start already.' I sat on the rocking chair. 'Where did you get the idea?'

'I study art and design at Solent University, and we're taught to think about colour and space and texture, but it still seems so dead. Like you judge a portrait by how lifelike it is, but it isn't alive is it? Not like gardens.'

'I get it.' I rocked in the chair, delighted with the idea. 'It's the colours and textures of the plants through the seasons, the smell of the roses and the honeysuckle.'

'Exactly. The taste of the food you grow, but also the rustle of the wind in the trees, the buzz of bees, the sound of birdsong, the glint of sunlight on water, the babbling of a brook.'

'I can't magic you up a babbling brook, but I could help with the rest of it.'

'Awesome.'

'Let's start with the bees. You need to have something for them all year round. Like lungwort and grape hyacinth for the spring, followed by geraniums, sweet smelling lavender, catmint and marjoram for the summer, and late-blooming Michaelmas daisies and sedum for the autumn.'

'Will we have enough space? Grandad won't want to lose his vegetable patch.'

I cast my eye around, the fence on the right looked a little bare.

'You could have runner beans in front of this fence, the scarlet flowers are pretty, and they'll attract certain types of bumblebees that have really long tongues. You could mix them up with a climbing native honeysuckle for scent in the evening.'

'I love that. I always felt the fence was a bit dead. It had no meaning other than to cut off next door. Not very Feng Shui. This will help screen it.'

'You know, you're not like any student I've come across.' I got up to look round a bit more. 'In a good way,' I added hastily.

Daisy followed me, chattering. 'I don't fit in really. The others think it's weird me living here with Grandad. But he needs a bit of help now, and I wanted to get away from home, because my mum is so dark, so I thought I'd come to Solent uni. It's cheaper living here than in the halls of residence but also Grandad is so wise. I feel like this is my spiritual home. I never met my grandma but apparently she was very crafty, and so is Grandad and he's good at gardening, and I'm good at art and design, so all we need is you to add some wildlife and then we have perfect harmony between sight, sound, texture and smell and life.'

Daisy looked at me sideways. 'Does this sound hippy dippy?'

'Not at all, I'm honoured to help.' Next to the vegetable

patch was a clear, grassy area. I walked over to it. 'This area here would be perfect for a pond.'

Daisy shrieked with excitement. 'I was hoping you'd suggest that. I knew there should be a pond here. I felt it with such certainty, but I didn't want to say, I wanted to see if you felt it too.'

'I definitely do. It would create an ideal habitat for many varieties of insects, which would attract birds.'

Daisy looked at the space as if through an imaginary camera lens. 'The water would mirror the garden back at us. Imagine the pallet of colours from the trees – orange, bronze, green, yellow, red, rippling back at us on the surface.'

I could visualise it easily, it would be stunning.

'Water also provides movement and sound, dragonflies skimming over the surface, the occasional plop of a frog visiting or the splash of a bird taking a bath,' she continued.

'You may not get frogs,' I felt obliged to tell her, 'at least not straightaway.'

Daisy waved away my caution. 'That's what I mean by Feng Shui gardening. To capture in a living garden that feeling you get when it all comes together. It's not just aesthetics, it's about life, soul, meaning, where everything is exactly where it should be and as it should be.'

I nodded slowly, looking around. For the second time since this project began, I felt a deep sense of satisfaction. Unseeing eyes, prejudiced eyes, might see a hippy dippy mess, but I saw perfect harmony. I felt privileged that I could play a part in the wonderful marriage between art and nature before me. I hadn't held out much hope for Charlotte's life coaching, but there was a magic when the three circles of the Venn diagram came together. What are you good at? What does the world need? What brings you joy?

'I get it. Water provides life as well as light and movement. The buzz of the bee isn't just a sound, it's a sign that your plants are being pollinated, that nature is flourishing. But I call it ecology, the vital inter-relationships between plants, animals, including humans and habitats that enable them all to thrive.'

'I prefer my term,' she smiled. 'Would a pond be expensive though?'

'No, there's a free pond basin going.'

Daisy looked thrilled. By the time we went back into the kitchen, she was brimming with plans for the pond and the garden. The smell of curry hit me when we entered the kitchen, making my mouth water.

'You can stay for some veggie curry if you like, as a thank you.'

That sounded good to me. We found her grandad dishing up.

'Some for you there, love.' He looked at me undecided.

Daisy broke in excitedly, 'We're going to dig a pond next to the vegetable patch, we—'

'No.'

'Come on, Grandad, Tim's given his time for free to help us help nature.'

He remained silent.

'But why not?'

I could see the stubborn set to his mouth, and a hint of something else I couldn't decipher. He looked... yes that was it, he looked furtive. I made my decision. It was his house. However puzzling his response, it was his call.

'No worries, I'll send you my report anyway, it will be up to you what you decide to do.' I nodded a goodbye at the old man.

Daisy led me to the front door, still apologising. I reassured her, but I had to admit it was a shame about the pond. That little spot seemed made for one. Regardless, it had been an experience. Something about the house and the garden had felt so full of love. Everywhere I looked, objects had been taken from nature and made into a thing of beauty. Branches of pussy willow in a jam jar on the sill; a collage of autumn leaves on the wall. Photos of Daisy as a girl, an old photo of what might be her grandmother, same dress sense! I did a double-take. A photo of a statue in Palmerstone Park covered in a knitted shroud.

When I unlocked my bike from the house next door, the man was still there, clearing out the dead plants from his pots. I put out my hand.

'Thanks, I'm Tim by the way.'

'I'm Samudrapati.'

I tried to pronounce it and he laughed. 'It's Sanskrit. When you get ordained as a Buddhist monk, they give you a name and you're stuck with it.'

'What does it mean?'

Embarrassment flooded his face, and he muttered something I didn't catch.

'Lordo – what sorry?'

'Lord of all wisdom,' he muttered, clearly feeling inadequate to the weight of expectation attached to his name.

Now he said it, he did look wise. He had an ageless face, could be twenty-five or forty, hard to tell. Just in case he was all-knowing, I couldn't resist a question. I nodded back at the house next door. 'Is that where the guerrilla knitter lived?'

He shrugged. 'I couldn't tell you.'

I wasn't sure I believed him. But one thing I did know, this was definitely another reason to call on Lori.

9

THE BAT BOX

I was nervous. Not just because Lori was standing close behind me; or because I was hanging halfway out the top window with Lori holding my legs; or that I wasn't at all sure that the bat box I was attempting to attach under the eaves wouldn't fall down. I was nervous because I felt like an invasive species in a hostile territory. I was in the very private, closely guarded, smelly and messy habitat of a teenager. On the desk inside was a laptop, host probably to many secrets in the browser history. I caught a hint of the unmistakeable smell of skunk – not the animal – under the more prevalent whiff of teenage boy.

'Still screwing it in, don't let go yet!' I hollered.

'Holding tight, don't worry.'

'You know the guerrilla knitter you never saw again?' I shouted into the room.

'Yeah?'

'I may have met her daughter, Daisy.'

'No!' Lori sounded gratifyingly amazed. 'What makes you think so?'

'There was knitting all over, and also a photo of the statue with the shroud on it.'

'Was she there?'

'No just Daisy and her grandad.' I tightened each screw in turn. 'What was the guerrilla knitter like? Did you actually know her?'

'Only by sight. I used to see her doing Tai Chi in the park when I was a kid. She was ethnic looking, colourful.'

'That's just like Daisy.'

'But she'd be seventy at least now.'

'Her grandmother? She said she died.'

'There was no funeral.'

Caw, caw!

I looked up to see a crow alighting on the roof above me. Another crow joined it, cawing harshly and looking down on me.

'I seem to have upset the crows.'

'OMG. There's a whole flock flying over.'

'Murder.'

'What? The guerrilla knitter?'

'No, the collective noun for crows.' I quickly tightened the last screw. With some inelegant contortions, I pulled myself back into the room.

'Did you get it up okay?'

Jo would never have let that question go unremarked, but I squashed a smirk – I was a still a relative stranger she'd let into her house. I was desperately fearful of crossing a line.

'I think so, but the last thing I'd want is for some bats to move in and then it come down. I'll get some extra fixings to be sure. I could pick you up a water butt too if you like; kill two birds with one stone?'

I cringed when I noticed Ethan's air rifle, remembering the magpie he'd shot. Probably an unfortunate metaphor.

'I'll get the fixings, especially as you're doing this for nothing.'

'Okay, shall I pop back next week?'

'I'll be at work, possibly Saturday.'

'Fine. What do you do, if you don't mind me asking?'

She started, a hint of worry in the quick furrow of the brow. 'I was hoping you wouldn't ask!'

My mind raced past funeral director, guerrilla knitting, mud wrestling – why was that in there? Oh yes, because she doesn't want me to know. Tax inspector…

'I'm a social worker.'

'Oh, right, but why wouldn't you want me to know?'

'I work with problem families where kids are at risk, and sometimes think I could be visiting me!'

'Ah.' I saw her concern. Ethan had a father who thought an air rifle was a suitable gift for a boy and his hobby seemed to be killing things. I looked out of the window at the crows on the lawn. I put myself in the shoes of a teenage boy with a gun. It was the perfect vantage point.

'Daisy was cool, I liked her,' I said, sensing a change of subject might be welcome.

'What about the grandad? Did he look shady?'

'Well he didn't let me have any vegetable curry.' I didn't mention his furtive look, I knew how toxic gossip could be.

'Not cool,' Lori laughed. 'Still, what is cool? I mean, what my son thinks is cool and me, well…'

I looked at her face as she pondered the question of what was 'cool'. I guessed she was in her early forties. I took in the soft lines around her mouth and eyes, lines of humour, lines of worry – about her son perhaps? Lines of strength, lines that made Botox seem like a crime against humanity.

'You're cool.' Shit. Shit, shit, shit. I've overstepped.

'You're cool too.'

There was a pause.

'What the fuck are you doing in my room? Who's that man?'

I turned round to see Ethan enter the room.

He grabbed his air rifle and pointed it at me.

'Ethan. Put that down!'

'We're just putting up a bat box.' I kept my voice calm.

Lori's face tightened – with fury? Embarrassment? Fear? I couldn't tell, but it was clear that it was time to go. I hurried out, fighting the urge to apologise – I wasn't guilty. But I kind of was and he knew it. He could tell I liked her. Lori hurried me out of the door with rushed murmurings of 'sorry,' and 'I'll email.' He was shouting as I made for my bike.

'If I catch you with my mum in a room with the door shut again, I'll fucking shoot you.'

It looked like I wouldn't have the opportunity to secure the bat box after all.

THE RANDOM RECIPE GENERATOR

It was Saturday afternoon and the drumming rain outside mirrored my mood. I'd sent off reports for the three gardens I'd done that week, and had run out of stuff to do. One downside I hadn't anticipated was how I'd feel meeting people who had everything I didn't. As if to rub it in, one father and husband was called Tim, ten years younger than me, three lovely kids, huge garden, a wife who looked like she still loved him. Was I too harsh on him when I told him that the magnificent insect hotel he'd made with tiny name plates over each doorway: beetles, ladybirds, earwigs, bees, would probably just get overrun with spiders? His children's faces had fallen when I'd told them that the varnished surface would repel most of them. I'd tried to make up for it by telling them how to create a hotel for solitary bees – a few bamboo canes tied together, which I'd promised to provide. Their faces remained disappointed even when I'd pushed some pine cones together to form a pyramid, and stuffed in twigs and dried leaves to make a home for ladybirds. I felt terrible about it now.

I might not have been that tactful either, I belatedly realised, with the happy couple with two lovely children who were so proud of all their bird feeders. Niger seeds for the thin-beaked finches; fat balls that all birds would adore; peanuts in wire meshes; sunflower hearts, a favourite of sparrows and greenfinches. It provided a banquet for birds that would be especially important in the winter months. Unfortunately, I'd informed them, it was a banquet served on dirty plates as they looked like they hadn't been cleaned for years.

I drummed my fingers on the windowsill gazing out into the rain. Should I contact Lori about the bat box? No, it would be too pushy. No point thinking about it.

I checked my email.

Finally!

Oh. Not Lori after all.

From: Lorraine Williams
To: Tim Redfern
Subject: Re Green Garden Consultancy –Report

Dear Tim,

Thanks so much for coming over and for the list of what plants would work in our garden. We took it down to the garden centre, but I couldn't resist a Blue Spruce and a gorgeous Japanese maple, and we got some pansies, primulas and asters. I'm afraid the kids just ran around putting all the prettiest ones they saw in the basket, you know what they're like! We had good intentions though 😊

For goodness' sake! I'd written up the report suggesting Mahonia, a food source for winter-active bumblebees; garden angelica, tall with large flowers enjoyed by all kinds of beetles, bees, hoverflies and wasps; bluebells with their creamy white pollen and nodding blue, sweet-smelling flowers. I'd felt good at the time visualising the happy buzz of pollinators enjoying the habitats and foods provided.

PS I forgot to get peat free compost – is that bad?

Is that bad?!

From: *Tim Redfern*
To: *Lorraine Williams*
Subject: *Re Green Garden Consultancy –Report*

Dear Lorraine,
I'm sorry to say that few of the plants you bought are likely to attract wildlife as you told me you'd like. The Asters will attract pollinators but won't like your shady, heavy clay soil. Maybe next time, when the plants fail to thrive, you could have another go with my list.
Kind regards
Tim

Oh no. That was too curt. Maybe she'll try again in spring with my suggestions, but for all I know, she'll make the same mistake again.

'I'm trying to crack on with my programming and all I can hear is you sighing.' Jo peered around the door, clutching a mug.

'Why didn't you make me one?' I complained.

'Now I can't even make a cup of tea without you wanting one. What's up?'

'This woman, she goes on about how she's worried about climate change and her poor sister whose house was just flooded in Yorkshire and then buys multi-purpose compost full of peat as if there's no connection.'

Jo shook her head tutting.

'It's frustrating being only able to advise. Daisy's garden cries out for a pond. I'll probably never get to secure the bat box, or pull down Lori's bamboo.'

'Thing is, mate, they're not your gardens.' Jo leant against the doorway, sipping her tea.

'She hasn't followed up on the water butt either. How useful am I being really? Giving advice that's ignored, making children cry—'

'What?'

'I was a bit mean about this guy's insect hotel.'

'You want good word of mouth, mate.'

'Here am I at fifty, no wife, no girlfriend even, no kids. Not even a garden of my own.'

She watched me pace up and down restlessly.

'You got the houseplants.'

'I wish you'd stop buying them, it doesn't make up for not having a garden. They just look bound, trapped inside their pots, they'd much rather be free to spread their roots.'

'You got too much time to think, that's the trouble,' Jo said.

'I'm going out.'

She glanced out the window at the rain pouring down. 'Good idea.'

Jo returned to her room and I donned waterproof trousers and coat and set off for the common. Walking under the tree-lined path provided enough cover to throw off my hood and feel the air on my face. This was where I'd seen the parakeets with Charlotte. I'd been subconsciously looking out for them for years, trying to talk myself out of my culpability in their spread across the UK, underplaying their negative impact on native songbirds. But now I was actively engaged in trying to put things right I could see that the guilt of that, on top of everything else, had been a subtle but pervasive drag on my spirits.

I'd felt so happy on Lori's decking, leaning over the balustrade taking in the garden, listening to the robin sing. I'd had a sense of rightness and peace, my past and my future coming together.

But this sense of rightness in one area of my life, instead of satisfying me was ripping my heart open to everything else I needed. It was intolerable, now I thought about it, that I'd spent so long in a job and in a flat that I didn't like. How had I managed to spend so many years half asleep? Jo and I had our funny moments, but it wasn't enough. Now I'd woken up, it felt like I'd stripped a plaster off a wound and I was painfully aware of everything else I yearned for.

My phone went, interrupting my musings over whether I could get another visit out of the bat box. It was a text from Jo.

RRG done. Get back here and start cooking!

The moment I got back, Jo called me up to her room. She shifted along her desk to make room for me.

'Right, Timbo, pull up a chair. Come and see my creation.'

I took a seat in front of the monitor. It looked like a simple Excel file with columns along the top labelled meat/fish; vegetables; pulses/beans; starch/carbs; herbs/spices; sauce/misc.

'I haven't done the weighting function yet because that's more complicated, but for now, press Shift and F9 and it will randomly come up with ingredients for each column.'

I went to press the keys.

'Wait!' she cried. 'Whatever you press, we must eat, otherwise it's pointless. Agreed?'

'Agreed.' I pressed Shift F9.

tripe
Brussel sprouts
gherkins
hazelnuts
millet
fenugreek
Marmite
garlic
Cinzano

Our mouths dropped as we took in the menu for tonight.

'Oh my days, Jobo. What the hell were you thinking?'

'We're allowed to drop one and add one though,' she said, as if that would help.

'We have to drop the tripe.' My stomach turned at the thought.

'Obviously.'

'Why did you even add it?'

'Some people like it.'

'No one does. And millet isn't even for humans, it's budgie food.'

'I just copied and pasted a list of cereals.'

'Then how do you explain Cinzano? What are we? In the seventies?'

'You're sounding a bit hysterical, Timbo, if you don't mind me saying.'

'Well we're supposed to eat this. And Marmite?'

'You're not thinking it through. Marmite can make a good stock for gravy.'

'Am I allowed to use gravy granules?'

'Not unless that's your extra ingredient. You'll have to think carefully about that, it might make all the difference.'

'Me?' I gazed at the screen, searching for inspiration.

'We agreed, you'd do first cook as I did the software.'

'So over this dish of millet, sprouts and Cinzano I pour Marmite dissolved in hot water?'

'Or you could do a little smear on the side like on *MasterChef*.'

'*MasterChef*? I'd like to see them have a go at this.'

'Yes!' She spun round to face me, eyes gleaming. 'A gameshow!'

'It would make a great game show.' Having for the first time in years had time to watch daytime TV, I could see this was just what the cooking show format needed.

'I could have a special joker column for all the weird foods, and program it to come up with one item each time that you have to use.' Her eyes lit up at the thought of the culinary pain she could inflict.

'That would be too gross for normal use. People like to enjoy their dinners.'

'But don't you get fed up when they take a bite and you know they're going to say "ooh how lervely, it's the best thing I've ever tasted." Whereas with this challenge…'

'There's a real chance it will be utter shit.'

'Utter shit!' repeated Jo with satisfaction.

'This is literally the most disgusting thing I've ever tasted.'

'It could be the Everest for chefs, the ultimate of all cooking challenges.'

'Anyone can cook up something decent when they can choose their ingredients but let's see what you can do with millet, Cinzano, gherkins, tripe and Marmite.'

'Yeah, Jamie.'

'Yeah, Nigella.'

'So go on then, Timbo.'

'What?'

'Get cooking.'

NO FOLK

From: *Walker. L*
To: *Tim Redfern*
Subject: *Sorry*

Hi Tim,
I'm so sorry about my son. The bat box has stayed up, although no bats yet. I got a water butt as you suggested, so will set that up. I see the butt and the drainpipe, but I haven't yet worked out how to connect the two. Am I being dim?
Sorry again about Ethan.
Cheers
Lori

From: *Tim Redfern*
To: *Walker. L*
Subject: *RE: Sorry*

Hello Lori,
Lovely to hear from you and glad to hear the bat box remains up. No worries about Ethan. Did you get a water diverter kit with the butt?

*If not, you'll need one. I'd be happy to pick one up and come and
fit it.*
Warm regards
Tim

From: *Walker. L*
To: *Tim Redfern*
Subject: *RE: Sorry*

Hi Tim,
*That would be great, I don't want you to think I was hinting
(although I totally was!). I'll get the diverter kit, but I'd welcome
help fitting it. Saturday morning is best if you're free? I'll be back
from walking Flo about nine-thirty so after that is good, but
Ethan will probably be back from his dad's around eleven, in
case you want to avoid him. Although I promise he won't
shoot you!*

I popped into the Share Shop to borrow a drill and saw, then set
off for Lori's. I was in no hurry to meet the man who'd given his
son a gun so I'd suggested doing the water butt first and then
joining her and Flo for a walk.

'I'm so sorry about Ethan,' Lori said, the moment I arrived.

'I was bad at his age too.'

She looked at me disbelieving.

'Really I was,' I insisted. 'I'm sure he'll grow out of it.'

'That gives me hope.'

'So where's your butt?' I smiled.

'On the decking, ready to go.'

It took little time to drill a hole in the water butt, saw off a
corresponding section of downpipe, install the water diverter and
fix the hose between the two.

'All done. The rainwater will now go into the water butt, and
when it's full it will go into the drain as before, but in the

meantime you have extra water which will be handy if there's another hosepipe ban.'

'Great. I should have got one years ago, so thanks for making me do it.'

'I didn't make you, I hope,' I began earnestly, then saw with relief she was smiling.

The moment we were done Florence ran around Lori's legs.

'I was going to offer you tea, but Flo says it's time for her walk,' Lori laughed, gathering the lead.

Was it that, or was she worried about me meeting Ethan, or her ex? Mindful of my last encounter with her son, I determined to retain a professional manner, and remember I was Habitat Man, not some Lothario who preys on single mothers.

We walked by the river, early frost crunching under our feet, admiring the trees in their autumn colours.

'I love this time of year,' Lori said. 'What's that tree?'

'The Holm Oak, non-native.' I pointed to a glorious oak in the distance. 'That native oak hosts hundreds of insect and lichen species, whereas the introduced Holm Oak hosts just one or two, because the local insects haven't evolved to deal with the oak's protective mechanisms.'

'Begone non-native tree,' she teased. 'Tell me, which plants do you hate most?'

'Bamboo. It's great in its native Asia but in the UK it's top of my hate list because it has almost zero wildlife value and it's so hard to get rid of once it's established.'

'Oh dear.'

'Many introduced plants have low wildlife value,' I added quickly. 'Such as rhododendrons, Japanese maple, non-native cherry laurel.'

'Is my cherry laurel non-native?'

I hesitated, then reminded myself I was Habitat Man.

'It is. Oh! Look at that.' I pointed to where the morning sun had lit up a spiderweb, the frosted dew on the web sparkling like diamonds.

Lori paused to admire it.

'Beautiful. Although that's one thing I don't like about autumn, all the spiders come into the house.'

'A common myth. They're always there, they just get about more this time of year.'

'Thanks for that, Tim.'

'One day we'll cherish even the most despised of species but sadly it will be because they've declined to the point of extinction.' I picked up a stick and threw it for Flo, who ran after it delighted. 'No longer will women shriek at a spider—'

'Don't say it like it's just women!'

'No longer will people shriek at spiders. No, they'll cosset it and say, weave your web you precious life form, for we now realise how much we need—'

'I mean, what do they even do for us?'

I opened my mouth to respond, but it seemed like the question was rhetorical.

'And don't say they eat the flies, because frankly I'd rather have the flies than those creepy corner huggers, I could just swat them anyway. Is it bad that I like swatting flies?'

'Dawn wouldn't approve,' I murmured, thinking of the attempt at a humane mousetrap.

'No she wouldn't.'

'You know Dawn?'

'Yes, I was the one who told her about you.'

Florence came trotting back, tail in the air, but refused to give me the stick.

'Did she make a pass at you?' she asked with a mischievous smile.

I shrugged ambiguously.

'Naughty Dawn. I knew she would.'

'You did?'

'I knew you'd be her type. She sits there watching her whodunits, doing her knitting then suddenly she'll get that glint in her eye.'

I didn't like to ask how she knew about the glint, but I wondered. Had Dawn made a pass at her? Had Lori said yes?

'She's got a kind heart though,' she continued.

I laughed in agreement and related the tale of the humane mousetrap. 'Yes, she'd put a wee bit of cheese in a tiny bottle and stuck a mini ladder with Sellotape—'

Lori guffawed with laughter. 'Dawn never actually did that? That was Ethan's ladder from his old Mouse Trap game. I told her it was rats.'

'And the rat was three times the size of the bottle.' I found myself embarrassingly convulsed with giggles all of a sudden. I quickly shifted to a manlier chuckle. She nudged me.

'Well did she? Dawn's polyamorous, she won't mind if you tell.'

'Poly…what?'

'It's a way of life that means you have several partners, but it's not like cheating, as everyone knows what's going on.'

I nodded wisely as if I totally knew all that.

'Yes, erm, I was invited to er… 'play' with her and her friend Kerry, but well…' I floundered, realising Lori was listening with interest.

'Are you erm, good friends?' I changed the subject.

'Mostly through our sons who went to school together, although they couldn't be more different. Dawn's son seems to accept all her shenanigans, but Ethan is the complete opposite.' Lori showed me her black boots. 'These are my whore boots apparently.'

'What?' They looked quite ordinary to me.

'My son is the Taliban.'

'Oh, right?'

'I met this guy online, and we started going out, then Ethan found him upstairs after dark and threatened him with the air rifle.'

'I'm glad it's not just me.'

'His dad brings home girlfriends and Ethan has no problem. Bloody double standard...'

'What happened? Are you and he still...?'

'Who? Ethan's dad?'

'No, the online dating guy?'

'Oh no. You'll think me shallow.'

'I'm sure I won't.'

'He kept making me listen to folk music. I said I didn't like it, so his response was to take me to folk music gigs. I mean, do I look like I like folk?'

'You do,' I shrugged. 'Sorry.'

'On what basis? Do I have long hair, wear floaty clothes and mope about pining for my true love who was drowned at sea?'

'No, but...'

'But what?'

'Nothing.'

'No, I insist, what made you think I like folk?' Lori was trying to look indignant but I saw the smile lurking underneath.

'I guess the question I asked myself is: do you wear handmade clothes and could I imagine you dancing around in a meadow while Clannad played in the background?' I ignored her snort of laughter and maintained a serious expression, a man must stand his ground. 'I'm sorry but the answer was yes on both counts.'

'Clannad isn't even folk.'

'You'll be glad to hear I don't claim to be an expert on folk, but you asked.'

'I am glad, but I don't wear handmade clothes.'

'What about the scarf?' I pointed to a hand-knitted scarf she was wearing.

'Dawn made me that during her epic knitting phase, I tried to give it away to a charity shop but they didn't want it.'

'Well, also because you like nature and look natural, no make-up.'

'Bless you,' said Lori enigmatically.

We'd circled back to the clock tower. It was nearly eleven. Lori put Flo back on the lead.

'Well, Tim, did you want to come back for a cuppa?'

'Better not. I'm due home now anyway.' I noticed sadly that Lori looked relieved. It was hard to tear myself away. 'But before I head off…'

'Yes?'

'What's so wrong with folk?'

'Don't you start! He'd send me constant playlists to educate me and then he wouldn't shut up asking if I'd listened to them all. It felt too much like homework.'

She turned to head back to her house and gave me a wave. 'Anyway, what with Ethan and the folk, well…' She shrugged and gave me a half smile, half grimace.

I had a sudden feeling that I wasn't being discouraged, but I was being warned. 'No folk then!' I shouted after her.

'No folk,' she responded, laughing.

I returned to find Charlotte waiting for me in the kitchen with Jo. I'd reluctantly agreed to follow up the life coaching session so she could fill in my backstory and raise her marks.

'Sorry I'm late.'

'I've been telling Charlotte about our random recipe generator.'

'I was saying you ought to write up each recipe and review it in a blog,' said Charlotte.

'I said it was a great idea,' Jo added.

'Yes, it is,' I agreed vaguely.

'Where have you been anyway?' Jo leant against the kitchen counter.

'Lori's,' I said, slightly defensively.

'I got up early to get here on time,' Charlotte said.

I looked at my watch – it was eleven-thirty. I made no comment. I had Charlotte after all to thank for my current life. I sighed and sat at the kitchen table.

'Okay, let's do this. What do you need to know?'

'Shall I leave you to it?' Jo asked.

'No,' I said quickly.

Jo nodded, understanding my need for moral support and sat at the table with us.

'You don't have to do this,' she murmured while Charlotte snapped open her laptop.

'I got a D! Can't have that!'

'Okay. Right. Erm. So you're not in financial trouble because of giving up your job?' Charlotte asked.

'I can last till my pension, no worries.'

'Can I have full details?'

'Of course not.'

Charlotte sighed but I wasn't being difficult.

Jo explained. 'You're not a financial consultant, Char. If you take too many details you'll seem like you're claiming to be an expert in areas where you're not, so you'd probably get a bad mark for that.'

'One would hope,' I muttered.

Charlotte seemed satisfied and scrolled down her list of questions and came to the ones I'd been dreading.

'Personal context. So you never married, you're still single?'

I sprang up. 'Cup of tea?'

'Not for me.'

I switched the kettle on anyway, my mind on how to respond. It sounded too lame to admit that after getting my fingers burned a few times, I'd settled for admiring from a distance. I thought of Lori and felt a sudden longing that took my breath away.

'We're all right as we are, aren't we, Timbo?'

I nodded, but I could see Charlotte thought we were a couple of saddos.

'You don't get it cos you're young, but once you're no longer thinking about if you want kids, the whole marriage and romance thing loses its appeal,' said Jo.

'I don't suppose you have any secret kids stashed in your past do you, Tim?' laughed Charlotte.

The kettle switched off and it was suddenly quiet. Jo shot me a look.

'No.'

Charlotte scrolled down some more and muttered to herself, 'Now for the job.' She looked up at me purposefully. 'Right, last one. Why did you spend so long in a job you hated?'

My stomach clenched with a feeling of desperate helplessness. I couldn't even manage a trite answer to distract her, and the truth was unthinkable. No one except Jo could ever understand. She saved me yet again.

'Fancy some lunch, Char, we got some leftover from yesterday we couldn't manage.'

'Ooh yes please. What is it?'

'Millet and sprout patty served with gherkins.'

'Actually I'm in a bit of a rush. Better head off.'

'We've got plenty.'

Charlotte made a run for it while she could.

THE FESTIVE SEASON

The pub had put up its Christmas decorations, and had a festive air. This was our last session before Jo disappeared off for a fortnight to her family up north. This time of year often sent me into a depression, but this year it was different. I was no longer evil financier, I was Habitat Man. Still single though.

'Get the pints in, Timbo, I've had some thoughts on the Random Recipe Generator.'

I wandered over to the bar deep in thought. Email first or just turn up? I was just passing, I'd say. I could imagine her chatting with Dawn. It was nice at first but now he keeps popping by. He's turned into a bit of a stalker, she'd say.

The landlord saw me approach and started pouring our pints. Lone-man-at-the-bar was quiet tonight.

'All right?' I asked him.

'Hectersded.' He shook his head sadly.

I nodded uncomprehendingly and returned to my musings. I'd ask Jo for her advice on if it would be okay to call in a capacity other than Habitat Man.

The landlord placed two pints on the counter and I nodded my thanks and carried them back.

'Jo—'

'Charlotte was right.' Jo supped her beer, thoughtfully.

'She was?'

'We should review each meal and do a blog to generate interest.'

'Not every day, though. My stomach couldn't handle it.'

'Twice a week, once each. But we write it up absolutely honestly, no cheating and see if we can get people interested.'

'Okay, but why?'

'So we can create an app of course.'

'Hang on, Jo, what happened to the environmental element? You've basically just put together an Excel sheet that probably took less than an hour. No one is going to pay for that!'

'That's the next thing. I can increase the probabilities that food in season will come up more often, but what else?'

'Input the carbon footprint of key ingredients. I can give you specific weightings if you like, but generally make beef and lamb very low probability, pork medium probability and chicken a higher probability.'

'Didn't I read somewhere that squirrel would be low carbon as we cull them anyway?'

I held her eye. She gazed back at me unblinking. 'Well people do have to get hold of it in the first place.' I shook off a brief image of Ethan and his air rifle. 'Although, you're right that most wild game would be locally sourced.'

'But we can't make it too posh,' said Jo. 'I'll add stuff like baked beans too. What about carbs?'

'Potatoes will have the lowest carbon footprint, pasta is okay. Rice is less good as it gives rise to methane emissions, and there's the transportation.'

'Anything else?'

'You should increase the number of potential vegetables up to six, as they're healthier and have a lower carbon footprint.'

'Okay, I can also add more dairy alternatives, or do a vegan version.'

'Social costs, like if it's Fairtrade or an ethical supplier?'

'People don't want to be preached at. I mean, Timbo, do you really want to know that your chocolate might contain slave labour?'

I saw her point. 'Okay, so, Jo, I wanted to ask your advice—'

'I'll do a free version which is very simple.'

'Would it be too stalkerish—'

'Then a more sophisticated version at a price.'

'Should I wait for Lori to contact me?'

'So they can weight what matters to them. Like environment, animal welfare, social impacts, financial cost, etc. and it will then be bespoke to their needs and values.'

'How will you promote it?' I asked, giving up.

'My social media following is in the thousands now. People really like the pets that look like their owner pics. Your Lori and her dog got me loads more followers.'

I choked on my beer. 'What?'

'Well that's why you gave it to me isn't it?'

'I didn't give it to you, I showed it to you.'

'Same difference.'

'But she'll find out. I didn't ask her permission to take the photo or put it online.'

'What kind of a person takes a picture of someone without them knowing anyway?' Jo stopped suddenly and got out her phone and tapped.

I had a bad feeling. 'What are you doing?'

'I noticed some comment, but didn't... no it's all right, just some guy called Ethan.'

My insides clenched. 'That's her son!' I grabbed the phone. My heart stopped as I read his comment: 'You fucking stalker. I'm telling her what you did.'

'Ah! I think tonight might be a four-pinter.' She rushed to the bar with uncharacteristic haste.

On the walk back, Jo tried to jolly me out of my gloom. 'Guess what song I'm singing in my head.'

I took in the sight of her strutting like a demented chicken and finally found the words to express my feelings. 'I fucking hate you.'

'Good one, but no. Try again.' She looked at me hopefully, stomping along, in an exaggerated rhythmic walk. 'It's 'We Will Rock You'. Your turn.'

I slouched along, gazing enviously at the usual happy couple holding hands ahead of us. Nothing's changed that much since my fiftieth birthday.

'Smiths. 'Heaven Knows I'm Miserable Now'?' she suggested.

I stopped walking and glared at her. 'I'm not playing. You've got me in trouble.'

Jo gave up on her strut. 'What was this Ethan chap like before this? Was he sweet as pie to you?'

'He threatened to shoot me with his air rifle.'

'Nothing's changed then has it? Just tell her that you sent the photo to a mate that had a thing for dogs that look like their owners. I'll take the blame. Don't tell her that I took it from your phone though cos that looks bad.'

'Because it is bad. Anyway, how am I going to see her to tell her that?'

'Tricky.' Jo set off walking again.

I followed her. 'Come on, Jo, you're good at this kind of thing.'

'You do my RRG blog, and I'll think about it. Don't worry.'

I felt better. Jo was the master of getting away with things. She'd find a way to put it right.

. . .

#RandomRecipeGenerator

I WILL NEVER, UNDER ANY CIRCUMSTANCES, COMPROMISE THE SPIRIT OF THE RANDOM RECIPE GENERATOR, BY DROPPING MORE THAN ONE INGREDIENT FROM ITS LIST, OR BY INCLUDING MORE THAN ONE INGREDIENT THAT IT HAS NOT COME UP WITH. NEITHER WILL I LOOK AT WHAT IT HAS GENERATED AND DECIDE TO IGNORE IT AND TRY AGAIN. WHAT THE RANDOM RECIPE GENERATOR DECIDES IS WHAT I SHALL DO.

That is my vow, and no matter how unlikely the combination, I shall give it a go.
Signed: *Tim Redfern*

mussels
red cabbage
onion
pear
bulgar
allspice
tarragon
sage
coconut milk
orange

My immediate thought is: I can't do this. However, this is closely followed by memories of a red cabbage dish my mum used to do with apples and red wine – perhaps I could do a similar version with red cabbage, orange, pear and allspice. I'll fry up onions, add the red cabbage and spices, sweat over a low heat then add the orange and pear at the end. I had to check what bulgar was – a bit like couscous, so that can be the base. That leaves the mussels and the coconut milk – I can drop one thing only. I'd like to consult Jo but that risks setting a precedent, and I'm not sure I want to cede control to her palate. No, best not to consult her, or then she'll demand it as her right to be consulted on every dish, and that would be disastrous.

Verdict

Jo **** I'm giving it four stars. It was inspired to do them as separate dishes. A starter of mussels steamed in coconut milk and Thai spice was delicious. Although as a purist I'm not sure that the Thai spice mix wasn't cheating as it was several ingredients in one. The red cabbage with pear and orange was also a warming winter dish. I was looking forward to saying how utterly disgusting it was, but Timbo pulled it off. A triumph!

Tim *** I hotly dispute that the Thai seasoning was more than one ingredient because Thai seasoning is actually listed on the RRG as an ingredient in its own right. Now that's cleared up, I give it three stars and I'm happy it wasn't disgusting. The red cabbage dish was nice but nothing like my mum used to make and now I'm thinking I could have done more with the mussels as they were delicious. Then I could have done a red cabbage, pear and orange salad on a bed of bulgar as a side dish. The random recipe generator really did encourage me to think outside the box using just seasonal and low carbon ingredients. I think Jo has hit upon a winner.

Jo was still in bed after a night's gaming, but I thought I'd done a decent blog. I noticed several new emails and felt suddenly optimistic. There was no one like Jo for getting out of a fix, she'll have thought of something I was sure. I made a cup of tea and sat back down to go through my inbox.

From: *Transition Southampton*

To: *Tim Redfern*
Subject: *Green Garden Consultancy*
Attachment: *Samudrapati, St Denys*

Dear Tim,
I heard from a Samudrapati who heard about us from his
neighbours. He said he's met you already. He's up for a visit in the
New Year sometime.
Warm regards
Karen

From: *Geoff Blackman*
To: *Tim Redfern*
Subject: *frogs*

Dear Tim,
I don't know if you were told, but I want to create a habitat for frogs
and bats. I might consider a pond. I'm away over Christmas, but can
we fix a date for the new year? I've paid my tenner.
Blessed be
Geoff

I responded straightaway to suggest some dates. I was
delighted that Geoff might be up for a pond, despite my slight
reservations about his plans for the frogs. Amphibians were
dangerously in decline due to habitat loss and pollution. Raw
sewage discharge, agricultural and industrial chemicals, increasing
quantities of poisons from pet treatments all posed threats to
these sensitive creatures.

I was also intrigued by the Buddhist chap. I thought back to
my days at work, when each email was more drudgery. Now I
opened each email with excitement – new visits, new houses,
each with habitats to create.

I heard Jo's heavy stomp, and the kettle switch on. I gave it a few minutes then joined her in the kitchen.

'Did you see my blog yet?'

'Yeah, top stuff.'

'Well?' I waited patiently while she swallowed her muesli.

'Well what?'

'Lori. How do I get to see her again?'

'Just turn up.'

'I did your blog for that?'

'You'd have done it anyway.'

'But she already thinks I'm a stalker so it will make it worse if I turn up at her house uninvited.'

'Okay, if she hasn't got in touch with you by Christmas, turn up with a Christmas card.'

'But she's probably away over Christmas.'

'Go after then, Christmas cards are valid up to New Year's Eve, everyone knows that.'

'No they don't, Jo. It really pisses everyone off.'

Jo shrugged. 'That's all I got.'

I remembered I had one more email yet to read. A distant hope sprung up that it was from Lori. I rushed back to take a look.

From: *Martin Brigham*
To: *Tim Redfern*
Subject: *Costing for Nature accounting*

Dear Tim

I expect you're surprised to hear from me, but I hope it will be a good surprise. We were disappointed at your sudden resignation, and since you left, we've noticed increasing concerns about climate change. On reflection, we regret not paying enough attention to your plans for a Costing for Nature policy. In fact, we think that formulating ways to

*include environmental costs alongside financial costs is exactly what
we need to be doing.*

*We'd be pleased to offer you your job back, plus a ten per cent
salary increase, effective immediately. We have no one else who has
the right combination of skills to do it well so we hope you'll
say yes.*

Oh.

'You all right?'

I looked up to see Jo standing at the door with a suitcase and
a letter.

'Huh?'

'You've been staring at the screen without moving for ages.'

'They've offered me my job back, they want to go with the
Costing for Nature software.'

'That's brilliant.' She noticed my expression. 'Or not?'

The thought of going back to work filled me with horror, but
it was Jo's software, it deserved a chance. More importantly it
would make a real difference.

'The thing is—'

'Sorry, Timbo mate, going to have to leave you with this one,
got a train to catch. Back after Christmas.'

I envied Jo her family. They were a great bunch, all as
eccentric as Jo in their own ways. I struggled with my two days in
Surrey with my family who were as squarely Middle England as
you could possibly get.

As if to rub it in, Jo handed me the annual Round Robin
Christmas card my brother sent to the whole family. He always
assumed, wrongly in my case, that we'd all be thrilled to hear
about how wonderfully his perfect children were doing at
university, what worthy hobbies his wife had taken up over the
past year, and all about the funny incidents that occurred during
their numerous family vacations in the latest upmarket resorts,
complete with smiling pictures.

'Enjoy.' Jo smiled, fully aware of how much I hated these missives. 'I'll be back for New Year's Eve.'

The door slammed behind her and I was left with myself, the email in front of me, and two weeks of emptiness.

From: Tim Redfern
To: Martin Brigham
Subject: RE: Costing for Nature accounting

Dear Martin
Adopting the Costing for Nature software is an excellent idea and I assure you this is the right way to go. I probably won't be interested in returning to work, but will be happy to talk you through the software, and train someone suitable to use it. I see you're beginning to realise the urgency of the climate crisis, so I can arrange a date to visit you before the end of the year.
Kind regards
Tim Redfern

Christmas shopping in town was the usual nightmare, the cheesy music of the German market competing with the buskers and the general din of too many people. I entered the shopping mall and the bracing air and white/grey sky was replaced by internal lighting and a herd of shoppers who all seemed to be walking straight at me. What was the point anyway of buying gifts? I never got them right. The worm explorer activity kits last year had been discarded the moment they'd been unwrapped. My family were from a different world. A world of relentlessly weeded borders, mown lawns, safe jobs. Discussions centred on catchment areas for the best schools, house prices and the performance of the latest four-wheel drive. Unlike Southampton, there everybody knew my past, even though it was never mentioned. But they had no idea who I really was. Jo was referred to as 'that strange girl', and my relationship with her was beyond their comprehension.

They would definitely be in favour of my going back to work. Although I realised I hadn't got around to telling them I'd given it up. I couldn't picture telling Mum, Dad, my brothers and sisters-in-law about Dawn the polyamorist or the guerrilla knitter, or Lori even.

Would she get on with them? She might think it was weird to feel so alienated from your family? It's normal for distance to develop as one moves away, but usually it's temporary. My brothers had both broken away then returned to the family fold in time with their wives and children. I could see Ethan starting the same process, but he'd be back, I could tell. What had entrenched the distance with me was the thing with young Danny. I'd desperately needed someone to confide in, but all they did was tell me that everything I was doing was wrong. Later on, they'd never even enquired about him. 'Best forgotten, you were an idiot, let's leave it at that.' The whole family were agreed. Sensible advice. Heartless.

I stopped abruptly, and turned round, heading in a fluid downhill motion towards the exit.

I was in no hurry to get home and gave in to the temptation to detour via Bitterne Park. I cycled over Cobden Bridge, then got off and walked to enjoy the sight of the fairy lights twinkling on the houseboats. They looked enchanting, the velvet blackness of the river reflecting the colours on the glassy water. A choir under the clock tower sang 'Silent Night'. I stood still and listened, wanting to weep with longing. I wheeled my bike over the bridge and leant it against the park railings and joined the group of people standing under the clock tower, some singing, some just listening. The peace and harmony of the scene was a far cry from the raucous hordes in the city centre.

During 'In the Deep Midwinter', I sank into a daydream of Lori walking by on her way back from Riverside Park. Any minute now, Lori would join me. I'd confess to her I wasn't going home this year. I imagined telling her the story about how my brother told me that I was adopted, trying to upset me, but I'd loved the idea and spent so long fantasising about my real family that they'd got out the birth video to prove I was theirs. We'd laugh about who would be the best fantasy parents. I wouldn't say that at the time I'd been hoping that my real dad was Rolf Harris.

We'd go walking in the New Forest, frost crunching against our boots, Florence gambolling ahead with that special jauntiness she got when she found a good stick. We'd pick chestnuts off the ground, then roast them over an open fire, drinking sloe gin made from our own sloes. Ethan would come in looking ridiculous in one of Dawn's knitted jumpers. He'd accidentally call me Dad. Lori and I exchange loving looks. She'd tell me that she didn't mind about the photo. I'd tell her how much nicer the Christmas vibe was here than in town. She'd agree. I'd take her hand in mine and we'd listen to the choir together.

13

THE GUERRILLA KNITTER

From: Transition
To: Tim Redfern
Subject: Another pond request

Dear Tim
Daisy has been back in touch. She says they do want a pond after all.
She was keen for you to come before New Year. I made her no
promises as this tends to be family time doesn't it. I'll leave it to you to
sort out details.
Happy Christmas
Karen

I was pleased to have something to do, and for an opportunity to find out more about the mysterious guerrilla knitter. I wonder what made her change her mind.

When Daisy opened the door, I sensed immediately that something was wrong. Daisy, and even the house itself had a sorrowful air. She led me through the house, which had an empty feel about it.

'You've changed your mind about the pond, is that right?'

'Yes, Grandad had a stroke. He's in hospital.'

'Oh Daisy.' I wanted to hug her, but it wouldn't be appropriate, so I just stood there helplessly. I was shocked and sad for her. She idolised her grandad. 'Is he going to be okay?'

She shook her head. 'He can't talk, he can't even communicate.' She blinked back tears. 'We'd fallen out. I was doing my Feng Shui gardening thing and I thought he'd be excited as he inspired it. But he was funny about it and I got cross. Now I realise he wasn't against it, he just wasn't feeling well. He wasn't up to it. The moment he comes back I'm going to make sure he knows how sorry I am. They say he can probably hear even if he can't talk.'

'What can I do to help?'

'I want to do the pond, I want to show him when he comes back, not tell him or make him think he has to help, I'll just do it and it will be the best surprise.'

'I'm really sorry, Daisy, but I wouldn't do anything without his permission.'

'He can't speak though.' She led me outside. The garden mirrored the despondent air. The trees were bare, the ground was soggy with rain and wet leaves, there was a damp chill that made me shiver, and a hole in the ground where she'd started digging.

'Look, I've already started it.'

'I can see. Still, I can't—'

'It was the digging that bothered him as he had a bad back.'

'Are you sure?'

'I need to do something for Grandad. I feel so helpless.' She started crying. 'I want to do it now, before Mum gets back. She's trying to schedule a discharge from the hospital. He hates hospitals.'

Daisy wiped her eyes, picked the spade up and started digging. Her technique was appalling. She'd get nowhere at that rate.

'Go on then, pass the spade. Let's do it together.'

'Thanks so much.' She passed me the big heavy spade and took a daintier one for herself, and we got stuck in.

Her efforts were negligible, for each spadeful I flung behind me, she matched with a tablespoonful. She was also getting in my way.

'Tell you what, how about you transfer the earth into the wheelbarrow as I dig it and then we can decide what to do with it. Maybe you could use it for a raised bed.'

'Are raised beds better then?' She pushed the wheelbarrow into position.

'They can help protect vegetables from slugs and snails, they're good for drainage, especially as you have clay soil here, and...' I stood up to stretch out for a bit, '...they're less backbreaking.'

I considered the pond-shaped hole in front of me. Still a way to go. I'd aim for two feet deep, otherwise the water might evaporate off if we had another hot, dry summer. Soon I'd got into a good rhythm – bend, dig, straighten and fling spadeful of soil over shoulder. Maybe I should suggest a pond again to Lori, we could fit in a small one, and it would bring some life into the garden. I hadn't wanted to overload her with too many suggestions, and frankly I'd got a bit obsessed with the bamboo. Would that be enough of a reason to call? Not on its own. Huh? What the hell is that...

'Ow!' shrieked Daisy, followed by, 'Oh my God!'

I looked up, Daisy was clutching her head with one hand and holding a grinning skull in the other. I looked down, there were bones in the earth, human bones, but no skull. I looked up. Daisy's mouth was open in a silent scream. I realised my mouth was wide open in my own Munch scream. She threw the skull back to me, I caught it, then dropped it quickly. It fell back in the hole and clinked against something. I bent down to look. It was a pair of knitting needles.

'What...'

We heard wind chimes.

'Oh shit,' said Daisy.

'Why?'

'I'm in trouble now.'

If she was in trouble then probably so was I.

'That will be Mum. I wanted to get this done before she arrived so it was a...'

'Fait accompli?'

'I couldn't see any reason why she wouldn't let me do a pond. I'm the one living here after all and it's all about wildlife, but now...'

More wind chimes, followed by a loud knocking on the door.

'Shit,' Daisy repeated, echoing my thoughts exactly.

She went to answer the door. I dropped the spade quickly, feeling like the innocent person caught with the gun when the police arrived. Although actually, hang on! There's a body in this garden. Who put it there? Maybe I should be worried about Daisy's mum for a completely different reason. I heard raised voices coming closer into the garden. I was trapped, there was no way out except through the house. Man up, Timbo. Stand your ground. You've done nothing wrong.

'I'm really sorry,' I said, the moment Daisy and her mum appeared in the garden. She looked cross... and worried. She stopped still and put her hand over her mouth when saw the hole in the earth. Englishman that I was, there was only one thing to say.

'Cup of tea?'

She nodded in a daze, walking up to the hole and gazing down at the bones. Daisy trailed behind her.

I dodged past her and into the kitchen and put the kettle on. I heard a gasping noise, then filled it up with water and put it back on. Clearly I should stay out of the way. Not leave immediately, even though there was now a clear route to the exit, because that would be rude. No, I'll give them time in the garden to sort everything out and bring out tea in a few minutes, then see if they notice my saying goodbye.

How would I explain doing a runner to Jo? She'd be disappointed at not knowing the explanation for the body, but I could tell her that it would have been inappropriate – yes, that was the word – inappropriate for me to intrude upon a family at this time. She'd see right through that, I was certain and home right in on my fear of being murdered with knitting needles.

Daisy's mum and Daisy came into the kitchen as I was pouring out the tea. You'd never guess they were related. Daisy was all the colours of the rainbow, short checked skirt over purple leggings, green hair today and a floaty cardigan over a multicoloured top, while her mother was attired in perfectly ironed black trousers, a crisp cream blouse with a navy jumper and tailored black leather jacket.

'Sugar?'

'Just milk for me,' said Daisy's mum in a clipped voice.

'I don't drink tea,' said Daisy.

Daisy's mum sat down and looked straight at me. 'I'm Fern, Daisy's mum. Daisy says she asked you to dig a pond?'

'Er, yes, I'm Tim R...' don't give her your last name you idiot. Daisy has your details anyway, you numbskull... 'Habitat Man.'

Daisy passed me the milk and I added some to both cups, slurping it round the edges.

'Sorry.'

For God's sake, man up and stop apologising, Jo said in my head. She was right, seize the initiative. I didn't care how stupid it sounded, it was time to ask.

'Is that the guerrilla knitter?'

Fern sighed and put her head in her hands.

'Mum?' Daisy hovered by the fridge with the milk.

'Yes, it's your granny in there, aka the guerrilla knitter.'

'Why was she called that?'

'For God's sake, Daisy, put the milk away and sit down.'

'Because she knitted a shroud to cover the statue of Lord Palmerston as a protest,' I told her.

'Among other things,' added Fern.

'Oh my God, the photo – that was her?' exclaimed Daisy, setting the milk on the table and sitting down to join us.

'She's a local legend. The Banksy of her time,' I added.

Fern relaxed slightly when she heard the admiration in my voice, and explained what happened.

'Mum had cancer, she knew she was dying, and went to the funeral parlour herself. But she couldn't stand the formal aura and polished coffins or the thought of her body being prepared for burial by strangers.'

'I can understand that, Mum, but why is it a secret?'

'We didn't know if you were allowed to do your own burial or prepare the body yourself, or weave your own coffin.'

'Why didn't you just google it?'

'This was a few years before all that started.'

'What do you mean?'

'There was no Google.'

'Oh my God? What did you do?'

'You saw what we did.'

'No, without the internet?'

'Libraries, asked around. But we didn't want to ask because if they said no, then we wouldn't be able to do what we wanted as they'd know we had a dead body so we did it ourselves.'

'Oh my God!' It was unclear if Daisy's amazement was at the burying of her grandma in the back garden or a world without Google.

'Mum knitted her own shroud and Dad wove the coffin out of willow, and we buried her in the garden where the pond was.'

'I knew there was a pond!' I blurted out. 'Sorry, go on.'

Fern looked at me sharply. 'You said she was a local legend. Are you saying there are rumours?'

'I've heard there wasn't a funeral, but I don't know if it's on the official radar.'

'Tim, I shouldn't ask you this, but would you keep this quiet?' Fern fixed me with an enquiring stare.

'I've got no urge to report you to the authorities if that's what you mean.'

'I meant keep it entirely to yourself?'

My face registered my doubt. I was going straight round Lori's. She was the one who'd told me about the rumour, she'd be thrilled to hear about the body. This was my way back in.

'Sorry I must dash,' I put on my coat.

'Wait!' barked Fern. 'Your contact details please?' She typed 'Tim' into her phone and held it out to me to add my number. I hesitated, tempted to put in a wrong number, then reluctantly typed it in. As if she'd read my mind, she rang the number and my phone went off in my pocket. She cut off the call and nodded. I hastened towards the door, jumped on my bike and pedalled over the bridge to Bitterne Park.

When I got to Lori's house, I could see it was empty. No car, no Florence looking out of the window. I gave up and went home.

14

BACK IN THE CITY

The next morning, I stood outside Lori's house in my smart city suit. Florence was at the window, but hadn't yet spotted me. If I went in, I'd probably miss the train I'd planned to catch, but I didn't care. They could wait. I needed to see her before I went up to London. I'd decided not to go back, but it was hard to think coherently while my mind kept slipping back to Lori and whether she thought I was a stalker.

I had the four versions of Christmas cards I'd written on me: a 'Happy Christmas to you and Ethan from Tim', a 'love from Tim,' a 'from Tim x', and, if I felt very confident, a 'love from Tim xx'. I walked up the path then hesitated. The thought of Ethan and his air rifle crossed my mind. Florence noticed me and barked, tail wagging. She's happy to see me at least, and I've the body in the garden to fall back on. I strode up the path and lifted up the vampire bat knocker.

I beamed when Lori and not Ethan answered the door. She didn't look cross, she looked just as pleased to see me as Florence, who ran up bringing me a stuffed squirrel, not resting until I'd tried to take it from her and she'd refused to let me.

'It's her new toy,' explained Lori. 'Come on in, good to see you. You look smart.'

'I can't stop long as I've got to go to London after this, but I wanted to wish you Happy Christmas and tell you the latest,' I jabbered nervously, following her into the kitchen, rummaging in my case for the card with the x. Lori pointed to a new speaker, playing music. 'My Christmas present. Pick a band.'

I wanted to go with Led Zeppelin but it had elements she might think were folk. I played safe. 'Coldplay.'

'Alexa, play songs by Coldplay.'

The familiar chords of the song 'Yellow', played, then another familiar sound of the kettle being filled. I began to relax, and sought out the card with 'love Tim xx'.

'Ethan showed me the picture you posted of me and Flo.' Lori shocked me back into nervous alertness.

'Jo, erm, Jo posted it,' I gabbled. 'Sorry I should have asked. I don't want you to think…' I put the card away quickly, and rummaged for the 'from Tim' version.

'I saw what Ethan posted about being a stalker.'

She handed me a cup of tea and I gulped it straightaway, burning my mouth. I yowled and spat it back in the mug in pain. She quickly poured me a glass of cold water. I took a gulp.

'Ethan and his dad are funny about that kind of thing.'

I held the cooling liquid in my mouth, waiting for the burning feeling to go away.

'My fault really, you know that previous guy I mentioned?'

I swallowed the water and nodded, 'Folk guy?'

'I jokingly said he was a bit of a stalker.'

'Stalker?'

'He wasn't really, I just bigged it up because it made me feel important. You know you've arrived if you've got a stalker. When I finished with him, I must have overdone the 'it's not you it's me thing,' because he started thinking – yes it is you – and he wouldn't leave me alone for a while. Then he kept singing that Coldplay song 'Fix You' to me. Anyway, all Ethan and his dad heard was the word 'stalker' and they used that basically as justification for banning me from having any kind of love life.'

I struggled to take in what she was saying over the clamour of my racing heart. She looked really pissed off. The word that kept jumping out at me was stalker. I gulped more cold water.

'They insisted on a full background check on any guy, because I can get access as a social worker. And I said that was totally unethical due to data protection...'

She can look up criminal records, restraining orders?

'Fix You' began on the speaker. Lori glowered.

'We had a bit of a row about it to be honest, so it wasn't the greatest Christmas.' She sat opposite me and looked straight at me. 'Alexa, stop!' she shouted suddenly.

Florence and I both jumped guiltily.

'Even Florence has turned weird on me – really jumpy.'

She'll find out. Maybe she already has.

'Do you have kids?'

Oh no. What does she know? I shook my head slowly.

'Good job. Alexa. Stop!' she yelled at the top of her voice.

The music subsided then resumed. '*Fix You*' promised Coldplay again.

'I'm fed up with men telling me what I can do and can't do, and that every bloke is some kind of stalker.'

She looks furious, positively furious.

'...*Fix you.*'

'Alexa!'

'I'm sorry—'

'Shut the fuck up!' she boomed. 'Sorry, it just makes me so mad.'

Florence fled and so did I.

Lori watched me leave. She was thinking, I was absolutely sure: I thought you looked like a nice guy, how could I have got you so wrong? You weirdo stalker. Get the hell out of my house.

. . .

The train arrived just as I got to the station. I sprinted along the platform, threw myself into the just-closing door and sank into a seat, heart pounding. I tried to slow my rapid breathing and calm my mind. My problems are nothing, I told myself. I mustn't let them get in the way of something as important as saving the planet through Costing for Nature accounting. I must stop thinking about what just happened and focus on the meeting ahead. I've got seventy minutes to work out what I'm going to do.

Seventy minutes later, I was sat in front of Martin in the same glass-partitioned conference room as before, having brooded pointlessly and unproductively on the fact that I'd left all four versions of my Christmas cards on Lori's table.

Martin was on a charm offensive. Once I'd been effusively welcomed, offered coffee from the fancy pot, and had a plate of the best biscuits placed in front of me, he got down to business.

'So, Tim. Have you decided if you're coming back to us? We have a contract ready here if you are, and we hope you will.'

'No it's not for me. What about Julian? He's a conscientious chap, I could train him up to use the Costing for Nature software.'

'He's left, but Sue from marketing could take it on?'

'Why would we get someone from marketing? This is about numbers.' I munched a biscuit doubtfully.

'Well obviously, CFN will be a unique selling point for our services, we want to able to maximise the reputational impact. Our thinking was that the person in charge of it is best placed to talk about it.' Martin saw my scepticism and moved in for the kill. 'Or are you thinking that you'd be the best man for the job? We do. As you say, what does marketing know about it? You gave a great pitch. You really convinced us.'

'No I didn't.'

'You had a point. You know, like holidays. I've just come back from skiing and the snow was shit quite frankly. And like you said, we can't escape it can we? It's everywhere now. Even I'm realising it so you can bet your bottom dollar everyone else is realising it. We need to get onto it. You're the man.'

I mindlessly munched another biscuit. Martin poured me more coffee, his persuasive patter washing over me.

'And if enough people go on holiday to tropical islands and find it's sunk and they think, "damn, this is where I was going to retire and play golf". Or you want to take the family swimming and the sea's chock full of plastic. Then you're going to have calls for green taxation, the consumers will kick up, there'll be green policies that will affect the way everyone does business and we need to be ahead of the curve. You sold it well, mate.'

Martin slid the contract over to me. I didn't pick it up, just looked at it. I took the last biscuit. Why not.

'Have a read.' He passed over an expensive pen. 'We added an extra twelve grand to your previous salary.'

I looked at the pen and the contract and swallowed down the last of the biscuits. 'I need a moment.'

'Of course.'

I headed to the gents to think, feeling like I was walking through water. It all felt wrong. The plush carpets, endless rows of desks and computers, the people; they weren't my people. I didn't belong here and I never had. I couldn't fathom how I'd stayed here for twenty-five years. Just this one visit and I wanted to run away.

Two of my former colleagues were leaving the gents.

'Hi, Tim, have you been on holiday?'

'I left two months ago.'

'Oh right. Thought I hadn't seen you for a bit. Anywhere nice?'

'Southampton.'

'Good house prices down there.'

'We're thinking of a second home in the New Forest.'

I was thankful when they walked on, debating best places for second homes, leaving me to my jumble of thoughts.

The sickly sweet smell of the air freshener hit me when I entered the gents. But I'd drunk a lot of coffee. Too much. Was it really me or Sue from marketing? The thought of the potential of the CFN software being lost to greenwash was intolerable. It would be easy to look good while making little difference by adjusting the settings. It was true that with a longer time frame, the Costing for Nature policy would start to save money, but who thought beyond the next quarter these days or even the next election cycle?

I washed my hands, then felt my phone buzz in my pocket. I took a look. I didn't recognise the number. I listened to the message as I walked back to the conference room. It was from Fern, mother of Daisy, daughter of the guerrilla knitter I'd dug up in the garden. I detected a note of hard desperation in her clipped tones. 'Tim, please will you get in touch with us. We need to talk to you.' My heart started racing again – the three cups of coffee, the accusations of being a stalker, bodies in the garden, maybe even police. I couldn't cope with any of it.

Martin was waiting for me in the conference room. The contract open on the table with the pen beside it. I knew why I'd stayed here for so long. Here no one knew or would even care about my past. These weren't people trained to think about the moral issues, not like say social workers. So what if I earn tons of money? I can give it to charity. That's what businesses do isn't it? Mess everything up making profits then do some corporate philanthropy to make it all okay. But the Costing for Nature software is better than that, it stops us creating the shit in the first place. It was clear what I had to do. I sat down, picked up the pen and signed the contract.

15

NEW YEAR'S EVE

It was often weird for a day or two when Jo came back after Christmas, and it took a while to get back into the groove.

'I've booked us a table at Ennios for New Year's Eve,' I told her when she got back.

'Don't fancy it. Anyway, it will be massively expensive.'

'I don't care, I'm earning again anyway, so might as well have something to spend it on.'

'It's all a bit hetero isn't it, Timbo? You're not planning to declare your love or anything are you?'

'Don't be stupid. We should celebrate that's all. I haven't seen you since they decided they want the software – your Costing for Nature software that you spent years developing.'

Jo agreed in the end, and the evening got off to a good start when she accidentally set her menu alight with the candle, causing a kerfuffle. When she lapsed into giggles afterwards I felt we were back on our usual terms. We compared notes on Christmas.

'Bit radical skipping Christmas isn't it? Was it the Round Robin that tipped you over?'

'That and they would have gone on about how stupid I was for giving up my job to be Habitat Man.'

'Wasn't it your brother who got you the job in the first place?'

'Yes, he expected me to be grateful because quite frankly I wouldn't have got it otherwise. Doing the books was only a small part of my job at the Environment Centre but he bigged it up.'

'I remember him – bit pleased with himself was my general impression.'

I'd once brought Jo back for a visit in the attempt to reconcile my Southampton life with my Surrey world. They hadn't known what to make of her.

'You were so mean to him,' I laughed.

'He deserved it. There he was, bragging on about the hundreds of job offers he had when you'd just been made redundant.'

'You were so sarcastic. I remember you saying how you felt so *terribly* sorry for him having to make such difficult decisions and being so *much* in demand.'

'He'd no clue, he just agreed.'

'Still, because of him at least they didn't check my record,' I said dully.

There was a silence that was broken when the waiter brought us our starters.

'Chicken liver parfait, figs, truffle honey and toast brioche with a chargrilled artichoke.'

I tried not to catch Jo's eye, for fear of setting her off. I knew she was thinking of her random recipe generator.

'And for you, sir, we have goat's cheese panna cotta with heritage beetroot carpaccio, beetroot sponge, candied walnuts marinated in Amaretto.'

I caught a muffled snort from Jo, which she converted into a cough.

Normally we'd have gone onto to compare foods and laugh about the menu, but I felt flat. Jo could see it too.

'The irony is that I stayed away to stop them trying to talk me into going back, but then I did anyway.'

'You don't have to do it you know,' Jo said.

'I do though don't I? You worked so hard on it, we both did. This is a great opportunity.'

'But don't do it if you're doing it for me. Obviously it would be nice to get some money for the software, and I'd bung you a massive rent cheque if it comes through, but if it doesn't, it isn't wasted. I'm using it on the random recipe generator anyway.'

'It will probably get easier once I'm back in the swing of it,' I sighed. 'Anyway, your turn. How were your family?'

'They've got so old. This is the trouble with being the youngest, you can see what's ahead. It literally took hours to say "how are you?" Back in the day it would be, "you all right?" They'd say "yeah, bit hungover," and that would be that. Now it's "how's your tennis elbow?" "On the mend thanks." "How's your plantar fasciitis?" "Getting worse." "Back?" "Learned to live with it." And the worse thing is, I was joining in.'

'How is your RSI?'

'Hurts when I use the mouse, but everything I want to do is on the computer.'

'This is like old times, first pint spent moaning,' I remarked.

Jo raised her wine glass, 'whining and dining!' I laughed but it didn't feel funny. The reason I'd wanted to come out and celebrate was to cheer myself up. The world of my colleagues was a world where joy can be bought in nice cars and fancy restaurants. I thought I may as well give it a go, but it seemed forced. Jo was trying her best, but the pub was her natural habitat. She was right, it would have been better down our local.

'Sod it, let's go,' I said.

'Thank God for that.'

I managed to catch the waiter's eye and we endured the painful process of paying and waiting while he got our coats with sad looks and endless comments of 'everything all right, sir?'

Jo pretended stomach ache to spare his feelings, then seeing his looks of alarm quickly changed it to back ache. I just wanted to get out of there. The whole restaurant seemed to be looking at us accusingly for spoiling the festive vibe.

'Pub?' suggested Jo hopefully once we were safely outside.

I wasn't sure the pub would be any better. The problem was me and wherever I went the gloom would follow. I had the horrible suspicion that the *joie de vivre* I'd experienced so many times in the last few months was to be a thing of the past. I was going back to my old life. It should be better as at least I'd feel my work was worthwhile, but it didn't feel better. It felt worse. Now I knew what I was missing. I couldn't bear the thought of the fake cheer I'd need to summon as we counted down the hours to the New Year, whether it was here or the pub.

'I just want to go home.'

#RandomRecipeGenerator

I WILL NEVER, UNDER ANY CIRCUMSTANCES, COMPROMISE THE SPIRIT OF THE RANDOM RECIPE GENERATOR, BY DROPPING MORE THAN ONE INGREDIENT FROM ITS LIST, OR BY INCLUDING MORE THAN ONE INGREDIENT THAT IT HAS NOT COME UP WITH. NEITHER WILL I LOOK AT WHAT IT HAS GENERATED AND DECIDE TO IGNORE IT AND TRY AGAIN. WHAT THE RANDOM RECIPE GENERATOR DECIDES IS WHAT I SHALL DO.

That is my vow, and no matter how unlikely the combination, I shall give it a go.

Signed: *Lyn French*

Jo, my strange and wonderful sister, has persuaded me into doing the random recipe generator and writing it up. She made me sign a statement that I won't on any account break the rules of not adding or omitting more than one ingredient. I think it's a wonderful idea – very 'Jo' so here goes.

pheasant
onion
spinach
celery
chilli
coriander
chutney
oats
bread

I guess it could be worse. After I heard about Tim's millet and Marmite, I was ready for anything. I'll have to drop the pheasant as I can't get hold of any locally and I've had too much sherry to drive. But, oh dear, that seems to leave me with curried porridge. Barry won't be happy. Curry has a sacred position in our household. This porridge, no, this Oatmeal Piquant, this Curried Surprise, it might work. Why should curry always be served with rice? Surely it's just a coincidence that the countries that grow curry spices also grow rice. Let's face it, if India had oat fields instead of rice paddies, we'd all be eating tandoori chicken masala with pilau oats. What was I thinking of? It will be delicious. This will turn the world of curry upside down. People will say 'who'd have thought it, curry and oats? Isn't it marvellous?' Madhur Jeffrey will have a chapter devoted to oat dishes in her next book. Curried porridge, here we go!

Method

Put all ingredients and my allowable extra ingredient of garam masala into a pan and cook for a while. Serve with bread.

Results:

Lyn ** There was something about the texture, rather slimy and gelatinous. But you know I think that was just unfamiliarity. Actually it wasn't that it tasted bad – in fact, the taste was quite nice really, if you ignore the texture.

Barry * Utterly disgusting.

Note: Barry refused to eat it, and I had only had a little bit, but it wasn't wasted. We took it to our neighbours' New Year's Eve party and it was used as a forfeit for losing at games.

16

THE BAMBOO WOO

From: *Walker. L*
To: *Tim Redfern*
Subject: *Bats!*

Hi Tim,
Did you see the full moon last night? Ethan saw a bat fly into the bat box! We were thrilled.
Hope all good with you.
Cheers
Lori

PS Come and visit – you don't need to do anything to the garden to earn your cuppa.
PPS I'll let you kill my bamboo!
PPPS Not trying to get you to do gardening for nothing (told Dawn off for that).
PPPPS Sorry about losing it last time. I wasn't mad at you, just Alexa and my ex and my son.
PPPPPS Thanks for all the cards

Yes! Excellent! No worries. Phew. Shit. I cringed with embarrassment at the last PS. But overall, this was good news. Maybe I don't have to stop being Habitat Man after all? I let myself get too down about things. I'll do the odd visit at the weekend to keep my hand in and, obviously, sort out Lori's bamboo as a top priority. It will be like old times. I won't mention the body in the garden though. I don't want her pushing me to respond to Fern's frantic call. It would end up a police issue and I don't want anyone raking up my past to discredit me. Everyone knows they always suspect the one who found the body. I hadn't even told Jo. I knew she'd understand, but suppression and avoidance had worked well for me over the last thirty years. I just didn't want to talk about it.

I got a rapturous welcome from Florence, who brought me her stuffed squirrel that now was missing its tail, offered it to me then wouldn't let me have it. We played that game for a while, then I was back at Lori's table, cup of tea in hand, filling her in on the latest turn my life had taken.

'You don't seem to have the same vibe as you had before,' said Lori, sitting down opposite me.

She was right. I was tired after my week back at work. Part of me was thinking 'would Lori like the random recipe generator,' and part of me was thinking 'is it too late to cancel Geoff?'

'Maybe it's because you're no longer plotting against my bamboo,' she laughed.

'Oh, but I am.'

'Glad to hear it.'

'The challenges of getting rid of it occupied my thoughts all the way from Southampton to Waterloo. Up to Winchester I was thinking 'just cut it down,' but then it would grow back, you'd have to keep cutting it down.'

'How often?' Lori leant back in her chair and sipped her tea thoughtfully.

'Weekly.'

'No way I'd keep that up, a few busy weeks at work and I'd forget.'

'It would take a good year. It would require commitment and patience.' I held her gaze, hoping she'd understand that I was thinking long term.

She nodded solemnly.

'So from Winchester to Basingstoke I thought about herbicide…'

'But?'

'But although it's quick, it would pollute the surrounding area so I'd avoid it.'

'Okay.' She clasped her tea, holding my gaze long enough for me to notice the hazel flecks in her eyes. The cares of the week fell away and that feeling I always had at her kitchen table returned. The feeling of being completely and utterly in the here and now, of having all the time in the world, thinking only of her, and her garden.

'I plotted, Lori, all the way to Woking. I'd want to go all the way and pull it up by the roots. Oh yes! And I'd take out the cherry laurel too. Then…' I took a sip of my tea and gazed at the garden visible through the patio doors. 'This took me all the way to Waterloo – I'd plant a beautiful guelder rose and a dog rose too, a lovely native rose, with a wonderful scent. The hoverflies would love that, and they'd eat the aphids.'

'I love roses.'

'Then we'd have to choose – a buddleia for the butterflies, or a native wayfarer tree. They add colour and have berries that birds love, especially the song thrush.'

'We hardly see them anymore,' she smiled into my eyes.

'I may even allow a ceanothus. They're not native…'

'Not native!' she cried, aghast, gently teasing.

'…but the pollinators love them.'

'That would provide a lovely splash of blue.'

'And if I take out your cherry laurel too, we'd have room for a blackthorn.'

'What are they like?'

'They produce sloes.'

'As in sloe gin?' Her eyes lit up.

'Yep.'

'I'd love to be drinking sloe gin right now.'

'It would take a season or two,' I warned her.

Lori shrugged, indicating she was prepared to wait.

I contemplated the following Christmas, the sweet, heady taste of sloe gin, going a little to our heads in the cosy kitchen, the warmth of the alcohol in our blood.

Sounds from upstairs disturbed the intimate air. Ethan bounded into the kitchen and stopped abruptly at the sight of Lori and me drinking tea. We watched as the basic social norm of not killing an innocent man battled with the urge to pummel me to death with extreme prejudice. I held my ground. The electricity in the air suddenly lost its charge and Ethan muttered something that contained the words 'bat box.'

The doorbell went. Lori shot Ethan a stern look and went to answer it. The hum of the refrigerator sounded oppressively loud all of a sudden. We heard her faintly talking to neighbour about a parcel.

A commotion outside provided a welcome distraction. Ethan followed me into the garden to take a look. The magpies were chattering frantically, flying down to the ground then back up again, clearly in great distress.

We walked down towards the noise, but had to step back when the magpies chattered at us angrily. Whatever was going on behind the hawthorn hedge, they weren't going to let us near.

'What's their problem?' asked Ethan.

'I can't see, but there's definitely something unusual going on.' I looked around for a better vantage point. 'We could see from up there.'

'My room.' He ran upstairs. I followed him and paused on the threshold.

Ethan peered out of the window. 'Fucking hell.'

I took it as an invitation and came in to look over his shoulder. The cause of the commotion was a baby magpie who'd fallen out of its nest. Two adult magpies strutted round the helpless chick.

'Oh no!' I exclaimed.

'It's gonna be cat food.' Ethan pointed at the neighbour's cat who was watching with interest from the fence.

'Maybe,' I murmured, but my dismay was to do with seeing a chick this time of year. I'd read that climate change was throwing the ecosystem out of balance – premature flowering exposing plants to frost, birds fooled by the warm winters into breeding early, putting them out of sync with their food supply – but this was the most extreme example I'd seen.

'It will probably be a week before it's big enough to fly,' I said.

'If it lasts that long.'

The cat leapt gracefully down heading towards the magpies who increased their racket. We held our breath, but it veered off at the last minute and jumped up to sit on the shed, right above the bird. It licked its paws and looked around as if it had no interest in the helpless chick below. It was fooling no one.

Ethan could take no more. He opened the window and I thought he was going to shout out, but instead he grabbed the air rifle.

'No! You can't shoot the neighbour's cat.'

He lowered the rifle and looked at me with anguished eyes. 'We gotta do something!'

This wasn't the moment to remind him that he'd shot a magpie without a second thought not long ago. I knew from experience, birds bear grudges. They probably wouldn't let anyone pick the chick up. I didn't know what to do.

Then we both watched astonished as one of the magpies flew up right into the cat's face and tried to scare it away.

'That was fucking bad ass,' he breathed. The cat jumped back and we both cheered.

'Go, birdy!' Ethan whooped.

'Once Jo and I saw a stag beetle fight off a cat,' I told him.

'Really?'

'The cat would have a swipe and then the beetle would stand up on its hind legs and pincer the cat's nose, and it would jump back. Went on for hours.'

'What happened?'

'No idea.'

The cat returned to stare at the baby magpie.

Ethan shot me a beseeching look. 'We gotta help.'

Lori appeared. 'What's happening?'

'Mum, they're fighting off the cat to protect their baby.'

I stood back to make room for her at the window. She saw the danger immediately.

'I'll ask the neighbours if they can keep their cat in for a bit.'

'But what about the one that comes over the back?'

'We do what we can do.'

I saw them standing, united in their desire to keep the chick safe and glanced at my watch with reluctance. I sighed, it was time to go see a wizard about some frogs.

17

THE WIZARD OF WOOLSTON

It used to be a lovely bike ride to Woolston, with views over the Solent to Ocean Village, the football stadium and the docks, giving way to long stretches of shoreline dominated by birds. Today I saw none of that. There had been several recent housing developments, but though they were nicely done, the view of Southampton, the river, and the sky was now blocked. I found myself on an unfamiliar roundabout, surrounded by high-rise flats and smart new eateries. Where was Weston Shore, the mudflats where the waders gather in their hordes to scrabble for worms and shellfish? Where was the sky? I was disorientated, and increasingly late. I cycled on blindly and eventually cleared the housing estate and was back on more familiar turf.

Geoff's house was a disappointingly ordinary, terraced house. Not even a vampire bat doorknob. I rang the bell and waited. I heard music – an eerie, witchy sound, spooky yet strangely beautiful. Geoff opened the door. He was a short, bald, barrel-chested man decorated with tattoos. Insistent whispering voices chanting spells enveloped me.

'I wanted to tune into the spirit of the Ancient Mother for our meeting,' he said, beckoning me in. 'Blessed be.'

The music was indeed working a bit of magic, quietening my jumbled thoughts about baby magpies and roses, and recalling me to the job in hand. This man wanted bats and frogs. He led me through the small house. Books were scattered everywhere. Books on runes, chakras, reiki, moonology – whatever that was.

'Oh, Dawn says "hi" no, er "blessed be".'

'I suppose she told you I'm a wizard?'

'She did.'

'I'm not a wizard.'

I breathed a sigh of relief.

'I identify as a witch.'

What? Jo would love that.

'It's not what you're thinking.'

I was thinking transgender wizard, but is that what he thought I was thinking?

'Wizards have a bad rep, the term wizard has been culturally co-opted.'

I felt out of my depth. What's wrong with Harry Potter?

'Er, right. And the bats and frogs?'

'I don't want them for spells if that's what you're thinking.'

'No, no of course not.'

'I'm not going to cook them up in a stew for Puck's sake!'

'No, I didn't think—'

'Now if I'd have asked for toads, you may have cause for concern. Toads have poison in their warts.'

The insistent whispering chanting music had stopped soothing me and become overwhelming. I was glad when he led me into the back garden and closed the door on the sound. It was tiny – a square of unpromising lawn with a garage blocking the light from one side and the new building development blocking the sky from another.

'Why do you want frogs and bats in particular?' I asked, keen to return to safe ground.

'They're my spirit animals.'

125

'Oh, okay, yes, hmm,' I nodded wisely. 'Er, how's that work?'

'The bat is my spirit guide, symbolising the power of seeing what other people can't, a second sight. I've lost it and now I need it back and being close to bats will help.'

He waved his hand at the skyline of Woolston. 'I used to sit out here of an evening watching the sun go down over Southampton Water. I'd see all the bats swooping around. It fuelled my spirit, now after a tarot reading, I can't replenish. I've lost the sight.'

It made complete sense to me. As he'd lost sight of the water and the wildlife and the bats, he'd lost his second sight too. I wondered about the frogs. I expect it was because they were amphibians, at home in two worlds.

'And the frogs?'

'They've got big eyes.'

Oh well.

'Right, well, even a small pond will provide a habitat for frogs, but I can't guarantee you'll get any,' I told him.

'Then what would be the point?'

'They've declined rapidly, due to water contamination, disease and lack of habitat mainly, and the increase in the rat population hasn't helped.'

'Can't I just get some?'

'Not that simple, it's against the law to trade frogs or even to transport them from one site to another.'

'Why build a pond for frogs if you can't bring me frogs?'

'It's a good habitat for all kinds of wildlife, and they should find the pond eventually—'

'You can't help me,' he said abruptly.

'It just means—'

'You've got sticky energy, I can feel it emanating from you.'

I was furious. I hadn't wanted to come anyway. I'd have much rather stayed at Lori's.

'I'm sorry you think I can't help,' I said stiffly.

Geoff turned abruptly and led me back into the small house. I tuned in sufficiently to note the slump of his shoulders and came off my high horse.

'You're right,' I admitted suddenly. 'I'm preoccupied.'

We entered the kitchen and he sat at the kitchen table that was covered with wizardy stuff – lush red velvet bags, crystals, pendulums, wood carvings of frogs, bat symbols in jewellery, what looked like a crystal ball. He beckoned me to join him. He looked me deep in the eyes then nodded.

'You came here to help me but maybe I need to help you first. What preoccupies you?' I hesitated. 'No need to tell me. The cards will tell you what you need to know.' He plucked a pack of tarot cards from the mess on the table and shuffled them.

I'd hoped for a cup of tea and a biscuit not a fortune telling. Jo would be happy though, she'd had a great laugh at my expense predicting all kinds of wizardry. My protest went unheeded and Geoff dealt out the cards. I nodded now and then to show interest while my mind wandered.

'Justice is in the third position representing balance.'

It will probably be too late to pick up the dry cleaning now.

'This card represents you the questioner, it's the juggler.'

Costing for Nature accounting would be a game changer. But I wanted to know what happened to the baby magpie and I really want to take down Lori's bamboo.

'This next card is the answer to your dilemma.'

Despite myself, I paid attention.

'The Fool.'

'The fool? What does that mean?'

'You'll have to interpret it yourself. Like I said, my powers have diminished.' He looked at me accusingly, which I thought was rather unfair. The fool? Jo often called me an idiot. Perhaps it meant the answer was in myself. That doesn't help at all. This was a waste of time.

He relented. 'The fool is often the wise person in disguise.'

That left me no wiser. He looked disappointed at my lack of reaction and tried to make amends.

'Let me try a bit of reiki on you.'

'It's fine honestly.'

'I can see your back hurts.'

It was true, sitting at a desk all week had taken its toll.

'I can try to unblock your chakras.'

'No, it's fine.'

'I insist.' He flicked his hands away in sharp thrusts and pumped himself up with deep breaths, then moved to stand behind me. There was a pause that seemed to get heavier. I craned my neck round to see. His face was intent with concentration.

'What are you doing?'

'I'm grounding myself.'

'Okay.' I turned back around and waited. 'Still?' I asked, unable to restrain my impatience.

'I'm visualising roots coming out of my legs.'

'Er. Okay.'

Eventually I heard sounds of movement again.

'Right. I'm ready to begin.'

Thank God for that. I saw out the corner of my eye his hands move around my back, never quite touching.

'Although with my powers diminished, it probably won't work,' he added.

He was right, it didn't.

Jo set two pints on the table. 'Right, enough of your news, time for me. A lot has happened while you've been gadding around.'

'You can't beat the Wizard of Woolston.'

'I can.'

'Go on then.'

'Charlotte life coached me. Yours was a bit rubbish, no offence, mate.'

'No offence! I've changed my entire life.' Shit I'd gone into soprano and risen to the bait. 'Or I had anyway,' I added, remembering I was no longer Habitat Man.

'You got a D, what can I say, but mine went superbly.'

'So what did she say?'

'She said that I should pull my finger out and stop drifting, which I thought was a fair point.'

'That's exactly what I've been saying for months!' I cried.

Jo continued as if I hadn't spoken. 'You remember the Venn diagram?'

'I do.'

'What am I good at?'

'Writing software.'

'Let me rephrase. What am I good at and what do I enjoy?'

'Being mean to people and making them suffer,' I said.

'Exactly. Good at it. Enjoy it. There's two circles right there.'

'What about what will make you money?'

'The Random Recipe Generator of course.'

'And dare I ask what does the world need?'

'Another cookery game show obviously.'

'You're not serious about that?'

'Oh yes. Charlotte has dreams of being the compere, but I told her I want to do it.'

I considered. Charlotte – slim, young, pretty, spangly. Jo – short, plump, charismatic and utterly hilarious at other people's expense. No contest.

'You'd be brilliant.'

Jo smiled, pleased to have her personal convictions confirmed.

'We'll set up a YouTube channel linked to the website, where I'll put up the videos of me cooking. Build up interest via the blog, do a bit of social media. Charlotte can help with that, and get people to share their own recipes and videos, then when we have a following, get the celebs on board.'

'How will you get a following though?'

'I've got in touch with everyone I've ever known, and told them to do the RRG challenge and get all their friends to do it. Even Luke Little Willy and Liz Big Willy.'

'Oh my days, I haven't heard those names since university.'

'Remember us throwing you out of the window?'

'I try not to.' I shuddered, remembering back to my twenty-first birthday. After a particularly brutal round of the insult game, she'd taken me out to get me drunk, and in the meantime, she'd got the others to replicate my room on the fifth floor exactly in a ground floor room. Then they'd thrown me out of the window in the room I'd thought was mine. The clarity of that moment, the split second where I was calculating whether it would be death or life in a wheelchair, stayed with me still.

'My proudest moment.' Jo's eyes gleamed.

I was lost for words. Her assumption that I'd find it amusing was still hard to contradict, even after all these years.

'They got married, which has a nice symmetry,' she continued.

'I guess being shared victims of the insult game, created an unbreakable bond.'

'A pleasingly simple game – guessing who wrote the insult.'

'Hmm.'

'Up in the Albanian Alps is a micro-species of flea called *cockus minutae*, and even that has a bigger willy than Luke,' Jo recited.

'Yes, that was one of your best, but—'

'How did Liz get her nickname? It wasn't one of mine.'

'Wasn't it something about her jeans?' I sighed, realising she wasn't going to stop until she'd dug out all the insults she could remember.

'That was it. They crumpled up at the crotch and made her look like she had a knob. Can you remember the ones about you, Timbo?'

Why does Tim like worms – because they look like his knob. There were many knob-gags. *Why is Jo a lesbian? – Tim.* That one hurt a bit actually.

'No, it was years ago.'

'Even Jo can grow a better beard than Tim,' said Jo grinning. 'That reminds me, Baby Face, did the wizard have a beard?'

'No he doesn't actually.'

'The Wizard of Woolston has good alliteration, but if I were a wizard, dancing round a fire summoning up the spirits of evil I'd do it in Netley,' she remarked, thankfully moving on from beards, or lack of.

She was right. Netley Abbey was down the road from Woolston, and was reputedly haunted, following claims of flitting white figures and ghostly chanting.

'Do you remember the duel we fought at dawn in Netley Abbey?' I laughed.

We'd been second year students, ready to leave the protection of the halls of residence and rent our own place. We'd summoned our reluctant seconds out of bed at six in the morning and headed off to the abbey. It was supposed to be a duel with sticks for who got the best room, but they'd broken straightaway and we ended up with a wheelbarrow race as the ultimate decider. I couldn't even remember our seconds, they'd faded into history, but Jo and I had stayed together.

'Look at that!' cried Jo.

'What?'

'Beard at two o'clock.'

It was glorious. Black, bushy, luxuriant.

'Never mind, Baby Face,' she soothed.

Sometimes I hated her.

18

COSTING FOR NATURE

My thoughts were a jumble on the morning commute. Lori, Ethan, the wizard. Did the cat get the magpie chick? I stumbled along with the hordes pouring out of the train, through the turnstile, across Waterloo station and out onto the street. I walked along Waterloo Bridge, buffeted by blasts of wind. I paused halfway, huddling in my jacket to enjoy the open vista and survey the murky brown river below. I'd heard that salmon migrated up the river this time of year, but I'd yet to see them. The gulls circled, also looking for fish, cawing loudly overhead, drowning out the noise of the city. This was my favourite bit of my commute to work. Soon, however, I'd be enclosed by buildings, then ensconced in a carpeted office amidst the incessant hum of computers, unmoving in my office chair gazing at a screen.

My mind strayed to Geoff. I empathised with him feeling disconnected from nature and losing his power. That was no way to feel. I'd never even had a chance to talk to him about bats. They'd feed mainly on moths and gnats. Nectar-rich flowers such as honeysuckle or evening primrose would attract moths at night and provide a lovely evening scent. I'd warn him to avoid non-native varieties such as Japonica. Ivy and heather, especially the winter-flowering varieties, would keep moths going through the year.

I left Waterloo Bridge and was surrounded by tall buildings. The sky shrank to a sliver and I realised that none of these suggestions dealt with his primary problem of losing sight of the sea, losing that sense of sky and space.

My musings were brought to a halt by a crowd of Extinction Rebellion protestors blocking the road, campaigning on climate change and marching towards Trafalgar Square. It recalled to mind why I was going into work and how important it was. Last time I hadn't been able to meet their eyes, but now it was different. I joined the mass of people waving banners. The protestor next to me was wearing a T-shirt which had a pagan symbol on it. He returned my smile with a glare – in my city suit he'd probably assumed I was part of the problem. I hadn't given up being Habitat Man to save the planet through Costing for Nature accounting to be condemned by an XR protestor.

'I like the pagan symbol,' I ventured.

'It's the pentacle, many of us are pagans.'

'I can see why – a shared love of nature,' I said, keen to demonstrate my enlightened views.

'It's an emergency!' bellowed the protestor suddenly, making me jump.

'Act now!' I yelled.

'You don't look like a pagan,' he commented.

'I'm not, but I know a wizard, well, he calls himself a witch because Harry Potter has co-opted the term.'

'What?'

'It's tainted by association,' I explained.

'What's wrong with Harry Potter?'

'I heard they don't like to use the term wizard.'

'That's because of the connotations of the Klu Klux Klan — they use the term Grand Wizard.'

That made much more sense. I felt like an idiot.

'Nothing to do with Harry Potter,' he drove his point home.

I changed the subject quickly, needing to prove myself. 'I'm not a protestor, but I'm doing my bit.' As we marched, I filled him in on the principles of Costing for Nature accounting and how it would save the planet.

'So you see,' I concluded eventually, 'once the environmental costs are assessed, then these costs can be offset and more informed decisions can be taken.'

I waited for the scales to drop from his eyes, for him to take me by the hand and proclaim me as a hero to the rest of the protestors. 'He's not just some city suit,' he'd cry. 'Not just some washed up middle-aged money broker destroying our young futures. No! He is a hero, fellow scruffy heroic twenty-year-olds. He's saving the world through Costing for Nature accounting.'

'It won't work.'

'You don't understand, you offset the carbon—'

'Yeah, I get that, but the cost of the carbon is too cheap to make a real difference. They'll give a tenner to plant some trees in Ethiopia to offset their flight to New York, but they don't factor in the time lag between using the carbon and the time it takes for the tree to grow.'

'But we'll just set a higher price. The UN propose eighty dollars per tonne for internal accounting purposes.'

'No, what will happen,' he continued relentlessly, 'is that businesses will no longer feel they have to curb their emissions because they're now offsetting them. The pressure will be off and emissions will continue to rise.'

I shook my head. He was wrong, of course he was.

. . .

I cycled fast trying to make the lights at the junction with Cobden Bridge – this was the junction with the road where the guerrilla knitter's body lay. Also, I was looking forward to seeing Lori. This time, I had no reason to rush off, and it would be lovely to sit in the kitchen, drink tea, plot against Lori's bamboo, and check out the magpie situation.

My eye was caught by a man waiting to cross at the lights. He had the most perfect facial hair I'd ever seen. I'd tried a few times to cultivate a beard and always ended up with bald areas. On beard-growing forums I'd been told if I toughed it out and let the rest grow, it would get bushy enough to hide the bare areas, but with Jo ever-ready to take the mick, I never saw it through.

I gazed at the beard with envious eyes. It must take careful snipping and precision tools to create this carefully sculpted thing of beauty that surrounded his mouth. Above the lips was a moustache that covered exactly the right amount of skin between his lips and nostrils. Below the lips was a little tuft that gently supported the bottom lip while the rest was cut away into a pleasingly curved shape that grew confidently and evenly up his face, thinning symmetrically as it met the ears.

The little green man appeared, and as he crossed, I allowed myself a tiny daydream where I was in possession of such a thing of beauty. Such facial hair would give one confidence, poise. I'd become a man of decisive action, allure. I wouldn't dither with a beard like that, I'd take Lori in my arms and be damned.

'Tim?' A voice hailed me. It was the helpful fellow who'd let me lock my bike up in his drive – the Lord of all Wisdom.

'Oh, er hi, erm Sumdipotty?'

'Samudrapati.'

'Sorry.'

'I wondered if we could fix a time for you to check out my garden. I was hoping to hear from you?'

'I've given it up now, er…'

'Oh, no worries, sorry for slowing you down.'

A flash of disappointment crossed his face to be replaced by an accepting smile. The lights turned green and I dithered. I didn't want to run into Fern. But he'd helped me out after all, and had an air of gentle serenity about him that was compelling. Maybe some of it would wash off on me and soothe my ceaseless ruminations on my life choices and Costing for Nature accounting. I checked my watch, I was early.

'I could take a quick look now if you like?'

'Brilliant, see you at mine.'

He started walking and I whizzed past him on my bike and quickly locked it to his gate as before, by which time he'd joined me. He led me through to the back garden.

Mindful of time, I waved away the offers of herbal tea and surveyed the space. I recognised the witch hazel on the left which provided such lovely colour to next door's garden too. I approved of the pussy willow further down. But on the right lurked my least favourite non-native shrub.

'What do you think?'

'I'm not that keen on the rhododendron you have there, it's unfriendly to wildlife. It actually has small amounts of poison in the nectar, enough to kill honeybees, though bumblebees seem to tolerate it. Otherwise, pretty well all native insects will avoid it. I'd say of all the popular UK shrubs, this is one of the worst.'

My slight feeling of rush had given the words a curtness I hadn't meant.

'Oh! Should I chop it down?' He looked crushed.

I regretted my harshness. It was a beautiful shrub and would look gorgeous when it flowered. I paced round the perimeter of the garden. Three fence panels bordering Daisy's garden were hanging down. Whatever we did here would affect next door. Her idea of the Feng Shui garden had inspired me. I'd ignored two more messages from Fern and was feeling guilty, maybe here was a way I could make it up to them.

'I have to sort out the fence. Are you thinking I should avoid panels treated with chemicals?'

'No. I'm thinking a living willow fence.'

'A wonderful idea.'

'Forget about fence panels and plant some willow saplings – they will grow into a beautiful, green living fence. You can do all sorts with it, grow vertically, horizontally or a criss-cross pattern. You can get quite arty with it if you're keen. But the best thing is that, next to the oak, willows have the highest wildlife value of all trees in the UK.'

'Really?'

'Yes, so if you do a willow fence, I reckon you could allow yourself to keep the rhododendron, just for beauty.'

His face was a picture and I was glad I'd made time for him.

'Willows ought not to be planted near a house or drain, but as this isn't going to be grown as a tree and controlled as a living fence, it should be fine.' I looked at the ground by the fence. 'Cheapest option would be to order willow saplings, or if you don't want to wait for them to grow, you can order willow, fedges I think they call them, online. You plant the thicker willow rods about a foot deep, then weave the smaller rods into a lattice. It would look lovely once the leaves start to sprout in the summer. Should cost you under a hundred pounds.'

I grabbed a trowel I'd spotted and knelt down and dug into the earthy border in front of the fence. The earth gave way easily, one push had cleared fifteen centimetres already. With my next spadeful, I came up against resistance. A hard layer this shallow would be tricky. I dug around with the trowel and realised I'd come up against a solid object.

'Hmm.'

'Have you found something?'

I dug round the edges of an object about six inches by four inches. It was a tin-box. I levered it out and handed it to him.

'I can't believe it! That's my time capsule.' He shook the dirt off it and held it up for me to see. It was an old tin money box.

'I can't even remember what I put in it. I was about ten when I did this. I'd seen the idea on *Blue Peter*.' He fumbled with the lid eagerly but it was wedged shut with grime. His excitement was contagious and I followed him into the house where he ran it under hot water to clear the mud off. He got out a knife and prised it open and pulled out sheets of paper from the box.

'What are they?'

'Lists of what pocket money I had and what I spent in on.'

'Oh.' I just about stopped myself from saying 'is that it'.

'I've always loved numbers. Making lists of income and expenditure.'

'Really? I'm an accountant and I hate numbers.'

'That's very sad.' He looked at me with concern in his warm brown eyes. Before I knew it, we were exchanging life stories over a cup of herbal tea. He'd studied accounting at university, got a first class degree and even spent a year in the city at a top accounting firm before giving it all up when he became a Buddhist and realised that the constant focus on money wasn't consistent with his values. When it was my turn, I tried to explain how I'd ended up doing a job I didn't like for twenty-five years.

'You must think I'm utterly ridiculous to have spent so much of my life doing something I hate.'

'Not at all, I can empathise.'

'How can you when you gave it up for what you believed in?'

'It didn't work out. The idea was that I'd hold meditation classes at the Buddhist centre, but it went wrong when I formally became a monk and was given my Buddhist name.'

'Lord of all Wisdom.'

'I shudder whenever anyone says it out loud. There'd always come this point when someone asked me what Samudrapati stood for and I'd feel such an imposter. So I stopped doing those

138

and started working at Café Thrive, the vegan café attached to the wholefood centre in town.'

I was aware of the shop, it allowed you to bring your own containers and fill them up from the big barrels of rice, cereals, nuts, etc. Now people were avoiding plastic, I suspected it must be doing well. I'd not tried the café though.

'Don't you enjoy it?'

'I'm bored. I long to go back to accounting, but we're supposed to be against material values, and I am, but as you can see from my nerdy time capsule, I love numbers.'

I couldn't help but laugh at the idea of a Buddhist monk with secret yearnings to be an accountant.

'I gave up my job when they turned down my plan to shift to an environmental accounting method. I won't bore you with the details,' I said.

'I know all about costing social and environment impacts.'

'You do?'

'I took on the Buddhist centre's accounts a few years ago to cheer myself up, and I adopted the triple bottom line method. All our projects are assessed on social, environmental and financial impacts. So you won't bore me.' He nodded at me encouragingly.

'I gave it up to start the Green Garden Consultancy which I loved, but then my old company decided to give Costing for Nature accounting a go and asked me back. I feel I have to do it now, as it would make such a difference.'

'Will it though?'

'What! How can you say that?' I felt like he'd punched me in the stomach. The sudden high I'd experienced when I at last found someone who appreciated the value of environmental accounting disappeared in an instant. I'd dismissed the XR protestor because yes, he knew about climate change but what did he know of accounting methods? But this Buddhist monk accountant chap should know better.

'The fact is that unless you measure something and add it up and include it in the costings, it is, to all respects and purposes, invisible in business terms. It's obvious that once we measure and cost impacts such as biodiversity and the carbon costs of activities, it will revolutionise how decisions are made.'

Samudrapati nodded, wisely not attempting to interrupt my rant. He gave me a moment to check if I was finished. I wasn't.

'In fact, to put it even more strongly, I can't see how any real progress could be made without Costing for Nature accounting.' I drained my cup of herbal tea too quickly and spluttered. I knew I was losing my cool, but couldn't help myself. 'I mean, you said, you use it yourself, you must see the value.' My knock-out blow delivered. I'd made my case and sat back.

After a moment's pause, he nodded again.

'In the business context it's different. It wouldn't work simply to measure the carbon footprint and offset it, they'd use that as license to continue to emit – you must see that.'

That was what the XR protestor had said.

'But it's a necessary first step. Surely something is better than nothing?'

'Not if it means you think you've done enough. It's like if you had reiki treatment thinking it will cure cancer, when what you really need is surgery. If it stops you seeking a solution that will actually work, it's worse than doing nothing. You have to do what's necessary.'

'It's easy to point out the problems, what about the solutions?'

'I'd go with a set carbon budget.'

'A carbon budget?'

'A limit, an actual ration they have to work within that is consistent with them achieving net zero carbon.'

Samudrapati was impressive. He'd been unfazed by my outburst, he'd made his case with calmness and authority. I had to concede.

'You truly are the Lord of all Wisdom.'

'Don't say that,' he laughed uneasily, 'it always makes me feel like a complete fool.'

Fool! Wisdom! What was it the wizard had said? The answer to my dilemma lies in the fool, who is often the wise one.

'I'm envious,' said Samudrapati, innocent of the plot I was hatching. 'I'd love your job. It would be absolutely perfect.'

19

THE MAGPIE

I cycled at top speed to Lori's, whizzing up over the bridge and right at the clock tower as if gravity didn't exist. Florence saw me approach from her lookout on the chair by the window and jumped up wagging her tail. A constant chatter of magpies sounded the alarm. Lori opened the door and I heard Ethan yelling from his bedroom window.

'Get away, you fucking cats, or I'll fucking have you!'

Lori shot me the now familiar apologetic look before shouting up the stairs.

'Don't shoot the cat!'

'I'm coming down!'

Ethan hared down the stairs. He paused when he saw me.

'It's still on the ground but we're keeping it safe, man.'

He rushed out into the garden and Lori and I shared a smile as we heard him shooing the cat away and crooning reassuringly at the magpies. We followed him and witnessed the spectacle of the cat fleeing over the fence.

'Ethan, don't throw stones at the cat,' Lori implored in a whispered yell.

'What?'

'For God's sake!' She stomped over and muttered in his ear, nodding towards the neighbours. I joined them, eager to see how the baby magpie was getting on. The scene was much the same as it had been a week earlier, the young magpie on the ground with the two adult magpies keeping guard.

'What do you think?' he asked. 'Is it big enough to fly?'

The magpie had grown substantially, it had all its feathers and was looking like a smart young bird now. It was remarkable that the parents had kept it safe for so long.

'I reckon it won't be long.'

'Thank God.' He gazed paternally at the chick. The adult magpies hopped around gazing at us beadily, keeping up a steady alarm call.

'I've done all I can for them, but they don't seem to appreciate it. Is it my imagination or are they giving me a dirty look?'

'Of course not, babe, they're just alarmed by all of us.'

I understood Lori's desire to quell Ethan's paranoia, but Ethan was right. He knew it too.

'Okay, then, I'll go in and you stay here and see if they still kick up.'

He went back in the house. The moment he was out of sight, the incessant din of the magpies' alarm call subsided. It started again when he came back out.

'See,' he said, over the din.

'Maybe we'd better all go back inside,' I suggested.

Back in the kitchen, Ethan stomped about indignantly.

'It seems ungrateful, man, like I've literally been putting myself out to help them, keep them safe and they treat me like shit.'

'I can't imagine what that feels like,' Lori said.

'Why do they give me this constant magpie shit?' he asked me, oblivious to his mum's sarcasm.

'Possibly because you shot one of them dead,' she said.

'They treat me like I'm their enemy, man.'

'It's like I'm not even here.' She waved her arms in his face.

'It's not fair!'

'La di da, don't mind me, I'm just your mum, I'm invisible.'

Ethan turned to me, puzzled. I'd clearly moved from being enemy number one, to man with the answers.

'Magpies are smart,' I told him. 'They recognise faces, lots of birds do. They know who is who, who puts out the bird food,' I remembered my teenage years, 'who kicks a football in their nest. Who shoots at them.'

'Really?'

'Yes, and they have long memories. And more than that, not only do they remember who is who and who did what, they can tell their mates, so you'll probably find even next door's magpies kick up when they see you.'

'Fuck! So I've got a bad rep!'

'Afraid so, among the magpies anyway.'

'I never thought it would have consequences.'

I shrugged, sensing the less I said the better. I suspected from Lori's look of frustration that this was something she'd repeatedly told him, but he'd needed to find it out for himself.

'Do you think I could make them forgive me?'

'I don't know, you could try.'

'I will! I'll never let them see the gun again. I'll put out food for them, be super nice.'

I shot Lori a look, He was growing up under our eyes.

'Would it work do you think?'

'I don't know, Ethan, but I'd be interested to find out.'

'Right. I'm off to google how to make magpies like me. I'm gonna fucking atone.' He stomped back up the stairs.

Lori turned to me, her expression was hard to read.

'I don't know whether to love you or hate you.'

Still hard to read.

'I've told him a thousand times that actions have

consequences. But he doesn't listen to me. Did you see how everything I say he completely ignores? Then you swan in and suddenly he listens to you as if you're the Lord of all Wisdom.'

I still couldn't tell if I was in trouble or not. She blinked back tears. 'And now he's transforming from a self-centred and worryingly violent boy, to this mature, compassionate kid.' She choked and fell silent.

I stood there, unsure what to say. Lori suddenly threw her arms around me and held me in a close hug. I held her back, as tight as I dared. A ray of sunlight came in through the Velux window above bathing us in a warm glow. I basked in the moment.

We heard Ethan rush back downstairs. She released me from her clasp.

'Mum, got any suet balls? Magpies like them.'

'I'll get some when I go shopping.'

'But let me put them out, when they're looking. Apparently magpies can make friends with humans,' he told me excitedly.

'Look!' cried Lori.

We followed her gaze out of the window. The young magpie was fluttering its wings, hopping along the ground, with its parents watching from an overhanging branch. It ran and fluttered and then suddenly took off into the tree. We cheered.

'Well done, Ethan. You helped make that happen, you really took care.'

'Cheers, Mum,' said Ethan, delighted.

He sped back upstairs and there was a sudden peace in the kitchen. I sat in my usual place at the table. Lori put the kettle on. Florence crept in once Ethan had left and her wet nose nuzzled my hand. I stroked her and scratched the back of her neck. Flo gazed up at me adoringly, wagging her tail softly. We heard birdsong, a welcome change from the magpies' alarm call. I still wanted to tell Lori so much, ask her so much, but was reluctant to disturb the peace. A weight had fallen from my shoulders, I was sure now, I'd soon be back to being Habitat Man. There was time to enjoy a moment to contemplate and daydream. The vibe coming off Lori was similarly peaceful. I suspected a weight had lifted a little from her shoulders too. It can't be easy being a single mum to a teenage boy, especially one who had a father who thought an air rifle was an appropriate gift.

She placed a mug of tea in front of me. I took an appreciative sip and sat back in my chair, gazing up at the sun's rays coming in through the Velux window. My eye was caught by the numerous spiderwebs and several spiders patrolling their territory.

'I do take notice you know.' She caught me looking at the spiderwebs. 'About welcoming insects.'

'So I see.' My phone vibrated. It was Geoff. I don't normally give out my number to the beneficiaries of my skills, but I'd felt guilty about Geoff.

Thanks for your report. I sent you a pagan playlist.

'Goodness.'

'What's that?'

'I just got sent a pagan playlist! Shall I?'

'Pagan! Is that like folk?'

'Let's find out.'

'Hang on, link up to my speaker.'

I looked at her, bemused. She took my phone, played with it and music flooded the room. The song spoke of the spirit of the wind, of the sea and sky. The plaintive melody reminded me that I hadn't really addressed the wizard's issues. He was trying to tell me something.

'Beware people sending unsolicited playlists,' warned Lori. But it was too late.

'I feel bad, I didn't do Geoff justice.' I told her about his disappointment over the frogs and losing the view of the sky.

'I'm sure he doesn't blame you though, it's not your fault.'

My phone vibrated, another text.

I demanded my money back from Transition. I feel bad about that now, but I'm a bit stressed lately.

'Seems like he does blame me.' I showed her the text.

'That's outrageous! You can't just magic up frogs.'

'He probably thinks I can.'

'OMG! Is this Dawn's wizard?' cried Lori.

'Yes. She calls him the Wizard of Woolston. Do you know him?'

'Not personally, but that's the fella Dawn had a threesome with. The wizard and his wife.'

'I didn't see a wife?'

'Maybe that's why he's stressed.'

She had a point. Perhaps it wasn't just the loss of the view over Southampton Water, and losing sight of the sky and the bats, maybe he'd lost his wife too.

'Alexa! Alexa, next!' she shouted again even louder. Flo ran off.

'You've upset her now.'

'Sorry, it's just... well, it sounded a bit folky.'

She nodded satisfied when the mournful melody was abruptly replaced by an upbeat rhythmic beat.

I drained my tea and checked my watch, time always flew when we were chatting, but I'd come with a purpose in mind.

'Now the chick has fledged, could we get rid of the bamboo?'

'All right, come on then.'

'Only if you're sure?'

'Let's do it.' She smiled and pulled on her coat. 'Ethan!' she bellowed at the ceiling. 'Come help with the bamboo!' She waited listening, then shrugged and headed outside.

When she handed me the lopping shears, rather than a spade, I realised with dismay that she just meant to chop the stems. I decided not to say anything, but it was far short of what I wanted to do with the bamboo.

She grabbed another pair of loppers and we got to work.

Some of the fronds were twelve feet tall, and we had to stand back as they crashed down onto the lawn. Once we'd got going, I caught her up with the backlog of news.

'Do you really think this Lord of all Wisdom, aka the Fool will take your job?' she asked, after I'd filled her in on the reason for my lateness.

'I really do.'

'You should tell the wizard.'

'Why?'

'He might think his powers have returned and stop sending you playlists.'

'Good point.'

'I'm here.' Ethan trod over the masses of bamboo canes littering the lawn. 'Can I chop something?'

Lori handed him her shears. 'You and Tim chop and I'll bundle the canes up.'

While we chopped, Ethan quizzed me about my guerrilla gardening exploits. I waxed nostalgically about our most ambitious project covering bus shelter roofs with sedum.

Ethan paused chopping and got out his phone and tapped into it. 'Green bus shelters. Cool!' He brandished his phone at me. I leant over and saw that some pictures of our efforts had ended up online. I'd had no idea. I felt a quiver of pride when Ethan showed the photos to Lori.

'OMG, was that you?'

'Not just me, but a bit yeah.' I shrugged modestly.

We got back to work. It felt good. Physical exercise, every felling of a cane bringing more light and space into the garden. Ethan and I, chopping side by side. Lori gathering the canes into bundles and stacking them under her decking. Ethan had called me cool. Well, he'd called my sedum roof cool. It was progress. Dare I see if Lori fancied a drink later?

My phone vibrated in my pocket. I paused to take a look – another text from Geoff.

Lori saw my expression. 'Another playlist?'

'Yes, this one is titled, *We won't wait any longer.*'

'You'd better sort him out.'

She was right, but it was easier said than done. How was I going to restore his view? How could I get the sky and the sea back for him?

'That's it,' said Ethan, chopping down the last of the bamboo.

We stood back and admired our work.

'It really makes the garden look bigger,' Lori said.

'You'll get a lot more light now the bamboo's down,' I remarked.

'Now I can plant some new stuff, right?' she asked.

I considered. The bamboo had provided cover, but who knew what was growing in the ground. There was always competition. I've made that mistake in the past.

'Best to see what's what first. Patience is needed.'

I'm assuming she's single, but she'd be wanting to hide anything of that sort from Ethan anyway. Although she did say she's fed up with him interfering in her love life. But how do I know she meant me? She's nice and smiley but maybe she's like that to everyone. It's too soon to ask her out.

Ethan had gone back to scrolling through pictures.

'Hey, Mum, look at all these gardens on roofs! Fucking cool, man.'

Yes, I'd better concentrate on my work. For best long-term results, one shouldn't rush things. Focus on getting out of my city job, back into being Habitat Man and sort out the wizard. I looked up at a few remaining bamboo fronds that had invaded the neighbour's garden silhouetted against the blue sky.

Hang on! Gardens on roofs. Geoff had a garage that looked pretty sturdy. If he sat up there, he'd be able to see the sky. He'd need to check out structural integrity, do a bit of work. Set up a ladder, lay a waterproof cover, cut in drainage outlets to flow into the gutter. He wouldn't need a lot of earth if he stuck with sedum. It's the perfect cover for roofs – shallow roots, hardy, made of draught resistant succulents, pollinators love it and sedum would attract moths which would attract the bats.

'Ethan, you're a genius!' I cried suddenly.

'Am I?'

'I'll make Geoff a roof garden, then he can see the sky.'

'Brilliant!' cried Lori.

With a renewed burst of energy, I gathered the last remaining fronds of bamboo and threw them on the pile of debris at the back of the garden. As I walked back, I overhead Lori talking to Ethan, who was shaking his head doubtfully. I caught the last few words 'Go on, you're okay with…' she stopped talking when I approached, shot Ethan a look and turned to me. 'Fancy staying for dinner, Tim?'

'I'd love to.'

Elated, I followed her and Ethan into the kitchen, brushing aside my brief speculation on who Ethan was okay with. 'I'd better wash my hands.'

'Upstairs, on your right.'

I returned to the kitchen, rubbing my hands, keen to impress Lori with my readiness to help. 'What can I do?'

'Erm, you got a text,' Lori said.

I looked at my phone on the table puzzled. No flashing notification light.

'Sorry, Ethan read it.'

'I thought it was my phone.'

I wasn't sure I believed him. His next words filled me with horror.

'What's this body she's talking about? Who's the guerrilla knitter?'

I read the text quickly. It was Fern asking why I hadn't responded and pleading with me to get in touch about the body. Lori and Ethan were looking at me with intense interest. I filled them in on what happened as briefly as I could.

'Why didn't you say?' asked Lori.

'I don't like to discuss clients' private business,' I said primly.

She looked unconvinced which was fair enough. We had after all discussed Dawn and her lovers and speculated on the wizard's marital problems.

'I get it, the police always suspect those who find the body,' contributed Ethan.

'But you've got nothing to hide, Tim, have you?' said Lori.

I looked down at my hands, I hadn't got all the garden dirt off.

'I'll just wash my hands again.'

In the bathroom I scrubbed away at the dirt under my fingernails, and made my decision.

'You know, Lori,' I said, when I returned to the kitchen. 'I won't stay after all. Jo's cooking for me tonight so erm, I'd better get back.'

Florence gazed at me sorrowfully from the dog basket, sensing with her animal intuition, my change in mood. I gave her a reassuring stroke.

'Oh, if you're sure. Thanks for helping with the bamboo.'

'My pleasure.' I forced a smile. 'Also, I've got a report to write for the wizard.' I shot a smile at Ethan, grabbed my phone and left.

20

HABITAT MAN RETURNS

Jo raised her glass to mine. 'Habitat Man!'

We clinked glasses.

'The contract has been drawn up, they've agreed the deal with your software, so you'll be quids in,' I informed her.

'So this Lord of Wisdom, Sumopotty fella…?'

'Samudrapati.'

'They're okay with him are they? I can't quite picture him in his orange robes among the suits.'

'He's a Buddhist lying low. I gave him a couple of my suits actually. So, that's it, I'm back to being Habitat Man.'

'Why don't you look happier? Shouldn't you be way-haying and jumping about a bit?'

'No, I'm pleased,' I insisted with a smile.

'You never told me how the other visit went, the guerrilla knitter one?'

There was a brief pause. Jo took a swig of her beer and laughed. 'You didn't dig up a body in the garden or anything?'

I froze, hoping she'd move on. I felt my eyebrows tilt, against my will, at their most anxious angle. 'Er…'

'Bloody hell, Timbo!' she exclaimed, her pint held frozen midway to her lips.

I filled her in on the details, and my decision not to go to the police.

'Of course. They always suspect the one who found the body.'

'I know. Obviously, I've done nothing wrong, but—'

'Although, Timbo, you'd be the only witness, what if she…'

'Stabbed me in the heart with a knitting needle?'

Jo nodded.

'I don't think she would,' I said uncertainly. 'But if the story came out it would be news and I'd be a key witness. They'll delve, Jo, and you know it doesn't look good on paper, let alone tied to a body in the garden. So I'm just going to lie low and hope it goes away.'

'You're worried about Lori finding out?'

'Yes. No. You know what? I'm going to leave it with Lori.' I took a fortifying slug of beer and set down my pint firmly. 'And I worked out the wizard problem. I'm doing him one of my roof gardens next week.'

'I agree with everything you've said.'

'You do?' I looked for the smirk. Jo never said this unless I'd been praising her for something.

'You're right about Lori. Don't forget her son wants to shoot you. And…' She raised her pint in the air again, 'Welcome back, Timbo! Habitat Man, Guerrilla Gardener, doing magic roof gardens for charity. Do what you do best, mate.'

My phone tinkled and my heart leapt.

'It's Lori.'

'She's got her own text tone?'

I ignored Jo's vexed air and read quickly.

As a result of the great bamboo massacre, I've piles of bamboo piled up. You left in a rush so I didn't get a chance to ask if some of your gardens would have a use for it? Come and pick it up if you want it. You can stop for some lunch Saturday if you like? If not I'll take it down the dump. L 😊

I started to text a reply.

'I thought you were going to leave it,' Jo said.

'Lori invited me for lunch next Saturday,' I told her with glowing eyes. 'Dinner would be better, but still…'

'We do Saturday nights though don't we?' She spoke as if Saturday nights down the pub were beyond question.

'Maybe it's just a thank-you for picking up her bamboo, but where will I store it?'

'Take it down the dump.'

'It could be useful. If we had a garden…'

'I'll do you a garden.'

'No,' I said hastily. I had visions of her dumping a pile of mud in my room with a flower stuck in the top.

'Get her to do a random recipe.'

'I don't want to put her off.'

'We gotta utilise our contacts.' Jo was insistent.

'I'm not going to ask her to spend ages cooking some weird concoction. She's a working woman, she was probably planning on a sandwich.'

'You sorted out her bat box, water butt, bush, chopped down her bamboo, and now she wants you to pick it up.'

'I was the one who wanted to chop down her bamboo. She was doing me a favour.'

'Course she was. Get the beers in.'

'Just because you take the piss, doesn't mean everyone else does.'

'All I'm saying is that she gets her gardening done so least she can do is a random recipe, write a blog and post it on my site.' She rattled her glass.

I compressed my irritation into a sigh, which I fear was lost on her and got in the drinks. I nodded to the guy at the bar.

'Awright?' he asked.

'All right?' I responded. He seemed relatively coherent today, so I took the opportunity to find out a little about him.

'Do you have a garden?'

He nodded. 'Yer, small one mind.'

'You're one up on me then.' I glanced at Jo to see if she was taking in this unprecedented move towards chatting to the guy at the bar and saw to my horror she was texting on my phone. Further conversation would have to wait. I hurried back and plonked the pints down spilling some onto her jeans.

'Take it easy.'

'What the hell?' I grabbed my phone off her and had a read.

Thanks, I'd love to come over for lunch. I'll have a think about your bamboo. If I can't use it immediately, could you store it a little longer? It would be a shame to chuck it.

Check out the random recipe generator we devised. Once the recipe comes up, there's no going back. You're allowed to add one ingredient and drop one but NO MORE! Write a review of any recipes you do on randomrecipe.com

'Keep your hair on, mate, I kept your beginning. I didn't add tons of kisses or anything,' she said, unrepentant.

I ignored her and sent off a quick message.

Hi Lori, Sorry for last text, Jo nicked phone off me and finished my draft. You don't have to do the RRG. Tim x

I turned to Jo. 'I added an x!'

'You slag!'

THE MAGIC POND

Geoff was keen to go ahead with a pond and delighted with the updated report, especially at the idea of a rooftop garden. I borrowed Jo's car to collect the pond basin, but called on Geoff first to make sure he'd dug the hole as directed.

A woman let me in. I assumed it must be Geoff's wife. She was as tall and slim, as he was short and stocky, and had a cheeky look about her that was endearing.

'Blessed be.'

I wondered if this meant she was a witch, but decided not to ask. It was gone four already and we had a lot to get through.

'Hi, I'm Tim.'

'I know. Come in, I'm Kerry.'

My ears pricked up. Kerry? The mysterious person in the room with Dawn? The one who wanted me to come and 'play'? I pleaded with my face not to blush. She flashed me a knowing smile as I hurried through into the kitchen. Geoff was already coming out to greet me, looking a much happier man than before.

'Tea?' enquired Kerry.

'Yes please, milk no sugar.'

Geoff led me out into the garden and showed me the means of access he'd constructed to his garage roof – a scaffolding ladder that had four legs and looked reassuringly stable.

'I wasn't sure you'd go for the roof garden, what with the safety issues and planning permission.'

'Don't worry about that, come and have a look.' I followed him up the ladder. He'd put out two chairs, but otherwise it was just a bare flat roof. We took in the view. To the right, the new housing development dominated the horizon, but straight ahead was now a clear view of Southampton Water and a wide expanse of sky. The wind buffeted my body. I turned to look at Geoff. It may have been my imagination, but it seemed that the wind was blowing energy into him, lifting him taller, broadening his chest and strengthening his spirit.

I didn't want to rain on his parade, but I felt a sense of responsibility for the suggestion. 'Are you sure about the weight-bearing potential of the roof? Has it been checked out by a builder?'

'I am a builder.' He nodded towards the housing development. 'I'm literally the architect of my own misfortune. Still, it pays the bills.'

We sat on the chairs and I talked him through the options.

'I'm not a gardener, but from the habitat perspective, there's a study that shows a higher bat activity over biodiverse roofs. As I said in my report, a simple and lightweight option would be sedum. That would attract pollinators such as bees, butterflies and moths which in turn would attract bats.'

'Anything else?'

'That depends upon how much weight it can bear, and how much time you have, because other vegetation would require either much deeper soil or frequent watering.'

'I'll keep it simple, the view, the wind and the bats.'

It was getting draughty and I was pleased when Kerry called us down for tea.

She handed me a mug then turned to Geoff. 'I'm just nipping out, love.'

'All right, love. Will you be long?'

'I, er yeah, probably.'

Kerry flashed me a quick smile and hurried back into the house. She'd put some lipstick on and I wondered where she was off to. Some witching business, a spot of polyamory, or maybe just shopping.

Either way, Geoff seemed happy enough and we turned to the business of the pond. He'd not started digging, but had at least marked out where it was to go.

'This area you've cleared here is perfect for the pond. It will be great for wildlife and water plants, and you may even attract some frogs if you're lucky. Keep this area of grass between the pond and your border overgrown to allow them cover to get to and from the pond,' I told him.

'Do we need a pond pump?'

'No need if you use oxygenating plants such as water starwort, hornwort, watermint or native pondweed. They'll also provide food and shelter for amphibians. Don't be tempted to add fish, as they'll eat any tadpoles you might get.'

'I'm confident I can attract frogs, now I have my power back.'

'Er, well, good. I'll get the pond basin now then. Are you okay to prepare the space while I go and fetch it?'

'I'll make the preparations.' Geoff nodded at the ground with an intense expression. I grabbed the spade and scraped out the perimeter with the end of the spade so it was clear where to dig.

'It's only a small preformed pond, about this size and about thirty centimetres deep.'

'Yes,' he breathed deeply in and out, maintaining his steady gaze at the ground.

'Okay, I'll let you get on with it. I've a few things to do but I'll be back shortly,' I said.

He broke away his gaze and walked with me back into the

house. He paused by his bookshelf to scan the shelves, still deep in thought.

I saw myself out, a faint premonition in the back of my mind that perhaps his view of preparing the area might not be the same as mine.

I decided on a detour past Lori's. She might be back from work by now and had a spare packet of seeds she'd offered, which could be handy, as the earth removed from the pond could create a bank for some flowers. 'Just passing through to pick up those seeds,' I'd say, adopting a friendly, professional air. 'Can't stop.' It was probably best to allow time for Geoff to dig the pond anyway, or I'd end up digging it myself.

I got a warm welcome from Florence, and Lori was surprised to see me, but pleased I think. I went through to the kitchen. Florence lay in her basket, and lured me over with her eyes. I submitted and squatted down for my usual cuddle.

'Who have you been rubbing up to?' I crooned, noticing a perfumed smell on her fur. She stuck her tongue out at me and rolled over, legs in the air for a belly rub.

Lori put a plate of sausages on the table, cut up into mouth-size pieces. I jumped up and took a seat, closely followed by Florence.

'This is a nice change from toast.' I smiled up at her.

'We had some left over from yesterday, help yourself. Let me get the seeds.'

It was always the right decision to pop in on Lori, I decided, munching the sausage pieces. Flo sat by my side, watching me intently with adoring eyes.

Ethan came and leant over, grabbing a couple of sausages.

Flo gave him a dirty look and redoubled the love for me with her eyes. 'She likes me most,' I thought.

'Any luck with the magpie, Ethan?'

'No, they still kick up, listen.' He stepped out onto the decking and the familiar chatter of the magpies started up. He returned to the kitchen, and it stopped.

'I'm sorry, maybe in time,' I said, not really believing it.

'Sod 'em. At least the robin likes me.'

'Oh yes?'

'Yeah, it takes mealworms right from my hand.'

'Cool.'

Lori returned with a packet of seeds. 'Which beneficiary of your skills is getting these then?'

'The wizard.'

'Tell him they're magic beans and will grow overnight.'

'He'd probably believe me.'

'Speaking of which, the bamboo is already growing back.'

'I knew it would, like I said, either you have to keep chopping it down at the roots till it gives up, or pull up by the roots, which is hard work.'

'Neither option sounds great.'

'Full disclosure, a professional gardener would probably tell you to apply the strongest herbicide they have, but it will kill everything else in your soil stone dead. Nothing would grow in the area for a year probably.'

'Best not do that then.' She looked out onto the garden wistfully. 'I quite miss the bamboo fronds waving against the sky.'

She was right, the garden did look bare. I'd better plant that dog rose quick before any undesirables colonise the space. I went to take another sausage and paused, there was one left.

'Go on, have it,' she said.

'Don't mind if I do.' I popped it in my mouth and munched appreciatively. I looked down at my watch, and saw with regret that I should be off. My eyes met Flo's, and I did a double take of shock. She was looking at me with intense hatred. I felt almost scared. What on earth had I done? I stood up to go.

'Thanks for the seeds, Lori, and the sausages.'

I looked down again. Florence's eyes remained like daggers. I hastened towards the door, then stopped dead, hearing a key turn in the lock. Ethan and Lori are right here, so who the hell is that? The door opened, and there he stood, silhouetted in the doorway. It was the man with the perfect beard.

'Hi,' Ethan said casually.

'Hey, Ethan?' His accent was charming, somewhere between Greek and Italian. 'Going to join us for *Downton Abbey* tonight?'

'Fuck off!'

But Ethan was smiling and so was bearded man.

He was so tanned. All my pride in the slight burnishing of my usually bright white skin to a freckly beige was squashed by his perfect olive skin, dark straight eyebrows and sculpted beard. And he'd said 'us'.

Florence was looking round desperately for something. She found it under the table, her favourite stuffed squirrel. She presented it to bearded man, tail wagging frantically.

I realised I was standing with my mouth open.

'This is Tim,' Lori said, no doubt wondering how to describe me. Friend, gardener, love interest?

'The gardener,' I added, conscious of Ethan.

Bearded man gave me a friendly nod. A nod that held mild interest. Not the nod of a man possessive of his woman who was thinking 'hello, who's this strange chap here that I don't know.' Clearly I wasn't considered a threat.

Squeezing past him out of the door, I recognised the smell from Flo's fur, a faint whiff of aftershave.

I could have sworn she liked me, thought I was special, but I was kidding myself. She wasn't looking at me lovingly, she wanted my sausage. She was obviously friendly to everyone. I got into the car, slammed the door and set off. Like woman like dog. Jo had warned me that I was being used. I berate myself sometimes for playing safe but I'm right to. I was right about there being competition, of course there would be for a woman like Lori. You never know what's lurking in the undergrowth.

Although, I'd not seen signs of another man previously, and I'd been on the lookout. He must be new, and unlike me a fast worker. Maybe she'd got fed up waiting for me to make a move. She'd looked disappointed when she found out about the body, and that I'd kept it from her. If he's new, there's still a chance. I could lay my cards on the table, tell her the whole story. The car behind tooted, I noticed the lights in front of me were green and drove on. All those times I'd congratulated myself on being professional, taking my time, not being pushy. What an idiot. I banged the wheel furiously and hit the horn. I'd missed my chance. That's what happens when you play it safe. I saw my futile self-deception for what it was, I was in love with Lori and she had another man.

Crushing disappointment overwhelmed me. I drove excessively slowly prompting another toot from behind, but I didn't care. The car swerved to overtake – a foolhardy, dangerous move that flipped a switch in me – the despondency gave way to anger and then a visceral jealousy that coursed through my blood. I sped up, raged at every traffic light, swore at cars that drove too slow or too fast. I scowled at every bearded man I spotted on the way, the world was suddenly full of them. I cursed at cyclists and at the crow that deposited a white package on my windscreen as it flew over. I raged out loud when I pulled up outside the Share Shop to see it was now closed, and was reluctant to stop raging even when I saw Karen had left a note for me on the door, saying she'd left the pond basin out round the back. I drove round to the back entrance to collect it. It was lighter than I'd assumed but bulky. I loaded it in the back of the car, battering my thumb and banging my head on the boot in an orgy of self-harm disguised as clumsiness.

My rage had subsided by the time I reached Woolston and given way to a melancholy self-pity. I leant the pond basin against the wall and rang the bell. Geoff let me in and together we manoeuvred the basin through to the garden. I'd become Buddhist, that's it. I'd take up the orange robes and my Sanskrit name would be Pond of Tears.

My stroppiness reignited when I saw the lack of progress that had been made on the hole. My suspicions had been proved correct.

'I'd hoped you'd have started digging. That's what I meant by preparing the ground.'

'I have been preparing. The earth is spiritually ready.' Geoff held my gaze as if challenging me to disagree.

I had no words. I grabbed a spade and began to dig. Pictures of Beard Man and Lori watching *Downton Abbey* crowded my mind. Florence on Beard Man's lap, then Lori... I pushed the images away and continued digging.

I sank into a familiar daydream of being a *Mastermind* contestant, answering confidently on my specialist subject of invertebrates. I was in darkness, a spotlight upon me. 'What is the biggest species of earthworm in the world?' John Humphrys was about to ask. My response was ready: 'The two metre long Australian Giant Gippsland,' possibly adding '*Megascolides australis*' for good measure.

Dum dum dum dummmm... Dum dum!

'Timothy Redfern, ex-accountant and ecologist from Southampton. Your specialist subject is how to be every woman's best friend and no one's lover.'

What?

Dum dum dum dummmm... Dum dum!

'What do you do when an opportunity presents itself?' asks John Humphrys.

'Nothing.'

'Correct.'

I threw the soil over my shoulder and tried to shake off the specialist subject I'd landed myself with, but the next one my mind irresistibly presented to me was even worse.

'Your specialist subject is how to end up fifty, single and alone.'

Dum dum dum dummmm… Dum dum!

Helpless under the demanding music and spotlight I submitted myself to the questions:

'Name three ways in which your first love ruined your life.'

I answer quickly. 'One, she got pregnant when we were sixteen and told me it was mine when it wasn't. Two, she let me get attached to what I thought was my son. Three, when a new man comes into her life she tells me I'm not allowed to see the boy again.'

'Correct.' The audience clap but I take no pleasure in it.

'But she never let me explain to him and I've spent years wanting to tell him I didn't abandon him.'

'Question number two.'

'But she said I'd be a stalker if I kept hanging round.'

'Question number two,' repeats JH sternly. 'What are you going to do about Lori and the guerrilla knitter?'

My thoughts circled endlessly. I'm in love with her. I don't just want to be friends. I couldn't tell her, but she'll keep asking, if it's not the guerrilla knitter that brings it out, something will. Maybe it's best she has another guy, a guy who can grow a beard and who has no past. I pictured the shock and horror on her face as she checked out my record. Saw a restraining order against a young boy. I dug like a madman, the frustration bubbling over.

'Answer please,' insists JH.

'Nothing,' I say at last.

'Correct.'

'See the progress we're making. It's all about preparation.' Geoff paced round the perimeter, flicking his hands sharply in a wizardy way at the hole as it grew under my frantic digging.

Dum dum dum dummmm… Dum dum!

'Is that the *Mastermind* tune you're humming?'

I nodded grimly and kept digging.

'What exactly did Jo say…' The beeper sounded, but I wasn't to be let off. 'I've started so I'll finish… when you declared your love for her?'

'My specialist subject would be Alistair Crowley.'

Dum dum dum dummmm… Dum dum!

'Pass,' I mutter, unable to speak out my final humiliation.

'He spied for us in the Second World War you know, because the Nazis were into the occult.'

'You have two correct answers and only one pass. When you declared your love for her, Jo said that she had just realised that she was a lesbian. You have scored two points,' says JH to much applause from an audience who are impressed by a man who's so lame he can turn a woman lesbian.

'Tim? Tim!' Geoff's voice intruded upon my daydream. 'Tim, I think we've dug enough now.'

I looked up at him, panting from the exertion, aware for the first time that my hands were blistered and my back aching. I looked down at the hole in the ground.

'That was magic.'

'What?' I croaked. I threw away the spade and with some difficulty straightened up.

'You cleared that earth with a preternatural force,' observed Geoff with the self-satisfied air of a man proved right.

I stumbled into the flat exhausted. My spirits sank when I heard Jo talking in the kitchen. I wasn't in the mood to chat. If I told her about the man with the beard, she'd most definitely take the piss, especially if there was company. Hunger overcame my reservations and I made my way into the kitchen to find her on her own, pointing her camera at her latest concoction and holding forth about the ingredients and preparation. I loitered in the doorway till she was finished.

'So you combine the rest of the ingredients and condense down into a sticky jus and voila!'

Jo poured a sticky purple liquid over a brown lump on the plate and then made a little smear on the side. She walked with the phone to a pot of fresh mint and tore off a few leaves and placed them with a flourish on top.

'Topped off with some fresh mint grown on our very own windowsill.' She spotted me in the doorway and sped towards me with the plate.

'Timbo – you can be the first to taste.' She nodded at me expectantly with the phone held in her hand. I gazed down at the brown and purple mess. I was starving so I took the plate handed to me and sat at the table. I picked up a knife and fork and tucked in. I don't know if it was the texture or the taste that hit me first. I gagged, looking up wide-eyed at Jo. What the hell was this? I needed a drink – anything would do. I took a swig from an open can of cider. It was a mistake. It all came up, a brown and purple spew that gushed out over the table. I found time to marvel as I vomited, how more was coming out of me than ever went in. Must have been the cider. When it was done, I dry-retched a couple of times and glared up at her as I saw she was filming the whole thing.

'Perfect!'

LOVE OR LUNCH

From: *Walker. L*
To: *Tim Redfern*
Subject: *lunch*

Hi Tim,
OMG – look what it came up with! Still want to come for lunch! 😊
x

> herring
> sweet potato
> leeks
> celeriac
> baked beans
> couscous
> turmeric
> apple
> red wine
> water chestnuts

X!

. . .

I stopped off on the way to Lori's to pick up some wine. In the Co-op, I had a change of heart. Yes I'd got an x after the smiley which was new. But was it a Florence type kiss? Was she just being friendly? This was just lunch after all. Lunch was business, lunch was water. Wine was for dinner and dinner was for men with perfect beards. I annoyed everyone at the queue by quickly substituting the wine for some grape juice, and then running off again at the last minute to dither over chocolates – yes – no. Yes.

Lori greeted me with a bright smile and a rushed hello, then hastened back into the kitchen leaving Florence to take care of the meet and greet. After the requisite amount of endearments, strokes and toy-throwing, I was eventually allowed to follow Lori into the kitchen.

'Hi, Tim. How are things? Lunch might be a while I'm afraid.'

'You're not…'

'Oh yes. I'm taking this random recipe challenge seriously.' She added chopped leeks to a pan.

'Sorry about that.'

How to phrase the question without seeming pushy? Who's that man with the beard? He's my boyfriend. Just the thought of her uttering those words was a dagger to the heart.

'Any news?' Lori broke the silence.

I paused, plucking up courage. 'Who…?'

Lori's smiling face turned towards me, flushed from the steam coming from the pot she was stirring. 'What was that?'

'Nothing.'

'Oh, Tim. Did you sort out work?'

'Yes. Er. Yes, all sorted.'

'Did the wizard get his roof garden?'

'Yes, and a pond.'

'Good. No more playlists then?'

'No. Er...'

'Are you okay? Is it the smell? Herring doesn't really go with – well – anything I'm cooking actually.'

'I'll have a look at the garden, see how it's coming on.' Maybe outside I'd work out how to broach the question. I had a horrible feeling that I wouldn't be able to relax until it had been answered.

'Sure, lunch will be a good fifteen minutes.'

I went out onto the decking and leant over the rails. The hawthorn hedge was growing nicely. Bamboo canes were amassed in a pile, needing a home. I heard Ethan in the kitchen.

'All right?' he asked, joining me on the deck.

We heard a coo.

'Is that a dove?'

'It's a wood pigeon.'

'It always says the same thing – woo, woo, woo, woo-woo.'

'My dad used to say it was saying "my toe hurts Betty".'

He laughed unexpectedly loudly when we heard it call again.

'Sounds exactly like that.'

'Does your dad have a beard?' Shit I'd said that out loud. Luckily he hadn't been paying attention.

'I got interested in birds now.'

'That's great.'

'I dunno. Since that magpie, I feel like they're all watching me. It's like bad enough with people.'

On cue, a magpie flew down onto the branch of a tree, looked at Ethan and set up a chattering alarm call.

'See what I mean?'

'I do.'

'A magpie shat on me the other day.'

'Really?'

'Was that random, Tim, or did it shit on me on purpose?'

'Is the shit random?' I mused. 'Good question.'

'Yesterday I saw this bird peck another bird on the bum. What was that all about?'

'What did it look like?'

Ethan pointed to a sparrow that had alighted on the lawn. 'Bit like that.'

'Sounds like a dunnock.'

'What was it doing? Some kind of weird sex play or something?'

'Female dunnocks are quite promiscuous – they do well out of having several male birds bringing resources to the nest, wrongly assuming it's their chick. This was most likely a male trying to peck another male's semen out.'

It probably wasn't appropriate for me to say, but Ethan was roughly the age I'd been when I'd been shat on. Better he should know the facts of life.

'Gross!'

'You asked.'

We leant against the decking rails together and gazed contemplatively at the back garden.

'Look at that?' He pointed at a spider spinning a web between one corner of the decking and another.

'I'd never have noticed that before. It's all different since the magpie. It's like I've pulled aside a magic curtain and seen a new world.' He dreamily watched the spider walk from one side of the developing web to the other.

I smelled something and leant forward for a surreptitious sniff – yep – skunk!

Ethan shifted his gaze upwards at the birds flying in formation across the sharp blue sky. I noticed a tell-tale flash of paranoia in his eyes.

'Is… the… shit… random?' he said again slowly as if he were asking a philosophical question. Perhaps he was.

'Birds have been known to mob perceived enemies by dive-bombing them or defecating on them, but if you mean on a deeper level…' I thought back. My life had been massively derailed by my own personal dunnock, and it didn't seem like anything I'd deserved or asked for, but... 'No, I don't think the shit's random, you can't escape cause and effect.'

'Heavy!'

'Look.'

Another spider clambered onto the newly-woven web. The spider who'd just finished it was resting at the other end. They contemplated each other.

'Is he trying to nick the web?'

'No, he wants to mate.'

The intruder tapped his legs on the web.

'What's he doing now?'

'He's signalling his amorous intentions.'

The larger spider approached the intruder and paused to consider her options.

'If he gets it wrong he'll be lunch, she'll go right over there and eat him. But if he gets it right it will be love.'

'Love or lunch!' he intoned.

We watched intently. 'It's a scary business,' I breathed. 'Will she like him or will she eat him all up?'

'Lunch,' cried Lori.

'Coming.' Ethan paused to watch a robin chase another robin over our heads, swooping down and up into trees then back out again.

'Are they fighting?'

'It can be hard to tell as both sexes look the same. It depends on the season. Either he's fighting another robin for territory or—'

'He's after shagging her.' He fixed me with a suspicious look. 'Just because I'm talking nice, it doesn't mean I won't kill you if you try it on with my mum.'

'Er, I understand.'

'That's why Dad gave me the air rifle. He agrees with me that it's not good for my mental health to have to deal with that kind of thing.'

I nodded mouth agape, stunned into silence by such a literal weaponisation of mental health.

'No offence.'

Another movement on the web caught our attention. The female spider was walking purposefully towards the male who was nervously tapping at the edge of the web. What was it to be?

'Lunch,' called Lori again, rubbing it in rather.

Lunch was interesting, and with the odd mix of ingredients, conversation centred on the random recipe generator. I explained how I'd pored for days over lists of ingredients, sorting them into high, medium and low carbon footprint for each season.

'It was your joker column that gave me the most trouble.'

'I love the joker column, man. You should put insects in there.'

'He's not joking.' Lori noticed my bemused face. 'We got some online for a Halloween party.'

'They were cool, instead of crisps we handed out dried crickets and mealworms,' Ethan said.

I sat up interested. I'd read several articles about the high carbon footprint of meat and suggestions that insects could form an alternative source of high fibre, low fat protein.

'You know that's a great idea,' I said. 'Insects are widely eaten around the world, and have a low carbon footprint.'

'Cool, man; you should put them in your Random Recipe thingy then.'

'You care about climate change?'

'It's a proper mental health issue, man!' Ethan did indeed have a worried expression, but I wasn't sure if that was still drug-induced paranoia.

'I'm sure Jo would be up for that.' I could picture her face, she'd be delighted to add insects to the list of ingredients.

'Oh, that would be banging, man. I'd like *MasterChef* it. Make something really cool, like foraged frittata of beetles. Or…' He gazed thoughtfully into the distance, moving his lips slightly as if to taste an invisible substance, 'deep-fried chilli mealworm balls with a redcurrant coulis, the acidity of the redcurrant balancing the nuttiness of the mealworms.'

I was surprised at first by the fervour with which he was embracing the idea, but then it began to make sense.

'I can picture it, man. I could like go hunting for beetles and stuff. It appeals to something… primal in me.' A wistful look appeared in his eye. 'I'd be killing them, lots of 'em and it would be all for a good cause.'

Ethan gazed into the distance, seemingly in a trance. There was a brief silence while I struggled for something to say.

'It was the baked beans gave me the most trouble,' said Lori eventually, passing over a side dish of baked beans in red wine and turmeric.

'You should have reduced the red wine down into a jus with the spices and put a little smear on the side,' he commented, coming out of his daydream.

'I'll get you to cook next time. Maybe you should be a chef?' She turned to me and explained. 'Ethan has to decide which college to go to and what his A levels will be next year—'

'If I go.'

'And what his work experience will be.'

I had lots of questions to ask. What his interests were, what he wanted to do in his A levels, what he'd do if he left school instead.

'Who was that man with a beard?' My heart was beating so loudly I was sure they'd hear.

'Arben. He's our new part-time lodger. He lives near Birmingham, but stays over when he has work down here.'

'He cries a lot,' said Ethan, 'especially when he watches *Downton Abbey* reruns, which is all the time.'

'There's nothing wrong with a man crying,' said Lori.

'Dad said that he used to cry all the time when he was young, then he just stopped and never cried again.'

I wasn't sure that was healthy either but Ethan looked proud on behalf of his dad. He shoved in a final mouthful, jumped up and went upstairs.

'Five minutes,' she yelled after him, then turned to me. 'We're off to a career's fair, to help Ethan decide what he wants to do.'

'Brilliant,' I said somewhat overenthusiastically, hoping she assumed I meant the careers fair and not that beard man was the lodger.

My phone buzzed, and I tensed, remembering the last message I'd received in this kitchen. I snuck a quick look. It was Jo.

'Guerrilla knitter?' she asked, loading the dishwasher.

'It's from Jo, saying to post a review of your recipe online. But really you don't—'

'Ethan! Now!' yelled Lori suddenly at the ceiling. 'We'd be happy to. Do I have to be nice about it?'

'Not at all, it's perfectly acceptable to say it was absolutely disgusting. It's turning into a bit of a catchphrase in fact.' I passed dishes over to her.

'It's a brilliant idea. I'll send the link to Dawn, she'd like it.'

'It was a lovely lunch though, you made it work.'

She shot me a disbelieving look and shut the dishwasher and turned it on. 'Eth—' Her cry was cut short when Ethan appeared. He was out the door in an instant and holding it open for us. I grabbed my phone and coat. Lori looked round for her keys.

'It's me waiting for you, Mum.'

Time for me to go.

I walked back, calculating my gains and losses. On the plus column, he was the lodger. On the minus column he was very handsome and they watched *Downton Abbey* together. Oh, and Ethan will definitely shoot me. I needed something to balance the numbers. I seized on the x on the email, and told myself it wasn't a Flo kiss.

23

GOOD WILL HUNTING

Jo thrust her phone into my face the moment I opened the door. 'Hugh's done the Random Recipe challenge.'

'What?'

She handed me the phone and sat me down at the kitchen table. I saw a tweet from Hugh Fearnley-Whittingstall with #RandomRecipeGenerator. While I read, she jabbered in my ear.

'Remember me doing my *MasterChef* bit with all the poncy prep and the smear of jus on the side? Then you came in and tried it and threw up instantly. I have to say, Timbo, it was hilarious. It was all in the timing.'

'You put that online?' I said aghast. 'You can't do that without asking me!'

'Oh, get off your high horse. Anyway, it went viral. Then a few other people had a go with the same recipe to try and make it taste good. And Hugh is into causes and such so I got in touch and mentioned the huge number of hits it got and how it's a fun way to promote seasonal, low carbon food and issued a challenge to him to make something that tasted good. And look. Look, Timbo.'

I tried to read what was on her phone but she was waving it around too much.

'He says: I did the Random Recipe challenge and it was absolutely disgusting. I gave it to the dog and he threw it up too. Look, he posted a video.'

She clicked on the link and showed me a video of a dog throwing up.

'It's hilarious isn't it?'

'Yes, it is,' I admitted.

'But that's not it, then Nigella joined in and said that it would work if you got rid of the kidneys, and used the sweetness of the beetroot and added some cream to make a delicious dessert. Then Hugh said go on then, so she filmed herself doing it, but she couldn't bring herself to eat it because she still had to deal with the onions at the end of the day.'

'That's great publicity.'

'Then Jamie had a go – he added curry leaves and took out the mint, but he couldn't eat his own concoction either – he said it was utterly disgusting. Then Delia came out of retirement, Timbo! Delia! She said all it needed was a bit of nutmeg to bring it all together. She didn't even get rid of anything – she just made it work.'

'That is actually quite impressive.'

'Isn't it? And now everyone's using it. We're going to have to up our game on the website, it's getting thousands of visitors. I'm getting requests for a vegan version, a vegetarian and flexitarian and pescatarian version.'

'What's flexitarian?'

'You eat whatever you like.'

'Right. Have you thought of adding—'

'Save it for the pub, mate. Gotta work on the website.'

'Sorry for keeping you,' I said after her retreating back.

I set up my laptop in the kitchen to look up uses for bamboo. I could make little hotels for bees out of bamboo cane tied together, but that would use up half a cane at the most. I could use a few to support climbing plants, runner beans, etc. I gave up and turned on the telly and flicked through the channels. A police officer stooping over a dead body. 'The killer got to him before he could talk,' she muttered, shaking her head over the stupidity of people who didn't go to the police straightaway.

I turned over quickly. Another murder mystery; a daytime cookery show; a drama with a young man threatening another man with a gun; a news programme hosted by a man with a beard. I watched unseeingly, thoughts see-sawing between the body in the garden and Lori. What to do about the repeated texts from Fern asking me to get in touch, and Ethan's desire to shoot me. Most of all, I brooded on the sheer handsomeness of Arben the lodger.

I had to earn my pint by listening to Jo bragging about the positive feedback her website was getting, and looking on her phone to see for myself how many thousands of views each video got of someone trying to eat the RRG concoctions.

'I'm a bit famous now. People liked you spewing, no doubt you did it well, but the feedback on YouTube about me was amazing.' She put her phone away finally.

'You're bad enough already without any more encouragement.'

'I'm getting an agent,' she leant back and tapped the table for emphasis.

'Don't be silly.'

'Really it's true. An agent got in touch already.'

This did actually sound encouraging and another day I'd have been more excited, but I was still preoccupied with the events earlier. I longed to talk to Jo about it, but there was no stopping the flow.

'I'm getting enough views to get money from adverts, but I need more content. How was the meal at Lori's?'

'The baked beans ruined it.'

'I told you not to add them.'

'You told me to,' I exploded, then noticed Jo's deadpan expression. Why did I fall for it each time? Jo allowed herself a little smirk.

'Anyway, Lori was fine, but Ethan—' I began.

'Are they going to write up the recipe and a review on the blog?'

'Ethan's a bit of *MasterChef* fan, he had some good ideas actually but—'

'What like?'

'He mentioned adding insects.'

'I like it.'

'He said he'd kill me if I tried it on with Lori—'

'You know I really do like the insect angle – it's novel.'

'It's his dad, that's the problem, he's the one who bought him an air rifle, who literally tells Ethan to shoot—'

'We could add them to the joker column. You should be more excited about this, Timbo, because of their low carbon footprint.'

'Jo – hear me out for God's sake!'

'Keep your hair on.'

'I really like her, Jo. But he couldn't be clearer. I'd risk getting shot, but what would it do to him? I don't want him to have shot a man before he's turned sixteen.'

She heard the urgency in my voice and sighed.

'Didn't Lori have another fella though, you said?'

'Turns out he's the lodger, but there's Ethan.'

She shrugged. 'Well, there you go.' She drained her glass meaningfully. 'Get the beers in.'

I stomped off to the bar, furious with her. All she thought about was herself and the random recipe generator. She only wanted to talk about what she wanted to talk about. She had no real interest in me, even the life coaching thing was just to help out her niece. It wasn't conceivable that she was jealous, our relationship wasn't like that, so she was just utterly self—

'All right?' asked the man at the bar.

I became suddenly paranoid that my internal rant had escaped. I had to know.

'Was I muttering just now?'

'Yeah.'

'What did I say?'

'Mmlywantlkself.'

Oh my days, I was the man at the bar muttering angrily to himself. Something had to be done.

I marched back to the table and banged the beers down. Jo pre-empted my attack.

'I saw it, Timbo, I saw you muttering at the bar.'

'I am that man.'

'I'm all ears, tell me about it, mate.'

My anger faded, Jo as usual had disarmed me.

'Is it the body in the garden?'

'It's not just that.'

'I heard you listening to Morrissey the other day,' she said gently. 'The day you puked up my dinner.'

It was true.

'And this afternoon. We threw out the Morrissey albums didn't we? It was a swap, remember? I smashed up my Civilisation disc and you chucked your Morrissey albums.'

'You're back on Civilisation,' I said defensively.

'I thought those days were over, I thought now you were Habitat Man you'd be happy.'

'It's not enough though, I need... don't take the piss...'

'I won't.'

'I need love.'

She nodded, her green eyes sympathetic. I was reassured by the lack of any stupid quip.

'I keep looking back. The other day when I was talking to Ethan, it came back again… young Danny…' it still hurt to say his name, 'he probably has kids of his own now.'

'There's been a lot of changes in your life lately, it's stirred things up.'

'I thought it was just my job I hated, but that's sorted and there's still a big hole. Every relationship I've had has been a disaster, I turned you lesbian—'

'You didn't turn me lesbian, you idiot. Listen, Timbo, some people just aren't meant for love, not the conventional kind. I'm the same. We try and it goes wrong. I don't know about you, but I look at married people and I don't envy them. Bored, trapped, affairs, divorce, timeshare kids. We get the best of both worlds – a stable home, someone to share the chores, to help out if you're sick, and then we can have affairs on the side without it being a problem.'

'But we don't though do we?'

'I concede there's not been much action on the old romance front for either of us, but we're okay aren't we? It's a good set up. You do your thing and I do mine and we have Saturday evenings.'

Jo's voice washed over me, reassuring, concerned, reasonable. I pulled myself together.

'You're right, Jobo, the insect angle – great source of protein, high fibre, low fat, low carbon footprint. Add them in.'

She gazed deeply into my eyes, and I saw her concern.

'About Danny,' she said. I felt the prick of tears at the back of my eyes.

'It's not your fault.'

'But I never got to explain.'

'It's not your fault, Timbo mate, you know that?'

I nodded, and swallowed down the lump in my throat.

She leant in again and gazed right into my eyes.

'It's not your fault.'

What? 'Jo, are you…?'

'It's not your fault,' she repeated, putting her hands on my shoulders.

'Are you *Good Will Hunting* me?'

'It's not your fault.'

The corner of her mouth twitched slightly and we collapsed into uncontrollable laughter. Big belly laughs that hurt my insides. Tears pouring from my eyes, struggling for breath. Fucking Jo!

The man at the bar raised his glass to us.

24

THE COMPOSTING TOILET

From: Transition
To: Tim Redfern
Subject: Dr Elena Moretti and Dr Eric Williams, Shirley

Dear Tim
This is a couple from Shirley who want to create habitats for children and wildlife.
Cheers
Karen

My route to Shirley took me down through the underpass into the west side of the common, a route I generally avoided due to the memories it conjured up. The council had given up trying to control the graffiti in the underpass and now it was like an additional art installation for those in the know. It followed the principle of survival of the fittest. The poor ones were painted over quickly, so the quality was pretty high. I used to take young Danny to the pond on the common, and the only way I could drag him away was by taking him back through the underpass, where we'd pretend to be art critics, analysing the swirls and patterns on the wall.

Chafing at the restrictions of young motherhood, Danny's mum was happy to let me take him out. Danny's new 'dad' though, was less keen, resenting, I suppose, that for the first four years of Danny's life, I'd been the father figure. The last time I'd had Danny for the day, he'd been delighted to see a graffiti artist painting on the walls, and even more delighted when he was allowed a spray himself. When I was 'caught' bringing him back, I'd thought the commotion had been about the paint he'd got on his clothes. That was the last time I saw Danny. Bewildered by all the shouting, tears streaming down his face, howling, pleading with me not to go.

I came out of the darkness of the underpass and ran doubled over with the memories towards a thicket of trees that offered cover. I fell to the ground, waiting for the waves of emotion to pass. Regret, bitterness, fear, anger, jealousy, love.

My phone went, another text from Fern. Furious, I deleted it immediately. She should have got the message by now. I don't want to be dragged into it. It's just another thing stirring everything up. I'd had enough of everyone thinking the worst in my home village. Not because they really believed it but because it makes for a better story. Why should I risk it all coming out just because I was the unlucky sod who'd dug up a body?

I stared up at the sky through the trees, noticing that the spring leaves were coming through. Gradually, I tuned into nature and let the sound of the wind in the trees calm me. Could I perhaps tell Lori? The thought set my heart hammering in my chest, and I abandoned it immediately. No, soon Fern will give up. I'll avoid the underpass and any visits where there are young children that might stir up memories. How would I phrase it? Green garden consultant – no families. That wouldn't wash. And what about my upcoming visit, asking for habitats for children and wildlife?

I scratched in the earth under my hand, remembering how I'd share with Danny all I'd been learning at university. We'd dig about in the ground and list all the creatures we found: earwigs, beetles, springtails, worms, millipedes, woodlice. Today, my scratching yielded a perturbing lack of life, just some ants.

'Man-up, Habitat Man,' I told myself sternly. This is your atonement, you're making a difference in people's back gardens, doing your bit for biodiversity and the environment. Focus on that and you'll be all right.

A jay chattered in the branches above, then an answering chatter from another tree. The sun came out and the leaves above me shimmered with a translucent green. Glimpses of blue sky appeared through the foliage. I picked out the thin high notes of a bird nearby, a tree creeper perhaps. Through the leaves I saw a flock of starlings high in the sky, swooping one way then another. I climbed to my feet and watched. Hundreds of them swirled and turned and dipped, as if to some inaudible music or hidden plan. Mesmerised, I started walking again.

I found myself in front of a house in Shirley. Eric, a tall blonde man in his thirties, answered the door. I looked up to point out the murmuration to him but the starlings had disappeared from sight. I shook off the fanciful idea that they'd led me there and introduced myself.

'I'm Tim, about your garden?'

'Hello. I'm Eric, come on in.'

In a blur, I allowed myself to be led to the back garden having vaguely taken in that his wife would be back soon with the boys. I pulled myself together and paid attention as he showed me around. If nothing else, I could make a difference here, although it seemed already to be a perfect habitat for wildlife. The grass was quite long. Garden debris had been piled up by the side providing a habitat for invertebrates. Half-buried logs for the vertebrates, water butt, bags of peat-free compost, a swift box under the eaves. They had a pond and the area between the pond and the shrubs by the fence had been allowed to grow over, providing cover to allow amphibians to travel to and from the pond without fear of being picked off by birds.

I should be pleased but instead I felt irritated. Not much atoning to be done here, it was already exemplary. This was the trouble with getting clients from the Transition list, I was preaching to the converted, not making a difference at all.

'How can I help?' I asked.

'It's the neighbours.'

I glanced over at the neat garden next door. 'Sorry, I don't understand?'

'It starts with an enquiry if our lawnmower is broken and would we like to borrow theirs, but what they really mean is cut your damn lawn.'

'Er...' I hesitated, unsure what was required.

'If we can say we paid someone to come and look over our garden as a professional habitat man, then that's different,' said Eric.

I got it at last. 'Long grass is only acceptable if it's on purpose, accredited by a professional habitat man?'

'Exactly.'

'Dad! Tell Matteo that caterpillars are green.'

We looked up as two boys ran into the garden, the eldest in school uniform. That's all I needed, two cute boys Danny's age to rub it in.

'This is Matteo and Christian. Boys, say hi to Tim.'

They ignored me, lost in their own argument.

'I don't see why they can't be red.'

'When you go to proper school, you'll have to draw them the right colour.'

'I know,' said Eric keen to distract them, 'find all the snails and throw them over the fence.'

I tried to tune out the sound of the boys' shrieks and find something useful to tell Eric.

'Right, so we need to make it look more managed.' I pointed to the untidy pile of vegetation at the side. 'If you chop your garden debris right down then you can pile it up under your hedges and shrubs to act as a mulch. It will create habitats and enrich the soil and look less messy.' I saw some secateurs and lifted an old branch and cut it into inch-long sections to demonstrate.

'There's something!'

I tried not to look, but small grubby hands cupping something were held out hopefully to me.

I couldn't resist and squatted down. It was a big black beetle with a shiny purplish sheen to its head.

'Do you know what that is?'

'A beetle?' suggested Christian.

Matteo ran up to look. 'Beetle,' he agreed.

'Well done. It's a violet ground beetle. It shows your garden has excellent biodiversity.'

'There's a snail,' shrieked Matteo and ran to throw it over the fence.

He must be about four, a sweet age. I gulped and focussed my attention on the lawn.

'You can have different mowing regimes for different parts of the lawn to delineate wildlife areas and make it look deliberate and managed, rather than unkempt,' I suggested to Eric.

'No, we already know what we're going to do...' Eric nodded next door where the neighbour had appeared to hang out her washing and spoke loudly, 'we should keep our grass long you say?'

I raised my voice slightly. 'Yes, one of the easiest things a gardener can do to enhance the wildlife value of their garden is to mow the lawn less frequently.'

'We're getting a meadow,' he added.

'For a meadow, you'll only need to cut the grass and compost the clippings once a year, in late August,' I said.

'Thank you for your professional opinion as wildlife consultant. We'll do as you say.' He winked at me.

I smiled politely. I'd done my bit, now I wanted to go. I wasn't going to be much more use here.

'Well good luck with your meadow. I'll send you a report with some suggestions as you may find that just planting wildflower seeds isn't that effective as grass out-competes the wildflowers. But there are solutions…'

'It's okay, we're buying one. I wanted to ask what the difference is between meadow mat and wildflower turf?'

'A more relevant question is whether you want an eco-friendly garden or an instant meadow?'

'Is it either or?' To his credit he looked concerned.

'Thing is, Eric, most wildflower or meadow mats are plastic-backed.'

'Yes, but they said it breaks down.'

I sighed, exasperated by what was essentially greenwash. 'It doesn't break down, it breaks up into micro-plastics, which is even worse for wildlife.' I shrugged and prepared to go.

He looked at me aghast. 'They should really say; the whole point was for us to benefit wildlife.'

I softened, perhaps I could do some good here after all.

'Meadows tend to develop over time in soil with low fertility—'

'Hello.'

I looked up to see an attractive lady come and join us.

'Tim, this is Elena, my wife.'

She surprised me by kissing both my cheeks. 'Ciao, Tim.'

'Erm, chow.'

'Darling, Tim says it's more eco-friendly to grow our own meadow,' said Eric, offering his cheeks for a kiss.

'Okay, then you must tell us what we need to do,' Elena said to me at once.

I'd been expecting resistance, and bit back a comment about

it also being much cheaper.

Elena noticed my surprise and shot Eric a pointed look, which he accepted with a shrug. 'Elena told me we couldn't invite you just for the neighbours,' he said.

She smiled at me charmingly. 'I tell him – darling, you are wasting the man's time when he could be doing more good elsewhere.'

I smiled and agreed, warming towards them.

'But, maybe the neighbours will want a visit too, and...' Eric looked for a moment like an excited child, 'I wanted to show him this.' He headed towards an intriguing wooden hut perched on a raised patio area at the bottom of the garden.

'It's a cool design. Is it a shed?' I asked.

'Come and see.'

Christian skipped down to join us, closely followed by Matteo. 'Do you want a wee?'

'Or pooh,' giggled Matteo and ran off shrieking.

Eric laughed. 'This is our composting toilet.'

It was beautifully designed, almost an arch shape, with a circular stained glass window towards the top of the door to allow in light. The way it curved into a point at the top gave it an ethereal *Lord of the Rings* look.

'I've heard of these, but I've not been in one.'

He looked at me expectantly so I opened the door and beheld the loo. The toilet was small but stylish – a square box painted in red, gold and white.

Eric's face was bursting with pride. He lifted up the slab of wood that the toilet seat was set into. Underneath were two compartments. At the front was a large plastic bottle and at the back in a separate section was a square plastic container, lined with a large bag and half full of wood shavings.

'We have a twin-bowl design that separates the solid from the urine, to keep it dry so you don't get flies. It goes dry and crumbly when it meets the oxygen and breaks down into germ-free compost, so you only need to empty it about once or twice a year, and you can use it to revitalise the soil.'

'This is Eric's new toy,' Elena told me smiling.

Eric returned to his explanation. 'When you go, you use toilet paper as usual, then instead of flushing, you put down two scoops of wood shavings. No water, no chemicals. It doesn't smell at all, does it?'

'No it doesn't.'

'Would you like a go?' he asked hopefully.

'Maybe later.'

'I'll just top up the wood shavings in case.'

Elena laughed and rolled her eyes. 'We leave it to him. Tim, come have a coffee and tell me what you think we should do.'

We headed back towards the house and I shared my vision for the garden with Elena.

'If you allow your grass to grow, daisies, clover, buttercups and dandelions will naturally proliferate, creating a meadow-like effect.'

Elena looked around nodding.

'For a wider variety like poppies, cornflowers, etc. you could remove some turf round the edges and replace with some horticultural grit or sand mix and sow wildflowers there.'

Eric stepped down from the hut to join us and I realised the patio outside the kitchen mirrored the raised patio the composting toilet was on.

'The path you walked on just now could be a raised decking, like a boardwalk from one patio to the other,' I told them when he joined us. 'That would protect the long grass and provide a sense of a designed garden rather than a garden left to run wild.'

'Yes, a path direct to the hut,' cried Eric, delighted.

'I know of some decking you can use,' I said, thinking of Lori's old decking that hadn't yet been taken down the dump.

'Perfetto… Matteo, stop that!' Elena rushed to stop him throwing a snail over the fence.

189

'But Dad said to.'

'Not when she in garden,' she hissed.

It began to rain softly.

'Christian, we all go in now, *avanti*.'

Christian sped past Matteo yelling, hitting him with a stick. Matteo howled and chased him inside.

We followed them in to a large kitchen/dining-room. Elena pushed aside paper and colouring pencils and set some amaretti biscuits on the table.

'Wash your hands first, and get changed,' said Elena when the children made a grab for them. They trooped upstairs and the kitchen was quiet.

Eric joined me at the table. 'Sorry about the neighbour thing, but we need them onside.'

'It's because lawns are a status symbol,' Elena said, setting out coffee cups.

Eric looked proudly at his wife. 'Elena is a psychologist at the university. She can explain the neighbours' attitude.'

Elena poured thick dark coffee into tiny cups as she spoke, 'My research is in conspicuous consumption and its symbolic value. Since lawns have no value for food or income, the larger the lawn and the less useful, the higher status it give.'

'That's why the neighbours have a go,' added Eric.

'Is a question of self-esteem. Showing off by having high status stuff only works if others want it too.'

I nodded, interested. It made sense of an attitude I'd come across at work. 'My ex-work colleagues used to take it as a personal affront that I wasn't interested in their latest sports car or four-wheel drive,' I told them.

'Here is because. If you don't want what they have, it lose symbolic value. So the neighbours think we dismiss their values by not caring about our lawn.'

The boys ran back in the kitchen and descended on the biscuits.

'We're bored,' said Matteo, crumbs falling out of his mouth.

'What can we do now?' said Christian.

I couldn't help myself. 'Do you want to play the caterpillar game?'

I took their shrieks as agreement. 'Draw ten caterpillars, cut them out and then colour them in, five in red and five in green.'

Eric shot me a grateful look and passed them over the paper and colouring pencils and they sat quietly colouring in.

'But what is so interesting,' continued Elena, 'is that with the turn against consumption, now when people see goods, they don't necessarily think, "that person is doing so well," they think, "that person is destroying the environment." Is no longer a status symbol but irresponsible.'

'Done it!' cried Christian.

'I done first!' Matteo, held out paper caterpillars for me to inspect.

I checked them quickly and nodded. 'Now, hide your caterpillars in the garden. Matteo, keep to the left and Christian to the right.'

'Okay!' The boys ran off to do my bidding.

Elena resumed her point smoothly, clearly used to constant interruptions. 'Or worse, conspicuous consumption is seen as pathetic, as if trying too hard.'

I considered this and sipped the coffee, wincing at its strength. I tried to picture my work colleagues. 'I only buy second hand,' Martin would brag. 'We're full-on minimalists.' Simon would respond, not to be outdone. 'I buy nothing at all.' 'I've given all my possessions away and donated my body and my family to the earth.' My inward chuckles at their imagined one-upmanship in non-consumption ceased abruptly when I was reminded again of the body I'd dug up.

'Tim, you look a little tense, how about some wine, if you don't have to rush off?' Elena said.

'Yes, have a drink and relax a little,' Eric urged.

I hesitated.

'We're your last call today, no?' enquired Elena.

I nodded and she grabbed some glasses and a bottle of Chianti and set them down on the table with some breadsticks.

The boys skipped back into the room.

'Hid them!'

'Now go find,' said Elena, pouring the wine.

'Hold on,' I said to the boys before they rushed off. 'Pretend you're both hungry birds collecting caterpillars to eat, but come back when you've found six of them.'

I accepted a glass of wine, feeling glad I'd come. I felt sorry now for misjudging them. Elena seemed to read my mind.

'You think we waste your time asking you just for neighbours no?'

I started to protest, but Eric jumped in. 'There's no point denying it, Tim, she can see through us. That's the trouble with being married to a psychologist!' he burst out laughing, clearly not too unhappy about it. 'But we'll do the meadow as you say.'

'If you plant yellow rattle seeds in autumn or some plugs in spring that will reduce the vigour of the grass, giving other wildflowers more of a chance. It wouldn't be long before your garden is alive with all kinds of butterflies,' I said.

'I like it. We can get the boys to identify,' Elena said.

'Moths too. Soak a cloth in a sugary drink and hang it from your washing line to attract them. Or hang a sheet from your washing line with a light behind it and at night all kinds of moths will be drawn to it, and your boys could have fun classifying them. They'd also attract bats, which they might like.'

Matteo rushed in with a triumphant cry. 'I found six first.'

Christian followed hot on his heels. 'I got five.'

'Let's see,' I said.

Matteo held out five red caterpillars and one green caterpillar.

'Now show me yours, Christian.'

Christian held out five caterpillars, all red.

'What do you notice?'

'They're all the red ones.'

'Well done. Why do you think that is?'

'Because they were hid easier.'

'Did you hide the green ones more carefully?'

They shook their heads.

'I know, red ones are easier to spot,' cried Matteo.

'Yes. And that's why caterpillars are green.'

The boys jumped up and down as they got it.

Eric clapped his hands, delighted. 'Do you have any more games like that? We could use you for the children's parties.'

'No,' I lied.

'You're so good with them. Do you have children?' Elena asked.

'Erm…' I put the wine down and shook my head. 'I think I will have a go at your composting toilet.'

Eric smiled delighted. The boys jumped up to follow me, but he held them back.

'Leave him in peace. It's his first time.'

I left the sounds of chattering children and walked outside. A few slow soft drops of rain remained, then petered out when the sun emerged, setting the raindrops sparkling against the vegetation. I walked down the garden to the hut and went in. I sat down. It was perfectly quiet except for the distant sound of a wood pigeon. It smelled of forests and fresh air. The feeling of calm and sanctuary in the toilet reminded me of Daisy's garden. That sense of perfect harmony between art and nature, soothing to the senses and the spirit. No harsh lights, whirr of fans, smell of urine overlaid with air freshener. Instead, daylight streamed in through the small window, which I now saw had a picture set into the glass, a frog on a lily pad amidst dragonflies and bulrushes. The sun caught the stained glass window and brought the scene suddenly to life creating an almost religious experience. The elusive frog so sensitive to water pollution, safe here where our waste was used to nurture life. A benign, quiet smell of wood shavings. I heard the characteristic chirp of a grasshopper and smiled. Danny would love that, and the pond too.

This time, I didn't push the memories away. I thought back to the decision I'd faced, try again to see him and risk a jail sentence and destabilising a new family, or walk away. In the sanctuary of the composting toilet, at last I forgave myself. There was no way I could have known then, or even know now, what the right answer was. But I knew that the decision had been made out of love.

Fern and the grandad had acted out of love too. She might end up in court, as I did, but on a possible murder enquiry. I remembered the desperation in her voicemail message. We make bad decisions when we make them from fear.

I looked at my list of unanswered calls from Fern, picked the latest and hit reply. She answered straightaway.

'Tim. I'm so glad you called.'

'I'm sorry I didn't get back to you earlier, I'll do all I can to help,' I assured her from the seat of the composting toilet.

'We need to talk, but not on the phone. Can you come round tomorrow, first thing?'

'There's something I need to do first. I'll aim for mid-morning. And don't worry, you acted out of love.' I ended the call.

It was time to tell Lori. I should give her some credit, and trust her to understand.

I breathed out for what felt like the first time in months and relaxed. I felt a swelling up, a feeling of rightness, of great joy, a letting go.

I used the paper then put two scoops of wood shavings down the toilet and used the hand sanitiser. I opened the door and walked out into the garden and back into the house.

Eric recognised something in my shining face and nodded, satisfied.

25

BAMBOO LOO

Saturday, I was round at Lori's first thing to collect her old decking. She took me via the side-gate to the back of the garden where the dumped wood remained, littered among the debris.

'Am I in trouble for not taking the decking down the dump?'

'Of course not.'

'You're just being nice. I know you said leaving treated wood there was bad for wildlife.' She handed me an almost pristine decking section.

'I'm not the wood police, Lori,' I said laughing, 'just here to provide advice.'

'Is this bit okay?' She held up a slightly rotten section.

'No, but put it aside to take down the dump later.'

We chatted and sorted all wood into piles: untreated wood for the wildlife, treated rotten wood for the dump and treated usable bits.

'Is it for one of your projects?'

'It's to create a boardwalk through long grass. It should look amazing, they're going for a meadow effect, and there should be enough decking to run from their patio to the composting toilet, which I have to say—'

'I'd love to see some of your gardens,' interrupted Lori, holding up a bit of decking for inspection. I shook my head and it went in the pile for the dump. 'What's, er, what's the guerrilla knitter's garden like?'

I hesitated. The first thing Lori would ask is why I hadn't gone straight to the police. I might be able to get away with telling her that I'd had a bad experience with the law once, but would she leave it at that? Doubtful. She'd probe, just like she's probing now. Or is it the perfect lead in? No, the worst. When I tell her about Danny, it mustn't be in the context of a probable crime.

'Sorry, I shouldn't be nosy. It's not like I'm interested to hear about the body or anything?' She looked at me hopefully.

'Let me just go round the back of your shed and pull out the bits stacked there. You can start taking the rest up to the gate ready for loading.'

Lori nodded, and carried bits of wood up the garden.

I crawled behind the shed and tugged at the wedged planks, heart pumping. Lori's a social worker, I reminded myself. She'll have seen a lot of abuse in families, so that's where her mind would go. That's where the police officers' minds had gone straightaway, I saw it on their faces when they came to arrest me. The policewoman had been a year below me at school, and the look of appalled disgust on her face had hurt more than the bruises I'd picked up later in the cell. She'd apologised after my court appearance when she understood the truth, but the damage had been done. I could explain to Lori and make her understand, but would it be like the invasive Japanese knotweed? Once the thought entered her mind, could she unthink it? I couldn't take the chance.

I crawled out, pulling the decking planks after me, and joined Lori carrying the wood up to the car. She looked at me a little warily. I had to give her something. I decided to take her question at face value, she'd only asked about the garden after all.

'Daisy has this plan for Feng Shui gardening.' I hauled the decking into the boot.

'What's that?'

'It's like gardening for all five senses – textures, colour, smells, in fact it's not even about the physical senses, it incorporates the idea of meaning, so when you hear the bees buzzing, it's not just the sound, but the knowledge that the eco-system is in harmony. I think ecological gardening is a better term.'

'I don't know, I prefer Feng Shui, sounds more mystical.'

'That's what she said.' I slammed my boot shut. 'All done.'

'Any ideas for my bamboo?'

'Not yet. But I'll think of something.'

'Tea?'

'Yes please.'

I reeled back when I stepped into the kitchen, and not just from the smell. 'Oh my days.' The kitchen looked like the scene of a crime, sharp knives, bones and blood.

'Sorry,' laughed Lori, putting the kettle on. She moved a plate piled high with bones to one side to set out two mugs. 'Ethan and his mate caught a carp and Ethan insisted we eat it, so I told him he could cook it as long as he cleans up after himself. He did the first…'

'What was it like?'

'Well the carp was only the half of it, they had some mealworms left over they'd used for bait so he fried them up in garlic and butter and then added the fish.'

'And the verdict?'

'Bony, bit muddy, but better than I expected.'

She handed me a mug of tea. 'Let's go to the lounge, escape the smell. We should be okay,' she looked nervously upstairs.

'Lovely idea.' The lounge was definitely a step up. Anyone can sit in the kitchen. Florence acknowledged my rise in status by following at my feet, then waited to see where I sat before making her decision. I went for the sofa and Lori sat beside me. Florence jumped up and squeezed herself between me and Lori and spread out to the maximum degree.

'Not you too,' Lori laughed, giving rise to a delighted flutter in my belly.

'How did Ethan's career fair go?'

'Not great, he's no idea what he wants to do, which makes it hard for him to be motivated to work towards his exams.'

'He should try Jo's niece Charlotte, she's a life coach.'

'Really?'

'She's doing an online course, so maybe I overstated it. But she's the reason why I'm Habitat Man and she got Jo onto the random recipe generator, although we're yet to see where that goes. I can't help thinking it's another excuse to avoid going back to work.'

'That's not a bad idea, it might really help him.'

'It's free because she's a beginner, but I think she'll find him quite easy to sort out.' I stroked Florence, who'd spread out, back legs in the air.

'Why? Do you have some ideas?' She gazed at me with her lovely eyes.

'I was thinking of his enthusiasm for killing insects.'

Lori groaned and I laughed. 'He could perhaps not personally hunt down individual beetles, but there are insect farms popping up – he could farm insects.'

'For that he'd need to study biology.' She scratched Flo's neck.

'Yes, there are loads of uses for mealworms – bait, food for hedgehogs, they're developing insect-based pet foods now and cooking. Ah, yes!'

'What?'

'I saw a programme once about an insect restaurant in Wales – they do bug burgers and are quite the tourist attraction,' I said.

'He could take domestic science A level, or go to catering college maybe?'

'You can't have too many strings to your bow.' My hand

caressing Florence met Lori's hand doing the same. We looked down. Flo was lapping it up. She had shifted onto her back so that all four legs were in the air, accepting all the strokes on offer. We smiled down at her doggy abandon. Flo's ear lifted up and angled itself towards the door. Lori pulled her hand away.

'So Lori, how come Ethan is okay with Arben?'

'Arben's gay,' declared Ethan, appearing in the doorway.

'Good,' I said without thinking.

'Why are you in the lounge?'

'Because you haven't cleaned up the kitchen. It stinks.'

I was still regretting my previous response and added quickly, 'When I mean good, I mean it's good that you have a lodger.'

'Yes and no,' said Lori. 'He spends hours in the bathroom.'

Ethan sat in an armchair, and leant back. 'Hours,' he repeated darkly.

'I'd like to put in another toilet, but there's nowhere it could go.'

'Yeah,' added Ethan. 'I'm like standing outside bursting, literally touching cloth.'

'Ethan!'

'Well, I am, and he's there tending his beard.'

I drank the last of my tea thoughtfully, an idea taking hold. I checked it for flaws, there were none.

'I've got it!' I declared.

'What?'

'A bamboo loo.'

'A what?'

I saw it in my mind's eye. 'You get yourself a basic composting toilet, and then you construct a two by four frame and tie the bamboo canes together and use it for cladding. Bung it by the gate, then when you get caught short by Arben's beard tending, you can use that!' I beamed at them. A perfect solution. And beard man was gay. It was an excuse to come round and mess about in the garden and build it. Okay, there was still Ethan and his air rifle, but at least there was no other man.

'A bamboo loo?' said Lori incredulously.

'Dad could help build it,' said Ethan. 'He's a carpenter.'

'Hmm,' she said doubtfully, which I took optimistically to mean doubts concerning the involvement of Ethan's dad. No one could doubt the brilliance of a bamboo loo.

My phone buzzed. I pulled it out of my pocket, and the name 'Guerrilla Knitter' appeared. *Are you still coming?*

Lori stood up. 'Come on, Ethan, let's sort the kitchen out together.'

It was my cue to leave, but now I had a reason to return.

I texted back. *I'm on my way.*

26

THE BODY IN THE GARDEN

Ten minutes later and I was setting off the wind chimes. Fern led me through to the garden where Daisy sat at the garden table working on the half-completed willow structure. The base had been done and thick rods stuck up vertically, through which she was weaving slender, more flexible rods. I realised what Grandad had been making, it was a coffin.

'Hi, Tim.' Daisy made room for me on the willow bench. I sat next to her and watched her deftly weave the willow to create the sides of the coffin. Fern pulled up a chair and sat opposite, passing rods to Daisy as she needed them.

'I checked online last night, Fern, it's legal to bury someone in your back garden if you own land, and it's not near a water supply.'

Fern shook her head, her face tight with worry. 'But the death and burial needs to be registered, and a record of the burial attached to the property deeds.'

'And it isn't,' added Daisy.

My stomach sank. 'What are you going to do?'

'The moment we report it, things are out of our control. We visited the Natural Death Centre, and they said in that situation the police would exhume the body and take it away to test it for DNA to check it's her. It would be a murder enquiry.'

Fern's words sounded ugly and out of place in this tranquil spot. I gazed into the half-dug hole. The bones had been covered up, but only roughly. The peaceful stone Buddha under the hazel tree watched the scene through lowered eyes. Early forget-me-nots were flowering in the border, and a fuzzy orange bee-fly hovered above them, sipping nectar through its long, straight tongue. A clump of butter-yellow primroses were in bloom beneath the willow. A blackbird sang from the roof. In the front gardens that lined this road, there may be dead plants, weeds, and discarded sofas, but this back garden was an oasis of tranquillity. If it seemed to me like a desecration of a holy space, goodness knows how it must feel to Fern and Daisy.

'You haven't covered up the hole?' I remarked.

'Dad's very ill, he wants to be buried here, but if we report the body it will be a crime scene.'

'Ah.'

'I don't want to say to you 'don't go to the police' as if we're murderers, because we're not. If I do that, you might think... well, you're the only witness,' Fern said.

'Erm...'

'There's no need to worry. I'm not going to murder you.'

'Of course not.' I tried to shake off the image of Fern coming at me with knitting needles in my bed.

'Mum. Stop saying that, now you've made a big deal of it, he's going to think we will, but we won't, honest.' Daisy smiled at me reassuringly, her young open face seeming fleetingly sinister.

'No it's fine,' I croaked.

Daisy stood up to go into the house. 'I'll just turn Grandad.'

'He's here?'

'Yes,' said Fern, 'he wanted to die at home.' She absentmindedly passed me a rod and I copied what I'd seen Daisy do, weaving it in and out of the vertical rods. It was strangely calming.

'Mum refused to see any doctors after the first diagnosis, so there's no one who can ascertain when and how she died. If we'd registered the death and the burial, we could have buried her here with no problem at all, but now we've covered it up for thirty years, we'd be in trouble. Daisy won't say anything.' She looked at me expectantly.

'So you want me to keep quiet?'

'Dad only has weeks to live probably. Then we can register his death and the burial site officially so it's all above board and no one needs to know there's another body buried beneath him.'

I wove the rods in and out and considered her request. Saying nothing might make me legally complicit. Although, it had already been months since it had been dug up. We'd have to explain the delay. But still, I'd seen enough crime dramas to know that if you cover it up and then it comes out it's always worse. I might not be doing them any favours by keeping quiet. I also noticed the willow fence I'd suggested for next door had been planted, and woven with a level of artistry that suggested Daisy may have helped. Surely Samudrapati must have seen something.

'I can't help thinking you should report it yourself. It would look better to own up. Then I'll support you any way I can.'

'But if the process takes ages, he may die before we're cleared. We may not be able to bury him next to Mum.' Fern choked a little on the last words. I realised that she wasn't just facing a possible court case and murder charge. Her dad was also dying. I felt ashamed that I'd waited so long to contact her.

'Okay, Fern. I won't say anything as it's not my secret to tell, but if anyone asks I won't lie.'

Her face lit up with relief. I remembered with a sense of foreboding all of the people who knew already: Lori, Ethan, Jo, Samudrapati, whoever they spoke to at the Natural Death Centre. I hoped it wasn't misplaced.

. . .

It was late by the time I'd dropped off the rotten wood at the dump and the usable decking in Shirley. I returned to find Charlotte in the kitchen with Jo.

'Meet my new social media director.' Jo pointed to Charlotte with a flourish. Charlotte was sat at the table, laptop open, tapping away, looking important.

'It's all about reach at this stage. Numbers, numbers, numbers.'

'I didn't know you were a social media expert, Charlotte?'

'You need to be if you run your own consultancy business.'

'Oh? Have you given up your life coaching course?'

'No, that's what I mean, life coaching is a kind of consultancy. I'm trying to pick up clients while I'm still training – it's about your portfolio and client feedback more than the qualification these days.'

'I may have got you a new client,' I said, thinking of Ethan. 'But I don't think you should charge until you have your qualifications.'

'Oh. Okay.'

'Char's promoting her life coaching via social media, so we're doing some cross-promotion with the RRG to increase our following,' Jo said.

'The trick is to piggyback on local celebrities and stories that are getting lots of views and tie it in somehow to what you do.' Charlotte rattled on about publicity, giving rise to a growing sense of alarm.

'Can we have a word in private?' I muttered to Jo.

Jo joined me by the door and whispered loudly.

'What?'

'You know what I told you the other day?'

'The body in the garden?'

'Shush. Well it mustn't go any further.'

I caught a glimpse of something on her face. 'You haven't said anything to Charlotte, have you?'

'Er…'

'What have you done?'

'Char? I think it's time for you to get going. Catch up with you later. Time for Timbo and me to have a pint.'

Charlotte packed her laptop away quickly and hastened out the door. 'Okay, see you, Aunty Jo; bye, Tim.' The speed of her departure was not reassuring.

'Pint then?' said Jo.

'We need to eat first.'

'Let's have some pub grub. Splash out for a change. My treat.'

'Oh God, you told her everything didn't you?'

'Let me grab my stuff. You got keys?'

I rattled them in my pocket. We headed down the stairs and a worse thought occurred to me. The guerrilla knitter was a local legend. I stopped dead in front of the door and grabbed Jo by her coat. 'This wasn't what she meant by tying into local stories to get publicity was it?'

'I'm sure it wasn't,' she soothed and opened the door.

The first thing I saw was Charlotte talking to a gaggle of people. She pointed at me.

'That's him,' she said, igniting a flurry of clicks and flashbulbs.

A woman thrust a microphone under my nose.

'Habitat Man?'

'Er, yes,' I said unwisely.

'Guerrilla gardener and digger-up of the body of the guerrilla knitter?' While I was blinking from the flash that went off in my face, she bombarded me with questions.

'Why has the body not been reported? Was it murder?'

I got my key out and scrabbled to get it back in the door.

'What about the rumours they wanted to shut her up before it spread?'

'What spread?'

'Guerrilla knitting. First it's covering statues with shrouds and then it's tearing them down.'

'No, she had cancer.' I finally got my key in the lock.

'Why wasn't it reported? Why was she secretly buried in the garden?'

I opened the door and threw myself inside and leant against the door panting. Where was Jo? I opened the door a fraction and saw them asking Jo questions, I reached out an arm and pulled her back in. They spotted me and resumed the questions.

'They did it out of love,' I blurted out and shut the door.

My phone went. It was a text from Fern. *Word has got out. The police have been round. They say there'll be an inquest, and possibly a prosecution. They want you to give a witness statement.*

I glared at Jo.

'I'll cook,' she said.

THE SUMMONS

From: *Mark@Rebellion.earth*
To: *Tim Redfern*
Subject: *joint XR, guerrilla knitta and guerrilla gardening stunt*

Dear Tim
I saw you on the news. Your message about love was spot on. You're a
hard man to contact, I didn't hear back from you on Twitter. I
eventually tracked you down via your testimonial on the life coaching
page (Charlotte sounds amazing – what a transformation to give up
working for the enemy and do your bit for nature. Respect man).
Extinction Rebellion want to build on what you're doing and join
forces with the guerrilla knittas to do a publicity stunt to boost XR
presence and awareness of the climate emergency in Southampton.
We can provide the resources, Habitat Man – tell us what to do and
we will do it. Can we meet asap? You're an inspiration.
With love and rage
Mark

'Jo – o! What the hell is going on?'

I bounded to her room. As usual she was at her PC, but this time not playing online games.

'We're trending like mad.' Jo turned to me with shining eyes. 'Charlotte has pulled a zinger.'

'I never provided any testimonial for her.'

'She wrote those herself, but they're all true though aren't they? Although I'm not yet a gameshow host, but soon, Timbo mate, soon. Look.'

She had several windows open and cycled through them at dizzying speed. Charlotte's life coaching page with glowing testimonials from me and Jo; random recipe YouTube videos with thousands of likes; Twitter pages with my anxious face, #SheDidItForLove.

'You're trending, mate. Everyone is on the bandwagon. You're being followed by Extinction Rebellion, the Natural Death Centre, the guerrilla knitters and gardeners, pagans, all the wildlife groups, the conspiracy theorists are all over it, and the polyamorists for some reason…'

'What?'

'What have you been up to, Timbo?'

'Nothing, and what do you mean followed?'

'I set up a Twitter account for you just for this, and immediately you got thousands of followers. Look, it's going up.'

I watched the numbers increase in real time under our gaze and felt sick.

'Sit down,' said Jo kindly. 'Look, you wanted more clients didn't you, well you'll get plenty now.'

'Take it down.'

'This is an opportunity to reach thousands, millions maybe with your tips. You can be the new David Attenborough.'

'Don't take his name in vain.'

'Ooh this is good.' Jo scanned an email that had come through.

'What?'

'My agent has sorted out an audition. Host of my very own cooking show.' She turned round to high five me, but I didn't oblige.

The doorbell rang.

'Best not to answer,' said Jo.

It rang again.

'Don't worry, they can't get in.'

I ran to the window and saw a neighbour leaving and two men slipping through the open door.

'They're in the block.'

There was a knock at the door. I froze, then heard something being slid under our door. I ran to take a look. It was an official-looking envelope with a crown on it. I tore it open. The contents jumped out at me in bold black type. Summons to appear as a witness. There was going to be an inquest.

I took it back to Jo.

'Jo?'

I sank into the chair and tried to tell her about the summons, but found I couldn't talk.

'The vegans have joined in the action. They've found my video of you throwing up the kidney dish and tagged it, this is what Habitat Man, Tim Redfern, thinks of meat. Sorry, mate, you'd better go vegan till this blows over or they'll accuse you of being a hypocrite. You're currently being hailed as a hero but the crowd can turn fast.'

I couldn't breathe. It felt like I was going to die. I clutched at Jo's arm. Finally she wrenched her gaze from the screen. Her eyes flickered over the court summons and back to me.

'Steady up, Timbo mate.'

My eyebrows I knew were going mental, seesawing wildly between seething rage at Jo and total panic.

'I'll come with you, mate. You'll be all right.'

I gazed at her open-mouthed. I could get through it with Jo, I reassured myself. She was the only person who saw my side. Jo knew I'd acted out of love. She picked up the summons.

'Ah. It's the same day as the audition.'

'Oh.'

I remembered our duel at dawn in Netley Abbey for who got the best room in our second year of university. What no one realised was that the winner got to take the worst room – we were both so delighted to have found a fellow kindred spirit that neither of us could tolerate the idea of the other having anything other than the spacious one at the front with the bay window. Thinking of those days brought a lump to my throat. Jo should go to the audition. It was an amazing opportunity. This was the world she was made for, a perfect fit.

'Jo.'

'Timbo Mate.'

'You go.'

'I'm going to the audition,' she said at the same time.

'You do the audition,' I gulped. 'I'll be fine.'

My thoughts veered wildly. Now I was vegan I had an overwhelming urge for meat. I had a sudden image of standing in McDonald's with dark glasses and cap pulled over my face. Other images flashed through my mind: running away, France maybe or South America. Fern and Daisy being interviewed in a police cell. Danny's face howling as I left, which turned into Ethan's face. His air rifle. I flashbacked to how it had felt being led handcuffed to the stand to explain why I'd broken the injunction. The bones I'd dug up. I gasped for breath.

'You'll love this, Timbo.' Jo looked from her screen back to me gleefully.

'What?' I gasped out. When Jo said I'd love it, it usually meant the opposite.

'I got an A.'

'You what?'

'From Charlotte's life coaching session.'

'You couldn't have.'

'I did.'

'But I got a D and mine was much more transformative.'

'Look at your face,' she jeered. 'You take these things too personally.'

I should pretend not to care. Showing a reaction always makes her worse, but I couldn't help myself.

'I do take it personally. This is my life. I earned a great salary, top London job, fantastic pension and you lived rent-free in my back room playing online games. I give it all up to create much-needed habitats, give nature a helping hand. You make a disgusting meal and film it and somehow you come out on top. I'm going to complain.'

'No one ever changes marks.'

'In the second year you wrote a letter to our tutor when you got a C and I got a B, and she allowed it.'

'That still pisses you off doesn't it?'

'You put more effort into that four-page letter than you did on your essay.'

'Exactly. It deserved a mark.' Jo grinned satisfied and went back to her screen.

'This isn't over,' I growled at her and stomped off to work on my letter of complaint. I spent the rest of the afternoon furiously writing up the notes I'd made since I'd begun my journey from accountant to Habitat Man.

NEEDLES AND NETTLES

Mark's house was walking distance to the station and city centre, handy for an extinction rebellion protestor. He opened the door before I had time to knock, looked up and down the street and hurried me into the house. The cloak and dagger wasn't necessary, I'd been on the alert for reporters the whole way.

'No one saw me, it's okay.'

'Come in.'

Mark looked about thirty, dressed in old jeans and a woolly jumper. He led me through a narrow hall into a shabby but spacious kitchen and sat me down at a solid old wooden table.

'We have a window of opportunity here. We want to draw attention to the climate emergency and bring together art, nature, the environment, guerrilla knitters and habitat. You're the man of the hour – what can we do?' He put the kettle on and looked at me hopefully.

I thought hard. A plate of green things on the table was distracting me. I couldn't work out if they were ornamental or edible.

'What are these?'

'Edamame beans. Try them.'

I tried a few, they were salty and lovely. One for the random recipe generator.

'Tea? I've got mint, camomile, fennel.'

I started to ask for my usual milk and no sugar and then remembered I was supposed to be vegan. 'Mint?'

'This inquest is going to be mental. There's news all over it so we want to make a statement. The guerrilla knitter is our hero and she's female so we're thinking something along the lines of Mother Nature but with a Southampton twist.'

'Right, yes.'

He placed the mint tea in front of me. I munched on a few beans and considered.

'Imagine you – Habitat Man, or Guerrilla Gardener?'

'I prefer Habitat Man,' I spluttered through a mouthful of beans.

'So imagine you – Habitat Man – are in charge of Southampton City Council. The city is your oyster. What would you do?'

'I'd stop mowing all the grass verges, let them grow.'

'That's no good.'

'I'd stop using pesticide.'

'Don't think what we won't do, think what we can do.'

'It's tricky, habitats tend to work best when we stop doing stuff, leave Mother Nature alone.'

Frustrated, Mark took my undrunk cup of mint tea and poured it away and poured me a glass of red wine.

'It's a bit early.'

'It's vegan wine and Fairtrade, don't worry. You're thinking too small. Think dramatic.'

'I'll need to line my stomach.'

Mark sped around the kitchen laying snacks before me. 'Olives. Ciabatta drizzled with virgin olive oil.'

'Ah, what are these?' I eyed some brown things on a plate.

'Falafels, drink up and think big.'

I drank obediently and made a dent in the snacks.

'The Yarn Bombers are working on a giant knitted statue of Mother Nature if that helps?'

It didn't really. I munched and mused.

'Anything?'

'Maybe if I look at your garden it would help, I think better outside.'

'Okay, follow me.' He led me through a back door into a small courtyard garden.

'It's a bit of mess, but we don't get much time.'

I surveyed the area, a few dandelions poked up through the paving, empty wine bottles and discarded banners. At the back it was fabulously unkempt, dominated by nettles and brambles. I paced around the perimeter, it was enclosed by a wall on three sides and a fence on the left. The nettles made it hard to check if there were gaps for a hedgehog.

'Well?' said Mark.

'That patch of nettles at the back will be a haven for insects, small birds and butterflies. The caterpillars of small tortoiseshell and red admirals especially depend upon nettles.'

'How's that relevant?'

'Have information boards in parks or by verges to teach people to see long grass and plants such as dandelions and nettles as valuable habitats and food source for wildlife, not as weeds. Get rid of the old-fashioned idea that it should look neat.'

Mark sighed. 'But that's hardly a protest. We need something more visible, something big.'

A faint tinkle of a bike bell was heard. 'Look, others are arriving now, maybe they'll give you some ideas.' He sped off to answer the door.

I sank onto the step, feeling put out. He'd asked what I'd do if I was in charge, and I'd told him. The absolute best thing, and Jo would like this, was nothing. Stop with the pesticides that killed the micro-organisms that everything else depended on, and let stuff grow.

I'd assumed it would just be me and Mark, but the hubbub coming from the kitchen indicated otherwise. I didn't feel able to go back in just yet and drained my wine, desperate to quiet the butterflies in my stomach at the thought that in two weeks' time I'd be back on the stand. I reminded myself that this time I'd be the witness, rather than the accused. It didn't help.

'Where's Habitat Man?' A thickset man with a beard and knitted jumper appeared in the garden and hailed me. 'There you are, the man of the moment. Very pleased to meet you, sir,' he boomed down at me.

I struggled unsteadily to my feet to accept the proffered hand. 'Hi, erm, Tim.'

'I'm Tri from the South Yorkshire Yarn Bombers.'

'You've come a long way.'

'Solidarity. The whole group will be down for the inquest. Can't wait. Come on.'

I followed Tri back inside. The kitchen was transformed with women knitting.

I stood uncertainly. My seat was now occupied by a trim lady who'd already got her knitting out and was clicking away. Mark brought in a seat from another room and everyone shifted up to make room.

'Everybody, this is Tim, he's going to help us decide what our statement will be for the inquest.'

'Hi, Tim,' said the trim lady. 'I'm from the Ninja Knitters – Isle of Wight Division.'

'They call her Fingers,' said a plump girl next to me. 'I'm Ashley from Knittas 4 Justice.' She nodded at Tri who had sat next to Fingers and pulled out his knitting. 'Why are you called Tri?'

'Because I only knit triangles.'

Fingers watched him knit critically. 'You're dropping a stitch when you change needles, that's why.' She held up her needles as she transferred the yarn from one needle to the next. 'So when you get to the end of the row—'

'I like knitting triangles.'

Mark went round the table distributing drinks and snacks, and poured me another glass of wine. 'Right, we're all here, and we only have two weeks. We need decisions. This is bigger than just knitting, this is about Mother Nature herself.'

'Just knitting!' cried Tri. 'It's this dismissive attitude towards women's crafts that we need to challenge. As a feminist—'

'Aren't we knitting a statue of Mother Nature?' interrupted a lady who looked to be at least seventy, and was clicking away with her knitting needles. 'I'm from the Graffiti Grannies,' she said to me. 'They call me Needles.'

I nodded, bemused.

'We should honour the original guerrilla knitter and knit shrouds for all statues of racists and colonialists. Like she did of Lord Palmerston,' said Ashley.

'Palmerston was actually a vocal opponent of slave labour, dear,' said the trim lady whose fingers moved so fast I could barely see them. Ashley looked disappointed. Fingers nodded to me.

'We're interested to hear what you have to say. You were the one who dug her up after all.'

They gazed at me expectantly but I had nothing.

'She was my hero,' said Needles, after a pause. 'I met her once when she came along to the first Urban Nitta event.'

'What was she like?' asked Tri.

'Just bones,' I said.

'An inspiration,' said Needles.

I flushed, realising the question hadn't been aimed at me. I buried my face in my wine and munched the snacks.

Another woman came into the kitchen with a baby in a sling. Mark introduced her as his wife Claire, and brought in a chair for her to join us at the table. I wondered what XR protestors would call their babies. Hope or Acorn. Or after a threatened species maybe. I sniggered to myself when my imagination came up with Hedgehog and realised I was quite drunk.

'What's she called?' asked Needles.

'Greta.'

'Good name,' I ventured.

I guzzled the snacks and drank, letting the conversation swim around me. Thoughts zigzagged from gut churning fear at the thought of the inquest ahead, to my sense of failure at not having a solution to Mark's request. The knitters had taken over and he kept looking at me hopefully and then looking disappointed.

I tuned into the raging debate over where the knitted statue of Mother Nature should be sited. Tri favoured a bank as the root of all evil. Mark favoured the court where the cameras would be. I tuned back out and pulled faces at the babe trying to make her laugh. After a while, I got what I thought was a smile, but it could have been wind. Meanwhile the debate had moved on to whether the knitted statue should look sexy or motherly.

'Habitat Man,' cried Tri, 'what do you think? Surely Mother Nature should be buxom at least, representing both maternal and sexual aspects?'

'It's not really a habitat issue.'

'Well it should be,' Mark asserted himself. 'We need to bring this back to what Extinction Rebellion stands for.'

'The trouble is,' I said, 'is that wool isn't especially environmentally friendly.'

'Rubbish,' shouted Needles, waving her needles in the air. 'Wool is renewable and recyclable.'

'But most of it is acrylic.'

'It's basically a plastic that takes decades to break down, and it uses fossil fuels,' said Mark. 'Also, sheep contribute a huge amount to greenhouse gas emissions. Tim is right, we have to abandon the whole knitting thing.'

The rest of the table glared at me. The steady click-clack of knitting needles sounded menacing in the brief silence that followed Mark's pronouncement.

'This is the guerrilla knitter who's been dug up may I remind you,' Needles' voice was ominously quiet.

'I came down from Yorkshire for this.'

'Any ideas, Tim?' pressed Mark. 'Did you think of anything when you were outside?'

'It's just you seem to want a big art installation, but the fact is that that leaving nature alone is the best thing for habitat. Like your garden, it may not look pretty but that thatch of nettles is great for wildlife.'

'You can make yarn from nettle fibre,' said Fingers casually.

Ashley googled it. 'Yes you can! Cut down the nettles near the base, remove the leaves.'

'You could use them as mulch, or make soup out of them,' I said, thinking of the random recipe generator.

'You soak the stalks, dry them, squeeze the stalk flat then comb it out and it goes soft and silky,' finished Ashley.

'Well then, that's perfect,' said Mark, 'you can knit the statue out of nettles. How long would they take to prepare, Tim?'

'You'd want to harvest them from August onwards when the stalks are woody.'

Mark's face fell.

'You can buy nettle yarn online,' said Ashley, scanning her phone.

'Let's focus on fashion then.' Claire took the baby out of the sling and turned it round to face her.

'Yes!' Mark started to pace, waving his arms. 'Forget your statue of Mother Nature, instead we surround the court building with cardboard cut-out people and dress them. We alternate green fabrics with non-green fabrics and show the environmental impacts. We know cotton is bad due to the pesticides and large water footprint, so next to the cotton outfit we can have a dustbin full of water with dead fish…'

The click-clack of needles paused.

'Not real fish obviously,' added Mark hastily, 'and next to nettles…'

'Get kids to colour in paper cut-outs of all the wildlife that thrives in nettle patches,' I suggested, thinking of Matteo and Christian. 'So by the nettle outfit, have a bucket of paper butterflies.'

Mark nodded, picturing it and I basked in the feeling of having finally contributed something useful.

'It doesn't have to be nettles, there are all kinds of eco-fabrics like Tencel and hemp,' said Ashley, scrolling down.

'And bamboo,' I added on a roll now.

Mark resumed pacing. 'We'll alternate these with non-green materials – cotton, leather, acrylics—'

'What about organic cotton?' Claire asked.

Ashley read from her phone. 'Less toxic, but more water-intensive… says here, it takes the water from a standard swimming pool just to produce one pair of jeans and a T-shirt, and double that for organic cotton.'

'The Graffiti Grannies only use donated wool, can I use that?' Needles asked.

Mark looked doubtful. 'It's still acrylic.'

'It stops wool going to waste,' I said, keen to redeem myself with Needles. 'What about promoting the idea of re-use over buying new, whatever the fabric?'

Mark nodded slowly.

'We could make space for a clothes swap,' said Claire.

'Yes, a rack where people can bring clothes they no longer wear and they can bring something and take something,' suggested Ashley. 'That will bring people in.'

Mark nodded more enthusiastically. 'This is coming together

nicely.' He poured me another generous glass of wine. 'Cheers, Habitat Man, this is perfect.'

I sank back into my chair relieved, slightly hypnotised by the sound of clicking needles and hum of conversation. The knitters debated who'd knit what. Mark made a series of short phone calls and texts to various people organising activities. Every now and then one of the knitters would congratulate me for the work I was doing or quiz me about the guerrilla knitter's family. Even Claire, who'd said little, leant over and we had a lovely chat about habitat benefits of shallow graves and willow coffins. For the first time I began to feel that maybe digging up the guerrilla knitter's body hadn't been such a disaster.

A slurping noise gave away that Claire was feeding the baby.

'I've got no problem with you feeding the baby at the table,' commented Tri. It didn't look like she cared if he did anyway, but he had a point to make. 'I'm an eco-crypto-feminist.'

'A what?' Ashley asked.

'It's the male drive for power and dominance that's destroying the planet. Eco-feminism isn't about equal pay or any of that, it's about running our institutions based on feminine values of nurture and care.' Tri changed needles and dropped a stitch.

Fingers leant over, unable to stop herself. 'Look if you just…'

Tri pulled his knitting away from her and continued. 'Crypto-feminism is about money, which is power, and that's in male hands. Crypto-currencies, bitcoin and blockchain, is totally male-dominated. They're calling it bloke-chain. The crypto-conferences are held in strip clubs, women are yet again excluded.'

The bread sticks were lovely with hummus. Mark noticed my appreciation and passed over some more. Interesting conversation, wine, snacks. A far cry from my days as a commuter, always in a rush for the train. I thought back to how worried I'd been about coming into people's homes I knew nothing about, but this was turning out to be a perk of the job. A few weeks ago, I'd never sat on a composting toilet, or heard of crypto-feminism.

Claire and the baby disappeared and another man joined us at the table with the XR logo on his T-shirt. He slapped me on the back and told me how great I was. The rhythmic sound of clicking needles created a tranquil atmosphere, conducive to conversation.

'Why do you knit?' new XR man asked Tri.

'It calms me.'

'Why triangles?' Fingers looked critically at the heap of wool triangles amassed around him.

'It symbolises my attempt to weave together the different aspects of my beliefs.'

'He's an eco-crypto-feminist,' Ashley told new guy.

'What like crypto-currencies?'

Tri nodded. 'Blockchain technology can redistribute power, take it away from the man and share it among the people.'

'The energy needed to process a bitcoin transaction is thousands of times more than the power needed to process a visa bill,' commented new guy.

'That's right,' I contributed. I knew this from the Costing for Nature software.

'So give up the crypto bit, just be an ecofeminist.'

'Then you can knit in a straight line,' added Fingers.

'Don't you have to be a woman to be a feminist?' commented Ashley.

'Don't you have to be black to attack racist statues?' countered Tri.

'Most of the Knittas 4 Justice group are black actually but they don't discriminate. Anyway, I have a bit of Native Indian in me on my mother's side.'

There was something restful about knitting that took the sting out of the exchanges. I mused that knitters should be a compulsory addition to all peace processes.

221

Fingers noticed my fascination and leant over. 'Shall I show you how?'

'I'm a bit pissed.'

'Doesn't matter if you get it wrong, have a go.' She rummaged in her bag and pulled out some knitting needles and a ball of wool and directed my hands to get me started. I was clumsy at first, but soon got the hang of it, and was able to tune back into the conversation while knitting. The new guy, Tri and Mark were competing to put the world to rights. It was amusing to watch, as each of them were clearly accustomed to an audience who disagreed with them.

'Classical economics only values what is paid for,' said Mark.

'But the market and paid work depends upon everything that economics ignores as worthless, like caring for the old and the young,' shouted new XR guy.

'Roles mostly fulfilled by women,' thundered Tri. 'Women shouldn't be kept down any longer, they are equal to men, in fact they're better than men, they're more ethical, more emotionally intelligent, more competent, more beautiful and I want to help them realise their power.' He slammed his glass down firmly.

'Without a functioning ecosystem, no economic work would even be possible, yet this is treated as non-existent by the GDP, which measures only consumption,' roared new XR guy.

'So we will be most successful when we have consumed our entire planet,' bellowed Mark.

'Where's the loo?' I asked.

I nodded uncomprehending at the instructions given and staggered into a cupboard, baby's bedroom and eventually the bathroom. Too unsteady to stand, I sank down onto the toilet, head in my hands, trying to keep the room steady around me while I emptied my bladder of all the wine. It was a relief, but not like the composting toilet. All toilets should be composting toilets. Definitely got to make one for Lori. If she'd let me. What would Lori make of Tri, the eco-crypto-feminist and Yarn

Bomber? I slumped back in the seat, and gazed at the toilet seat. It was made from wood. Bamboo perhaps? The bathroom was like the kitchen, solid, functional, old fixtures. Maybe Elena was right. Anti-consumption is the new aspiration. These properties weren't cheap so they chose not to buy new stuff. They'd be proud of their battered but functional table. It wouldn't occur to them to buy a new mahogany table when virgin forests were being cut down. Bamboo though, fast-growing, that might work.

Nettles. That was a brilliant idea, if I say so myself. Jo would like that too for her joker column. You could use them like spinach. It would be seasonal though as you'd want to pick them early spring before the flower heads appeared. No sod her. I'm not doing her any favours. The whole life coach thing for God's sake. Why did she even tell me she got an A? Talk about kicking a man when he's down.

There was a tentative a knock on the door. It was Claire. 'Tim, do you mind, we need to use the bathroom.'

I pulled myself upright from my position slumped over my knees, and stood up carefully.

'Sorry. Okay, sorry.' I washed my hands and splashed my face with cold water, shocked at the sight of my face. My eyes gazed back at me, red-rimmed and unfocused.

I staggered back to find Needles, Ashley and Fingers had departed. I considered leaving but wasn't in any hurry to get back to Jo, I was still pissed off at her. Tri, Mark and the XR guy were still putting the world to rights.

'The issue is what we count as success. It's totally cockeyed.'

I sat down. This was a subject I felt able to contribute to. I told them at great length about the injustice of Jo having received an A for her life coaching session, while I'd got a mere D.

'Mine was much more transformational,' I raged. 'I've created habitats, put up water butts, bat boxes, taken down some pretty dodgy bamboo and she just cooks disgusting food that people throw up. Yes it's entertaining but it's food waste.'

I scrabbled round in the now empty dish, searching blindly for more snacks. Claire reappeared in the kitchen without young Greta and set down some falafels in front of me.

'Food waste is nearly ten per cent of total emissions.'

'I lost it in the supermarket last week – they had two for one offers on milk; who can drink all that before it goes off.'

'No point shouting at staff, email via the website, then it goes to the right person.'

'I've dug ponds, habitats for all kinds of creatures threatened with extinction, and she's just a YouTube celebrity!'

'I'm in complete agreement with you, Tim. It's all wrong.'

Satisfied, I drained my glass.

Clare placed a cup of coffee in front of me.

'Milk?'

'Yesh pleash.'

She poured in some soya milk. I absent-mindedly pulled the knitting off my needle and used it to stir the coffee.

'Is it true what you said?' asked Tri.

'Wassat?'

'That the guerrilla knitter had cancer.'

'Yesh, what you gotta understand is they did it out of love.'

'They wanted to spare her any more suffering?'

'Contentious,' said Tri.

'Contentious means publicity,' said Mark.

'It's like on the composting toilet. We should have them, Mark, put that in the plan. But you don't always know what's best, you just know if you act out of love, even if it is illegal. Like...' I stopped mid-sentence. Without the gentle click-clack of the women knitting, I felt less at ease. Tri was looking far too interested and Mark looked like he was tweeting. I glared at them suspiciously. 'You're trying to get me to say stuff cos I've had a few.' I staggered to my feet, and lurched towards the door. I'd nearly told them everything, my criminal record, Danny.

'Are you okay, Tim?' asked Mark.

'I'm saying nothing else.'

I pocketed the knitting needles and wool, grabbed the last falafel and departed.

'Hi,' I spoke carefully into the phone. 'Issat Lori?'

'Tim?'

'Sorry, issit late.' I looked around, realising it was dark.

'No, no it's fine. Are you okay?'

'I'm ringing about the composting toilet.'

'Oh?'

'I want to make one for your garden.'

'Erm, right. How's it all going?'

'Yeah, er.'

'Where are you?'

Her voice sounded so soft and concerned I wanted to cry. I noticed I was sitting on a bench in a park. Behind me was the statue of Lord Palmerston, so far just wearing a knitted scarf.

'Palmerston Park. Been putting the world to rights.'

'So I see.'

'What?'

'I'm seeing a lot of you in the media.'

'Huh?'

'I understand now why you kept quiet about digging up the body. You didn't want me to be complicit. I was a bit... well it all makes sense now.'

'Does it?' That worried me. What did she mean it all made sense. Before I could follow up, she'd moved on.

'You haven't seen Ethan in town have you?'

'No.'

'We had a row and he stormed out, and I don't know where he is.'

'I'll keep an eye out for him.'

'It's all right. Best keep your head down at the moment, Tim.

It's just I can't find my blowtorch. He got it for me for Christmas. He said it was to caramelise crème brûlées.'

Oh my days. That was funny. My burst of laughter was broken by a hiccup.

'What?'

'Freeze!' I spluttered through my laughter.

'What?' Lori started to laugh herself.

'Freeze, or I'll burn you to a crisp and dish you up with ice cream.'

'It's not funny.'

I managed a snort and a hiccup in disagreement.

'Still though, if you do see him just lie low.'

My laughter stopped in my throat. I tried to process what she was saying. Sudden shouts from the city centre broke the peace.

'Anyway, you wouldn't do ice cream with a crème brûlée, it's a dessert unto itself.' Lori continued, after a short pause.

'Oh well. I stand corrected.'

'Your wizard has been calling you the magic gardener.'

'What? Geoff?'

'That's him. He said you restored his powers of second sight.'

'For Puck's sake.'

She chuckled. 'Is that what he says? You should do him a composting toilet as revenge for sending you folky playlists.'

'A composting toilet isn't a punishment, Lori.' I relaxed back into the bench, pleasantly aware of the swaying of the branches of trees against the clear night sky. The noises from the city centre had subsided, leaving just the sound of the light breeze whispering through the leaves.

'Oh and your mate's random recipe thing has really taken off. Dawn sent it to me with hashtag RevengeCooking.'

Lori's voice was warm caramel in my ear. It made me feel hungry. Phone clutched against my ear, and still talking, I headed towards the bright lights of the nearest takeaway.

'What do you think about men who are feminists?' I

asked her.

'Instinctive distrust, I'm afraid.'

'That doesn't seem fair.'

'It's experience, Tim, not prejudice. If a man truly respects women he need never fear what to say. We can tell. He can be as blokey as he likes, and he won't go wrong because his heart is in the right place. But the guys who claim to be feminists, maybe it's wrong but instinctively I take against them.'

'It is wrong, Lori, it's prejudice.'

'Instinct.'

'May I hazard a guess that your folk-obsessed ex claimed to be a feminist.'

'Yes, he did. Totally proves my point.'

'I think you'll find it proves mine.'

'And how's that?'

'Sheer prejudice,' I maintained, enjoying myself hugely.

'And, Tim, do you claim to be a feminist?'

'I wouldn't dare!'

I reached the end of the park and pulled back just in time to avoid a cab whizzing past, then hastened across the road.

'What are you doing?'

'Getting a takeaway. By the way, did I tell you Jo got an A for her life coaching and I got a D? Isn't that outrageous. I—'

'None of your business.' Lori's voice hissed.

'What?'

'Sorry, Ethan's just come in. Yes I know! I will. Shut up.'

I paused outside a kebab shop wondering what was going on. Eventually I gathered that Lori was once again addressing me.

'Sorry, look erm. Tim. You must think me totally pathetic, but I'm getting flack. I don't know about the composting toilet. It's not that anyway.'

There was a long pause. I waited patiently trying to understand what was going on. 'I've told them you're not a murderer. Like what the hell. This was thirty years ago for God's sake. He's threatening to move to his dad's, so I feel I have to, well, I think it's best to not come round.'

I listened and waited.

'Do you understand?'

I nodded down the phone.

'Not for ever. You know maybe I will have a composting toilet one day, when things have quietened down. Sorry.'

Jo hailed me the moment I came in.

'Look at this, Timbo. *Habitat Man Tim Redfern enjoys a selection of vegan snacks.*'

I staggered into Jo's room and gazed blearily at her screen.

'Is that me?'

'*You got to try edamame beans he says,*' she read from the screen, 'and there's a picture of you stuffing your face looking rather sozzled.' Jo looked up at me. 'Are you drunk?'

'I told you to take it all down.'

'I tried, mate. I closed down your Twitter account but there's a Facebook page now devoted entirely to the inquest. Tons of groups have joined. The guerrilla knitters obviously – who knew there were so many of them? Hello! Is this is photo of you knitting?'

I sank into a chair and gazed blankly at the back of Jo's head as she scrolled thorough the page.

'Extinction Rebellion have loads of posts, the Natural Death Centre are promoting green funerals, you got Black Lives Matter – not sure of their connection, vegans, feminists, the conspiracy theorists claim the guerrilla knitter was murdered to stop her knitting shrouds over more statues of imperialists. They claim the fact they're doing an inquest is proof. The assisted euthanasia and right to die groups are on there too. Suddenly they're a big presence, no idea why.' Jo looked at me enquiringly. I shrugged and shook my head.

'Extinction Rebellion are going mad with the tweets. *Habitat Man says crypto-currencies are sexist and bad for the environment.*'

'Mark took everything I said and hashtagged it?'

'He's milking it, mate. Here's another. *Habitat Man says tell your council to stop using pesticides #PesticideActionNetwork.*'

'That's not so bad.'

'*Habitat Man says sheep are bad for the environment. Knit with nettles, says Tim Redfern.*' She glanced at me incredulously. Her phone dinged.

'Oh no.'

'What?'

'A photo has popped up of you eating a kebab. *#HabitatManHypocrite.* Shit, the vegans have forwarded it. *#LambMurderer.*'

'What?'

'They're turning nasty.'

I felt sick. It all made sense. This was why Ethan wouldn't let Lori see me. 'This is all your fault.'

'It's okay, Timbo mate.'

'I'm not your mate,' I hissed furiously.

'I can salvage it. Just tell me you didn't have lamb.'

'I don't know.'

'Do you have a greasy residue in your mouth and feel over-full and slightly sick?'

I ran my tongue round my mouth. 'Chilli sauce.'

'That could go either way. I'm going to claim it was hummus.' She tapped rapidly into her phone. There was another ding. 'Oh and you're being accused of supporting the murder of the guerrilla knitter, although the assisted suicide people are for you. The crowd's divided.'

I could stand no more and rushed for the toilet. I hung over the bowl, hoping to throw up. Throw it all up and out of my system, the wine, the kebab, the bile, my rage and fear and desolation, but it stuck in my throat.

FALLING

Dum dum dum dummmm... Dum dum! went the *Mastermind* tune. I was sitting in the black chair, spotlight upon me. Magnus Magnusson, the original host from my childhood, was asking the questions.

'Tim Redfern, final year student at the University of Southampton, your specialist subject is Earthworms,' recited Magnus Magnusson quickly. I was leaning precariously over the railings of Itchen Bridge, it was dark and windy.

'What is the largest species of Earthworm in the World?'

'Pass.' Shit. A revision schedule of *Mastermind* musings at midnight while drunk wasn't going to compensate for losing a whole semester.

Dum dum dum dummmm... Dum dum!

'What are three top tips for dealing with trauma?' Magnus deftly switched topic.

'Suppression, avoidance...' Magnus nods, I paused and looked up, recognising the jaunty gait of Jo coming to get me. I stared into the glittering water below. What would she do if I jumped? Leap in unhesitatingly to save me, or be the one to push me in?

Even as I dreamt, I knew I was on familiar terrain, this was a dream I'd had many times and it was a nightmare. I was falling off the bridge, tumbling down through the night air, down towards the inky black water. I made barely a splash, the water seeming to open up and welcome me in. I sank down, bubbles popping out from all over, past sheaves of seagrass bending this way and that with the tide, past colourful coral, swaying anemones and cheerful fish. When I got to a singing lobster, I realised I'd recreated a scene from the *Little Mermaid* and a terrible sadness overtook me. Watching children's films with Danny was one of the many delights of being an almost-dad, and I'd never watch it again. Then I was falling once more, this time out of a window.

Jo and I are in the lift of our student block of flats and seem to have been going up and down forever.

We lurch into my room, packed with the usual group. 'Surprise,' they shout.

'Initiate Plan B.' Jo nods at the others, who swarm round me, ushering me towards the window.

I laugh nervously. 'What's going on?'

'Open the window,' Jo orders. The window creaks as it's heaved up, and I'm being dragged to the windowsill.

'Go on, chuck him out.'

'What?'

They hoist me onto the sill. I feel the draught from the night air on my face, and the sash locks digging into my hip. My room is five storeys up.

'Mercy killing!'

'Put him out of his misery.'

'Happy twenty-first.'

'Bye, Timbo.'

The pressure pushing me over the edge is unrelenting. Terror takes over, this is for real. I struggle with everything I have, my panic-stricken eyes meet Jo's mocking gaze.

'Let him go.'

But they continue to push me, and I realise what she said was ambiguous, they think she means to drop me. Then she removes all ambiguity.

'Go on, chuck him out.'

Jo prises my hands off the sill where they cling. As my fingers lose their grip, I notice my poster of earthworms has been torn. The one I bought for Danny, but never got to give him.

I woke in a cold sweat, dry-mouthed, my heart still hammering from that primal terror, the bracing for impact.

I crawled out of bed, downed a glass of water that had been placed on my bedside table, then tripped over a washing-up bowl on the floor, presumably put there by Jo.

'All right?' said Jo brightly, when I slouched into the kitchen. She waved her phone at me. 'Have you seen this? The random recipe challenge has gone viral. It's a thing now, everyone's doing it.'

I couldn't bear to look at her. It was her fault, all of this. She'd got Fern into trouble by blabbing, she'd got me on the news. She was the reason Lori wouldn't see me. She'd thrown me out of a window for God's sake. I made myself a cup of tea and bowl of muesli and ate in silence. Then I put on dark glasses and a hoody, grabbed my bike and cycled over to St Denys. The least I could do was to try to make it up to Fern, the innocent, well probably innocent victim of Jo's quest for fame and fortune.

I lost my nerve when I got there and saw a police car outside. It belatedly occurred to me that I might not be allowed to talk to her. I'd glanced at the court summons but had been too stressed to take in the details. Hurriedly I turned around and cycled home.

A lurid pink jacket was hanging on the peg when I got back. I heard a low murmur of voices from the kitchen.

'Are you all right, Tim? I'm sorry about the court case,' Charlotte spotted me tiptoeing past.

'There are police cars outside Fern's,' I told her, suddenly terrified of what lay ahead.

Jo nudged her. 'Go on, Char, tell him about my A.'

Fury replaced my fear and I stomped to my room and slammed the door. Cut out the outside world, cut out Jo, cut out everything. I worked on my letter of complaint.

From: *Transition*
To: *Tim Redfern*
Subject: *email bombardment*

Dear Tim
We've had literally hundreds of emails for you, but as per your request we created a junk folder and all those that had the word 'body', 'knitter', or 'inquest' in the message went in there. I understand your concerns, but I think they included some genuine requests, so maybe when you're feeling less overwhelmed I could forward them onto you? Good luck at the inquest.
Karen

From: *Tim Redfern.*
To: *Makelifecount@outlook.com*
To: Subject: *Mark for life coaching course*

To whom it may concern,
With respect to the life coaching case studies of Charlotte French. I was the first subject for Charlotte's life coaching course, and I'm writing to complain about the mark. I'm not writing from the perspective of someone who's taking your course. Charlotte is taking the course. She said she had to do some practicals, or case studies I think you call them, and I was the first participant. So I'm aware that Charlotte's mark in no way affects me. It affects her, and she

233

seems to be fine with it. I have to make that clear. I'm not writing from the position of being personally affected – I'm simply a participant.

Sorry for the long introduction, but Jo thought you wouldn't understand what I was talking about because, why would someone who was a participant care what Charlotte had got. But I'm not just a participant because that case study was my life. So I'm afraid I've taken it personally that Charlotte got a D. I'd originally been prepared to accept the mark with good grace, because I concede that I was reticent about some aspects of my past, which don't look good on paper and are in fact very private. But when I heard that Jo had got an A, I felt a stand had to be made. This is Jo Clarke, Charlotte's second case study (and aunt).

In what kind of world can inventing a cookery challenge whose catchphrase is 'this tastes utterly disgusting', compare with the changes wrought in my own life – not just in the total change of career and lifestyle, but also in the secondary impacts on all those households I visited? I should also mention that it was me who insisted upon the seasonal produce element of Jo's random recipe challenge, which if adhered to, lowers the carbon footprint of food choices by several hundred per cent.

I know from my own university days that it's not usual to adjust marks after they've been awarded, but for me this is about a wider issue of what counts as success. My original aim was to simply provide a few examples, but I got rather carried away. Still it's all relevant to my claim, so I present the case to you in its entirety. It's too big a file to email, so please access it via the downloadable link below.

Kind regards
Tim Redfern

PS I've been careful to give due credit to Jo and showed the file to her so she could double-check that I'd been accurate and fair but she just laughed at me and told me I was overreacting. But that's just her way to pretend she isn't bothered. But she does care. You should have seen the waves of smugness rolling off her when she told me she got an A.

I awoke with a feeling of dread. A heavy pendulum hung from my heart, dragging it down to meet a writhing, squirming feeling in my gut. Why did my body feel so heavy, yet also so charged up? In the fleeting moments after waking, I ran through the usual suspects: Danny – nothing new on that front; work – I left my job months ago; gut-wrenching rejection – again nothing new to report. Inquest. There it was. Today the inquest began. I rolled over and shut my eyes.

'Tim!' Jo appeared at the door. 'Aren't you going to court?'

'No,' I said into the pillow.

'I can take a later train so I can go with you for the first hour if you want?'

'My bit isn't till tomorrow.' I stayed under the covers.

'Okay, well good luck.'

There was no sound of her leaving. Perhaps she was waiting for me to wish her luck at the audition. Eventually there was a sigh and the sound of her heavy tread down the corridor.

An hour later I'd managed to get dressed but took my muesli back to bed where I calmed myself by scrolling through the latest news from the Earthworm Society.

'Tim!' called Jo, another hour later. 'The landline's going.'

'Don't answer it.' I rushed over to prevent her from picking up. Only my parents called the landline, specifically my mother.

'I'm off now anyhow.'

We listened to it ring, waiting for it to go to answerphone. Jo hesitated, checked her watch and reluctantly opened the door to leave. 'Good luck, mate.' She waited for a moment then left.

The door shut behind her.

'Timothy?' came my mother's querulous voice. 'What's all this about a murder in Southampton? My hairdresser said you had something to do with it. I told her I knew nothing about it and that of course you're not a guerrilla gardener or whatever she called it, you work in finance. Anyway, dear, please call me back as soon as you can.'

The flat seemed ominously quiet after the final click of the answerphone. I pottered around, watering houseplants, emptying bins, not daring to venture out to place the bin bags out the back. Who knew who or what lay in wait outside? It had been two weeks since I'd left the flat. Most of the time had been taken up by compiling a tally of all the impacts from my garden visits to accompany my letter of complaint to the life coaching course tutor, but now that was sent off, there was little to occupy me. I sat and knitted for a while in front of a daytime cookery show.

It made me hungry but the fridge offered up little apart from the leftovers from last night's random concoction. Jo had tried making bug burgers so she could talk from experience at her audition. She claimed they were disappointingly delicious, but I'd been too hyped up to taste anything. Yesterday I hadn't even noticed the little cricket heads poking out, but now they seemed to be looking at me. Surely she should have liquidised them or something. I settled for another bowl of muesli and some nuts and slumped back in the sofa to watch the news.

The sheer spectacle of the inquest had given it a prime spot. The camera panned over the crowd of people milling round the court building, then cut to an angry-looking woman standing outside. She spoke into the mic that was thrust under her nose.

'This case has come to court in record time. We've said for years there was a cover up, and this is proof.'

The news reporter addressed the camera.

'But there are many reasons to hurry. The guerrilla knitter's husband, who buried his wife illegally, and perhaps more, has just days to live, and there's no hope of him being able to testify. The focus is now on Fern the guerrilla knitter's daughter.'

A photo of Fern that made her look like a terrorist filled the screen over the reporter's fast-talking patter. 'The authorities want this to go away as quickly as possible as it has attracted unprecedented attention. Guerrilla knitters from all over have emerged and are wreaking havoc. Statues of male imperialists and warmongers across the UK have been covered in knitting.'

I jumped when I saw the statue of Lord Palmerston, now fully covered in a knitted shroud. I stuffed a handful of peanuts into my mouth and watched, nervously munching.

'Knitting needles have been confiscated from the courtroom to protect the staff who have complained of being harassed.'

I identified Fingers among the mob who were crowding into the courtroom. The camera fixed on a nervous policeman trying to retain control.

'Madam, would you please hand over the needles. Step away from the knitting!'

I recognised Needles approaching the policeman from behind. She hooked off his helmet in the mayhem and replaced it with a knitted tea cosy. The camera lingered on his confusion and discomfort. Suddenly the image cut to a suburban Surrey street that looked frighteningly familiar.

'The man at the heart of this, Tim Redfern, aka Guerrilla Gardener, aka Habitat Man also has a secret to hide.'

My face flashed up on the screen, I recognised it from the time the reporter had collared me outside the flat. I looked ridiculous – eyebrows almost up into my hair and my mouth open with surprise.

'We spoke to his mother.'

I choked on a peanut. Through my coughs, splutters and tears, I caught glimpses of my mother's outraged face.

'Of course he's not a guerrilla gardener, he's an accountant in the City.'

'Clearly she had no idea of her son Tim's secret identity. But he hasn't been seen at his work place for months.'

Simon's face appeared on the screen, with the caption 'ex-colleague' written below.

'He had a bit of a nervous breakdown. First he wanted my beard and then he said something about setting the parakeets free.'

'Another fact,' said the reporter, 'that Tim's family had no idea about.'

I watched appalled as they cut back to my parents' house.

'He should have told us about the parakeets, we thought someone had broken in didn't we, Bill?' A glimpse of my dad was visible hovering behind the open door.

'Shut the door, Barbara, this is all nonsense.'

We were back in front of the courthouse, and the reporter turned to Charlotte who was hanging about hoping to get a word. The reporter thrust a mic in her face. 'You were the life coach who got Tim on the path to being Habitat Man?'

'Yes, that was me.' Charlotte gazed earnestly at the camera. 'The incident with the parakeets obviously affected him deeply and during one of my life coaching sessions we discovered a way for him to atone by becoming Habitat Man. I've coached many famous people – Jo Clarke, creator of the random recipe challenge which at this moment is being developed as a brand new gameshow called 'That Tastes Absolutely Disgusting'.'

'That brings us up to date on happenings so far. Today we heard from Fern, the guerrilla knitter's daughter and tomorrow, Habitat Man himself will testify in court about the body he dug up in the garden.'

Her words hung in the air. The landline rang again. I should pick up really, she wouldn't leave me alone until she'd spoken to me. I stood motionless gazing at the phone. The answerphone clicked in.

'Timothy? It's the answerphone again, Bill. What's all this

about the parakeets? You must call us back. It's no use trying to avoid us. That's what your brother says and he's right, this is what you always do. Don't make us have to come down ourselves. Bill, tell—' Beep.

I paced round the flat unable to settle. Why did we never keep any alcohol in the house? In desperation I poured the only drink available, a glass of the Cinzano that we'd got for our first random recipe. I sat in front of my laptop and scrolled through the endless emails. Mark from Extinction Rebellion had got in touch to express his disappointment in me for freeing the parakeets and tainting Extinction Rebellion by association. I deleted all the spam then stopped when I saw the next email. I poured another glass of Cinzano. This was what I'd been waiting for.

Dear Mr Redfern. Thank you for your letter. We remember the case as it gave rise to discussions on whether we should be letting our students loose on the general population at such an early stage as you did indeed give up your entire livelihood on the basis of her advice. But with respect to the rest of your letter, we're confused. No one 'gave you a D' as you assert, or Jo an A. That isn't how it works – the students submit three case studies and we give an overall mark on the whole thing. We aren't sure where you got that impression but we're glad that you feel the life coaching session had such as positive impact, not forgetting the secondary impacts, as you so painstakingly point out.
Kind regards
Paula Webb

What?!

The phone rang again. I stood and listened sixty miles away to my parents argue down the phone.

'Timothy? What on earth have you been doing?'

'Leave it, Barbara, he's not picking up.'

'We don't want all that nasty business to come out.'

'It will have something to do with that Jo, I tell you.'

'Don't be prejudiced. She's strange, but she stands by him.'

'No she doesn't!' I shouted at the phone, waving my glass in the air, spilling Cinzano over the floor. 'It's her fault I'm in this mess.'

30

LONE MAN MUTTERING AT THE BAR

I downed the Cinzano, pulled a cap over my face, grabbed my keys, coat and wallet and stormed out. Thankfully there were no reporters outside, and five minutes later I entered the local. To my surprise, lone-man-at-the-bar wasn't there. It was years since I'd been to our local on a weeknight, and never, I realised, by myself. The bartender poured me a bitter.

'No Jo tonight?'

'No.' I felt suddenly lost. Our usual table was empty but it seemed too sad to sit there on my own. I stayed at the bar. 'She's auditioning to be a cookery game show host.'

'She'd be brilliant. My missus did her random recipe challenge. I didn't even realise it were nettles in the soup till she said.'

'The nettles was my idea.'

'It'll be good for business having a celebrity here.'

'I'm a celebrity too. I'm Habitat Man,' I said rather too loudly, fed up of being upstaged by Jo. I'd lost my audience, the bartender was now serving a young couple. I supped my beer, my mother's words about Jo resonating in my head. She's not standing by me. The exact opposite in fact. It's not that she should be here, I get the audition, but that's not even it. She says she has my back but it's bollocks. She gets a bloody A for being a celebrity gameshow host. Then instead of trying to hide it so as to spare my feelings at this difficult time – she knows I was upset by my D – she bloody rubs it in. A time that only she knows how bloody difficult it is, although my family knows too. Mum just cares about what the neighbours or her bloody hairdresser thinks.

'Hi, are you Habitat Man?'

A girl came up to me, with bright enquiring eyes, her more reserved boyfriend hovering behind her. It was the young couple.

I nodded uncertainly.

'I knew it was. Can we have a photo?'

Before I knew it, she'd pulled her boyfriend over and they were standing behind me smiling into her phone as she took a picture.

'Us with Habitat Man! Is it true you're the magic gardener?'

Sod it. 'Yeah, that's me.' I took another gulp of beer.

'I'm Ally, this is Josh.'

'I loved that video of you throwing up meat,' ventured Josh, taking a seat next to me.

'We're vegans.'

'We all talk about how eating meat is disgusting and bad for the planet and that.'

'But like the violence with which you spewed it out, was worth more than words.'

'It was sick. Proper sick.'

'You're the real deal, Habitat Man.' Ally gazed at me admiringly. I shrugged modestly, all thoughts of mentioning that this was a response to Jo's randomly generated recipe fleeing from my mind.

'And no one knew you were Habitat Man, not even your parents?' asked Josh wide-eyed.

'Well it's not exactly like I'm Batman,' I laughed, 'although I did put up a bat box and create a habitat for bats for the wizard.'

I took another slug of beer and felt much better. What was I getting so worked up about anyway? Who cares what my parents think, that boat sailed long ago. I'm now gardener to the magicians, ecologist to the guerrilla knitters, vegan saviour. I finished off my second pint and found a third was waiting for me, courtesy of the young couple. I made them laugh by telling them about the wizard identifying as a witch and threw in a hilarious pun about being Batman and the robin in Lori's garden. They seemed interested in my description of how to rat-proof a compost bin, so I told them that any food produce that went to landfill would produce methane, a greenhouse gas, many times more damaging than carbon dioxide.

'But if it gets incinerated, then wet waste lowers the temperature of the burn requiring more energy, so that's why all food-based waste should be properly composted. And this is important for habitats because the compost, through the magic power of the humble worm, turns waste into rich fertile soil, alive with—'

'Sorry, did you want another?'

I looked up into the bartender's concerned face. The nice couple seemed to have departed.

'Yer awright, and crisps.'

'Cheese and onion?'

Did crisps contain cheese? I looked round furtively. No sign of them.

'Yeah.'

My buoyant mood departed as rapidly as it had arrived. I returned to my musings about Jo. Something didn't make sense. Hang on! What about that email?

'It doesn't make any sense,' I told the bartender.

'Nothing does, mate,' he said, refilling my glass.

'It said she never even got an A!' The bartender nodded and took my fiver.

I got out my phone to try and access my emails, but couldn't focus. Still I was pretty sure it had said that I hadn't got a D and she hadn't got an A. Why would she wind me up? The more I thought about it, the more furious I felt. Talk about kicking a man when he's down.

'It's like that time when she threw me out of the window,' I told the bartender, then saw he was at the far end of the bar serving other customers. She knows how I must be feeling going into court, and this is what she does.

Out of the corner of my eye, I saw the couple leave the pub. I raised my glass to them and they nodded back, smiling uncertainly.

'She tells me she got an A and then she fucks off,' I tell the empty bar. 'I just won't do it,' I mutter into my pint. 'I'll just google what happens if you break a court summons. At least we can do that now. Not like the guerrilla knitters, that's why they got into this mess – no Google.' I got out my phone and tapped into it. *Can I do a bunk on being a witness?* I peered at the phone, it had come up with a load of pages on bunk beds.

'Shit. No. Hang On!' That was a lucky escape. If they find out I searched this then I couldn't get away with pleading temporary terror under mental illness. It would be premeditated. I'd be back in jail again. I muttered into my pint over and over, 'I can't. I must.' The bartender, shot me a strange look. Suddenly I felt as trapped in the bar as I'd felt in the flat. I lurched out of the pub and into the night air.

I headed in the opposite direction to home. Like the wizard, I needed sky – a big empty sky.

The blue LED lights on Itchen Bridge twinkled eerily, drawing me in. The wind blew into my face from the east, making my eyes water, setting off a tinkle of bells from sailing boats from the yacht club. I turned to face west. The lights from the city and the docks shimmered on the dark water, then further west, like a mirage hovering on the water, were the glittering lights of Fawley Power Station. Not much has changed, I mused when I found myself at the top of the bridge, looking down. Twenty-nine years, the same inky black water. The only thing different now were the words *You Are Loved* etched into the concrete sill. I wanted to believe them so much it made me cry.

My phone buzzed, a text from Jo. *I don't have to throw you out of the window again do I?*

I thought friends and family were supposed to console you when you're down. Jo had thrown me out a window. My brothers had been real dicks over the Danny business and almost gleeful when I'd been banned from seeing him. Dad had been the biggest dick and Mum still just cares what the precious neighbours think.

A pipistrelle bat! It could be flying inland heading for Ethan's bat box. I need to fix that properly. A sharp breeze jolted me back to reality. I won't, because I can't, I'm not allowed round.

My rage at Jo reignited. It was her fault. She was the one who'd blabbed to get publicity. I stood stock still, fists clenched, fury overwhelming me. She hasn't even texted to say good luck or ask how I am. I never wished her good luck, but it's not like an audition to be a celebrity TV game show host compares to what I'm going through. I found a stone and threw it with force into the river. I heard the faint plop and watched the ripples spread out.

'I'm not doing it!' I yelled into the night, the wind deadening my words.

But what if it's contempt of court or something? My family had been mortified the first time. It had only been a weekend in jail but it had derailed everything, although in fairness, it had been derailed anyway. My parents were right I suppose. I was guilty of avoidance. I'd avoided them ever since they told me during the whole Danny business that everything I did and said was 180 degrees wrong. What was I supposed to do with that information? My brows tilted up towards each other. I might as well face it, I wasn't going to be in court tomorrow.

The inky blackness of the water below was like that black hole in my head where I put all the things I didn't want to think about. A dark pit that you have to avoid because it can pull you in if you don't give it a wide berth. It was gaining in force, beyond my control, dragging me into the place where all the thoughts and images I filtered out before they reached full consciousness went to live. The flash of hatred I'd seen in Ethan's eyes the first time I'd knocked on Lori's door. I'd immediately suppressed the thought that these were Danny's eyes. No matter that Danny would be in his thirties now, I knew that's how he'd look at me, with hate because I'd let him down. The niggling doubts I had from time to time about Jo, which now seemed like certainties. She wasn't my friend, she didn't care about me, never had. I was free rent, that's all.

I felt suddenly exhausted, as if all the life had gone out of me. The lights from the other coast shone brightly on the water, looking so pretty. I imagined jumping in and sinking down, but it wouldn't be like my dream. The twinkly lights were from Fawley Power Station. The water would be polluted, not just from that, but from the many cruise ships. There would be no shoals of fish, let alone singing lobsters, but instead discarded shopping trolleys, plastic packaging and abandoned bikes. I threw in another pebble, it took a long time before it hit the water, but the splash was satisfying. Salty water ran from my eyes and into my mouth. The vision of the inky black water blurred. The breeze died down and there was a moment of stillness.

A familiar stillness. Twenty-nine years ago it had been interrupted by Jo's jaunty gait, hailing me, berating me for being a party pooper, taking me back and throwing me from the window. My phone went. Jo again. *Good luck for tomorrow. Just remember I got an A and you got a D* 😊.

For fuck's sake! It really was the window all over again,

kicking a man when he's down. The terror, feeling my fingers lose their grip, noticing the tear on the earthworm poster, not realising its significance, thinking only that it would be the last thing I saw before I died. But I hadn't died. I'd fallen onto the ground just two feet below. I remembered that moment of euphoria when I realised I was alive. The grinning faces in the window, the laughing banter seeming to come from far away.

'Classic Jo gag.'

'We swapped rooms!'

Jo's green eyes gleaming and she's saying something but I couldn't hear her over my pounding heart. It sounded like, 'I saved you,' but it made no sense, because she'd pushed me.

After that I'd been all right. The adrenaline rush of my presumed brush with death had jolted me out of the depression I'd fallen into. Got me back on track with my degree. I shook my head, grasping at new interpretations that hovered within my reach then dropped away. I looked again at the text, mouth opening as the light dawned. *I got an A and you got a D.*

I shouted with laughter, finally understanding. Oh my days! I can't believe I fell for it, but she knew I would, because I did every time. I thought it through. The long hours I'd spent writing my letter of complaint. My obsessive compiling of all the gardens I'd visited, the impacts that I'd had, and also learning from other people. It had been my lifeline, distracting me from my fears, keeping alive hope and a sense of purpose. She knew what she was doing and she'd had my back all along. You never knew with Jo. Years could go by while she sat quietly on some wind-up she'd pulled on me, but this time it was the opposite. For the first time I saw her pushing me out of the window in a different light. She hadn't been trying to kill me, she'd been trying to save me.

I fumbled with my phone to respond, then jumped when it rang. I tried to focus on the screen to see who it was. Lori. I jabbed frantically at the screen trying to answer it before she rang off. In my haste it nearly slipped into the water and I lurched for a precarious moment over the rail to grab it.

'Yes?'

'Sorry, is it too late?'

My insides melted at the warmth of her voice. 'No, No. Good to hear from you.'

'I saw on the news. You're in court tomorrow?'

'Er…'

'You weren't there today, Dawn and I took the morning off to go along.'

'Really?'

'It was amazing, we loved the protest with the eco-fashion. Dawn says she's only going to knit with eco-fibres now. I think it will really change people's fashion habits.'

'You do?'

'Totally. So what are you going to say tomorrow?'

'Depends what they ask?'

'Haven't you thought about it?'

'I've tried not to.'

'I reckon that the more reasons you can give for them burying her in their garden, other than murder that is, the less suspicious it will look.'

'Maybe I could talk about the habitat implications of home burials?'

'Good idea. Practice on me.'

I gulped, and took a deep breath. Then a deeper breath, feeling it fill my chest. I am Habitat Man, I told myself. Do your work. Tim Redfern, you are up on the stand as digger-up of body and expert ecologist to tell the court about the habitat implications of natural burial. I finally allowed myself to exhale and began to pace to and fro.

'Are you okay?' asked Lori. 'You've gone quiet.'

'It's important for habitats, biodiversity, and indeed life on this planet to have a biologically active soil,' I began.

'Yes,' Lori encouraged.

'Conventional burials use embalming fluid which includes toxic chemicals such as formaldehyde. The reason they do their job well is the same reason they're toxic – they kill life. So adding such chemicals to the soil would kill off many micro-organisms. Also, typical coffins made of hardwood are a wasteful use of a precious resource.'

'Good, perfect,' Lori's voice infused me with a new sense of confidence. I found some left-over edamame beans in my pocket and crammed them into my mouth.

'It's good to have as many micro-organisms in the soil as possible.'

'What are you eating?'

'Edamame beans.'

'Go on.'

'They do the work of breaking down organic matter and provide food for other micro-organisms. You have for example tiny ciliates that swim around in the soil, and eat the bacteria and provide food for nematodes and worms—'

'You probably don't need that much detail.' Lori's voice sounded muffled.

'Are you eating too?'

'Toast. Go on.'

'Well the point is that allowing the body to return to the earth in as natural a way as possible with fewest chemicals is better for habitats, biodiversity and the environment. It's the most natural thing in the world for the nutrients in a corpse to be recycled, broken down into the soil, and absorbed by the roots of growing plants. Many families, mine included, have trees planted in the garden where they buried a family pet, because the decaying body nourishes growth. That's the cycle of life.'

'That's lovely. That's really good, Tim.'

'Thanks.'

'Is your mate Jo going with you?'

'No, but she threw me out of my bedroom window once to save me.'

'Sorry, it sounds really windy at your end. Did you just say Jo threw you out of a window?'

'Yeah.'

'Why?'

'Well—'

'Sorry, Tim. The wind keeps drowning you out. Where are you?'

'Itchen Bridge, I'll head back. Can you hear me now?'

'Yes. Shall I go along to the court with you? Keep you company?'

'You'd do that?'

'Of course, I want to look round the stalls anyway. Don't come to the house. Nine o'clock, Palmerstone Park by the knitted statue.'

'I'd love that.'

She rang off.

A spring breeze, with a hint of chill sprang up and blew life back into me. I paced up and down the bridge to keep warm, mesmerised once more by the way the city lights danced upon the mirror-black surface of the water far below. What would it take to transform the current murky, lifeless reality to the abundant, colourful, underwater life of my daydream? You'd want to clean up the sewage outfalls flowing into Southampton waters for a start. Eric's composting toilet had been a real eye-opener. I allowed myself a dream where every garden had a composting toilet – instead of waste getting flushed down the drain, all those lovely nutrients would be recycled. I vowed anew to build one for Lori. We'd also need to halt the poisoning of streams feeding into the estuary with pesticides flowing from farmland and gardens. If people followed Mark's suggestion to email the council to ban pesticides, and stopped using them in their gardens, wildlife could recover. Yes, the waters are filled with plastics and junk, but it could be cleaned out, one rusting supermarket trolley at a time. I imagined a team of smiling, chatting local volunteers, hauling out the rubbish for recycling, taking pride in cleaning up the river.

I walked back down the bridge, thinking of the fashion protest. Even if we just moved away from the trend of fast fashion and the associated waste that would be something. Or better still, maybe non-consumption is becoming the new aspiration as Elena had claimed. With community enterprises like Karen's Share Shop, we could access what we needed without the burden of ownership. Retailers were already beginning to switch their fashion departments to fashion libraries. Even my old firm had taken up Costing for Nature accounting and with Samudrapati in charge, I had faith he'd make it work as intended.

My vision of abundant life suddenly seemed possible. With a little encouragement, these familiar streets and gardens could burst into life; more native trees and wildflowers, more ponds, more organic vegetable and fruit patches, and piles of rotting wood. I imagined a healthy, green city, alive with birdsong, the buzz of bumblebees, the metallic glint of dashing dragonflies and the colourful flash of butterflies' wings. A place where children could grow up surrounded by nature. How wonderful it could be.

I left the bridge and cut through the back streets of Southampton. I passed a flowering hawthorn in a front garden, the honeyed scent filling my nostrils. Lori's new hedge that we'd planted together would flower next year. A blackbird sang melodically, perched on a chimney stack. It was either very late to bed or a very early riser. The dawn chorus would soon be starting, heralding a new day. Tomorrow, I'd tell the court about the biodiversity benefits of willow coffins and home burial. I couldn't wait.

31

THE INQUEST

I sat on the bench near the shrouded statue of Lord Palmerston, watching a park gardener spraying the roses. Lori arrived just as I was about to suggest to him that planting garlic among the roses would deter the aphids without the need for pesticides.

'Hi, Tim.'

'Lori!' I stood up and beheld her with delight. She stepped forward and I enfolded her in my arms for a lovely moment. A faint chant of 'Fashion is Ecocide,' grew louder, and we quickly found ourselves in the midst of Extinction Rebellion protestors marching towards the courthouse waving banners.

'Shall we?'

Lori nodded and we followed them towards the courthouse. It hadn't been possible to completely surround the building, but the knitters had taken over the park next door for their eco-fashion exhibition. By XR standards it was very peaceful. Instead of the angry speeches and chants I'd heard in the London protests, there was the steady click-clack of knitting needles and murmur of information being passed on to the numerous people who were passing by or heading for the courthouse.

Lori paused by a cardboard cut-out of a figure dressed in

denim jeans. 'This one has double the carbon footprint of the nylon trousers, I wouldn't have expected that.'

'Even more if you include the laundry, dear,' explained the lady sitting by the cut-out figure knitting away. 'Jeans are heavy so they take more energy to transport and use a lot of water washing and lots of energy drying. Those lightweight nylon ones use a fraction of energy in the laundry costs.'

'Heating water is very energy intensive,' I added, remembering my Costing for Nature calculations.

'That's right, my sweet. Best not to over-wash clothes, increases wear and often unnecessary. Dry on the line outside if you can, as jeans take ages in the dryer. Your nylon trousers are much lighter, use less energy, dry in minutes.'

'I thought acrylics were bad.'

'So they are, my lovely. They're toxic to the people making it, non-biodegradable and carbon intensive, but cotton uses so much water, and causes terrible water pollution in the process.'

'What are you knitting with?' I asked her, pocketing a leaflet.

'I'm knitting with recycled yarn, but see the lady over there?'

I recognised Fingers. 'Knitting with nettles?' I ventured.

'Yes she is, and further on you'll see clothes made out of hemp, bamboo, flax and Tencel fibres.'

I saw Mark with another band of protestors, their fearful banners proclaiming the end of the world seeming out of place. While Lori was browsing the stands, I went over to say hello. His greeting was muted, so I got it out of the way. 'Sorry about the parakeets and the kebab.'

He relented. 'This was a great idea of yours, Habitat Man.'

'It was a team effort.'

'The fashion swap really brought in the crowds.' Mark nodded towards the far corner which thronged with people carrying clothes.

'Habitat Man!' I heard a familiar booming voice. It was Tri.

Lori returned to my side. 'Lori, this is Mark who organised this, and Tri, from the, what was it?'

'South Yorkshire Yarn Bombers.'

'This is wonderful,' Lori told them.

'It's just,' Mark looked round disappointed, 'well there's not much shouting.'

'It's the feminine influence,' proclaimed Tri. 'Whereas men want to dominate and shout, here we persuade.' He bounded off to speak to a couple who'd approached his cut-out.

'Is that the crypto-feminist?' whispered Lori.

I nodded and jumped as the clock on the civic centre struck the half hour.

'We'd better go.' Lori hurried towards the court building. I was spotted by a huddle of journalists that hovered around the entrance. Cameras flashed and cries of 'Habitat Man,' 'what did she do for love?' and 'was it lamb in that kebab?' rained down on me. A mic was thrust into my face. Before I could speak, an official whisked me inside and through a door marked private. Lori was being herded into the courtroom, along with a mish-mash of knitters, protestors and general public. She turned round and looked quizzically at me. I managed a reassuring smile before I was ushered into a private waiting room and told to wait for the coroner's assistant. I regretted now not reading the information on my summons. Everything related to the case had been accompanied by a buzz of panic that had prevented me from taking any of it in. What a drama queen I'd been about the whole thing.

I entertained myself by reading the leaflets handed out at the protest. Linen yarn is made from the flax plant and is good for knitting summer clothes due to its thermo-regulating properties. I'd tell Jo – she hated the heat. I laughed out loud when I thought how she'd wound me up over the life coaching mark. I texted her an LOL and enquired after her audition. I moved onto the leaflet about the Global Organic Textile Standards certification scheme, and how a GOTS logo means the fibres have met environmental and labour standards.

Jo texted back. *They love me.*

Of course they do, I responded. *You're an evil genius.*

I paced around, rehearsing speeches in my head, and wondering what was going on in the courtroom. I'd just purchased some bamboo socks on my phone for my dad's birthday and was partway through ordering a hemp shirt for myself, when an officious man with a clipboard came in and frowned at me.

'Mr Redfern?'

'Yes?'

'We can't find your witness statement. Did you send it in?'

'No, sorry.' I didn't admit that I hadn't read beyond the time and place.

He sighed. 'Have you brought it with you?'

I shook my head apologetically. 'Could I write it now?'

'Looks like you'll have to. I have a blank form here. But write quickly, and legibly. I'll wait.'

I started writing my account of finding the body. 'I can't remember the day—'

'Twenty-eighth December.'

'That's it.'

'You get in much more trouble trying to avoid...' he petered out when I glared at him. He'd sounded just like my mother. I felt like I was fifteen again. He shook his head and glanced up at the clock, not bothering to conceal his air of being put upon.

I concluded my brief statement. *Called to advise on a pond by Daisy, ended up digging it. Found bones. Daisy's mother Fern arrived and told me it was her mother buried there who'd died of cancer but wanted a home burial. They didn't know if it was allowed so they just did it themselves. I went home.*

'Is that it?' he asked when I handed him the form. I was

reminded again of my mother gazing critically at my school homework.

'It's concise,' I claimed defensively, 'but accurate.'

'Come with me.' He led me out of the side room and into the courtroom.

I paused to check for the anticipated feeling of panic. It wasn't there. I was ready to do my bit.

He tutted when we entered and saw a man on the stand already answering questions. 'He was supposed to be after you.'

'Sorry.'

'Just sit anywhere till you're called.' He gave me one last accusing look, took my witness statement up to the coroner and handed it to him discreetly. I looked around, no jury, no wigs. Excellent. The benches were full of people, some of whom I recognised from Mark's house. Lori waved at me from the far end and I headed towards her. As I squeezed past a couple of elderly ladies, one of them grabbed my wrist and pulled me down.

'Timothy!'

'Mum?'

'Sit next to us.'

'No I'm—'

'Sit down!'

I gave in and sat down. Next to her I recognised her neighbour, Mrs Lacey. I'd not had much to do with her in the past, but she beamed at me as if we were old friends. I looked over at Lori who was watching bemused and shrugged helplessly.

'Look, Mum—'

'Shush.'

'He's from the Natural Death Centre,' Mrs Lacey whispered over to me.

'What did she ask you?' the coroner was asking the man.

'She asked about burying bodies in gardens.'

'Did anything strike you as unusual?'

'Not at all. We have discussions every day with relatives who hate the idea of a standard funeral. Most people are unaware of how much they can do themselves. It's perfectly legal to keep a dead body in your house, and wash and prepare it yourself, and do your own funeral and we assist with this. Many people find that it's an expression of love for the deceased to take on these functions and return them to the earth naturally and in a way that cherishes both the environment and the family.'

The stenographer was typing rapidly. Soon she'd be typing my words. I felt a tap on my shoulder and looked round. It was Tri, burly and bearded amidst a row of lady knitters.

I smiled quickly and turned back round.

'It's only in our developed cultures that the idea of death is distasteful,' the man continued. 'We're taught to feel squeamish at the sight, or even the thought of a dead body. I suspect that these feelings of distaste and avoidance are actively encouraged to feed a profitable funeral industry. They can make people feel like they're not respecting their loved ones unless they order the most expensive mahogany coffin.'

Mrs Lacey was nodding avidly. I wondered where Mr Lacey was. Mum took her hand and squeezed it, and I guessed.

'They pour toxic chemicals into the deceased bodies and bury them six-feet deep where the aerobic bacteria can't penetrate. This means that the process of breaking down releases methane which is a greenhouse gas many times more potent than carbon dioxide, and we're encouraged to think of this as the natural, loving way to dispose of our loved ones, when it's anything but. Also consider the emissions associated with cremation; the stone for memorials, often shipped long distance from overseas quarries—'

'Yes, yes,' interrupted the coroner, looking up from his notes. 'But the real question is, did Ms Fern Donovan Brown tell you about the body in the garden?'

'No, she said her father was dying and she wanted to bury him in the garden.'

'Did she mention anything about registering, or more precisely, not registering the burial and the death?'

'No. Well, kind of. I thought it was hypothetical. I can't remember exactly what she asked, but I told her that it was legal to bury bodies in a garden, as long as it's not near a water supply and the burial site is registered, and obviously the death needs to be registered.'

'Obviously is my least favourite word. I find whenever someone says "obviously" it's far from obvious. Let me be more precise in my question. During your discussion, was she made aware that an unregistered death and burial would be illegal?'

'I suppose she was.'

'Did you tell her how to find out if a body had been registered?'

He shot an apologetic look at Fern. 'Yes.'

'Did that not raise alarm bells?'

'No. Why?'

'Why would she want to know how to find out if a death had been registered if her father hadn't yet died?'

'Oh. I don't know.'

'To confirm, Ms Donovan Brown was aware of the illegality of not registering the death of her mother, and of the illegality of not registering the burial site, and aware of how she could check, in the face of her father's inability to tell her due to his illness, whether or not the death and burial had been correctly registered?'

'Yes, that's correct.' Was I imagining it or did his glance over at Fern look slightly more suspicious this time.

'Thank you for your testimony; you may sit down. Now I'd like to recall Ms Donovan Brown to the stand.'

The man sat down and all eyes turned to Fern as she took the stand. Her gaze alighted on me. I smiled at her but she looked away grim-faced.

'Oh dear,' whispered Mrs Lacey, nudging me. 'She's not happy with you is she?'

I didn't deign to answer, and leant forward to hear what the coroner was asking.

'In your statement yesterday, you testified that you didn't know that the death wasn't registered.'

'That's right.'

'But we just heard that you knew exactly how to find out if a death had been registered, and in the police report it indicates that someone checked the records the day after you visited the Natural Death Centre.'

A buzz went round the court. It looked like Fern had been caught out in a lie.

'Sorry. Yesterday when you asked if I knew the death hadn't been registered, I thought you meant at the time. Dad took care of that.'

'But we just had testimony that you found out a few months ago that it hadn't.'

'Yes, I knew later.'

'So you were aware the death wasn't registered and yet you didn't go to the police.'

'I was worried it would look bad. I told Daisy not to dig in the garden,' cried Fern in a fit of frustration.

'It's not your daughter Daisy on trial for disobeying your instructions, it's you who must answer the questions raised by your covering up of the body, of how exactly your mother died.'

His voice held a sternness that hadn't been there before. I worried for her.

'Your father secretly and illegally buried his wife in the back garden. And you then continued the cover up. Was it kept a secret because it wasn't in fact a natural death?'

'No, of course not, she died of cancer like I said yesterday. All we did was bury her ourselves.'

'Thank you, you may step down. Mr Redfern, please take the

stand.'

Fern didn't meet my eye as we crossed each other. She was angry I could tell. I would do all I could to put things right for her.

I was sworn in and then the questions began.

'Can you tell the court why you were digging?'

'Daisy wanted a pond. I'm not supposed to do the digging myself but she wasn't very good at it.' I looked out for Daisy hoping to smile at her to show no offence was intended. I couldn't see her, and realised she must be at home tending to her grandad.

'Just to be straight, you had no idea a body was buried in the garden?'

'Erm. No?'

'You don't seem sure?'

'Well, it's just her grandad wasn't keen for anyone to dig in the garden.'

'In what way did he show that?'

'He told Daisy not to dig a pond and, well, he glared at me.'

'So after being told not to dig a pond, you went ahead and did so the moment he wasn't able to object?'

'I thought it was okay?'

'What made you think so?'

I hesitated, I didn't want to get Daisy into trouble.

'Go on,' pressed the coroner.

'Daisy said it was okay.' I gulped, my pause had made Daisy's request sound dodgy. I spoke quickly, trying to make up for it. 'She was crying as her grandad was ill and said she wanted to make the garden nice for him. It's a lovely garden, and that area is perfect for a pond. Ponds create a host of habitats and it's the first thing I'd advise when visiting any garden if you want to increase its wildlife potential.'

'When you came across the bones, what happened?'

'I was shocked, and so was Daisy, then Fern turned up.'

'And how did Fern explain the body?'

'She said that her mother had been ill but wanted to be buried in the back garden, naturally with just her family, and a lovely willow coffin.'

I remembered what Lori had said about providing benign reasons for the home burial.

'Willow itself has high wildlife value as a tree and willow coffins and shallow burials are better for habitat and the soil. Also—'

'Thank you, the court has been made aware of the benefits of willow coffins.'

'But it's not just that, they wove their own coffin and she knitted her own shroud. This garden where they live, I wish you could see it. It's nurtured with love. Fern's mother, her body is replenishing the soil, making it fertile. It's not carted off like something shameful. It's like… it's like composting toilets. Do you put your waste far away where you can't smell it, or do you use it to nurture the earth? We flush our waste away so we don't see, but you can't disguise the stink. Like when you're in Riverside Park and sometimes there's a faint acrid pong from the water-processing treatment. If we all had composting toilets, you wouldn't have that.'

I glanced towards Lori. She was smiling and I continued encouraged. 'Instead, the waste would, after an appropriate period of time in the correct conditions, nourish and enrich the soil and not smell at all, as long as the wet waste is kept separate from the solid. You can put the wet waste on your compost bin and stir it around a bit. That will create heat and nitrogen which gets the process going nicely. But if it's your main toilet, I wouldn't, you don't want to drown your compost with wee. It's a question of balance.'

The coroner was reading his notes, and frowning slightly. 'I'm sorry I don't see the relevance. Do the family have a composting toilet?'

'No, but they should. We all should.' I saw my mother shaking her head.

'What is the relevance?'

'It's about loving our...' I hesitated, not wanting to say shit and losing faith suddenly in the point I was trying to make.

'Shall we move on?'

'No.' I had it now, back on track. 'The point is that they didn't want to hand the body over to strangers who didn't care for her. Instead they made her body part of the beautiful environment they'd created for themselves in the back garden of a slightly grubby suburb. Birds sang, Your Honour, bees buzzed, trees rustled and the earth was rich with life because they didn't poison the soil with chemicals but nurtured it with her body that was not really dead, but now a life-giving force to the soil. Just like,' I said triumphantly, 'our shit, instead of being flushed away like something shameful, processed with chemicals and creating an acrid pong in what is rather a beautiful part of Southampton, can with the composting toilet, nourish the soil leading to new growth and flourishing of life, in what has become, in many gardens, a worryingly barren soil. They did it out of love, Your Honour, out of love for her and love for the environment and Mother Nature herself.'

A smattering of applause came from the benches at the back. Lori was wiping tears from her eyes, although it looked like she was laughing rather than crying. My mother still looked puzzled, but Mrs Lacey was clapping. I smiled around, pleased with my speech. Habitat Man, you've done good, I told myself and turned to leave.

'Before you go, Mr Redfern, can we return to that phrase, which I believe you have uttered several times, "they did it out of love." What did they do?'

'Buried her in the back garden.'

'Just buried?'

'What do you mean?'

'What were you told about the manner of her death?'

'Fern told me that her mother was dying of cancer, that she knew she was going to die.'

'Is that all?'

'Yes.'

'Did they tell you if she went to hospital or was treated by doctors or died at home?'

'I'm not sure, I was still quite shocked about finding the bones.'

'You don't remember?'

'No, but I don't think so, no.'

'Is it fair to say that you admire their actions?'

'The family were wise, Your Honour, wiser than most of us. We hide away the things we don't want to think about like death and human waste, but if we face them squarely they become opportunities for renewal and regeneration. Their garden was one of the loveliest I'd visited. There was a balance, a harmony a Feng Shui if you will, it just needed a po—'

'So you admire their actions in terms of the home burial?'

'Yes I do,' I claimed stoutly.

'And the fact that they didn't register the burial, or the death?'

'I didn't know about that at the time.'

'At the time? Mr Redfern, did you know that the death hadn't been registered later?'

I hesitated. 'Yes,' I admitted.

'How did you find out?'

'Fern told me.'

'How? Were you in regular communication? Friends perhaps?'

'No, not at all, she wanted me to come round.'

'Why?'

'To er, to ask me not to tell anybody about the body.'

'I see. Did that strike you as suspicious?'

'Her explanation made sense, she was worried her father

would die soon and he wanted to be buried with his wife in the garden. They didn't want it to be a crime scene.'

'Crime scene? What kind of crime?'

I flustered and cursed myself again for not having read the paperwork. I didn't even know if she was being charged with something. I took a guess. 'Wrongful burial?'

'Not assisted suicide?'

'What?' I shook my head, trying to process the suggestions being made.

'Thank you that is all.'

I was ushered off the stand.

A quick glance revealed that there were no seats left next to Lori. I sighed and made my way back to where my mother was waiting for me.

'What on earth—' she began, but was interrupted by Tri hissing my name. I looked round.

'Well done, Habitat Man,' he whispered loudly.

'Told you,' whispered Mrs Lacey to my mother.

'Look, it's the wizard now,' said one of the women behind us.

'What?' This was a new world to my mother and she was struggling to take it all in.

I heard the familiar irritated voice of Geoff and tuned into the proceedings. The coroner was reading the notes in front of him with a sceptical expression. He looked over at Geoff on the stand. 'It says here that you're a... wizard?'

'I identify as a witch.'

The cackling from Tri and the knitters behind me drowned out the coroner's next question. I looked round, a couple of them looked rather witchy themselves. Tri was shaking his head. 'Not right,' he muttered indignantly, 'co-opting the female experience.'

Lori shot me a quizzical look. I longed to be sat next to her, she'd love this. The coroner gave the knitters a stern look and they subsided.

'I can testify that she was very ill,' Geoff was saying. 'I was just starting out, she was one of my first reiki—'

'Victims?' heckled Tri, smirking and nudging his neighbour.

'That's religious intolerance,' claimed Geoff testily, glaring up at the benches.

'Withdrawn,' he shouted.

The coroner treated the back benches to a stern gaze. 'Quiet please.'

Geoff pursed his lips in annoyance and continued. 'The point is that I can testify that she was ill. I knew Fern and she asked me to do some reiki on her mother.'

'I assume it didn't work?'

It was the coroner's turn to be treated to one of Geoff's glares.

'She was pissed off when it didn't make any difference. She said: "It didn't bloody work. We're going to have to take things into our own hands".'

'This was a long time ago, how can you be sure you remembered her words correctly?'

'It was my first time, for Puck's sake, and the woman was dying of cancer. She needn't have been so harsh.'

I caught Lori's eye and grinned.

'Is it possible that your interpretation is affected by your hurt feelings at the insult to your skills?'

'Thanks to Tim, my powers are restored now.'

The eyes of the court turned to me. I shrugged modestly, and self-consciously looked back at Geoff.

'This is not an opportunity for you to promote your reiki practice.'

'I don't see why not, the other fella promoted his natural death business didn't he? He had ages on it.' He had a point and I felt a little responsible. I suspected the coroner had let him run on to give himself a chance to read my witness statement. 'Everyone's going to go off and do a green funeral now. So what's wrong with people coming to me for a bit of reiki? And I do spells.'

Out of the corner of my eye I saw Fern scribbling a note and handing it to a smartly dressed man sat beside her. He read it, then stood up.

'Fern would like to take the stand for a moment.'

Geoff stepped down and Fern took his place.

'Ms Donovan Brown, you want to add something?'

'He asked me out, and I said no, that's why he's trying to land us in it.'

Geoff rose up from the bench. 'You were pretty mean.'

'My mother was dying for goodness' sake, and you're making a pass? After you failed to cure her?'

The court was agog with the drama, heads looking to and fro at Geoff and Fern. She looked indignant and he sat upright, his face taut with relived rejection.

'Thank you, you may sit back down. I'd like to recall Mr Geoffrey Blackman to the stand.'

Looks of dislike were exchanged as they crossed each other.

'Is it true that you asked Ms Donovan Brown out after failing to cure her mother, and she turned you down?' asked the coroner.

'Yes, bu—'

'Is it fair to say that you harbour resentment against her for rejecting you?'

'I admit she hurt my feelings. Her mother did too. I think it's important that men are finally allowed to express hurt feelings. But that doesn't change what I heard. They said they were going to take it into their own hands.'

'And what did you take that to mean?'

'Murder.'

A hum of shock went round the court. I looked at Fern with new suspicion. There had been a fierceness about the grandad when he'd been stirring his vegetable curry, he'd given me a nasty look – he didn't even give me any curry, and Fern had been insistent, she'd asked me to keep it quiet. Could Geoff be right?

VERDICT

The coroner called lunch and everyone made for the exits. I found myself trapped between my mother and Mrs Lacey as we inched our way to the doors.

'It was even busier yesterday,' said Mrs Lacey.

'You were here?'

'Your mother wouldn't believe you were Habitat Man, so I came with my daughter to prove it.' She wagged her finger in my face. 'I knew it was you who let the parakeets out.'

My mother turned to Mrs Lacey indignantly. 'You never said anything to me.'

'Well one doesn't, does one?'

'Er,' I began, unsure what to say to my mother. 'I wasn't expecting you.'

'She had to see it for herself before she'd believe it,' said Mrs Lacey.

'I should have known when you got the kids those worm explorer kits,' said my mother.

'Which they all hated,' I said.

'Hannah loved hers.'

'Really?' I felt absurdly delighted.

We finally squeezed through the door and into the foyer. I noticed Lori emerging from the other door.

'Yes, she's got the whole set now. But Timothy—'

Journalists descended on me, all speaking at once.

'Habitat Man.' 'Do you think she did it?' 'Were there knitting needles among the bones?'

Grateful for an excuse to escape my mother's baleful look, I tried to answer each of them as best I could. 'That's me, no, er, yes there were knitting needles yes.' I looked over their shoulders for Lori. The journalists spotted Fern and rushed over to her. I beamed as Lori hurried towards me.

'OMG!' cried Lori, the moment she reached me.

I laughed knowing what she was referring to. 'Geoff?'

'He was exactly as I imagined him.'

'Surely you pictured him tall and thin with a long flowing beard.'

'No, I knew he'd be short and squat and tetchy.'

'No you didn't. That's just hindsight.'

'Was it that crypto-feminist who was heckling him?'

'He was indignant that he was co-opting the feminine experience.'

'For Puck's sake,' she imitated, and we burst into laughter again. 'And Geoff was so stroppy!'

'I knew exactly what you were thinking,' I challenged her. 'I was observing you. First you laughed and you were thinking about the playlists Geoff sent me—'

'We won't wait any longer,' she laughed.

'And he demanded his money—'

'Charity money—'

'Charity money back. Then I saw you look annoyed for a second, and I just knew you were thinking of your ex who sent you folk playlists.'

'I totally was,' she declared, surprised and delighted.

'Do you know what I was thinking?'

'Please no—'

'I was thinking, what's so wrong with folk?'

'Not you please.'

'What about Mumford and Son? You must like them? Or Led Zep?'

'That's rock surely?'

'They have folky bits, and...' I paused and added daringly 'they're the best bits.'

Lori looked over my shoulder, noticing my mother and Mrs Lacey watching with great interest. Sighing, I made the introductions.

'Lori, this is my mum, and Mrs Lacey from next door.'

Lori stepped forward to greet them, but was interrupted by the journalists who had rushed back. I steeled myself, but it was my mother they were after.

'How does it feel, finding out your son's secret identity as Habitat Man?'

'Of course, I knew all along,' she declared, ignoring Mrs Lacey's incredulous look. 'What kind of mother doesn't know what her son is up to?'

'Me for one,' muttered Lori in my ear.

'But it wasn't my secret to reveal,' said my mother solemnly.

I stifled my laughter. Jo would love this, it was so ridiculous. I turned back to Lori. 'Did you like my bit about the composting toilet?'

'It was...' she paused, lost for words, 'well it was something.'

'I didn't want you to think it was aimed at you.'

'I must have imagined the meaningful look you shot in my direction,' Lori smiled. She glanced at her watch. 'Sorry I've got to go.'

'I'm so glad you came.'

'I wouldn't have missed it for anything.' She nodded at my mother, who was waving away the journalists. 'Bye, er, Mrs

Redfern. Bye, Mrs Lacey.' She shot me an amused look and dashed off.

I gazed after her, guessing that she wanted to get back before Ethan got home. I suspected she hadn't told him she was coming to the court. I turned round and was faced immediately with the enquiring gaze of my mother and Mrs Lacey.

To forestall the inevitable questions I took a chance and turned to Mrs Lacey. 'Sorry about Mr Lacey.'

'Thank you, dear. When Fern described their home burial, it brought it all back.' She gazed wistfully into the distance. 'Fern made it sound so peaceful and intimate, outdoors, and no one rushing you and a lovely willow coffin.' She looked back at us, tears in her eyes. 'Arthur's funeral was like a conveyor belt, they wanted us in and out as quick as possible so the next lot could start. The vicar didn't even know him, and it did strike me at the time that a lot of good wood was going into the ground. What with the rainforests and poor orangutans without a home, I wish I could go back and do his funeral over.' Mrs Lacey pulled out a hanky and dabbed at her eyes.

Mum squeezed her hand. 'There's no way I'd want my sons dressing my dead body though,' she shook her head in horror.

I agreed. I wouldn't want my brothers anywhere near my naked dead body either.

A bench became free and we took the opportunity to sit. My mother pulled out a lunchbox and handed out sandwiches.

Conscious of the unlikelihood of it being vegan and the press's eyes upon me I stuffed a sandwich into my mouth in one.

'Timothy!'

Fern was making her way through the crowd towards me, her face taut with anger. I stood up, desperately wanting to apologise for setting off this whole charade.

'Tim.'

I struggled to chew the sandwich fast enough to be able to swallow, and proclaim my abject apologies. I nodded.

'My father just died.'

I masticated frantically, trying to convey my sympathy with a few facial contortions.

'And it's because of you and your big mouth that I wasn't able to be with him at his deathbed.' She turned and walked away. By the time I'd swallowed, she'd gone. I sat back down.

'That will teach you to stuff your face,' said my mother. 'Shall we?' she said to Mrs Lacey, and with orders to watch their bags they headed off to the ladies.

Grateful to be left alone, I enjoyed a bit of people-watching. The journalists were talking to Geoff, but getting restless, looking round for new angles.

A group of mostly black women, Ashley standing out white among them, were in a vigorous debate with a local historian. I recognised Needles from the Graffiti Grannies walking past, too busy holding forth to the Urban Knitta group to notice me.

'We're an underground movement,' Needles was telling them. 'Literally. Our last project was on the London Underground, to make it cosier. We did the knitted bench.'

Mark came in full of restless energy, and tried to get the journalists' attention, but they were now talking to the assisted suicide people. He collared the knitting groups instead and encouraged them back outside for the fashion protest.

'But it's lunch hour,' several of them protested.

'Exactly, that's when we need people on the stalls. You can eat your lunch by your cut-outs.'

My mother and Mrs Lacey returned. It was clear what they'd been talking about. My mother had the unmistakeable look of a mother interested in her son's love life.

'My turn,' I headed for the gents. Geoff was washing his hands and a couple of blokes occupied the urinals. To escape attention, I locked myself into a cubical. Geoff left and the other two immediately started talking.

'I've got a bad back, maybe I should ask.'

'It didn't sound like he was any good. Didn't he kill someone with it?'

'No, that was cancer.'

'It sounds a bit risky to me.'

'Habitat Man restored his powers.'

'How can a gardener give someone reiki powers?'

'It's about tuning into nature and accessing the vibe.'

'Oh right.'

I heard the sound of the hand-dryer, then the door closing and I ventured out, the coast was clear. I washed my hands, slowly, in no rush to face the inevitable questions.

When I came out I was pleased to see people heading back into the courtroom. I collected my mother and Mrs Lacey and we filed in.

'While you were taking your time in the toilet, we overheard that there's one more witness then the judge—'

'Coroner,' corrected Mrs Lacey.

'Coroner, will sum up. They want to conclude it quickly so Fern can deal with her dad's death.'

'Quite right. Poor girl after what she's being out through, it's not right.' Mrs Lacey's words weren't aimed at me, but I felt the sting of culpability.

Up on the stand was a man I didn't recognise. He was dressed in a smart suit and had a self-important manner.

'And you are Mr Briar Donovan?' asked the coroner.

'Brian.'

The coroner donned his glasses and peered down at his notes. 'It says Briar here, we can't proceed until we're clear on your name.'

'They named me Briar, but I go by Brian.'

'Right. Then let us proceed.'

'Firstly I want to make it clear that this is ridiculous. I came back from Australia where I've been living quite happily for twenty years away from my hippy dippy family, because Fern says

Dad is on his deathbed and find myself instead here in this court.' Brian glared at the coroner challengingly.

'He's got a point,' whispered Mrs Lacey. I nodded, but any sympathy for him vanished at his next comment.

'I'm a busy man, I charge my time at a thousand pounds a day. I've given that up to be by the side of my dying father as befits an eldest son, but some idiot has decided that a thirty-year-old case needs an inquest and I'm required to attend!'

There was a collective gasp at the word 'idiot'. The stenographer stopped typing and looked apprehensively up at the coroner whose expression had hardened.

Tri tapped me on the shoulder and hissed down at me. 'This is an alpha-male-off!' I shivered with fearful anticipation. I'd seen it before with my brothers and at work. 'Self-important-rich-tosser versus the man-in-position-of-authority,' I whispered back.

'What can you tell us about the home burial of your mother?' the coroner asked stiffly.

'Very little because I wasn't there.'

Eyebrows were raised at his disrespectful tone.

'You didn't attend your own mother's funeral?'

'Oh he's sticking in the knife,' murmured Mrs Lacey gleefully.

'Well I loved her, of course I did, although she was embarrassing. A bit hippy dippy, you know.' He looked at the public benches expecting sympathetic nods, but got glares from the massed ranks of guerrilla knitters. He carried on, slightly less confidently. 'I knew they weren't registering it, that's why I didn't go.'

'You didn't go to your mother's funeral in protest at its illegality?'

'Correct.'

'Let me get this straight. You knew an illegal burial was taking place. The daughter here, just turned eighteen, blinded by grief for her mother does what she thinks is right, but you were older, in your twenties, and you did nothing?'

Tri muttered in my ear. 'Never challenge a fella on his home turf.'

'Definitely,' I whispered back.

'Shush,' whispered my mother. 'He's getting to the nitty gritty.'

'It was them who buried her in the garden.'

We turned as one to look at Fern. How must she feel, being landed in it by her brother? Suddenly she was the object of sympathy, not only had she lost her mother and now her father, she had this man for a brother.

The coroner went in for the kill. 'Buried or killed?'

There was a kerfuffle from the far benches. The assisted suicide squad stood up and clumsily unrolled their banner. This was their moment, but they spoilt it by all shouting at once.

'We object to the term kill.' 'It's an act of love.' 'Legalise voluntary euthanasia.'

Counter arguments and accusations were thrown by others in the benches.

'You just want your inheritance early.'

'No we don't.'

'Good comeback,' I whispered to Mrs Lacey, who laughed.

'Yeah! Bet you've all got rich relatives you want to die.'

I jumped at a bellow from my right. 'Like that tosser down there with the fake Ozzy accent,' yelled Mrs Lacey.

My mother threw her an appalled look. 'It's not a pantomime,' she whispered disapprovingly. Mrs Lacey shrugged and shot me a mischievous look.

The assisted suicide squad sat back down, murmuring and nodding among themselves, seemingly satisfied with their protest.

The coroner called the court to order and pressed on with his questions.

'You say you weren't there for the burial. Were you present when your mum died?'

'Yes.'

'He's respectful now,' whispered my mother.

'Did she die of natural causes?'

'She died of cancer. Shortly after the reiki session.'

All eyes turned to Geoff who glared belligerently at anyone who caught his eye. He looked like he was muttering under his breath.

'He's casting spells on him,' Tri said behind me.

'They won't work if they're anything like his reiki,' responded a knitter. They all sniggered.

'Shush,' said my mother turning round, 'he's summing up.'

Brian had stepped down and the coroner shuffled his notes for effect and looked round the court. When he got to Fern, he adopted an expression of sympathy, which hardened when his gaze fell upon her brother. The stenographer sat alert, her fingers suspended over the keypad. The press at the back leant forward, waiting for the verdict. I found a few edamame beans in the bottom of my pocket and munched expectantly.

'Ladies and gentlemen—'

'Witches and wizards,' I heard them whisper behind me.

'No one can know why the burial wasn't registered, the man who could tell us has sadly died. But it seems from the testimony that this is a family that liked to live self-sufficiently and outside of the system, doing things their own way. Some of them anyway. This is a case that has attracted much speculation. Some have blamed the authorities, wrongly as it must now be clear, for the disappearance of the woman known as the guerrilla knitter. I hope that these ridiculous conspiracy theories can now be put to rest, because her family have themselves testified that she died a natural death and was buried by themselves in the garden. As for whether it really was a natural death, it seems that a mixture of accusations from a rejected suitor,' he glanced at Geoff who glared back, 'and some ill-chosen words from a well-meaning gardener,' he glanced up at me, 'led to suspicions of assisted suicide which we have no reason to give credence to. So in the absence of any clear evidence to the contrary, I rule that this was a natural death. The person who is really to blame for it not being registered has just died and this court extends its deepest sympathy to his family and genuine sorrow that these proceedings meant they were unable to keep him company in his final hours. But I understand that his granddaughter Daisy kept vigil by his side. It's true that Ms Donavan Brown has made some poor decisions in covering up the body, but allowances must be made for the personal grief she must be feeling as she knows her father is dying. The purpose of this inquest is to satisfactorily explain a death so that rumours can be quelled, justice can be seen to be served and the family can move on. This inquest is now concluded, and the death can now be officially registered.'

Everyone clapped and there were whoops from the back benches. Fern looked exhausted but relieved.

A party air prevailed in the foyer, except for Mark, who looked harried, still trying to round up all the protestors and knitters he could find for the fashion protest. I managed to lose my mother and Mrs Lacey who'd got into a debate with the assisted suicide squad. 'It's about quality of life,' one of them was saying earnestly to Mrs Lacey, who was dabbing her eyes.

'Arthur's last months were very painful for him,' she agreed. 'It would have been nice to spare him those.' My mother looked less convinced, and I suspected she was thinking that her mercenary eldest son might be too quick to pull the plug if given the chance.

A throng of guerrilla knitters and reporters clustered round Fern competing for her attention.

The man from the Natural Death Centre came up and held out his hand. 'Hi, I'm Andrew, you did brilliantly.'

'Thanks, you too.'

Another lady with blonde hair, dyed pink was beside him. 'I'm Carla. I loved your composting toilet spiel. We're getting one for our houseboat.'

'We've got to go, but see you at the funeral.' Andrew smiled and left with Carla.

I presumed he meant the grandad's, but I'd be the last person to be invited I was sure. I looked around, the courthouse was clearing now, and there was the music to face. My mother headed towards me purposefully, followed by Mrs Lacey.

The civic centre clock chimed the hour. Mrs Lacey checked her watch and put her hand on Mum's arm. 'If you want to come back with me on the train I'll probably head back in a minute.'

Mum looked at me. This was the moment when I was supposed to acknowledge that she'd come down to see me and offer to take her out to dinner. Or both of them probably. What I really wanted to do, which I knew was impossible anyway, was to head over to Lori's. My mood fell flat, the ever-present problem of how to see her remained. The last thing I felt like doing now was enduring my mother's opinions on my life choices.

She waited a bit longer and then she said, 'Right I'm coming. By the way, Tim, don't forget your dad's birthday. He'd have come down himself, but he doesn't get out much these days.'

I flared up. I'd forgotten his birthday one time when I was twenty and she'd never let me forget it. 'You don't always have to remind me.'

My words lingered in the air harsh and accusing. Mrs Lacey shot my mother a sympathetic look. I recognised something in my churlish tone. I sounded like Ethan, the way he talked to Lori. I gave my mother a sudden hug. 'Sorry. I got him bamboo socks.'

She laughed in surprise. 'So did I!'

'Never!' My mother buying any socks that weren't from Marks and Spencer's was a revelation.

Mrs Lacey nodded over to my left and I saw Fern coming

over. Thankfully she was smiling. The lines of worry that had been etched into her forehead since I met her had disappeared.

'Fern, I'm so sorry—'

'No it's fine. I was angry with you earlier, but now I'm glad. This had to come out. Maybe his death is a symbol that it's the end of all this now. Would you like to come to the funeral?'

'Could I bring a friend?'

'Of course you can.'

'I'd love to.'

'Saturday, two pm, back garden.' She headed off purposefully. Home, I presumed, to be with Daisy. I wondered if her brother would be there.

Cheered, I turned back to my mother and gave in to the inevitable. 'Stay and eat and we'll catch up.'

'Really?'

I always thought of my mum as indestructible but it struck me that she was well into her seventies. I didn't want her on the train alone. Mrs Lacey was even older, and she'd just lost her husband. 'You too, Mrs Lacey, both come and eat with me.'

Journalists' eyes were upon me and the XR lot. It was going to have to be vegan.

'We'll go to Café Thrive. It's close to the station so I can drop you both off after and you can go back together.'

'I don't want to get back in the dark,' said Mrs Lacey.

'It's only four, I'll get you on the six o'clock train okay?'

My mother beamed at me. 'That would be lovely. We have so much to catch up on.'

What had I let myself in for?

33

CAFÉ THRIVE

My concerns about how my conservative mother and her neighbour would respond to the unfamiliar food were unfounded. They oohed and ahhed over the menu, and after a consultation with the waiter, a hipster with a wispy beard, decided upon a sandwich of Mediterranean cashew 'cheese', roasted balsamic mushrooms, pumpkin seed pesto and sundried tomatoes for my mother, a bowl of roasted vegetables, balsamic mushrooms, hummus, avocado, lemon quinoa, salad leaves, seeds, falafel and pea shoots with tahini dressing for Mrs Lacey, and I treated myself to deep fried southern style meat-free seitan with coleslaw and chips, loaded with sour 'cream', salsa and jalapenos, with a pineapple, mango, papaya and apple smoothie.

The moment the food ordering was out of the way, my mother looked around then leant towards me and said in a low voice, 'I was worried that your Danny business would get out.'

I flicked a glance at Mrs Lacey.

'Don't worry, she knows all about it.'

Mrs Lacey nodded. 'I agree with your mother, that girl treated you abominably, it wasn't fair the way you took the rap because she lied.'

Then my mother was off, a rant I'd heard several times a day years back. 'You never saw how manipulative she was, she had you at her beck and call with that kid.'

I willed myself not to respond.

'I kept telling him,' Mum told Mrs Lacey, 'the trouble with Timothy is that he lets himself be taken advantage of. He's still the same.'

'Oh yes, with that lesbian flatmate who doesn't pay rent.'

'Jo does pay rent now actually,' I informed her through clenched teeth.

'Where is she anyway? I'd have thought she'd have been here to support you.'

'You know the random recipe challenge?'

'What's that?'

'I know,' cried Mrs Lacey. 'That tastes utterly disgusting.'

'What?' My mother was bemused.

'You get a random list of ingredients, always with one really weird one and you have to cook with just those. My daughter did it.'

'That sounds like a Jo thing. But why isn't she here? Have you fallen out over that woman – Lori?' my mother was clearly fishing.

'Jo's at an audition to be a cookery game show host.'

'Ooh it would make a great show,' agreed Mrs Lacey.

'Still, we like Jo, but I'm not sure she's good for you.'

'That's not really your business.'

Mrs Lacey hissed with shock and shot Mum a look.

'And while I'm at it, with respect to Danny, all you ever told me was that I was doing everything wrong. I knew I was being manipulated but what was I supposed to do? And don't answer, because I'm not interested in your opinions.'

My mother flashed me her 'be quiet' look and nodded up at the waiter, who I realised had been hanging round with our meals perched uncomfortably all on one hand, not wanting to interrupt my outburst.

'Your food,' he whispered. He set it down carefully and departed at great speed.

The tense silence was broken by murmurs of appreciation while we tucked in. I felt like a dick, but I couldn't unbend yet. The issue of me giving up my job still hung over us. I wasn't going to get away with that.

'I felt like a complete idiot with those journalists at my door—'

'Mum, just drop it.'

'No I won't. How do you think I felt, not knowing what my own son was doing?'

Mrs Lacey nodded in agreement.

'I couldn't face you all ganging up on me for giving up my job.'

'This is what you do, you avoid conflict, but it leads to something worse. Anyway, you're wrong.'

'What?'

'I think you being Habitat Man is wonderful. I never thought finance suited you.'

'You didn't?'

'I do know you a little, Timothy. Your brothers love money but you never cared about it. This is one area where I don't agree with them.'

'Huh?'

'You weren't right for that job, we can't believe you stuck it for so long,' added Mrs Lacey.

What did she know about it? I barely knew her but she seemed to know everything about me.

'We tried to tell you but you never listened to a word we said.'

'I just assumed—'

'You should have chucked it in long ago,' said Mrs Lacey.

I'd had enough. 'That's easy to say, but I had a record, where else could I have gone? And how come you know so much about it anyway?'

'Mothers talk. Your mum knows all about Jemima.'

'Who the hell is Jemima?'

'Mrs Lacey's daughter. We're a little worried about her shopping habit.'

I had a vague memory of a girl a few years older than me.

'But Timothy,' my mother continued. 'Surely you know it doesn't stay on your record forever.'

'What about when I applied to be a biology teacher, and they turned me down when they checked my background?' To my chagrin I felt tears pricking my eyes.

'Obviously they dig deeper when you're dealing with children, but only for that kind of job.'

'That was the job I wanted!' I cried.

It had been like a dagger in the heart. I'd done five years as an accountant then, with exhortations from Jo to 'man up', I'd tried for the job I really wanted. I couldn't pass on my love of nature to Danny anymore but perhaps I could to other children. I remembered that moment of hope after my interview had gone so well, followed two weeks later by a curt letter of rejection.

Mrs Lacey's look of deep sympathy undid all my defences and I found myself crying like a baby as I relived the hurt and despair I'd felt all those years ago.

Mrs Lacey put her arms round me and patted me on the back as I wept into her shoulder. 'There, there. Let it all out. You've buried it for so long.'

'I have,' I wept, the stress and exhaustion from the previous few weeks catching up with me.

My mother shot a look at the waiter who was waiting to collect our plates and he stepped back quickly.

I pulled away, realising how ridiculous I must seem. Mum

passed me a tissue and I blew my nose loudly, scaring off the waiter who'd cautiously approached again.

'It's okay,' said my mother brutal as always, 'he's done crying.'

Mrs Lacey nodded up at him and then patted my hand in sympathy. We sat back in silence as the waiter cleared the table as rapidly as he could.

'You see this is what happens when you avoid things and bury them,' said my mother the moment he was gone. 'It's like you said with the composting toilet.'

I had a moment of sudden hope. My conservative, middle-England, middle-class mother approved of my new job, was buying bamboo socks, eating vegan food…

'You're not going to get a composting toilet are you, Mum?'

'Don't be ridiculous.'

34

CINZANO AND KNITTING

I was delighted to see Jo's coat and boots in the hall when I got home. It seemed like an age since I'd seen her. I found her in the lounge, sprawled out on the sofa. She gestured towards the abandoned knitting and bottle of Cinzano.

'Has your mother been down?'

'Yes.' I left it at that. No point asking for it. I dropped into the chair and let out a long, slow breath.

'That bad?'

'No, actually. I reconciled with Mum, Fern got off, case dismissed. I gave a brilliant speech if I say so myself. Lori came.' I grinned involuntarily at the memory of our exchange.

'Excellent.'

'How was your audition?'

'Fine.' Jo grinned, clearly delighted with herself. 'So, Timbo, when did you realise my A was a wind-up?'

I smiled, thinking back to that moment of relief when I finally understood.

'I had your back didn't I?'

'Yes you did,' I admitted, starting to chuckle at the effort I'd put into my letter of complaint.

'I saw you looking up the impacts of home composting and native species on biodiversity. It kept you happy for hours.'

'Do you want to see their response?'

'Definitely.'

While I searched for their email on my phone, Jo bragged on happily.

'It was a finely tuned wind-up. It needed to last exactly the right amount of time as I knew your anxiety would get worse the closer it got to the inquest, so I had to drag it out. I was worried it peaked too soon, because when you sent off your letter there was nothing to do but wait, and you still had a day to go. The danger time. Hence the texts. Brilliant, if I say so myself.'

'I have to hand it to you, Jo, it was one of your best. Up there with pushing me out of my bedroom window.'

'It was wasn't it?'

The email loaded and I showed it to Jo. As she read it out loud, laughing her head off, I couldn't help remembering my initial bemusement and anger. I had a moment's flashback to the windy bridge and shuddered.

'You didn't doubt me?' asked Jo suddenly, looking up.

'I totally doubted you. I hated you with a passion for two weeks.' I caught a flicker of something akin to uncertainty in her expression, then realised I'd misread it when she reverted to her usual buoyant smugness.

'So gullible. It's your most endearing feature.'

'You seem way more excited about your plan for stopping me having a nervous breakdown than you are about being a game show host. How did it all go?'

'Pub?'

'I don't know, it's a weekday.'

'And I have to get up early tomorrow.'

'Really?'

'Yeah,' she sighed.

'But there's no alcohol in the house, except...'

'Sod it, pour us a Cinzano will you?'

I obliged, and poured one for myself. 'Go on, Jobo, what happened?'

'It was great. They wanted to do a pilot so we ran through it Monday, then they took me out for dinner and put me up in a hotel so we could get cracking first thing. Bloody hell, Timbo, they wanted me at Shepperton studios by seven am.'

'So that's why you look tired.'

'It's been a long day.'

'It certainly has.' I took a sip of Cinzano and absent-mindedly picked up my knitting.

'What's going on? I go away two days and you turn into your mother.'

'It's calming,' I said, clicking away with the needles. 'How did they know what food to do for the pilot? Isn't it supposed to be random?'

Jo tore her eyes away from my knitting. 'Well that's the thing, they'd pre-planned it and got the most disgusting foods. They basically did the recipe you threw up.'

'Isn't that cheating?'

'That's what I said. I told them my fans would know it was fake. But they said not to worry and that they'd add the graphics of the RRG later so it looked spontaneous.'

'Hmm. Did you have an audience?'

'We will tomorrow. People turn up at studios hoping to be part of TV shows, and they were hoping we'd get some today but the morning show ran over so we just did some to-camera stuff. Anyway, I'm back up there tomorrow to finish the pilot, and then if the powers-that-be like it, they'll do me a contract. I should know by the end of the week.'

'That's quick. I always assumed these things take ages.'

'They want to catch the trend, they said.'

Jo didn't seem as excited about it all as I'd have expected. Still, as a basically idle person, maybe the two days up in London had taken it out of her. It takes a while to adapt to the commuting life. Funny to think our positions may be reversed if all went well.

'Did you get into trouble with your mother?'

'No. She approved of me being Habitat Man actually.'

'I told you she would.'

I was about to protest, but something about knitting calmed me down and gave me time to realise I'd be falling for it again. 'Turns out my worm explorer kits went down quite well in the end with the kids, well my niece at least.'

'I knew they would.' Jo tried again to provoke me. She'd said the exact opposite at the time.

I disappointed her by nodding mildly.

'What are you knitting?'

'Summer trousers, made out of flax.'

'What? You can't knit trousers?' Jo was incredulous.

I grinned. 'Of course not, it's a scarf.'

'Lori came with you today?' Jo quickly changed tack to cover up the fact that for once I'd got her.

'Yes, for the first half.'

'What's the deal with you and Lori? Is it plain lust?'

I stopped knitting, overwhelmed by a flood of images, not just images – feelings, taste, touch, smell. The all-enveloping look and touch and feel of Lori naked in my arms with her big brown eyes looking up at me, or possibly down at me. Or maybe sideways, as we lay next to each other. Would she sleep on the left or right…?

'Okay, Timbo, I get it, you feel lust. Is it just that?'

'I can have a laugh with her. But it's more than that.' I put down the knitting and tried to explain. 'It's like immediately we're together, everything flows perfectly and smoothly. We're in a perfect Tim and Lori bubble and it's like it's meant to be.'

Jo looked at me, her expression inscrutable. 'Does Ethan still want to shoot you?'

'He does.'

'Another glass of Cinzano?'

'I think I will, Jo, thank you.'

She pulled out a bag and poured some dodgy looking snacks on a plate. 'Fancy some bar snacks?'

'What the hell are they?' Little heads poked out of green things, surrounded by a creamy substance.

'It's jalapenos stuffed with crickets with a dollop of soured cream.'

'Go on then.'

We chatted and I knitted, and it felt like old times, although not quite.

The next day I woke again to a quiet flat. Jo had departed for London and I had the place to myself. I had a pile of emails to get through, but it was a beautiful spring day, and after the claustrophobia of the last few weeks, I needed to be outside. I welcomed the trees and birds on the common like old friends. No one glanced my way, thankfully it looked like my five minutes of fame were over.

My first call was to my favourite goat willow. Its catkins were now the upright buds of fur that gave it the alternative name 'pussy willow', a mature, curvaceous tree that was bursting to release its cotton-wool-clad progeny. The catkins had been gestating since being pollinated by fat bumblebee queens in early spring, and now were releasing tiny seeds, each attached to a puff of silky white threads that helped them to drift on the gentle breeze, settling on the nearby grass like a light powdering of snow. I rubbed the supple leaves, full of spring life, between my fingers, causing a cascade of fluffy seeds to float onto the air. A flash of red caught my eye, a few leaves down, two ten-spot ladybirds were mating.

I left them to it and walked on. A rustle on the ground gave away a smart young blackbird poking through the leaf litter looking for grubs, worms and insects. It found something it liked and flew into the canopy to feed its young.

The nettle patches were flowering, meaning the leaves would be too bitter for cooking, but in the shade were still some I could use for tonight's dinner of spinach, nettle and mushroom pasta. I put on some gloves and picked off a few and put them in my bag.

I continued on towards the wild bit of the pond to search for tadpoles. At this time of year, they'd be at my favourite stage, when the stubs turned into tiny little legs. Danny used to watch them for hours, hoping to see that moment of transformation. I sat quietly under a hornbeam tree gazing into the water, but couldn't see any. I watched instead the ducks herd their young across the pond. Two dragonflies mated rapidly on the wing, forming a heart shape as the male clasped the female to him. I felt suddenly lonely and lay back, looking into the canopy of leaves above.

My phone went, the tinkle of wind chimes indicating it was from Lori. At last. I held it up to my face and squinted to see.

I'd love to come to the funeral. Ethan's at his dad's so it should be OK to pick me up. L x

The sun sparkled through the leaves, lighting up the myriad of life dancing in the air. Infinitesimal hairs from catkin seeds dispersed by the wind, miniscule flies and midges, fern and fungal spores, remnants of tufty white dandelion seed heads. A pair of painted lady butterflies fluttered round each other, and a song thrush whistled its love song from the branches above.

35

THE NATURAL BURIAL

It was a warm day so I was pleased that Fern had insisted that no one wore black. In the spirit of the occasion I donned my new hemp shirt which Jo told me brought out the blue of my eyes. Despite her mocking tone, I decided to take the comment at face value, and was looking as good as I knew how. The stress of the last few weeks and my vegan diet had lost me a few pounds, and the slight belly I'd carried with me for the last two decades had disappeared. A soft bark and frantic tail wagging from Florence stationed at the window must have alerted Lori to my presence and she opened the door before I could knock. She wore a floral print wraparound dress that emphasised her perfect curves. Confident in my new shirt and from the x from her last text, I allowed myself the luxury of a proper admiring look.

'You look good in a dress.'

'And your shirt brings out the blue of your eyes.'

'So Jo told me.'

'Nettle by any chance?'

'Hemp.'

I felt a small thrill when Lori came close to rub the fabric between her fingers. 'Cool.'

I held out my arm. 'Shall we?' She took my arm and we set off on the ten minute walk to Daisy's house. By the time we arrived, I'd filled her in on what had happened at the inquest after she'd gone.

I pulled the wind chimes, setting off the now familiar harmonies. A woman came to the door I didn't recognise. To my surprise she embraced me in a hug. 'Tim, so lovely to see you.'

I recognised the voice, no longer clipped but the same low-pitched tone.

'Fern?' She was transformed. Where there had been stern suits was now a tie-dye T-shirt, floor-length flowing skirt, a bandana and flowers in her hair.

'Come on through, is this your plus-one?'

'Yes, this is Lori.'

We walked through the hallway to the kitchen, Lori looked round taking in all the nature-based decorations and craft work. Then she spotted the photo.

'OMG. The original knitted shroud. You must be so proud of your mother.'

I tensed, remembering how curt Fern had been before, but I needn't have worried.

'Yes, she was remarkable, I'm so thrilled we can now re-bury her alongside Dad, and do it properly.'

'I'm honoured to be invited.'

'You look so different,' I told Fern as we entered the kitchen. Fern's brother was rummaging impatiently through cupboards looking out of place with his formal black suit and tie.

'She's reverted to type,' he said, overhearing. 'It was only a matter of time.'

Lori looked at me enquiringly, and I remembered she hadn't seen him on the stand.

'This is Brian my brother,' Fern told her.

'Fern, I'm on the lookout for some proper booze, got any gin?' he asked, giving us a cursory nod.

'We have raspberry vodka, dandelion wine, or elderflower cordial if you're not drinking,' Fern told us, ignoring him. 'All made from Dad's garden. Help yourself.' The wind chimes were heard again and Fern hurried off.

We poured ourselves some dandelion wine. I didn't fancy being left with Brian so I led Lori to the lounge where I'd overheard Daisy. She was talking to an older man and rushed over when she saw me and took my arm. 'Tim, this is my dad.'

'Paul,' he said, holding out this hand.

'Nice to meet you. This is Lori.'

'I love your house. Everywhere I look, I see such lovely things,' Lori told Daisy.

I heard another familiar voice and looked round, it was Samudrapati heading to the kitchen with Fern. I was longing to find out how he'd been getting on at my old firm. Daisy was showing Lori all their handmade arts and crafts, so I returned to the kitchen for a chat.

'How's it going with the Costing for Nature software?' I asked Samudrapati, the moment the pleasantries were over.

'Good and bad. They're volt-heads now.'

'Volt-heads?'

'Obsessed with electric vehicles.'

'That's good isn't it?'

'You'd think. I showed Simon this volt-head vlog, *Fully Charged* and he tried out the latest Nissan Leaf. Then he started raving about the acceleration and the braking and was scathing of anyone who was stuck with ICE dinosaur tech?'

'Ice?'

'Internal combustion engine. It's all acronyms. Simon has his own photo voltaic panels now and he's like "I'm using my PVs to power my EVs".'

'EVs?'

'Oh yes, it's not just a car, he's got an electric motorbike now which he comes to work on. I had a go, it's amazing actually.'

Brian barged in on us, raspberry vodka in hand. 'Thank God for that, someone talking about proper stuff, not all this hippy shit. What kind of bike?'

'It's a lithium battery sports bike. It's so clean, no oil, cruise control, the braking is superb, and quiet. It's surreal. You go really fast really quickly and with just a quiet hum.'

'Have you heard of the EV they have in California where you can summon it to come to you all by itself? And they've got a sentry function to catch out anyone who gets too close,' said Brian.

I felt like I was back at work surrounded by not petrolheads this time, but volt-heads.

'What do you drive?' Brian asked me.

'I car-share with my mate Jo. She rents out her VW via an app, makes a fortune actually, and I borrow it when I need to. Once it's over ten years old it's not eligible for the drive app, then we'll go for an EV.'

'You'd be an idiot to buy ICE now,' said Brian knowledgeably. 'By the way, I'm Brian,' he held out his hand to Samudrapati.

He took it, and paused, knowing the expected response. 'Samudrapati,' he said reluctantly. I waited, fearful on Samudrapati's behalf, for the next question. I could imagine the snort of disdain that would come once he found out what it meant.

Brian's face expressed his thoughts clearly.

'Should have known,' he sighed and took his drink next door.

'But the thing is...' Samudrapati gazed thoughtfully into his drink.

I didn't like his doubtful tone. I prayed he wasn't going to ask me to take my job back.

'Fuck it.' Brian stomped back into the kitchen. 'I have to know, what does Sodomopitty mean?'

Samudrapati was saved by the arrival of Andrew and Carla

who came in carrying violin cases, followed by a younger woman, who looked just like Andrew.

'Tim, the Habitat Man,' cried Carla. 'Wonderful to see you.' I smiled, a little nervous that her exuberant air might not be fitting for the occasion.

'Don't worry,' said Andrew, reading my expression, 'we agreed with the family, this is an opportunity to celebrate two wonderful lives. This is my daughter Katie, she's doing the music.'

Katie gave me a shy smile and turned to Andrew. 'We'd better tune up outside.'

I left them to it and went to find Lori to check she wasn't feeling abandoned. I needn't have worried, she was chatting happily with Daisy and her dad in the lounge. We exchanged smiles, then I got waylaid by Fern in the hall.

She sat on the stairs and patted the space next to her. 'Come and have a seat, Tim, I need to apologise.'

'No you don't, I should apologise if anything,' I sat next to her.

'I shouldn't have asked you to keep quiet. Now it's all out, I see how toxic secrets can be. I feel free now, liberated.' She looked like she could break into an exuberant twirl at any moment. 'It's only now it's all over that I realise how much keeping my mum's burial secret was taking from my life-force.'

'Life-force,' scoffed Brian squeezing past us up the stairs on his way to the bathroom.

Fern just laughed up at him. She turned to me and took my hand and gazed into my eyes. 'It takes energy to keep something covered up. It's heavy, and I put that heaviness on you. I could feel it in your aura.'

I felt suddenly envious of her. Lori was standing in the doorway of the lounge still chatting to Fern's husband. I'd tell her about Danny, I vowed to myself. At the first possible opportunity. I'll tell her today. Paul was looking over at Fern bewildered. He must be wondering what had happened to his wife. Lori looked over too and caught my eye and smiled.

Fern was oblivious of her husband's gaze. 'But now I feel weightless,' she continued, laughing. 'Like I could float up into the sky with the puffy white clouds.'

'For fuck's sake,' commented Brian, squeezing past us on the stairs on his way back down.

'How's Daisy doing?' I asked Fern. 'I haven't had a chance to talk to her yet.'

'She's going to miss her grandad a lot. They were real soulmates. But she's excited about taking over the house and garden. She's going to invite some of her student friends to live here and use the rent money to keep herself going.'

The sound of fiddles tuning in the garden was heard. Everyone looked towards Fern.

'It's time,' she stood up. We all followed her through the kitchen into the garden.

There was a collective gasp of surprise and delight as we stepped outside. Long willow rods wedged high between opposing trees provided a natural curtain rail which hid the hole in the ground from sight. From the rods hung colourful twines, strewn with daisy chains and scented creamy white clusters of elderflower from the tree that had come into bloom. Photos and mementos were tied into them. Spring flowers squeezed into glass bottles hung from willow, elderflower and hazel trees. Vegetable snacks were set out in coconut husks on the homemade table, a huge bower of pussy willow, adorned with an abundance of spring flowers created an archway that buzzed with life. I edged towards the snacks for a quick bite. Daisy bounded over and gave me a hug, brushing aside my condolences. 'Look at the flowers, do you recognise them?'

'Lily of the valley, forget-me-nots, oh yes, here's the lungwort and there's the grape hyacinth.'

'They're the ones you recommended for the bees, and they love them.'

'Who's this?' Lori picked out a photo entwined in the willow. It was a young couple with flowers in their long hair, he was holding a guitar and wearing a kaftan and she had multicoloured bell bottoms and a tie-dye T-shirt strewn with beads.

'That's Grandad and Grandma. I wish I'd have known her.'

'Your mum looks just like her.' We looked over at Fern who was laughing and showing Carla photos hanging in the willow curtain.

'She's so different now, it's weird,' said Daisy.

I explained to Lori. 'Fern was quite, well severe, sorry, Daisy, obviously I saw her at a bad time.'

'No you're right, she was.'

'Is it strange having her change like that?' asked Lori gently.

'Yes, I've lost Grandad, but I had time to come to terms with it, and now it's like I've lost my old mum and got someone new. I mean, I'm glad obviously, she looks so happy and before she was dark. It's weird that's all. Still at least Uncle Brian will never change.'

'Don't you just long for a burger rather than all this rabbit food,' Brian appeared by our side.

'Uncle Brian, try the asparagus. Grandad grew it himself.' Daisy handed him a spear.

'If I must.'

Now that snacks were officially open, I grabbed a plate and filled it up and passed it to Lori. We stood there quietly, feeling the gentle spring sun on our skin, taking in the scene. Brian decided against talking to us and cast his eye round for his next victim, moving quickly over Carla, whose pink hair gave her away as having hippyish tendencies. He homed in on Paul as his best bet and barged in on the conversation he'd been having with Samudrapati.

'What do you think of your wife turning into a hippy?' we heard him asking.

'He's like a wasp,' murmured Lori in my ear. 'Just when you're beginning to relax and everything's lovely, he comes buzzing around.'

'Wasps are important predators of greenfly, and they pollinate too.'

'I knew you were going to say that.'

The intermittent sound of fiddles tuning gave way to a proper tune, and gradually the chatter subsided and everyone looked towards Andrew and Katie. They brought their fiddling to a graceful close and we stood before the curtain of flowers and willow. Brian's voice still taking to Paul was discordant in the sudden quiet, and he bumbled to a halt.

The music of the garden took over from the fiddles. Undeterred by the crowd, a tiny brown wren, tail cocked in the air, trilled its liquid song from the new willow fence. Nearby, a chiff-chaff chanted the repetitive call of its name. A queen bumblebee burred, her legs loaded with balls of pollen for her hungry offspring. A brimstone butterfly fluttered by, investigating the flowers on the willow bower, its bright yellow wings a flash of sunshine.

A roar of a plane flying overhead reminded us that we weren't in the deep countryside, but in a suburban small garden, underneath the flight path from the airport a few miles down the road. When the plane had passed, we tuned again into the sounds of nature. After a few moments Fern nodded at Andrew and Daisy and together they carefully lifted the willow curtain down from the branches and walked it to the end of the garden.

I steeled myself to look. But it wasn't the deep, dark, rectangular coffin-shaped hole I'd pictured in my head. The hole in the ground was just as I'd left it, pond-shaped and three feet deep, except now Grandad, as I thought of him, was laid out in his baggy trousers and a colourful knitted jumper in the willow coffin, surrounded by the bones of his wife. I exhaled with relief. This was absolutely right. The shallow pond-shaped hole was like nature's opening arms welcoming them back to the earth.

Lori was gazing open-mouthed at the dead figure in front of us. To the side, much as I'd left it, was a mound of earth, with several spades dug in.

'I helped to weave the coffin,' I whispered to her.

'Morbid isn't it.' Brian appeared behind us, sipping a fresh glass of raspberry vodka.

'I think it's magical,' said Lori. 'I thought it would be creepy, but somehow it isn't.'

Daisy jumped down into the hole, stepped carefully over the bones, kissed her grandad's cheek tenderly and then pulled down the lid of the coffin. Her father helped pull her out. Fern reached over and held her hand tightly, and spoke.

'Thirty years ago, I buried my mother right here. Dad played a song on his guitar, we wrapped her in her knitted shroud and placed her gently in the willow coffin that we'd woven, and just like today, it was a beautiful spring day, I swear even the same wood pigeon.' We laughed softly hearing the familiar cooing. 'When Mum died, it seemed like the most natural thing in the world to follow her wishes and bury her in her beloved garden. We didn't question it, well Brian did.' Fern glanced over at her brother who was sipping his vodka blank-faced. 'But Mum and Dad seemed so certain, and they'd done all that knitting. Then when Mum was in the ground and we couldn't even plant a tree to mark the spot because Dad wanted to be buried next to her, it didn't seem so great. I became a bit of a loner to avoid questions, like from people like Geoff. I'd loved their way of life, but the secret turned it sour and I changed. Although I called my daughter 'Daisy',' Fern gave Daisy a warm smile and hugged her close, 'so I suppose I was always waiting to return to the person I'd been before, once it was safe. And now it feels safe, thanks to Habitat Man.' Fern looked at me. 'It's thanks to you, Tim, that the secret is out, and I'm sorry that you and Daisy never got your pond, but I'm glad you tried.'

I'd noticed a spot by the willow tree in dappled sunlight that would be perfect for a mini-pond. It would provide the aesthetics for Daisy as the sunlight glinted over the water, and a bath and drinking spot for passing birds and hedgehogs. Reluctantly, I decided this wasn't the time to mention it, and contented myself with a self-deprecating smile.

'Without you spilling the beans,' continued Fern, 'I'd have done to Daisy what Dad did to me and she doesn't deserve that. Daisy, you deserve a life lived in the light.'

Daisy hugged her mum back and gazed at the coffin. 'I love you, Grandad.'

Fern handed Daisy a spade and with it she threw some earth onto the top of the coffin. Fern handed me a spade and offered one to Brian who shook his head and stepped back, glugging his vodka. Samudrapati and Carla also took a spade and Fern kept one for herself.

'Bye, Dad,' she said simply and threw another spadeful of earth onto the coffin.

Andrew nodded at Katie and they started to fiddle with a rhythmic tune that kept pace with the spadefuls of earth being shovelled onto the coffin. I joined in, and passed the spade to Lori who added another spadeful. Samudrapati, Paul, Daisy, Carla, Fern, everyone except Brian took turns. Andrew picked up the pace of the music and earth got thrown in faster. Katie sang, a keening, high note that blended in with the music and the birds and bees and expressed in wordless harmony the bittersweet recognition that a precious life had passed. I looked up into the sky and saw swifts had arrived, they were swooping and swirling like arrows through the sky. Katie noticed and she stopped her bow and just sang, her voice swooping up and down like the birds above, while Andrew's rhythmic fiddling provided the underlying pulse. The shallow grave filled up with earth and she let her voice soar, getting thinner and higher. She took up her bow again and drew it along the strings so that her voice and the fiddle blended into one and it was impossible to hear which was which. Then, emerging out of the long final note came a wail. I was impressed. How had she done that without moving her lips? But it was Brian. He'd come out of the stupor he'd been in since the digging had started and grabbed a spade and shovelled the earth back out.

'Oh my God!' he howled. 'Nooooo.'

Everyone stood back to give him space as he gave vent to his grief. He looked a ridiculous figure in his formal black suit and tie, wailing and digging red-faced. But there was nothing ridiculous in his grief. He cried and howled and dug. 'Oh my God! Daddy!'

Katie's bow held Brian's wail just as it had held her voice and played it in harmony, giving it dignity and weight. Brian threw off his jacket, rolled up his sleeves and dug and cried and dug and wailed. Andrew improvised, allowing the music to become less directed, but coming back again and again to the beat, providing the continuity, reminding us of the inexorable, inescapable rhythms of life and death. Katie played the high, long notes, the sweet beauty of love and loss.

Brian opened up the willow lid of the coffin and clasped his dead father in his arms. Andrew softened the tempo, and Katie kept the top notes going with her bow while he wept. I felt a moment's empathy with Brian. Like me, he'd clearly felt disconnected from his family. He'd gone all the way to Australia to escape that feeling of alienation but he'd come back and I knew what he was thinking, well we all knew because he was shouting it into the grave.

'It's too late. I left it too late. I missed my chance.' The enormity of this realisation was filling his soul with sorrow and he wailed it to the heavens. The fiddles picked it up and played it out. I marvelled at their mastery of their craft, the music carefully designed to bring out the grief that needed to be felt, to be expressed. Andrew stopped his bow and gave the floor to Katie. Her bow picked out a melody that I'd swear was improvised, wandering for a while, then getting a sense of itself and developing its own structure, tuning into the ebb and flow of Brian's grief that swelled and abated and then swelled again as the realisation hit him again and again and again. We were hearing music being spun out of pure human emotion. The note dropped into a lower key, Andrew picked up his bow and boosted it with a bass note and it was transcendental. The music redeeming the brutality and rawness of the loss, turning it into something exalted and sublime.

Brian let his father go, placed the lid back and shovelled the earth back in. The fiddles played as we picked up our spades and joined in till the hole was covered again. Andrew upped the tempo and introduced a hint of something else.

Brian jumped on the earth and stamped it down. 'You were so embarrassing, all of you, that's why I left,' he yelled at the ground. 'I just wanted you to be normal. But I don't want you to be normal now. I want you not to be dead. I want to say I'm sorry. I want to talk to you and I can't.' He struggled with his tie and pulled it off and tied it round his head. 'See I have a bandana now, Dad, I have a bandana.'

The music played on, and, sensing it was time, Andrew introduced another hint of something and I felt my foot tap. Brian stamped down on the ground again. Andrew repeated the motif and I tapped my foot again. Carla nodded at Andrew and he played it again, a clear hint of a jig. She jumped on the grave with Brian and took his hand. Andrew and Katie launched into the full-blown jig and suddenly they were off, Carla twirled Brian round in a circle, and he couldn't resist. I held out an arm to Lori, and we joined in as everyone twirled and jigged on the grave to the music. We danced it out all of us, all our griefs, both for the loss of the man lying in the earth and for our own personal losses, past, present and imagined. We danced and laughed and cried and the swifts swirled overhead, heralding that the striving of spring was giving way to the warmth of summer. Andrew and Katie played like demons slowing us down, then reeling us back in again and again, and then when we were ready to drop, brought us home with a final flourish leaving us collapsing sobbing and laughing with the sheer wonder of it all.

Fern brought out a small fruit tree in a pot. She stepped forward and dug a hole, which reached down a few inches short of the coffin, then pulled the tree out of the pot, teased out the roots and planted it in the hole. She handed the spade to her brother and smiled.

'Mum and Dad can still give you your favourite pudding.'

'Damson tart?'

'And damson gin,' she smiled at him.

Brian took the spade, filled in around the hole with the earth and patted it down. Daisy stepped up with the watering can and watered it thoroughly. It wasn't the pond we'd initially wanted, but the tree looked right there, and as Daisy said, it was about meaning not just looks. The damson tree would take the sustenance from the earth and use it to provide creamy blossoms for bees in spring, summer fruit and a perching place for the birds, and damson pie and gin for the family.

After that, it was time to go. We turned to leave, looked back and saw Brian still jigging with a bandana on his head, and Daisy watching with a horrified expression.

'It's the folk,' said Lori.

On the walk back, Lori quizzed me about the conversation I'd been having with Fern.

'Did you see her husband staring at you and Fern talking on the stairs? I wondered if he was worried about you and Fern – you looked like you were in a really intense conversation.' Lori's voice was gently questioning. I held a faint hope that she might be jealous. Fern had after all taken my arm on the stairs and gazed deep in my eyes. Was this a good time to let her know that she was the beating heart of my universe? First I had to tell her about Danny, and then we'd see where we stood.

'But he wasn't worried about you,' she continued, 'he was just freaked out by the change in his wife.'

Hmm. No one wants to be thought predatory, but I'd like to be considered a bit of a threat. Although once I told Lori, I might be considered a different kind of threat.

Lori paused when we got to Cobden Bridge. Left was Lori's house, right was home.

'Shall I walk you back?'

'I'm not sure if Ethan will be in. He might kick up if he sees you.'

'No worries.'

'I'm sorry, things seem to be going backwards. You must think I'm ridiculous being bossed around by my own son.'

'Shall I just walk with you to the clock tower?'

She set off up the road, which I took as agreement.

'I know I'm allowing myself to be manipulated by him but what can you do? Knowing that doesn't help does it?'

'No it doesn't,' I said with some warmth.

'You're so understanding.'

We walked in silence, but it wasn't restful, I sensed that Lori was having an argument in her head, maybe with Ethan, or his dad, or herself. Either way, we marched right past the clock tower and by the time we reached her front door she'd decided in my favour. 'This is ridiculous. Tim, if you're brave enough, you're welcome to come in. He probably won't be back anyway.'

Florence saw us at the top of the path and jumped down from her sentry position at the front window, tail wagging madly.

'Well, I can't disappoint Flo.'

Florence gave a little howl when we opened the door as if to chide me for my long absence. Then, like a coquette playing hard to get she ran back to her favourite chair in the lounge and threw herself in it, her body angled sideways, a hint of legs in the air and gazed at me with her liquid brown eyes, putting every ounce of her doggy will into luring me over to stroke her.

'I won't come to you,' her eyes told me, 'because I'm so beautiful that I know you'll come to me.'

'Tea?' asked Lori, heading for the kitchen.

'Yes please.'

There was a quick bark and I turned to Florence, who pretended she hadn't said a word. She slightly shifted her position, belly on show, two back legs ready to raise themselves into the air, the moment proper contact was made between my hand and her belly. Her brown eyes willed me over.

I went to follow Lori into the kitchen but I couldn't resist it, I looked back. Florence remained there, calmly certain I'd relent and give her some love. She waited patiently, all four paws now up in the air, a quick glance over to me. Did I imagine it or was there a hint of self-doubt starting in those kohl-rimmed eyes, the tufty little ginger beard and little black button nose? Who was I kidding? I turned back and rubbed her belly and crooned to her how beautiful she was. Satisfied, she jumped up to follow Lori into the kitchen, leaving me to admire her swaying walk and jaunty tail. She reccied the kitchen quickly with a glance round to check no snacks were on offer and settled herself with a happy sigh into her basket. Lori had the kettle on already and was digging out some biscuits.

'That dog gets more love than I do!'

I detected a note of bitterness. It was hard to imagine that Lori might yearn after my freckled white body in the same way I yearned for hers. Even so, piecing together everything she'd said about Ethan's vigilance regarding other men, she may have gone many years without any action.

'Why do you allow Ethan to keep the air rifle?' I asked, following my train of thought.

'Well, put it this way, after I confiscated his magnifying glass because he used it to fry beetles to death, his dad got him a sling. I confiscated that when he used it on a squirrel. Then he bought him a knife, then when I confiscated that he got him the air rifle.'

'But there's nothing his dad could get him worse than that is there?' My image of Ethan's dad was getting blacker by the moment.

'One would hope not, but I worry about Ethan deciding to stay with him instead. He worships him. That's where he is now, and he never lets me know when he's going to bring Ethan back. He likes to turn up unexpectedly.' She set two mugs of tea on the table and sat opposite me.

Confessions could wait, it was time to find out more about this ex-husband of hers.

'Is that because he doesn't like to plan things?' Jo was like that. Apart from our Saturday evenings, she was reluctant to be pinned down to any time or date. Probably because she knew she'd be immersed in some game and forget.

'No, it's deliberate. He likes to keep me on my toes, make it hard for me to have anyone over.'

'Does he want you back?' Silly question, of course he'd want her back.

'No.'

'He must do.'

'He has a girlfriend.'

'Consolation prize.'

'No, it's because of his mother, I'm sure. He has a bit of a mother fixation. She had him when she was just a kid herself, and apparently was a bit of a goer – his words.'

'I can't imagine you going for someone like that.' This man was clearly a complete misogynist. What on earth had Lori seen in him? He must be superbly handsome, probably bearded.

'It was a holiday romance and I got pregnant. I'd no idea he was only eighteen. He was really swarthy and muscular.'

I knew it.

'He felt strongly that he wanted the kid to have a proper dad, so we tried to make a go of it, but with our age difference, he just put me in the role of mother then rebelled against me. It was like he was punishing me for how his mother made him feel.'

'Hmm.' I wasn't sympathetic. He sounded like a bully, and they always blame it on their childhoods. What kind of dad gives a teenage boy a rifle?

'That's why I'm happy to have Arben here as an alternative male role model. I suppose it's two extremes – Arben with his obsession with *Downton Abbey* and his endless hair products and Dan's toxic manhood, but maybe they'll balance each other out.'

Lori's hopes were misplaced. This Dan fella was turning a bright young lad into a murderous thug. Boys at that age were so easily influenced. What happens at that age can affect one's life for ever. Despite Ethan's threats, I felt protective of him and of Lori.

'He didn't hit you did he?'

'No, but his anger was so explosive, it was scary at times. I know he sounds like a dick but he has this vulnerable side. He had no proper dad, a manipulative mum. It made him really touchy.'

I admit I had a vested interest in proceedings but to my mind it most certainly didn't justify telling his son to shoot me. I contented myself with another 'Hmm.'

'I was walking on eggshells the whole time, trying not to upset him. He said it was my fault because I kept pushing his buttons but it's like his buttons stuck out a foot long – you couldn't avoid them.'

'He should try living with Jo, he wouldn't last a minute.'

'Oh yes? Tell me more.' Lori's eyes were attentive.

'Okay, one time I was moaning on about wanting to live

somewhere with a garden and a pond and then the next thing I knew there was a pond in my room.'

'What?'

'Yup. Jo had carefully constructed this pond in my room with tarpaulin, rocks, even a plastic duck floating. It must have taken hours to fill it up. No efforts were spared. It took me ages to get rid of it, but I suppose it had the desired effect.'

'What was that?'

'I shut up about wanting a garden.'

'It's such a shame you don't have one. Is that why you do this?'

'I hadn't thought about it that way, but it's a perk, although I only advise, I have no control.'

'You'd like one though?' she asked softly.

'I'd love one.'

'Well, I let you take down my bamboo. Who knows what else I'd let you do.' The twinkle in her eye gave rise to a flutter in my belly. 'Funny though, I always assumed you lived alone.'

I realised what it must look like to her and hastened to explain. I had a sense we were moving onto the next level and this was not the time for misunderstandings.

'I probably never told you, but Jo is gay.'

'What?' Lori looked confused.

'I didn't want you to get the wrong idea.'

'Wrong idea?'

'I mean there's nothing between us.' I gazed earnestly into her eyes, trying to read her expression.

She suddenly looked absolutely gutted. 'Oh.'

This wasn't the reaction I'd been expecting.

'We're just friends, nothing else. Obviously there's a lot of affection between us, and we have a real laugh sometimes, but nothing of a romantic nature.' I pressed my point home, trying to catch her eye, but she was staring intently into her cup, her fingers white from clenching it.

There was a long pause. She looked up eventually and fixed me with a look, impossible to decipher. 'Okay, so we're talking faghag are we?'

I wasn't sure what the term meant. It must mean a man who lives with a gay woman.

'I suppose.'

She seemed to be having a hard time processing the information. Much harder than I'd anticipated. I wished I could read her mind. She looked down into her cup and muttered, 'Faghag.' It sounded as if she were trying to convince herself.

'I mean we do have a laugh don't we?' she said, sounding for a moment like Jo. 'That's something I suppose,' she muttered back into her cup.

'Is that a problem?'

Lori maintained an intense gaze at the cup in her hand.

'No, of course not.'

I had to say, it looked like it was, which surprised me. But that's what we do when we fall for someone. We assume all the things we don't know about them must be exactly as we like them. I didn't know her tastes in music, apart from not liking folk, but obviously she'd be a Led Zep fan, and obviously she'd like long walks in the country and obviously she wouldn't be homophobic.

'Do you like Arben?' she asked out of the blue.

I lit up. Of course she's not homophobic, she has a gay lodger. I suspect my eyebrows were tilted up at the angle of wistful yearning as I confided to Lori my admiration for the precise quality and cut of his facial hair.

She started to cry.

We heard a key in the lock then Ethan came in. Lori wiped her eyes quickly, but it was too late. He glared at me and I felt a strong desire to get out of the kitchen.

'Hi, Ethan. I'll just er… just nip to the loo.'

I was flummoxed, no other word for it. What on earth had

happened? More to the point, what should I do? I aimed carefully in the bowl and waited. As often happens, and I'm not sure which was cause and which was effect, the solution came at the same time as the flow. I realised that the root of the problem was that my life had been running on parallel lines – Jo and Lori. Jo who represented my past, Saturday evenings down the pub, everything I'd been and done before Habitat Man. Lori was my present and maybe my future. I needed to bring those two lines together and then, I was sure, all would be resolved. It was time for Jo and Lori to meet. But there was still Ethan to contend with.

When I came back Ethan smiled at me like I was his best friend.

'Good to see you, Tim. You can come round anytime, you know that?'

'Erm, thanks.'

'Cos you're cool, man. Also, can I do that life coaching thing you said?'

'Yes, I can arrange it.'

'Cos I don't know what the fuck I want to do.'

'Ethan!' chastised Lori.

I'd no idea what had brought on Ethan's change of heart but decided to test it out. No more messing around.

'Would you like to come to the pub tonight, Lori? Meet Jo?'

'I don't think I could, not tonight.'

'You should,' urged Ethan. 'You don't get out enough.' Lori glared at him.

'Next Saturday then?'

'Go on, Mum, or he'll think you're homophobic.' He turned to me. 'We're not, honestly.'

'Okay,' she said at last.

I decided to focus on the good news of Ethan's mysterious turnaround. Confessions could wait. I'd quit while I was ahead.

36

ABSOLUTELY DISGUSTING

It used to be that so little happened in my life, or Jo's, that we'd wring the last drop of drama or fun from any titbit of news. But now so much was happening, I didn't know where to start. I had little idea how her week had gone, she'd been away early and back late each day, then had retired to her computer exhausted. Role reversal from my city days.

Recent events should surely be enough to keep us going for hours. Yet having set down the first two pints of the evening on our usual table, I found myself lost for words. Could it be that I didn't actually want to tell Jo everything? I couldn't undo those moments of doubt, even if they'd proved to be unfounded. I realised again that the trouble was that I'd been leading a double life, one with Jo and one as Habitat Man. Next Saturday, I was sure, when Jo and Lori met, this feeling of living parallel lives would be resolved one way or another. I was terrified.

'Next week, I asked Lori along.' I took a nervous sip of beer.

'Well that's a break with tradition.'

Jo's expression was inscrutable. I resisted the urge to beg her to be good, to take it easy on Lori. If she realised how important it was to me she might decide to 'have my back' and God knows what that might lead to. No, play it casual.

'Yeah.'

'The son no longer wants to shoot you then?'

'No...?'

She looked alert at the hint of puzzlement in my tone. I longed to confide in her my mystification. Why was Ethan suddenly friendly? What had made Lori cry? But that would mean admitting that her tears had followed the revelation Jo was gay, which would put Lori in a bad light. They needed to like each other.

'How's it gone with the game show?' I asked instead.

'It took ages to shoot the pilot. Not because of me. I was doing funny stuff, bit of patter, a few insults and of course the audience laughed their heads off, but that wasn't good enough for them. The director kept making them do laughs on demand till it sounded really fake, so they were roaring away with laughter while I just sat about.'

'The point is, did they like it? Are you in?'

'Yes, I got the contract through yesterday.'

'Amazing, Jo, I knew you'd get it. No one could be more perfect for a show that makes people eat disgusting food.' I raised my glass to celebrate, then lowered it when Jo didn't respond.

'I dunno, Timbo. The contract, I don't like it.'

'Is it exploitative? Poor pay?'

'Great pay actually, but I have to turn up at a ridiculous hour, five days a week and it's hard work, and actually mostly boring.'

'I did that for years, it's called earning a living.'

'This is why I haven't said anything, I knew you'd be judgemental.'

'Since when do you care what I think?'

'You underestimate yourself, mate. Look, I saw what it did to you, all that commuting. Last week was hell and that would be my life. All the canned laughter, it wasn't real. I'd have to travel up to London every day and basically be fake. I can't be arsed.' She drained her pint.

'Steady on, Jo, I've barely started mine.'

'See, that's what work does to me. Drives me to drink. So don't be a dick about it.'

I'd had to go to the inquest alone so she could pursue her dream, and now she didn't want it. This was just another example of her laziness. Although, Lori had come with me…

I softened. 'I'm not being a dick. I understand.'

'Good. It was an insult. I'd made this audience authentically laugh. I was on good form and said some pretty funny stuff, mean mind—'

'Of course mean, that's your thing.'

'It is my thing and they really laughed. But no, they had to have it canned on demand. It's all happening with YouTube anyway. TV is so last century.'

'Can you make enough from YouTube though?'

'My followers are growing each week, and it's fun.'

'I must admit, now I have more time on my hands, it is fun to experiment a bit.'

'You see, this is what I love about you, Timbo, you're not as boring as you look.'

'Cheers.'

'I mean it, you're always up for these things, the software, the random recipe generator, I couldn't have done it without you.'

I shrugged, feeling self-conscious, pleased and slightly puzzled. 'Are you okay?'

'Don't worry, I've not gone soft, but I was remembering back to our university days when we were both cooking for the first time. You'd try all kinds of things. You peaked with that strawberry ice cream made with real strawberries and real cream.'

'Now it would be nettle and hemp milk ice cream. With a locust sticking out instead of a Flake,' I laughed.

'Oh my God! Yes!' cried Jo.

'I was joking.'

'No, it's perfect.'

'Please don't make me eat it.'

'That will be the new Timbo special, nettle, locust and hemp.' She leant forward, green eyes gleaming. 'I think...' She gazed into the distance thinking hard, then caught my eye again. 'Yes... I may have a plan.'

'Go on.'

'Get the pints in and I'll tell you.'

I looked down at her empty pint and my half-drunk one, and bowed to the inevitable.

I waited while the bartender pretended to listen to the indecipherable mutterings of the lone man at the bar, uncomfortably aware that last time, that had been me.

'Two pints of the usual,' I enunciated clearly when the bartender looked my way. He started pouring, and grinned ready to make a jocular remark referring to my last visit.

'Please don't tell Jo,' I pleaded, before he could speak. He tapped his nose and winked and handed over the pints.

'Cheers,' I nodded at him gratefully and headed back.

'So? What's the plan?' I asked, sitting back down.

Jo beamed. 'It's the best idea ever.'

'And?'

'Did you like those bar snacks we had the other day?'

'The jalapenos stuffed with crickets and served with sour cream?'

'Yep.'

'Quite tasty.'

'Let's launch a brand of snacks called "absolutely disgusting".' Jo slammed down her pint with a flourish.

I paused, beer halfway to my mouth considering. 'It could work.'

'Timbo! This is why I love you! Yes it could!'

'Lori was saying they got in some insect snacks for a

Halloween party, so there's that market.'

'Good idea. My sister used one of the random recipes as a forfeit at games, we can promote that idea.'

I noted the 'we', but didn't comment. 'You've got your YouTube following, you could market to them via that channel.'

'I can do an ad for my snacks at the end of each random recipe video.'

'The insects should be a staple. Ticks all boxes, cheap, disgusting and tasty at the same time, healthy and low carbon.'

'The only thing is we need to source a local supply chain.'

'I might be able to get you a local supplier,' I said, thinking of Ethan's imminent life coaching event.

'See, it's all coming together.'

'But what about all the legal bits, health and safety, packaging, transport?'

Jo's face fell. 'Yeah. Well, we can get someone else in to handle the boring bits.'

It was time to confront it. 'We?'

'Go on, let's do it together. You're always complaining you don't have enough gardens to visit, and you're better at cooking than me. It'll be a laugh.'

'I've got hundreds of emails to get through since the inquest, I'll be busy now for months.'

'Most of them won't be genuine. They'll all be conspiracy theorists wanting the inside story on the guerrilla knitter.'

'Some will no doubt, but even if half want a visit…'

'But do you want to wade through them all? What if there's trolls and nasty comments?'

'I can cope with a few negative comments you know,' I protested, getting fed up with this idea I was constantly on the verge of a nervous breakdown.

'Yeah, but you may get the vegans saying they saw you eat meat?'

'I never even said I was vegan—'

'We can't have you being vegan if we're selling insect-based snacks.'

'I shall eat what I want, and read through the emails, because I'm not a snowflake, and I want to create habitats in people's gardens, because that's what I do.'

'Hark at him.'

I ignored her grinning face. 'And I shall help you come up with disgusting snack ideas, because, as you say, it's fun, and I'll think about the sourcing aspect, but the rest is down to you.'

'Ooh I love you when you're masterful.' Jo smirked and added, 'But obviously in a lesbian way, just in case you're getting excited.'

'I'm not getting… Oh shut up.'

It looked like we back to normal.

37

TRIANGLES

After a week going through my emails and arranging visits, it was finally the big day. We'd arranged to meet Lori at our local. It had been a long time since there'd been anyone else at our Saturday evening pints. I hid my nervousness on the walk over, no point giving Jo the opportunity to wind me up, although she seemed too distracted by her plans for world domination by YouTube to pay as much heed as she normally would to such an unprecedented change of routine.

'I earned my first hundred quid from YouTube,' boasted Jo.

'But that's for months of work.'

'Yes, but now I've reached fifty thousand views, it will grow exponentially, then I can start on the merchandise.'

'I can't believe people are paying to watch videos of people cooking food and throwing it up.'

'Well they're not yet, this is mostly from ad revenue, but once my subscribers grow, then that's another income stream. I'm a star now. In fact, I feel the urge to strut.' She put on her headphones, fiddled with her phone then started to march.

'Guess what I'm listening to,' she shouted. This was a regular game of ours, but usually it was reserved for the walk home with a few beers inside us.

'I see a swagger. A lot of attitude – is it 'We Will Rock You'?'

'Nope,' she exaggerated her rhythmic walk, reminding me of a chicken.

'Okay… thrusting chin – a Rolling Stones number.'

'No.'

She put the headphones on me and immediately I got it.

"Walk This Way', Run DMC and Aerosmith version. Good one.'

'Your turn.'

I plugged the headphones into my phone. I chose 'Stayin' Alive' by the Bee Gees, turned the volume up and strutted.

'Bob Marley?' suggested Jo.

'Nope. I swung my shoulders side to side rhythmically, and relaxed my stride a little more.

'Okay,' mused Jo. 'I see a little dip in your knee between each step. Relaxed strut. Jaunty even. Disco?'

'Yep. Imagine my arse in tight white trousers.' I tried to make it obvious, swinging my hips from side to side in an exaggerated fashion.

"Night Fever'?'

'Right band, wrong song.' I sashayed along, head held high, looking from right to left, swinging shoulders and hips side to side.

"Stayin' Alive'!' She got it just as we reached the pub. I turned to give her a high five and saw with horror Lori following us.

I turned to introduce Jo, but she'd gone through the door. Lori looked taken aback. Goodness knows what we must have looked like from behind.

'Sorry, we must have looked very gay.'

Lori smiled brightly, it looked rather forced. 'Yes.'

I tried an apologetic smile and ushered her into our local.

'Lori meet Jo.' I waved her over to our table, where Jo was sitting down.

'Where?'

'There.'

'But that's a woman.'

'Yes, that's Jo.'

Lori's face was blank for a moment then it lit up. She rushed over and shook her hand.

'Hi. I'm Lori and you're Jo?'

'Hi, Lori. Yes, that's me.' Jo raised her eyebrows at me in amused acknowledgement of Lori's excessive enthusiasm.

'I thought you were a bloke,' said Lori, her eyes shining.

Jo does look blokish, especially from behind but still it seemed a little rude.

'A bloke. That's nice,' said Jo with no hint of a smile.

'Oh, no, that's not what I meant. I'm sorry.'

'Stop it, Jo.' I sat next to Lori.

She smiled at Lori. 'I'm just joshing you, I'm not upset.'

'Good.' Lori smiled, relieved.

'You can call me Joseph if you prefer.'

'Oh, okay.'

'Not really.'

Lori turned to me unsure. 'I can't tell if she's winding me up.'

'Welcome to my world.'

Jo grinned at Lori. 'She's even more fun than you, Tim.'

'Tim said you were gay but then I thought you were a bloke so...'

'You thought Timbo was gay? Hysterical!'

Everything began to make sense. I relaxed a little. Jo and Lori were immediately in a laughing huddle.

'Well, the way you were walking!'

'It's a game we play called: what am I listening to?'

'What on earth was it?'

'"Stayin' Alive".'

'Ah yes, makes sense.'

'Timbo mate, get the drinks in.' Jo turned back to Lori, 'What's your tipple?'

'White wine and soda for me.'

'Off you go, Timbo. Look the bloke at the bar isn't happy we've bought a third along.'

I took my place at the bar. Jo was right, the lone man propping up the bar looked definitely put out.

'Nosorry,' he said, shaking his head.

'No,' I agreed, humouring him. Jo was chatting away with Lori. My fears had all been about what would happen if they didn't get on. Now I was worried that they were getting on too well. I wanted to get back to the table as soon as possible, but the landlord was taking his time.

'Slippnblowalline,' the man at the bar said to me, in a sorrowful tone.

Thankfully the drinks arrived and I returned to the table. I heard the words 'composting toilet' and laughter. Lori was telling Jo about the court case and what Jo had missed.

'You never told me about that crypto-feminist,' accused Jo, when I sat down.

'I wasn't talking to you then.'

'Tim was mad at me for leaking the guerrilla knitter story,' Jo told Lori, unabashed. 'I bet he was a dick. I can't stand blokes who want to muscle in on feminism.'

'Me too,' agreed Lori.

'It's like with Greenham Common Peace Camp. Do you remember, Timbo? All those sad guys who were peeved it was women only?'

I did remember. I'd felt a twinge of left-outness myself but hadn't dared to admit it.

Jo laughed. 'Some of them tried to get away with dressing up as women, cheeky bastards! What is it with guys that the moment they dress up as women they go all coy? They always overdo it.'

I thought back to my time as a female avatar and my pink tutu – she had a point.

'I never told you about Dawn.' Lori touched my arm. 'You know she came with me on day one of the inquest?'

'Ah Dawn.'

'That's the one who asked him to play,' Lori told Jo.

'Play? What Monopoly? Scrabble?'

'No 'play' with her and Kerry.' Lori smiled.

'Kerry? Male or female?'

'That's what I wondered too,' I said. 'Female it turned out.'

'Bloody hell, Timbo, you've been living a double life.'

'Well I thought you were a bloke,' Lori told her laughing.

'This meeting has come none too soon,' declared Jo.

'Anyway, what about Dawn?' I asked.

'You know she had a thing with the wizard and his wife?'

'This Dawn sounds like a right one.'

'She's polyamorous,' I explained to Jo. 'It means—'

'I know what it means.' Jo then asked Lori the question I'd been longing to ask. 'Go on then, would you?'

'What?' said Lori innocently, fully aware what Jo was referring to.

'Have a threesome with your mate Dawn?'

'Stop it, Jo.' I didn't like the way she was listening avidly for the answer.

Lori laughed and shook her head.

'Are you sure,' Jo insinuated, 'that there hasn't been a bit of girl play.'

I could tell she was getting off on the idea. 'Stop it at once.'

'Tim wouldn't, obviously,' said Jo.

'I might.'

Jo turned back to Lori with a gleam in her eye. 'So… would you? Or perhaps you already have?'

'Well, Dawn set up a threesome with the wizard and Tri,' continued Lori, not deigning to acknowledge Jo's smiling query.

'Oh my days!' My mind boggled at the thought.

Jo shook her head, confused.

'Tri's the eco-crypto-feminist, so called because he only knits triangles,' I explained.

'Dawn was impressed by his knitting at the exhibition and flirted outrageously with him, like she does, and invited him to a threesome with a witch. And apparently she'd told Geoff that one of the guerrilla knitters was joining them that evening so he also assumed a woman, so they both had a bit of a shock.'

I burst into laughter at the thought of Geoff and Tri's faces when they saw each other.

'Geoff wasn't happy when Dawn was enthusing over the triangles on Tri's knitted jumper.'

'Obviously, she likes the three-part configuration,' said Jo.

I remembered my only experience of a love triangle and how I'd raided Mum's larder for goodies to take over when Danny was born. 'Who brought the food?'

'She didn't say, I don't think they were planning on food.'

'Ah, that's because they weren't expecting competition, she caught them unawares so they had to improvise. I'm guessing Geoff offered her some reiki,' I said.

Lori, laughed, impressed. 'He did, then Tri offered to knit Dawn a bed throw.'

'He would, yes.' I wished I had a beard to stroke. 'Demonstrating his skills for the female. Much like the Bower bird who fills his nest with brightly coloured ornaments to attract a mate.'

'Then Tri took the piss out of Geoff's reiki, and Geoff got upset and put a spell on him.'

I shouted with laughter. 'So that's why Tri was heckling Geoff in the court. Sabotage. Also a tactic of the Bower bird, who will often destroy a rival's nest.'

'Really?' Lori looked unconvinced. 'He lives up in Yorkshire doesn't he? Why would he care?'

'Maybe he's looking for a new nest. Dawn has her own place, they share an interest in knitting.'

'Could be.'

'The alert male must never takes these things for granted. Robins are very territorial, and will defend their territory aggressively against intruders.'

'Hang on,' interjected Jo. 'Is Geoff the robin?' She smiled at Lori and rolled her eyes.

'Obviously,' I said testily, not wanting to be the butt of Jo's piss-taking in front of Lori. 'But will the spell scare him off?'

'Well, if his healing ceremony killed her, then a curse from the wizard might be like the elixir of life,' laughed Lori.

'You're reading too much into this,' scoffed Jo. 'The wizard has a wife of his own doesn't he?'

'It's not always about the female, it may be the chicks,' I said, unable to resist a final bird analogy. 'Geoff doesn't have kids of his own does he? He's probably got very fond of Dawn's son. Men have feelings too.'

'Why are you getting defensive, mate?' asked Jo innocently.

I blanched. This was an unexpected shot across the bow. Jo knew damn well why I might be defensive. Time to bring some food to the table. I jumped up. 'Another drink, Lori? Crisps?'

'It's my round,' Jo stood up.

'I insist.'

'You bought one already.'

I gave up, and took the opportunity to visit the gents. I'd been dying to go, but hadn't dared leave Jo alone with Lori in case she told her about the wind-up with the life coach marks. She was so pleased with herself about it, but I was the one who looked an idiot, getting so worked up about a D. That was trivial though compared with this new threat. As I urinated, I pondered the age-old question – how far could I trust her? When Jo had my back it could be a brutal experience. Although, she could do it better than anybody, she said I'd been the hero. If Jo tells her about Danny, it might not sound so bad. She'd say it kindly, 'You don't know this, Lori, but…'

Then again, she'd been cross pestering Lori about her relationship with Dawn, she'd undermined me by rolling her eyes, and she'd pretty well de-sexed me by saying it was obvious I wouldn't 'play' with Dawn. It would be natural to be threatened by a new person coming in.

I washed my hands, wishing I was in a composting toilet rather than a smelly urinal. In a bamboo loo in Lori's garden, listening to the birds singing outside, the robin that we'd seen on that first visit, eyeing up the worm, the wood pigeon cooing in the background.

I hurried back towards the table. Jo had returned already with the drinks.

'But why was he so worried about the inquest anyway?' I heard Lori say.

'Sorry about your D,' she giggled, when I sat back down.

'Don't, Lori,' Jo's voice was serious. 'Tim gets very upset.'

'Not at all,' I forced a smile. 'Ha-ha.'

'See.' She winked at Lori. 'Sounds like I missed out, but I was in London auditioning to be a host for a cooking show.'

'Really? No!' Lori gazed at Jo, open-mouthed.

'They gave me a contract for one season with an option to extend.'

'That's amazing,' breathed Lori. 'I'd no idea I was sat here with a celebrity game show host.'

'Don't, it will go to her head. Anyway, she's not going to do it.'

'Why not?'

'Too much work,' I said.

'No, Lori, it wasn't just that. I can make as much on YouTube and on my own terms.'

'You mean your random recipe generator?'

'Yes, and add some merchandising. We're looking into a brand of snacks based on my catchphrase, 'absolutely disgusting'.'

'My son would totally subscribe to that. Although I'm not sure I'd want him to. He's literally using cooking as a form of revenge against me.'

'Why? What have you done?' Jo asked.

'No clue. Being his mum?'

'Hang on, is this the carp and cricket bony surprise?'

'Yes. Did Tim tell you?'

'No, he posted it on my site.'

'He never did? OMG!'

'Ooh I feel an idea coming on.' Jo's eyes gleamed.

'Go on,' encouraged Lori.

'Well, Lori, what's been holding me back on my merchandising idea I was telling you about, was that, frankly, it's a lot of slog, but maybe I could get my subscribers to do the work.'

'What? Co-create recipes? A brilliant idea,' cried Lori.

'So you exploit their work to get money,' I said.

'No, you can name the dish after them, like it could be Ethan's carp and cricket bony surprise.'

'He'd like that.'

'What's the surprise?' I asked.

'That's it's not as disgusting as you'd think,' Jo said.

'Brilliant,' said Lori.

I had to hand it to Jo, she did it so effortlessly, you became complicit in your own exploitation. Lori was taken in by Jo's buoyant charisma, but I didn't want Ethan taken advantage of.

'Or perhaps the creators of the successful snacks could have a share in profits?' I suggested.

'A co-operative,' said Lori. 'Crowd-source the recipes, then people are invested in their success, so you expand your networks as they promote it to all the people they know. Win-win.'

'Oh Lori, you're fitting in very well,' Jo grinned at her.

Lori grinned back, basking in the glow of contributing to a Grand Idea. I had new worries now. Lori was supplanting me as chief plotter.

'Tkmenmarmsnluvme' shouted the man at the bar, picking up on the air of excitement. I noticed we were the object of interest for several of the regulars who were wondering about this new configuration.

'Lone-man-at-the-bar is lively tonight,' commented Jo.

'I saw him once at the Brook, he's a singer,' said Lori, surprising us both. 'I worked it out when he said "let me kiss you".'

'He said what?'

'He's a Morrissey tribute artist. They're lyrics.'

'Oh my days, they are,' I exclaimed in wonder. I thought back through all the strange things he'd ever said. 'They're all from *You are the Quarry*.'

'See, that's what happens to you if you listen to too much Morrissey,' said Jo.

'Oh no!' I looked over at him concerned.

'What?'

'He said "I'm not sorry" earlier.'

'I always thought that one was about suicide.'

'I should be extra nice to him.'

'He'll be all right, he's been muttering at the bar for years,' said Jo.

'Did you ever like the Smiths?' I asked Lori.

'Tim used to like 'Heaven Knows I'm Miserable Now'.'

'Shut up.'

'I wasn't into the Smiths so much, but I used to like Morrissey.'

'At least he's not folk.' We both laughed.

'No you couldn't accuse him of that.'

My worries faded and we were back in our bubble, swapping

lyrics and interpretations, conversation flowing like sweet honey, effortless and perfect.

Jo was unusually quiet, following our conversation with a pensive smile. 'See you in a mo,' she said after a while, and headed towards the ladies.

The moment she was gone, Lori leant in towards me.

'Jo's brilliant, she's so funny.'

'Watch it though, if she finds your weak spot, she'll mine it for all it's worth.'

'I can well believe it. What's her weak spot?'

'I don't believe she has one.'

'Everyone has one, Tim.' She looked at me hesitantly. 'If Dawn asks, would you really?'

'No.'

'Good.' She squeezed my hand, then jumped up. 'I'll just nip to the ladies too.'

I sipped at my pint trying not to worry what they might talk about. After an endless five minutes, they appeared again, laughing together as they walked back to the table.

'Jo was telling me how long you two have known each other.' Lori sat down.

'Thirty-one years – since our university days.'

'It must be a really strong friendship.'

'Yes, it is.' But it isn't enough, I longed to tell her.

'We know exactly what the other person is thinking,' declared Jo.

'Okay, so what's Tim thinking now?'

'Look at his eyebrows. It's obvious.'

Lori shook her head bewildered.

'He's worried I'm going to turn you lesbian.'

Lori laughed out loud in shock and turned to me. 'Is that true?'

'Of course not.'

It was.

Jo smiled knowingly. 'Tim's convinced he turned me lesbian.'

My heart stopped. Jo has my back, I can trust her, she won't say more than that.

'No!' laughed Lori incredulously.

Please don't tell her it was when I declared my love for you, I begged Jo silently. I tried to catch her eye but she wasn't looking at me.

'Back when I was slim and pretty, not that Tim is lookist you understand, he went through a wee phase when he thought he was in love with me.'

There was no time to process the shock of the betrayal. I jumped in quickly, determined to make a joke of it. 'It was so funny,' I hooted. 'She literally turned lesbian right in front of my eyes.'

Lori was laughing. Thank goodness! She was laughing and so was Jo.

'Did you ever see that scene on *Kevin and Perry Go Large* when Kevin turns thirteen and turns into a monster?' I asked her.

'I did, Ethan was exactly like that.'

'That was Jo. Before my eyes she turned.'

'It's like all this time it had been repressed—'

'Her hair turned blokey, clothes, posture—'

'My inner bloke came out. It could no longer be denied.'

'And then the bodily functions began—'

'The belching, the farting.'

Lori by this time was helpless with laughter in the face of our double act. 'Did hairs pop up on her chin?' she asked gleefully.

'Literally as I watched.'

I could keep my straight face no longer and laughed in a mixture of hysteria and relief until tears were pouring down my face.

'I grew a nice little moustache,' Jo managed to splutter out, setting us off in giggles again. Wave after wave it came until it expended itself in fits and starts. Jo wiped tears of laughter from her eyes and got out a large hankie and blew her nose in it with a noisy boom, setting us off again.

'On that note,' said Lori, 'another round?'

'Yes please.'

Lori headed off to the bar. Jo was still chuckling to herself, but eventually noticed the cold stare I was fixing her with.

'For God's sake, Jo, what are you trying to do?'

'I've done you a favour. It's much the best way. Get these things out in the open from the start.'

'What else do you plan on telling her?' My stomach was churning.

'You can trust me with that.'

'Can I?'

Lori returned with the drinks.

'What have I missed?' she asked sensing the change in atmosphere.

'I want to be serious for a moment,' Jo addressed Lori and shot me a quick look.

Oh God! What was she going to say next?

'There's some truth to what Tim said. But not in the way he thinks.'

'Go on,' said Lori.

'He didn't exactly turn me lesbian, but he did make me realise that I was.'

Jo had our full attention, which usually she would revel in. She fiddled with her glass. Oh my days, was she looking defensive?

'Go on,' I said.

'I'd not been interested in most of the guys who'd made a pass before Tim, cos frankly, they were dicks. But Timbo is brilliant. He's funny, he's smart, he's solid. He's not even that bad-looking. I bloody loved him and I still do. So when he declared his lervv, I couldn't pretend it was because he was a dick. I realised then I just wasn't into men.'

I was poleaxed. Lost for words.

'OMG!' Lori looked at Jo. 'That's your weak spot isn't it?'

Jo nodded.

'You feel guilty!'

'There's not many Timbos out there and I've hogged him all to myself.'

I couldn't believe what I was hearing. Had Lori felled the mighty Jo? Had she in one evening discovered her Achilles heel? Something I'd been looking for in vain for the last thirty years?

'I bequeath him to you, Lori, you are worthy,' Jo declared.

'Thank you,' said Lori gravely.

'I have a new life now anyway as a YouTube superstar.'

'There's still Ethan though?' I felt obliged to point out.

'We don't have to tell him you're not gay,' Lori suggested.

'When's his life coaching session with Charlotte?' I asked.

'His dad's taking him Saturday morning. Will she say anything?'

'She's not the sharpest tool in the box,' said Jo, 'if I tell her to keep quiet, she's more likely to let something slip.'

'Fancy a date with me Saturday afternoon?'

'I'd love that.' She put her hand on my arm.

'An epic date – whatever you like.'

'I'd like to see your gardens.'

'I'll organise it.'

I held her gaze, so happy I couldn't speak.

'Here's to Tim being gay for one more week.' Jo raised her glass.

'Cheers,' we said, neither of us choosing to think about what would happen after that.

38

LIFE COACHING ETHAN

Ten minutes to go before I set off for my date with Lori. Eric and Elena had offered us lunch as thanks for the decking so we'd start there – an opportunity to show Lori the composting toilet, and it would be a lovely cycle ride across the common to Shirley. After that she was keen to see Samudrapati's willow fence. Then a break for Lori to change and sort out Florence and I'd pick her up again later for dinner at Café Thrive. After that, a walk along Weston Shore for a romantic sunset over Southampton water, then we'd be well placed to check out the Wizard of Woolston's roof garden. I didn't actually want to call in on Geoff, but we could walk past. Then, if all went as hoped, we'd go back to hers.

Jo and Charlotte came in while I was peering in the mirror, checking for stray nostril hairs.

'How did it go with Ethan?' I asked Charlotte, following them into the kitchen.

'Fine.'

'What did you advise?' I grinned, waiting to hear how Ethan was now set on his own unique path, that perfect sweet spot in the centre of the Venn diagram where it all came together.

'He's going into hairdressing.' She hung her faux fur jacket over the back of the chair.

'Hairdressing?' I tried to imagine Ethan making polite conversation with a pair of scissors in his hand. I struggled to find words that would express my views without offending Charlotte. 'That's... crap.' I looked over at Jo to see what she thought. She was leaning against the counter, looking amused.

'Well, it's safe isn't it? People always need their hair cut,' Charlotte said, unabashed. 'They didn't like you giving up your job. Hairdressing is a growth sector. It will compensate for your one.'

'Compensate?' I cried, my voice high and squeaky.

'It will give balance to my case-study portfolio. They can't all be like yours.'

I was furious with her. 'What about Ethan? What about his hopes, his dreams? What you said made a difference, Charlotte.'

She looked at me open-mouthed.

'What you do has consequences!' I yelled. I'd mapped out a lovely path for Ethan. 'It makes all the difference in the world finding the right employment, whether it's paid or not. Finding that spot where it all comes together. What do you love? Killing things – tick. What are you good at? Cookery and killing things – tick. What does the world need? Low-carbon, low-fat, high-fibre source of protein – tick. What will make you money? Starting an insect farm with its own restaurant attached, selling bug burgers farmed on the premises. Tick!'

'I never would have got that.'

'How could you not? It brings everything together, all those disparate elements. It's like the perfect recipe.'

'Come on, Char, it's obvious now, girl, isn't it?' Jo gazed sadly at her, shaking her head.

'It would fulfil him, it would redeem that poor messed up boy. He can't help his dad. And now he'll go into hairdressing.' I was gutted for Ethan, destined to live a life he wasn't suited to.

I tried to calm down. She was only young, what did she know? Even so there was one thing I didn't get.

'Sorry for yelling, but how could the Venn diagram... how could you have come up with that?'

'I don't always do that, it's one of many techniques. Sometimes we take a psychological approach.'

'I still don't get it.'

'He seemed to really like gay men. That's what made me think of hairdressing.'

'What?'

'Not in a gay way. Maybe it's a reaction against his macho dad, but he just likes to be around them. He liked you, Tim.'

I heard a loud snort and turned to see Jo, whose straight face had deserted her.

'Oh my God, that's hilarious,' she managed to wheeze through her laughter.

'Huh?' said Charlotte confused.

'Ethan thinks Tim is gay,' said Jo.

'What? Actually that makes sense now. I couldn't work out what he was on about.'

'You didn't tell him I wasn't did you?' I asked Charlotte urgently.

'I dunno.'

'Think!'

Charlotte had had enough of being yelled at. 'Stop having a go. If you're pretending to be gay, then that's on you.'

'But I'm not...'

'You'd better get on with your date pronto,' said Jo, nodding at the clock.

I gave up. Jo was right, time to go. I gazed at the mirror once more, smoothing down my eyebrows and checking my teeth and hair. I smiled broadly at my reflection, suddenly excited about what was ahead. I'm sure it would all be fine. I grabbed my bike helmet, patted my bumbag and set off.

39

GARDENS

'Snap!' cried Lori when she opened the door. I laughed delighted, we were both wearing shorts and almost identical T-shirts.

'Is that linen?' I asked.

'It is.'

'I bought it after the fashion expo.'

'Me too.'

'Ready?' I waved my bike helmet.

'Yep.'

Florence barged through, fed up with being ignored, and managed to get in a quick lick of my knees before she was shushed back into the house.

We put on our cycle helmets and set off. It was a warm balmy day, and much quicker to cycle across the common to Shirley than have to drive all the way round, waiting at traffic lights.

'Shall we go via the underpass, see the graffiti?' suggested Lori, when we neared the common. I shook my head, and she followed me via the alternative route across the pedestrian lights. Soon we were cycling through the lush greenery of the common, dodging toddlers and dogs.

Eric and Elena gave us a hearty welcome when we arrived.

'Tim, the man who's saved me from mowing the lawn. I'm in your debt.' Eric patted me on the back.

Elena put her hands on Lori's shoulders and kissed both cheeks. 'You have to be Lori, who we must thank for our upcycled decking.'

Elena only managed my left cheek, before Matteo hurtled into my legs.

'Play the caterpillar game with us again.'

Christian ran to the door and grabbed my hand to pull me inside. 'Tim, Tim! We drew pictures of what we've found in our meadow.'

I smiled helplessly at the adults while the boys dragged me into the kitchen to show me their efforts.

'We were very grateful to you, Tim, it kept the boys busy drawing all those butterflies and moths for the fashion exhibition,' Elena said.

'We told everyone that the butterflies by the nettle stand were ours,' Christian told us proudly.

'We played your moth game, and this is what we found.' Elena pulled down a list she'd stuck on the fridge.

Lori read them out: 'Elephant Hawkmoth, Burnished Brass, Cinnabar moth, Garden carpet, Brimstone moth. I love the names, they sound really exotic.'

'Boys, who needs pictures when we can show them the real thing.' Eric led us outside with the air of introducing a great spectacle. 'Ta da!'

I stood at the door, mouth open. Charlotte's words ran through my mind, *when was the last time you felt joy?*

'It's exactly as I'd pictured.'

Lori's decking led the way from the patio outside the kitchen door towards the hut at the end. It was about a foot off the ground, the same height as the grass. Bees buzzed around the wildflowers they'd planted and every now and then an unmistakeable sound was heard.

'Is that a cricket?' Lori asked.

'Grasshoppers,' I told her.

'You like what we make?' Elena asked me.

'To see this come together just as I'd imagined, it's pure joy.'

'So that's what my old decking was used for?' Lori looked around entranced. 'It looks fabulous.'

'The boys love it,' said Elena.

'There's the composting toilet.' I led Lori along the boardwalk.

'Yes, you must try,' said Eric.

'All right then.'

She entered the hut and we waited for her gasps of admiration.

Eric spouted facts outside the door. 'As climate change progresses, water will become a scarce resource. Composting toilets reduce household water consumption by about thirty thousand litres a year, and reduce pressure on water-treatment systems.'

'Uh huh,' came faintly from inside.

'You must sit down,' Matteo knelt on the ground and shouted under the door.

'She's a lady silly,' said Christian.

'Will do!'

'Urine is sterile and a good fertiliser. We have a twin bowl you see that separates the shit from the urine,' shouted Eric.

'Right.'

'So the shit stays dry and breaks down quickly, and makes good compost for the garden, so it's stupid to just dump it in the water, right?'

'Stupid, yes.'

We clustered outside waiting for her to give us her verdict.

Lori stepped out and was confronted with our expectant faces. She looked a bit overwhelmed. It clearly wasn't the religious experience for her that it had been for me.

'You like?'

'Erm, there was no flush?'

'You put the wood shavings down, depending on what you did.'

'It was hard to do anything to be honest.'

'Certainly it was, they crowd you.' Elena waved us all back up the garden. 'Come on, I have lunch nearly ready.'

Matteo hung back. 'I want to show Tim our pond dragon.'

'I definitely want to see that.' I let him lead me to the pond that nestled between the patio and shrubs, and we gazed into the water.

'That's a pond skater,' he pointed out the little insect that really did look like it was skating on the water, 'and that's a water boatman?'

'It looks like it's swimming backwards,' I hinted.

Christian appeared. 'It's a backswimmer,' he declared.

'That's right.'

Matteo put his hands in the water to feel around. 'I'm looking for the dragon.'

Christian grabbed a net and dragged it through the water, intense concentration on his face. 'I've got something.'

Matteo squealed with excitement when he saw a creature in the net. He grabbed its wriggling body and held it tightly in his chubby hands.

'Oh my days. It's a newt.'

I remembered how excited Danny had been the first time we'd found a newt in the pond on the common. I swallowed down a lump in my throat.

'We just pretend it's a dragon, we know it's not really.'

'Is it a great crusted one?' asked Matteo. 'Look, it has a crust.'

'That's a crest, but no it's the common newt, it just gets this in the breeding season to attract the ladies. Still, how wonderful to have newts.'

'You have to put it back now,' Christian said.

336

'I know.' He plopped it back in the water and it disappeared crossly into the depths.

I gazed after it into the water, searching.

'Are you looking for frogs?' Matteo asked.

'Yes, or they may still be tadpoles.'

'I never seen one.'

'I did, when I was little,' piped up Christian.

'I knew a little boy once who loved frogs, and one day he hid a couple in a jar and took them to his grandparents' house.'

'Poor frogs.'

'Yes indeed. And then in the evening when everyone was watching television, his grandmother hears 'ribit' and she says, 'Oh my goodness what is that?'.'

The boys giggled at my grandma voice and I continued. "Nothing,' he says. And then she hears it again. 'Ribit', and cries out. And Grandad says, 'don't be so silly,' and just as he says that they both see a silhouette of a frog jumping across the screen and they all scream.'

'Was he in trouble?'

'He laughed and laughed. But then we asked him if he'd like being kept in a jar, and he promised not to do it again.'

'Could you get us some frogs?' Matteo looked at me hopefully.

'I wish I could, but you're doing everything right. They have plenty of food in your garden, and lots of places to shelter and this lovely pond. One day they might come back.'

'Tim! Boys! Lunch is waiting.'

'Whoops.' Christian looked at me guiltily. 'I forgot. Mum sent me out to get you.'

'You'll be in trouble.' Matteo was gleeful.

'It's easy to get lost in a pond. I used to get in trouble for that,' I confided.

'Did you have a pond?' asked Matteo.

'Hurry up, we'll get told off.' Christian tugged at my hand.

I'd been fighting the memories since Matteo had shown me the pond, but Christian's worried words undid me.

Hurry up, we'll get in trouble, Danny had cried when he found out we were late. The boyfriend arrived just as we got back, and it was then I'd realised that she'd never told him I was taking Danny. To save face she'd insisted that I'd taken him without her permission. I'd let the lie go unchallenged, thinking that it was best for Danny that his mum had a stable relationship, even if it wasn't with me. I'd had no idea what it would lead to: allegations of child abduction, the new boyfriend taking out an injunction in an overzealous show of protectiveness, Danny's mum unwilling to confess to the truth. Then being arrested for breaking the injunction, explaining to the judge after a weekend in jail that I'd been desperate for an opportunity to explain to Danny, to say a proper goodbye. My never seeing Danny again.

I felt a hand slip into mine. 'It's all right,' Matteo told me solemnly. 'Mum won't be that cross.'

'Phew.' I forced a smile, and let him lead me back to the kitchen, where Elena was ladling tomato sauce onto bowls of spaghetti and handing them out.

Lori waved a slice of ciabatta. 'Try the bread with olive oil. It's delicious.'

'Pass me some then.' I sat next to her. 'Sorry we're late.'

'It wasn't Tim's fault,' Matteo said. 'It was Christian.'

Christian gave Matteo a sharp dig in the ribs, but kept quiet.

I smiled at them, feeling better once I'd eaten some bread. Low blood sugar, that's all it was.

I turned to Eric. 'How does your neighbour like your garden?'

'Now they want to copy us.'

'It proves my research, I think.' Elena set down a bowl of steaming pasta in front of me.

'What's your research?' Lori asked.

'It was psychology of consumption, wasn't it?' I said.

'You remember well, but now I look at new tendency to non-consumption.'

'Like the Share Shop?'

'Not quite. For example, our neighbour tell me they also want upcycled decking, but before, she'd insist for new. And it's because the meaning has change. The story behind new decking might be rainforest destruction, air pollution, climate change, is not a nice story, but the story behind your decking is a lovely story. We don't just buy the product, we buy the story.'

'Mum, he took my bit!'

Christian had taken the last piece of bread. Elena fixed him with a stern look and he tore a bit off and offered it to Matteo, who ate it quickly.

'I began though with psychology of competition,' continued Elena smoothly. 'That's how I and Eric meet.'

'I'm a criminologist and Elena explained to me why anti-social behavioural orders weren't working,' Eric said.

'I tell them that ASBOs are seen as a badge of honour, they compete to get them.'

'I reckon my son would be proud rather than ashamed if he got an ASBO,' agreed Lori.

I mopped up the last of the tomato sauce with the bread and sat back replete.

'That was lovely, thank you.'

'Coffee?'

'We should be seeing Samudrapati now shouldn't we?' Lori said.

'We don't have to.'

'We can't let him down.'

'He's this Buddhist chap who took over my job in finance,' I explained to them. 'I'm a bit concerned he might hate it as much as I did and want to give it back.'

Lori laughed and rose to go.

'She thinks I'm joking,' I laughed and accepted the inevitable.

. . .

Twenty minutes later we were drinking iced water in Samudrapati's kitchen, and I realised I was right to be worried.

'I'm not making as much progress as I'd hoped,' he told me sadly.

'But you said you were making a difference. Haven't you got them into electric vehicles?'

'They've got three apiece.'

'Ah.'

'They're chucking their cars away keen to get the latest EV. They use renewable energy which is great, but the environmental impacts of making any car in the first place is huge. This is the problem I was saying earlier. It's no good offsetting or switching to renewable if you just use it as an excuse to consume loads more. We need to tread lightly on the earth. But it's not in their nature.'

'Sorry, work talk must be boring for you. Shall we change the subject?' I asked Lori hopefully.

'You go ahead. You never talk about your work before Habitat Man, but it must have been a big part of your life. I'm interested.'

'No, really.'

'Don't worry about me, I'm all ears.'

'They're begging me to go back at Café Thrive,' Samudrapati continued relentlessly. 'They're struggling as they can't get good staff on their wages. Maybe I'd do more good there.'

'But you're over qualified to be a waiter. This is a challenge surely?'

'What are they like at work?' Lori asked.

Change the subject, I willed her with my eyes.

'Simon and Martin are ridiculously competitive,' Samudrapati told her.

'Hmm,' Lori raised her eyebrows at me.

'They're very competitive,' I began slowly.

'Yes, that's the problem.'

'But could it be a solution?' I mused.

'What do you mean?'

'This will probably sound stupid…'

'Try me,' Samudrapati said.

'What if you get them competing about who can live lightest on the earth?'

'That's a Buddhist thing, non-attachment to stuff, but I can't come out as a Buddhist, they wouldn't take me seriously.'

'You got them going with that vlog for volt-heads, couldn't you try them on someone trendy, like that Japanese minimalist lady?'

'You know, it could just work,' he said.

That was good enough for me. I jumped up. 'Shall we have a look at your garden?'

'Of course, you must see the willow fence.' Samudrapati led us outside.

Lori was impressed when she saw it. 'This is so cool, I didn't notice it at the burial.'

'The idea was to provide both a barrier, but also a sense of continuity with next door's garden,' I told her. I'd seen images of living willow fences that adopted a lattice design, but this was far more creative. I turned to Samudrapati. 'Daisy did this didn't she?'

'Yes, she was in charge and I helped, it was great fun.'

'From this side I can really appreciate the pattern.' I stood back to admire the artistry. She'd started off with a web-like design, with rods radiating out from the centre, and looping back. Then she'd clearly thrown out the instructions and taken a long thin rod off in another direction right out to one edge, then woven it back in and done a loop in the centre, then off again in the other direction, resulting in a beautiful bow, reminiscent of a butterfly.

'She's an artist,' I declared.

'Just like her grandad,' agreed Samudrapati.

'Did you run out of rods?' Lori asked.

'No, why?'

'This rod doesn't loop back like the rest.'

Samudrapati smiled. 'Maybe it was on purpose. Do you know what I think?'

We shook our heads.

'Look closely.'

The fact that the rod hadn't been woven back allowed a gap in the foliage through which the Buddha could be seen under the hazel tree next door, serenely meditating. A sight that would have meaning for Samudrapati.

'Oh she's good,' I breathed.

'What?' Lori cried, frustrated.

'Don't look at the fence, look through it.'

'Ah that's lovely,' said Lori finally seeing.

When I'd suggested the living willow, I'd wanted to do something for Daisy and Fern, and with this she'd done something for her neighbour who'd been so loyal to the family. It was beautiful, and not just to look at, but the sense of connection behind it.

I caught the sweet scent of the honeysuckle Daisy had planted on her side. Tendrils of the tubular pink and cream flowers were creeping through. The buzz of a passing long-tongued bumblebee ceased when it alighted on the mouth of the flower. I knew it was unfolding its long proboscis to probe deep into the corolla of the flower, dipping and retracting it to lap up the nectar.

My eyes met Lori's warm brown eyes.

'We'd better be getting on,' I said.

THE SECRET

I'd reluctantly decided against inviting myself along for the dog walk and shower and took the opportunity to go home and freshen up too. The linen shirt had been perfect for a hot day and cycling but I was taking no chances.

I picked Lori up later, this time in the car and noticed she'd changed into her figure-hugging wraparound dress.

Café Thrive was busy and I was starving by the time I managed to get the order in. Wholefood burger, sweet potato fries and onion rings for me. Halloumi burger, side salad and passionate pink smoothie for Lori.

'Will it take long?' I asked the bearded man at the counter. It was a wispy beard, not impressive, but friendly and vegan looking. I thought it was the same guy I saw last time, but I couldn't be sure, perhaps they all looked like that.

'We're short-staffed. The food may take a while.'

My heart sank as my stomach grumbled. I went back to the table.

'Dinner may be slow,' I told Lori, 'they're short staffed.'

'Never mind, at least it's not insects.'

I sat back and gazed across the table at her, basking in the moment. I was taking Lori out to dinner. Okay, it wasn't a posh restaurant with white tablecloths, candles and fawning waiters. It was bare wooden tables, bright lights and order at the counter. But the vibe was cool, the staff were friendly, the food smelled lovely, and Lori was sat opposite me, with her warm, dark eyes and melting smile. She looked, I'd say, even more beautiful than Florence tonight, and I took the opportunity to tell her so. She appeared flabbergasted at this extravagant accolade, opened her mouth to speak, then paused, apparently lost for words. I had a sudden idea.

'Hold that thought.' I dashed back to the counter.

'Could you do with some extra help at the weekends?' I asked.

'We certainly could. It's supposed to be my free night. We couldn't pay full rate though.'

'How would you feel about a fifteen-year-old boy with an interest in cooking, helping out as part of his work experience?'

'Definitely. Call on a weekday and you'll get my boss.'

'Brilliant. Any chance of fast-tracking dinner.'

'I'll do my best.'

I sat back at the table, and resumed gazing at Lori.

'It's true, even without a little ginger beard, you look absolutely lovely.'

'I can't believe I'm flattered at being compared to a dog, but then again it is Florence, so having run through several responses I'm going to settle with… thank you, and you don't look so bad yourself.'

'I don't?'

'You've picked up a bit of a tan, you've got those bright blue eyes going on.'

Her hand lay on the table and I took it and brought it to my lips. 'Mmm, you smell good enough to eat.'

'That would be my cinnamon and ginger soap bar.'

The thought of Lori in the shower flickered in my mind.

Mentally I'd joined her and was gently lathering her down when the food arrived.

'Oh!' I said somewhat ungraciously, letting go of Lori's hands so young bearded man could set down the plates. His expectant smiling expression suggested he was waiting for a flurry of thanks for rushing the food through, but my grumbling stomach was now the last thing on my mind.

'Thank you so much, we were starving,' Lori smiled graciously up at him. Satisfied, he smiled back, and set off to bring the drinks.

Still, food was food. We tucked in.

The waiter returned with Lori's dairy-free strawberry and passion fruit smoothie. She offered me a taste – it was like nectar.

'I'll have a smoothie too,' I told the waiter, 'any flavour, surprise me.'

'Will do,' he hurried off to do my bidding.

'How did you get him to hurry it up?'

'He's desperate for his Saturday nights back.' Between mouthfuls I told her of my idea for work experience for Ethan. 'He doesn't have to do it. I know a vegan café might seem an odd choice for—'

'A boy that likes killing things, I know. But maybe they'd be a good influence on him.'

'That's what I thought. I also thought they probably have to be quite innovative to get vegan food to taste as nice as meat. It might be good experience for Ethan, if he goes ahead with the insect restaurant idea.'

I belatedly realised that Ethan as yet had no idea of the future we'd mapped out for him, and still thought he was going into hairdressing. I told Lori about the life coaching session with Charlotte, which like Jo, she found hilarious, rather than tragic. She stopped laughing when she saw me looking serious.

'Look, he's not going into hairdressing just because Charlotte said so. Trust me, he's much more likely to listen to you.'

'Really?'

'Oh yes, he really looks up to you.'

'Especially now I'm gay.' At this, we burst out laughing, surprising the waiter who'd returned with my drink.

'Super Green Smoothie.' He set a murky green concoction reverently down on the table. 'Enjoy,' he said confidently and returned to his counter.

I took a sip.

'What's it like?'

'Disgusting,' I declared, provoking more giggles. I gazed longingly at her passion fruit and strawberry smoothie. Lori leant over and had a sip from mine.

'It's lovely, want to swap?'

I fell in love a little bit more.

'Are you sure you want to go all the way to Woolston after this?'

'Oh, I have to see the wizard and his green roof.'

'It will be getting dark by then, though.'

'All the better to see the bats.'

We drove over Itchen Bridge to the other side of the river. The LED lights on the bridge switched on, bathing it in pale blue light, adding to the sense that this had been a magical day and was set to be a magical evening. The enchantment dimmed when we slowed down through Woolston High Street, a soulless mix of gambling shops, beauty parlours and takeaways. Then, after the usual period of getting lost in the new housing development we reached Weston Shore.

I parked up and we got out and headed for the section where meadows and scrubland separated the shore from the housing estates. Soon there was just the wide expanse of Southampton Water in front of us and the sound of the gentle breeze in the trees behind. I took her hand and we walked in comfortable silence, both of us reluctant to disturb the peace around us.

We sat on a bench and watched the sun set over the Solent. Pipistrelle bats swooped along the water, locating the insects via their second sight, as Geoff called it. Among the gulls, we picked out oystercatchers, turnstones and curlews pecking for food on the exposed shingle.

'It's been a lovely day.' Lori leant against me.

'Which was the best bit?' I asked her, hoping she might say something about the composting toilet.

'It's not over yet.' She shot me a grin that made me go weak at the knees. 'I loved seeing what you've been doing in other gardens.'

'Which was your favourite?'

'Daisy's garden was special – the burial was magic. It turned sorrow into something beautiful – a mirror of love.'

Her smile was pensive as she watched the sun disappear into the horizon. I put my hand over hers.

'Did you lose someone?'

'My dad died when I was young.'

'I'm sorry.' I squeezed her hand.

'I'm so aware of what it's like to grow up without a male influence. I don't want that for Ethan.'

'Is that why you got married?'

'I thought at least he'll have a dad that way. I knew it wasn't a good idea really.' Lori caressed my hand with her thumb, sending shivers down my spine. 'Ethan needs a positive role model. Make him realise that being a man isn't about being muscular, hairy and dominating.'

'Phew.'

'Someone who takes disappointment like a man, who has enough confidence in himself not to have to be so controlling.'

'Tick,' I laughed. 'Tick, tick, tick.'

'I love that you think about Ethan,' I felt a jolt when her eyes caught mine. 'Most guys just see him as an obstacle. Me too sometimes.' Lori sighed wistfully.

'He's a great kid. He reminds me of…' I tailed away.

'Who?'

'You can't see him as a hairdresser then?' I laughed quickly.

'No,' she smiled. 'He's got a lot of choices ahead, but I like your ones.'

'A bug burger restaurant with food locally sourced from his own insect farm?'

'Exactly,' she leant into me. 'I'm a bit jealous actually?'

'Of me?'

'Your work. You have this vision and then it comes to life. But last week I had to tell a woman that if she didn't stop seeing her abusive partner, her kids would be taken away. And I suspect she won't, and then what do I do? Every choice seems wrong.'

'All you can do is have good motivation,' I told her earnestly.

'We shouldn't bring our baggage to the job but I do. I sometimes feel like my whole life has been shaped by losing my dad. Choosing to stay with Ethan's dad, social work, keeping families together. Sorry, this is getting really deep.'

'It's all right. I understand.'

'Do you?' She turned to face me, hearing something in my voice.

I looked away, and gazed back out over the darkening water. This was the moment to tell her. But I was the one that had walked away. How things come full circle. I'd left sweet little Danny in the hands of man who I hoped against hope hadn't been abusive, but had definitely seemed overly controlling. Maybe that's why I felt so protective of Ethan. He reminded me of the boy I'd left.

I felt the familiar melancholy overtake me. This was my long-awaited date with Lori. Visiting the gardens, sitting here watching the sun go down, and the best bit was to come. The anticipation had been building all day and I'd swear it wasn't just me. A knee rub here, a hand squeeze there. Eyes catching for a moment. I should tell her, but I didn't want to ruin it. There was no way I could tell the story and make it sound good. I knew because I'd tried in my head hundreds of times.

'Are you okay?' I heard her ask softly.

'Fine.'

Even if, best case scenario, she understood. Even if she could see beyond the label to the truth, even then, I don't think I could tell her and not fall apart.

'Let's go see this wizard then.' I jumped up, surprising her with my briskness. I looked around, trying to work out a shortcut to Geoff's. A cut-through into a housing estate looked promising.

'Do you know where you're going?'

'I think so.' I hadn't a clue. I consoled myself that it was a beautiful night for a walk. The air was soft and humid, the plants and trees, bare the last time I'd been here, had burst into life. The trees were in full leaf, and in every garden, flowers were blooming, releasing their scent into the air.

'Identify the smell.' Lori held her hand over my eyes as we walked past another garden.

'Roses. Too easy.'

'This one?'

'Honeysuckle.'

She removed her hand from my eyes and entertained herself by teasing me. 'Ooh look at that lovely bit of scrub, and those weeds, aren't they lovely.'

I was about to cave in to the temptation to list the invertebrates who'd make a nice home there, but had to stop and think as we'd reached a junction – left or right? I wasn't sure but if we went right, then we should at least be able to enjoy the sight of the full moon while it was still large and low in the sky.

We turned right, I looked around and suddenly there he was. I nudged Lori and pointed. Surely there couldn't be a more wondrous sight. Geoff – aka the Wizard of Woolston – sat upright in a chair on his rooftop garden, outlined against the full moon, looking out over the water. His bald head glistened with sweat. The breeze up there must be welcome on this balmy night. From there, he'd be looking over the dark expanse of sky over Southampton Water. He'd see the colourful lights of Fawley Power Station seeming to hover in the distance, twinkling against the dark water, the gulls and the bats swooping down through the sky in their search for food. I felt the pride a woman must feel upon giving birth. I'd made this happen.

We walked closer.

'Look!' cried Lori. 'Look at the bats.'

Five pipistrelle bats circled his head.

'OMG, it's magical.'

'It's not magic, they're after the midges attracted by his sweaty head.' I caught a faint strain of music. 'Or perhaps the sound coming from his headphones.'

Lori's shining eyes reflected the moon in their dark depths. I drank in the sight. She gazed back at me. I couldn't wait any longer. I took her in my arms and leant in to kiss her. I paused just before our lips met, savouring the sensation of her warm breath on my mouth. She leant in towards me until our lips touched gently. A passion rose up through me like a spring storm, strong and sudden. It met with Lori's soft, yielding lips. Her relaxed mouth, subtly slowing me down, encouraging me to lose myself in the moment. We seemed to melt slowly into each other in the gentle warmth of the evening. A slight breeze blew up, the welcome cool air contrasting with our warm skin and hot mouths. Her mouth opened a little more, I allowed a moment for our open mouths to pause against each other, then gently explored her lips with my tongue. She did the same, and suddenly the storm seemed to rise up through her too and we kissed with an urgency I hadn't felt since I was sixteen. One of us, maybe both, let out a small groan. My hands took in the curve of her back, and moved down. There was a moment of delicious tension as my urge to conjure a broomstick from the wizard and transport ourselves to the nearest bed, grappled with my desire to savour the present. Tomorrow Ethan would find out the truth, but we had this one night. It wouldn't be rushed.

I saw a movement out of the corner of my eye. Geoff had got up.

'Quick.' I pulled her out of sight. 'I don't want him to see us.'

'I feel like a teenager,' she laughed. 'Shall we go back to my place?'

'Oh yes.'

We got a vigorous welcome from Florence when we got back.

'Poor thing,' I said stroking her, 'have you been on your own all day?'

'She's just making a fuss to make me feel guilty.'

I followed her into the kitchen. She held up a half-bottle of wine. 'Fancy a drink?'

I hesitated.

'Don't worry, you can stay over.'

I couldn't control the beaming smile that spread across my face. 'Go on then, a small one.'

'What a perfect day. I can see why you love what you do.' Lori poured me a glass of red wine, and handed it over. 'You were so different when you went back to working in London.'

'I hated it.'

'How long did you work there?' She poured herself a glass and leant next to me against the kitchen counter.

'Twenty-five years.' I put down my glass and pulled her gently so she was standing in front of me and I could gaze into her mesmerising eyes. Yes, there was definitely a hint of hazel in their depths. I held her hips gently as I leant back against the counter.

'I suppose it was well paid. Is that why you stuck it?'

Lori was a social worker doing good, useful work. I'd been making rich people richer. I couldn't have her thinking I was in it for the money.

'No, not really.'

'Why did you stay in a job you hated for so long then?'

Oh. I should have seen this coming and headed it off.

She waited expectantly.

The pause was too long now for me to get away with a change of subject.

Her eyes changed expression from interested and a little bit sexy to perplexed.

This was the time to speak.

The pause had taken on a life of its own. Lori stepped back slightly, sensing something was up. My hands were still on her hips, and I resisted the temptation to pull her back in close.

Time to spill the beans, Tim. Time!

'Erm, I had something on my record, I was er, worried employers might see it if they did a check. I er, I couldn't cope with that.' I waited, with no real expectation, but yet a slight hope that that would be enough.

'What?' Lori put down her glass and stepped back. My hands fell down to my side.

She wants more. I need to tell her. But it didn't sound good. How can I make it sound okay? I'll start off by warning her, prepare the ground, warm her up for a shock and let her know it's not as bad as it sounds.

'It doesn't look good on paper you see,' I said pleadingly.

'Well?' Lori clearly needed more.

'It sounds worse than it was. Jo said I was the hero actually. I took it on the chin for the sake of the boy.'

'What boy?' Her eyes hadn't yet turned cold, but they were puzzled, guarded.

I have to say now, she's a social worker, she could look me up herself. Better coming from me than in black and white, or maybe it would come up in capitals, red font, underlined. STALKER.

'There may be, I'm not sure, some kind of restraining order thingy on my file. I don't know if it's still there because I er, well, I was very young.'

I was right, that didn't sound good.

I heard a key turning in the lock, probably Arben.

Lori gave no sign of hearing the door. She gazed at me in wide-eyed horror.

'Against who?'

I shook my head, reluctant to say more. She mustn't know I'd been in jail.

I heard steps, two lots, run down the hall towards the kitchen.

Her words rang out incredulous and loud, 'Are you saying you're some kind of stalker?'

Ethan burst into the kitchen shouting. 'He's not gay, Mum. Tim's not gay!'

He was closely followed by a man. An angry-looking man. Well-built. A man who'd obviously heard Lori's last words. A man who was glaring down at me from his six foot and three inches with dark ferocious eyes.

I shook my head helplessly at Lori and at the fabled Dan.

'What the fuck?' he said.

I smiled placating as one does with a very muscular man whose potential for violence is clear. His eyes narrowed and his fist curled. Oh my days, I'm going to die. His fist hurtled towards me and I ducked. While I was down there I threw my arms around his knees to bring him down. He wasn't expecting it and it kind of worked, he buckled slightly. I felt him hit my back and I stood up quickly throwing him off balance. Then it was a blur as we both struggled to hold the other down. We found ourselves caught up in a mutual headlock and our eyes met. There was something familiar about him. Was it the resemblance to Ethan? No, it was more than that. The light dawned.

'Danny?' I choked in wonder. He loosened his grip slightly and gazed back at me. I saw a similar moment of recognition.

'Dad?'

His dark brown almost black eyes looked into mine. He hadn't worked it out, but I'd done my biology, my blue eyes, his mum's blue eyes. It wasn't possible.

'Afraid not, but I'd like to have been.' It broke my heart to say it.

'But why didn't you come round?' he asked, still absent-mindedly holding me in the headlock.

'I wasn't allowed to,' I managed to gasp.

'You should have tried!' he yelled, throwing his arms up and releasing me.

'That's what the restraining order was about. Don't think I didn't try.' I was desperate to convince him. I straightened up still holding his gaze. In his moist dark eyes my worst fears were confirmed. He had felt abandoned.

'I'd do anything to make it up to you!' I cried.

Dan, my Danny, the man who never cried, gazed at me with a sudden vulnerability and shy hope and burst into tears. I looked at my not-really son whom I'd loved and missed so much. I burst into tears. Ethan saved us from ourselves.

'For fuck's sake!'

We looked at Ethan's outraged face and pulled ourselves together.

I could see in Ethan's unthinking confidence that, unlike Dan, he'd not lost a father figure. Yes, Dan had bought him an air rifle at the age of fourteen. Yes, he'd been unreasonably controlling, and set Ethan to spy on his mum to stop her having any sex, but Dan loved Ethan, and Ethan never had cause to doubt it. Dan caught my eye again and what I saw made my heart sink. She hadn't told him the truth. He'd had no idea, he'd thought I'd just left him. Poor, abandoned Danny. We started to weep again. Ethan stared at us in disgust.

'Er...' There was a slight cough. We all turned to look at Lori, who was looking at Dan in horror. 'Are you saying this is him? The one who walked away without a word when you were young?'

Dan wiped his eyes and nodded.

She turned to me, speaking slowly, spelling out the horrible truth. 'So, Dan's ridiculous insecurity is your fault? You're the reason I've been in forced celibacy for five bloody years?'

'I tried to see him.'

'You should have tried harder.'

'I went to jail trying!' There was no hiss of shock, in fact they both seemed satisfied, Ethan even looked impressed. Then she asked the question that hadn't yet formed in my mind.

'So where does that leave me?'

I gazed at her, shaking my head helplessly, my mind boggling. Dan/Danny. My not-quite son, Ethan's dad and Lori's ex-husband. Where did that leave me and Lori?

Maybe Jo was right, some people just aren't destined for love. Jo would know what to do. She'd say to wait. It would be wise to take a step back, I realised. Give what's in the ground time to grow, to work out what it is.

'I'm so sorry. I'll make it up to you, both of you,' I croaked.

'Yes you will,' said Lori and did the only possible thing that could have saved us. She kissed me. Out of the corner of my eye I could see Ethan and Dan staring at her in disbelief. Lori wanted my full attention. She held me as close as she could, very close. Her right arm caressed my head, neck and back and then jerked me in even closer. Her left hand left my buttocks and slowly and deliberately lifted, middle finger first, into the appalled faces of Ethan and Dan.

God I love that woman.

READING GROUP QUESTIONS

1. Would you like a friend like Jo? In chapter 1, Tim admits he can't tell if Jo has his back or is just exploiting him. What do you think? Did your views change across the course of the book?

2. Did you learn anything about green solutions or environmental issues? Did this book lead to any changes in your own behaviour such as gardening for wildlife, eating seasonal food or make you aware of greener options such as car sharing, home composting, composting toilets, natural burials etc.?

3. The book ends with an interesting configuration. What do you think happens next for Tim and Lori, bearing in mind the complicated web of relationships at play?

4. Many books are set in glamorous locations, but *Habitat Man* makes a point of showing how beauty and ecology can be attained even in an ordinary terraced back garden. Do you think the choice of Southampton as a location worked?

5. Who would you cast for the role of Tim, Lori and Jo in a TV adaptation?

We'd love to hear back from book clubs and reading groups on their discussions, so feel free to send your group's thoughts on the above questions to hello@dabaden.com.

Sign up to the mailing list on www.dabaden.com and get access to more activities, quizzes and questions, plus a 'what happened next' taster download, exclusive to subscribers who've finished *Habitat Man* and can't wait for the sequel.

If you enjoyed this book, please help to spread the word by leaving a review on Amazon, Goodreads, Waterstones online or any other suitable forum. These are a huge help to authors.

For more information about the author and the inspiration for *Habitat Man*, go to www.dabaden.com or connect on:

facebook.com/greenstoriessoton

twitter.com/DABadenauthor

instagram.com/greenstoriessoton

ACKNOWLEDGEMENTS

This book was inspired by the real life Green Garden Consultancy that started in Southampton in November 2019 and is managed by Transition, Southampton. I am particularly indebted to Kevin who advised me and sent me details of some of the gardens he visited (with the owners' permission).

Particular thanks go to Dave Goulson, Professor of Biology at the University of Sussex, whose numerous books, including *The Garden Jungle: or Gardening to Save the Planet* provided great source material. Dave generously offered his help with the manuscript, especially the nature bits, reading through, checking for accuracy, and writing the occasional lyrical passage himself.

Gratitude is also extended to Rosie from the Natural Death Centre who freely gave her time to tell me about the environmental benefits of natural burials and the legal issues surrounding home burial. Also to Chris and Debs, a couple of house boaters with a healthy obsession with death, nature and music who inspired sections of this book.

In the process of writing this story, I've found that people who love nature and the environment tend to be lovely people and Dave, Kevin, Rosie, Chris and Debs illustrate this beautifully.

I also thank the Wizards and Witches from Southampton Pagan Moot for helping me with my research. Rest assured the Wizard of Woolston is not based upon any of you, although you may recognise the odd quote!

Thanks to Alex T a fellow greeny who alerted me to the tantalising concept of cryptofeminism and another Alex, the guerrilla gardener who risked a socially distant meeting to tell me of their secret exploits.

I am also indebted to Heather Conway, an expert on death law and Gary Leonard a consultant solicitor who were both kind enough to help with legal research, although I confess that plot needs have triumphed over legal accuracy, especially with regard to timescale.

Last but not least, thanks go to my partner Chris who was brave enough to tell me my first draft was rubbish, and by the final draft delighted me with several LOLs and a surreptitious tear.